"Daniel Church evokes a terrifying scenario with deft pacing and endless horrors, laced with trademark wit. Dare you discover the secrets of Warden Fell? Tread carefully, as there may be no going back if you do…"

Alison Littlewood, author of Mistletoe *and* A Cold Season

"Deliciously creepy with characters to really care about. Daniel Church is on my "must buy" list."

Shona Kinsella, author of The Heart of Winter

"Daniel Church's skill lies in taking a folk horror theme and putting his own unique slant on it, building layer upon layer of suspense and psychological terror that transports the reader from the modern-day world into a universe of ancient darkness."

Catherine Cavendish, author of The Stones of Landane

"A twisty chimera of a novel, *The Sound of the Dark* is at once an intriguing mystery and an exploration of the wounds that the past leaves on the present. Church deftly weaves elements of folk horror, true crime, haunted technology, and body horror into an existential nightmare as epic as it is harrowing. Reader, be warned: no one can hear the sound of the dark and remain unchanged…"

Jo Kaplan, Shirley Jackson Award nominated author of
It Will Just Be Us *and* When the Night Bells Ring

"*The Sound of the Dark* will give you anxiety, but in a good way. It's an addictive mixture of folk horror and hauntology, a black broadcast beamed to your mental ears straight from the hungry mouth of night. I loved it unrestrainedly."

Gemma Files, award-winning author of
Our End *and* Blood From the Air

"*The Sound of the Dark* by Daniel Church is gripping, gleefully gothic and unsettling. Comparisons with King and Tremblay are on the mark. A book that's testament to the fact that the darkness has its own song, and it's impossible not to listen."
Angela "A.G." Slatter, author of The Crimson Road

"In *The Sound of The Dark*, voices from the past whisper secrets that should have been left buried ... secrets of a cold murder case grown warm once again, a brutal slaying that's not what it seems, and terrifying, shadowy wraiths. Daniel Church has outdone himself with this haunting, chilling new novel, and those echoes from the past will stay with me for some time."
Tim Lebbon, author of Secret Lives of The Dead

"A gripping, slow-burn descent into madness and memory, *The Sound of the Dark* is folk horror meets true crime obsession. Atmospheric, haunting, and razor-sharp, with 3D characters dealing with real, human issues."
Conrad Williams, author of Hell Is Empty

"Daniel Church takes you on a hell for leather, nonstop ride into horror, where all you can hear is *The Sound of the Dark*."
Marie O'Regan, author of Celeste *and* Resurrection Blues

"Daniel Church takes the reader into 'Darker' territory in this haunting tale. Fans of *The Stone Tape* and the Cthulhu Mythos won't want to miss this! A chilling read from start to finish."
Samantha Lee Howe, USA Today bestselling author of
The Stranger in Our Bed

The Sound of the Dark

Daniel Church

ANGRY
ROBOT

ANGRY ROBOT
An imprint of Watkins Media Ltd

Unit 11, Shepperton House
89-93 Shepperton Road
London N1 3DF
UK

angryrobotbooks.com
Listen closely

An Angry Robot paperback original, 2025

Edited by Dan Hanks and Shona Kinsella
Cover by Sarah O'Flaherty
Set in Meridien

ISBN 978 1 91599 840 8
Ebook ISBN 978 1 91599 841 5

Printed and bound in the United Kingdom by CPI Group (UK) Ltd, Croydon CR0 4YY

The manufacturer's authorised representative in the EU for product safety is eucomply OÜ - Pärnu mnt 139b-14, 11317 Tallinn, Estonia, hello@eucompliancepartner.com; www.eucompliancepartner.com

9 8 7 6 5 4 3 2 1

For Hannah Dennerly,
With love from the Filth Wizard

"Hell is discovered."

STAGE DIRECTION TO DR FAUSTUS,
ACT V, SCENE II, BY CHRISTOPHER MARLOWE.

1.

June, 1983

Statement of Leonard Bainbridge, taken Friday 10ᵗʰ June 1983, Scorbridge Police Station, Lancashire. Interviewed by DCI Rose Bennison, DS Graham Harrower and DC Peter Culleton attending.

BAINBRIDGE: I was mowing the grass out front when it all started – had my back to Tony's caravan, so I wouldn't have seen anything, not to begin with. And the mower makes a hell of a noise, so I didn't hear anything either. Not till it all kicked off.

BENNISON: That's okay, Mr Bainbridge.

BAINBRIDGE: I honestly can't understand it. I didn't know them *that* well, but they'd always seemed such a nice family. Happy. Never a cross word. Lindsay always seemed very much at ease – not frightened of him or anything like that. I know all sorts goes on behind closed doors, but I've some idea of the warning signs – sunglasses on cloudy days, that sort of thing – and there was none of that. And their kids – they were such lovely children. I still can't believe –

(*Breaks off. Pause.*)

BENNISON: Do you need to take a break, Mr Bainbridge?

BAINBRIDGE: No. No. Thank you, but I'd honestly prefer to get this over with. Every time I think about it – God. I'm just glad Irene had gone into town to vote when it all kicked off. If she'd seen that, I can't imagine what... she's in pieces over what she *did* see, as it is.

BENNISON: Okay. Just – in your own time.

BAINBRIDGE: All right. Where was I?

BENNISON: You were mowing the lawn.

BAINBRIDGE: That's right.

BENNISON: And you hadn't heard or seen anything amiss, hadn't had any idea there was anything wrong with the Mathias family before that afternoon.

BAINBRIDGE: That's right. And then it all started. There was this racket, all of a sudden, from their caravan. Banging around, shouting, raised voices. Not the usual kind of things – kids playing and so forth. Agitated-sounding, if you know what I mean. And then someone – one of the kids, I think – screamed.

BENNISON: What happened then?

BAINBRIDGE: Well, I stopped the mower and turned around. Thought one of the kids might've had an accident. I couldn't see anything – they were all inside the caravan, and the doors were shut. I hadn't seen any of them that day. Or the best part of the past fortnight, now I think about it. And that wasn't usual – they were very outdoorsy, especially the little ones. Anyway, there was another scream. Not one of the children this time. Must have been Lindsay. And then, this terrific bang.

BENNISON: A gunshot?

BAINBRIDGE: Must've been. Then both kids started screaming, and I could hear Tony shouting. I'd started towards the caravan when I heard the first scream, but that bang stopped me in my tracks. I couldn't decide whether to go and help, or hide. So in the end I just stood there like a lemon, and then the caravan door flew open and the children ran out.

(*Pause.*)

BAINBRIDGE: Alison, the youngest, she just came tearing ahead. Always was a right little thunderbolt, that girl. Ran like the clappers. Neal was lagging behind her. I'm not sure, but he might have been injured – couldn't see too clearly because the sun was behind them, you see. They were more or less silhouettes at first. He might have had something wrong with his leg. I remember thinking his head looked a bit wonky too, somehow, but that couldn't have been right. Must have been his hair. They were both shouting at me, but I couldn't make out what. I took a step towards them, but then Tony showed up in the doorway. With the rifle.

(*Pause.*)

BENNISON: Would you like some more water?

BAINBRIDGE: No. You're alright. Now, I saw *him* clearly enough. Muffled up like it was the dead of winter. Gloves, a parka with the hood up, a scarf over his nose and mouth. All I could see were his eyes, and God almighty – there was *Hell* in his eyes, it's the only way I can put it. And then he put the rifle to his shoulder and –

(*Pause.*)

BAINBRIDGE: There was a flash and a bang, and Neal sort of threw his head back and flapped his arms and then fell down. Little Alison had almost reached me – I was going to grab her and run for my place – but she stopped and looked back. Checking on her brother, maybe.

Tony pulled back the bolt on the rifle. I remember seeing the empty cartridge fall out. I actually heard the brass tinkle when it fell on the caravan steps. Then he pushed the bolt forward, put the rifle to his shoulder and fired again, and her head, that little girl's *head*, it just –

(*BAINBRIDGE hyperventilates, begins to cry.*)

BAINBRIDGE: Sorry. Like I was saying, her head just – it seemed to burst. Her blood went all over me. Her blood and – oh, God.

(*BAINBRIDGE hyperventilates.*)

BENNISON: Take your time, Mr Bainbridge.

(*Pause. Deep breath.*)

BAINBRIDGE: She dropped like a sack of spuds, of course. Wouldn't have known what hit her. That's the only good thing you can say of it. And that was that. The two of them just lay there on the grass between the caravans, and Tony stood there with his rifle, looking at me. I thought bloody hell, this is it. I remember thinking thank God Irene wasn't here, but he – he didn't shoot at me. I'm not sure how long we just stood there like that. Felt like ages. I knew I should run, but I was afraid if I moved he'd shoot me after all. And then he just lowered the rifle. And he said – no idea why, it doesn't make the slightest sense, but what does, about any of this?

BENNISON: What did he say, Mr Bainbridge?

BAINBRIDGE: He said: "Don't put your radio on, or the telly." That's it. That was all.

BENNISON: He didn't say anything else?

BAINBRIDGE: Not a word.

BENNISON: What happened then?

BAINBRIDGE: He stepped back inside, and shut the door. That was that. I stood there a bit longer – maybe as long as a minute – trying to make my mind up what to do. Go hide in the caravan, or try and leg it to the road. Went for the second option in the end, in case he changed his mind. And anyway,

I didn't want Irene coming back and walking into that. I was almost at the road, when I heard another shot and looked back. He'd come back out of the caravan and he was shooting at Neal. I think... I think Neal was still alive. I'm sure I saw him move. Then Tony shot him again. I didn't see the boy move after that. Best thing I could think of was to ring you lot, so I did. There was a phone box round the corner from the gate. And a bus stand, with a seat. I had to sit down there and wait after I'd called. I was shaking too much.

Part One:

World's End
June, 2023

2.

Cally Darker slipped out of bed, leaving Iain snoring, and padded downstairs with her shoulder-bag and laptop.

She'd only fallen asleep in the small hours. Sunday night syndrome, Iain called it: you wanted an early night because it was Monday tomorrow, so – Sod's Law – you couldn't settle. But, despite having barely slept four hours, she was up and alert, a good hour before her alarm went off.

Not that she *had* a day job any longer, but she tried to get up at a reasonable time and do the housework and cooking. Besides, Iain loved his office job and found conditions like depression or stress absurd, let alone the idea they could make even the simplest tasks seem near-impossible.

Red-haired, pale and full-figured – 'statuesque,' one ex had said, back when Cally had hit the gym twice a week – she stood a good inch taller than Iain even in her socks and the feminist in her rebelled at playing the domestic goddess, but depression wore you down; besides, the past couple of months had strained the relationship enough already.

Cally's mother had always said she and Iain weren't 'suited.' While Millicent Darker had said that about every partner she'd had, Cally suspected she was right about Iain. But if they split up, she'd need a place to stay, and she'd only two options. Dad and his partner Lucy lived in North Wales; Millicent lived in spitting distance of Manchester, but Cally would rather gargle bleach and swim in a crocodile pit than go through that again.

Cally's parents had divorced when she was thirteen, and she'd spent the next three years under her mother's roof. That had been pure hell, especially as she'd been an outsider at school as well. She'd left Millicent's house the day she turned sixteen, moved in with Dad, gone on to sixth-form college, then University. Everything going up, up, and away – until suddenly, it hadn't been.

That had been when the depression and anxiety had first reared their heads. They didn't do much for your judgement, which Cally guessed was why she'd moved back in with Millicent – Dad and Lucy, by then, had relocated to Wales, and Cally had wanted to stay in Manchester. She'd reasoned she was older and wiser now: living with her mother for a couple of months couldn't be *that* bad.

But it had been.

Cally brewed coffee, curled up on the sofa with her laptop, then rummaged through her shoulder-bag for her meds. She kept everything she considered essential in her shoulder-bag, which was rarely out of arm's reach. She'd once had to do a panicky midnight flit to get away from an ex-boyfriend, and had left her pills behind, causing several days of horrible discontinuation symptoms.

Cally logged into her Anchor and YouTube accounts to view the podcast's stats. *You Want It Darker's* figures were growing slowly but steadily. People loved true crime: serial killers, unsolved murders, cold cases finally cracked after years of mystery and silence. Cally understood; after all, she loved them too.

She used a separate email account for podcast correspondence, and checked it every Monday. That was today, so she logged in there as well.

You have [17] unread messages.

"They're slowing down," she muttered, sipping her coffee. She marked most of the emails for deletion straight off. Six were outright spam. Seven were notifications from YouTube: three new followers, four new comments. The other four were direct messages from actual people. Not that that was much to crow about. The subject line of the first two messages were variations on the theme of 'get back in the kitchen u ugly bitch,' but with worse spelling and grammar. The third said Check this out Cally and had a picture attached; she almost deleted it unread, then decided to give the sender the benefit of the doubt.

"I'm going to regret this," she muttered, and clicked the email.

A dick pic. Talk about hope triumphing over experience. But they didn't even bother her anymore; they were just boring. She emailed back her standard response – *Why have you sent me a picture of a child's penis? I've informed the police* – before blocking the sender, which with any luck would ruin the bastard's morning. Cally smiled to herself: she'd take her victories, and dopamine hits, wherever she could find them.

One email remained.

Subject: The Other World's End Murders.

"Well," she muttered, "that's different."

Her last podcast had been on the 1977 'World's End' Murders of Christine Eadie and Helen Scott in Edinburgh, and the 2014 conviction of Angus Sinclair for the killings. They hadn't been Sinclair's only victims, but the email's title suggested something else.

The biggest problem for a true crime podcast was that virtually every serial killer and high-profile single crime had already been done to death (ha-ha,) and Cally was still fighting to catch people's attention. To do that, she needed to pique their interest with less familiar cases.

Such cases were often less-known for good reason – not as sensational, or there was less information in the public domain – but while Cally had wandered for years from undemanding office job to undemanding office job, she could summon vast reserves of dedication for what Iain liked to call 'the weird shit you're into.' The digging and research that went into preparing a podcast, for Cally, was actual *fun*.

She'd been particularly proud of her work on one recent case, so seeing it mentioned in the email both brightened her Monday and put her in a receptive mood for the message as a whole.

Hi Cally,

Just wanted to let you know I love the podcast and I think it's getting better with every episode. I was particularly impressed by the Miles Giffard one. That case is nowhere near as well-known as it should be, and you did a great job providing the background and detail that brought it to life.

The World's End Murders one was excellent, too, but have you ever thought of doing one on the 'other' World's End Murders, from 1983? There's hardly anything about them out there (maybe because some idiot journalist used that name for them, so they always get pushed to the back of the search results by the 1977 case) but what's there's pretty interesting. My family used to live near Blackpool, which is how I heard about it. Here's a couple of links, anyway – practically all I could find online.

Keep up the great work!

Best,

Pete.

Cally moved the cursor to the first link, hesitating. The email address was a word salad – p56283@gnetmail.org – but the message itself seemed genuine enough.

Decisions, decisions.

Her coffee mug was empty, which gave her time to think, or an excuse to delay. Cally padded back into the kitchen and brewed another cup, but the same links and the same decision were waiting on her return: to click or not to click?

Cally sighed, put the mug down and moved the cursor to the first hyperlink. She hesitated once more, then wagged a finger at the laptop screen.

"If I end up with a computer virus," she muttered, "I'm bloody well hunting you down."

And then she clicked the link.

3.

The first link, via the Wayback Machine, was to the long-defunct *gore.net*, a late '90s/early Noughties website that had prided itself on displaying the most graphic images imaginable in the name of 'Documenting Reality.' The 'Fresh posts' listed down one side of the webpage included 'Poop fetish' (no way was Cally clicking *that*,) 'helicopter decapitation' and 'shotgun suicide.' The page she'd arrived on, however, was headed 'murder scene photos.'

The first shot showed an expanse of grass, with the very end of a white-painted metal structure protruding into either side of the frame. The sky was blue, turning dark directly overhead; beyond the grass was the sea, into which the sun was setting, a dull red smear.

On the open ground in the middle of the picture lay two bodies. One lay on its back, arms outflung, legs tangled together. The other was face-down, feet splayed apart. Even at that distance it was clear both victims were young.

Not so much graphic as arresting and deeply sad. The empty grass, the empty sky, the empty sea, the two bodies the only objects of note. The one on the right wore jeans or dungarees. The one on the left wore a pink-and-white gingham dress, the kind Cally had worn at primary school. She scrolled down to the next picture, to find herself viewing a close-up of the child in the gingham dress.

The head was gone. There was a stump of a neck with rags of skin and hair attached. The surrounding grass was sodden, blackish-red, strewn with dark lumps and pale, china-like shards.

"Jesus, Cally, what the bloody hell's that?"

Cally jumped in the act of picking up her coffee. Thankfully, none went on the laptop – she couldn't have afforded a replacement. Some landed on the carpet, but most of it splashed on her bare thigh. "Fuck!"

Iain backed away as Cally dabbed at her leg. Fortunately she'd been engrossed in p56283's email and links so long that the coffee was no longer scalding hot.

"You okay?" he said at last.

"Yeah. Jesus, don't sneak up on me."

Iain nodded at the laptop screen, grimacing. "Maybe you wouldn't *be* jumpy if you weren't googling shit like that."

"I didn't google it. It's a link from a fan."

"You really want fans like *that*?"

"It's a murder case."

"No shit."

"I mean, he thought I might want to cover it for the podcast."

Iain managed not to roll his eyes, but only just. "And are you?"

"Don't know yet."

Iain looked at the screen again and grimaced. "Jesus, Cally, switch it off."

Trying not to grit her teeth, she slammed the laptop shut before going into the kitchen for paper towels.

"Why on earth would you look at that stuff?" said Iain, following; Cally ducked past him on her way back out to the living room. "I'm sorry, darling, I just don't like seeing people's brains blown out before I've had breakfast."

She was tempted to ask what he'd expected to find her looking at, but Iain would consider that to be proving his point. "Fine," Cally said, laying paper towels on the stained carpet. "Sorry you were upset."

"I'm not upset, love." He came out of the kitchen. "I'm *worried* about you."

And he genuinely was. He looked adorably earnest in

his clean suit and tie, especially as it was slightly oversized. Combined with Iain's smooth face, it made him look about fifteen. Which wasn't a thought Cally wanted to dwell on. She already wondered daily how she'd got into the relationship and, more importantly, how to get out of it.

The first part wasn't really a mystery: she'd been lost, scared and in need of stability. Even so, Cally would have pulled the plug months ago except that she'd been about to be sacked from her job and was in no shape to secure another. A lousy reason to move in with someone, but she'd done it anyway. She wasn't proud of herself.

Iain was sweet, and adventurous in bed if nowhere else, but that was really all they had in common and the cracks were showing. It wasn't good for either of them, or fair to him.

"I mean, you keep saying you're depressed."

"I *am*."

He sighed. "Honestly, love, you need to take some responsibility for yourself." She heard him shaking cereal into a bowl, and the click as he put the kettle on. "If you were *really* ill, *seriously* ill, you'd be in hospital."

Cally opened her mouth and shut it, having lost count of how often she'd tried to explain that it didn't work that way.

"You spend all day moping round the house and looking at this awful stuff online. How's *that* going to help? You're *not* mentally ill, love, but you *do* need to snap yourself out of all this. Get out of the house, get yourself a new job."

"Right," she said. *Snap out of it* and *get a job* were Iain's catch-all solutions; as he didn't really believe in depression, whatever doctors said, he struggled with the idea work could make it worse. Alien concepts to a nice middle-class boy who'd never known a day's mental health trouble in his life. Easier just to agree with him at times like this.

Thankfully he'd now set about his breakfast and had been raised not to speak with his mouth full, so Cally grunted non-committally and sat with her hands in her lap. She wanted to open the computer up again, but had no desire for another lecture.

The kettle boiled. As always, Iain made his coffee with a ridiculous amount of milk so he could gulp it down as soon as it was made. Cally wanted to go back upstairs and lie down (ideally sneaking the laptop with her to continue her gorehounding without interference) but Iain would only lecture her about staying in bed all day. Like an idiot, she'd left her phone upstairs; she could have at least looked at her Instagram.

Iain slurped his coffee. "Maybe I should stay home today, look after you."

Mother of God, not that. "I'm *fine*." Iain's face stiffened at the sharpness in Cally's voice. "Sorry. I'll be okay, honestly."

For a horrible moment she thought she'd insist on staying home, guaranteeing a truly unbearable day, but then he glanced at his watch, said "Shit," drained the last of his coffee and scurried back into the kitchen to leave his empty mug in the sink. "All right, if you're sure." He pecked her on the lips en route to the door. "What's for tea tonight? Lasagna?"

"Uh-huh." She couldn't remember if the ingredients in the fridge, but again, it was easiest to agree.

"Lovely. See you later."

The front door clicked and, mercifully, he was gone.

Cally slumped back on the sofa, eyes closed.

If she stayed with Iain any longer she'd completely wreck her mental health, and then she'd *have* to move back in with Dad and Lucy. She didn't want to leave Manchester; it would be twice as hard to come back if she did. But needs must.

She'd have to ring Dad, tell Iain they were finished, pack her stuff and make her way to Wales with it (unless Dad came and got her, which would make her feel guilty as hell). Cally groaned. Leaving or staying: both involved far more hassle, stress and work than she currently felt equipped to handle.

So she did what she always did in such circumstances, and

retreated, crawling back upstairs with the laptop, a bottle of water and the heel of a toasting loaf to bury herself in bed – physically in a cocoon of bedsheets, and mentally in p56283's links. She didn't leave the bedroom, except for bathroom breaks, for the rest of the day. She was still there when Iain got home.

4.

When the front door opened, Cally groaned. She'd vaguely resolved to get up and cook tea before Iain returned, but like her earlier resolutions to shower and get dressed, it had been forgotten.

"Cally?"

She shut the laptop, switched off the bedside lamp and pulled the bedclothes over her head.

It was a small house and sound carried, so she could hear Iain irritably muttering downstairs. He was a neat freak, and not only the dishes he'd left in the sink but the paper towels she'd put down to soak up the spilled coffee would still be where she'd left them.

Cally heard him climb the stairs and shut her eyes, even though the bedroom lights were off and her head covered. She'd done the same as a little girl, too. At least until she'd been sure the footsteps were Dad's, and not Millicent's.

"Cally?" Iain tapped at the door, then opened it. "Darling?"

She mumbled vaguely, as if just woken. Iain sighed. "Jesus. Have you been here all day?"

"Mm."

"Love, you said you were going to get yourself up and about. Do something about getting a job."

No, you *harped on about it. As usual.* Iain sighed again: *I'm not angry, darling, just disappointed.* "Okay," he said. "I'll get us a takeaway. Pizza all right?"

"Pizza sounds great." Better to agree for the sake of a quiet life.

"Right."

The bedroom door clicked shut. Cally closed her eyes again, and listened to his footsteps recede down the stairs.

She forced herself under the shower for two minutes and dragged a brush through her hair. Dressing or changing clothes seemed like huge, exhausting tasks on bad days like this, but she'd opted for minimal effort and maximum impact, donning a blue thong and the black silk cheongsam he'd bought her for her birthday.

Again, she wasn't proud of herself – a recurring theme in this relationship – but sex was near-enough all they had left in common; if it gave Cally a much-needed dopamine hit too, she wouldn't complain. The outfit caught Iain's attention, anyway, and improved his mood. They snuggled on the sofa while he told her about his day (in one ear, out the other,) and were necking passionately when the pizza arrived.

With dinner underway, she slipped out of the cheongsam to avoid getting pizza grease on the silk, which made Iain happier still. An early night looked increasingly on the cards, with all sins forgiven in the morning. Happy For Now, if not Happy Ever After.

But she'd spent all day researching and making notes, and once Cally fixated on a subject, she couldn't stop herself talking about it. That'd been true ever since childhood, much to Dad's amusement and Millicent's annoyance.

"Think I've got my next podcast sorted," she said.

"Oh yeah?" said Iain.

The living room grew cold.

You and your big mouth, Cally thought miserably. To Iain, the podcast was just a peculiar hobby, and an unhealthy one at that. But she'd gone and said it now. Maybe she could always things back; she was fairly sure her current state of undress could have distracted Iain from anything short of his parents' severed heads on pikes. "Yeah," she said. "That email I got before? The links I was looking at?"

Iain put his half-eaten slice of pizza down. "Oh. Yeah."

"It's a murder case from the '80s, but no one else has written about it. I'd never even heard of it, but it's really interesting."

"Yeah?" Iain took a sip of beer.

"This guy, Tony Mathias. He was an artist. Pretty successful, one to watch and all that. And then, out of the blue, he had this massive psychotic break. Killed his whole family, set fire to his caravan and shot himself."

"*Caravan*?"

Cally tried not to laugh at how that was what had stood out most for Iain. "Yeah."

"Thought he was successful?"

"He'd won awards."

"Right, so no money."

"Maybe he *liked* living in a caravan."

"I suppose." Iain's tone suggested he'd rather attach giant leeches to his genitals. "What's so interesting, though? Some batty artist type flips out and kills everyone? Big whoop."

"Yeah, but *why* did he go mad?"

"He was an artist, wasn't he?" Iain reached for his pizza slice. "Probably on drugs."

"He hadn't had any trouble before. No sign of anything wrong."

"Apart from being an artist," Iain mumbled through a mouthful of pepperoni and onion.

"Ha-ha. Seriously, he did okay. Married, kids. Everyone who knew them said how nice they were, how happy. And then, 9th June 1983, he took a rifle and shot his wife. His kids ran out of the caravan. He shot *them* both, right in front of the next-door neighbour, then went back inside and–"

"Shot himself." Iain grimaced.

"Set it on fire first."

"Glad we didn't order the BBQ wings."

That was quite witty for Iain. "Not everything burned, though," said Cally. "He'd been writing all over his bedroom walls. Most of it was gone, except two words, written over and over again. *World's End.*"

"So he thought it was Judgement Day?"

"This was the '80s, dude. The Cold War? Have you listened to half the pop music from then? Besides, 9th June 1983 was General Election night. Maggie Thatcher won a second term by a landslide. Nothing short of World War Three was keeping *that* off the front page. I suppose one horrible tragedy was enough."

"She did a lot of good for the country," mumbled Iain, leaving Cally wondering how she could have *ever* thought dating him a good idea. Luckily all around, Iain was too busy eyeing the rest of her to notice her expression.

"Point is, there was no history of mental illness, nothing to indicate Tony Mathias was a danger to anyone. Something must have set him off. If I can find out what, I might have something interesting."

"Not my cup of tea," said Iain. "Horses for courses, though, I suppose." He reached out and cupped her breast. "How about dessert?"

She chuckled and slid astride him. "This is what happens when you bottle-feed babies."

"Oh shurrup," he muttered, then took a nipple in his mouth and sucked.

Cally moaned softly. Depression and medication dampened her libido, but the right kind of kissing and caressing could wake it up. And this definitely qualified. Iain handled her as though he couldn't believe his luck: half near-holy reverence, half-kid-in-a-sweetshop.

She wasn't trying to distract him anymore; she was genuinely enjoying herself. They squirmed and grappled on the sofa for a few more minutes; she undid his shirt, then his belt and slipped to her knees in front of him, taking his cock in her hand. He groaned and shut his eyes.

"Shall we go upstairs?" she said in the sexiest whisper she could manage. Iain couldn't get up the staircase fast enough, which was no mean feat with your trousers and boxer shorts around your knees.

Afterward they snuggled contentedly for a few minutes before Iain rolled over, checked his alarm was set for the morning and began to snore.

Probably for the best; pillow talk would only have exposed the gaps between them again. Her situation was still the same: stay here, or run home to Daddy. Wherever she went, there was neither purpose nor direction in her life. Except, perhaps, in one area.

Cally slid out of bed, pulled on a dressing gown, then took her laptop back downstairs.

5.

She spent the night trying to learn more about the case, but information proved frustratingly thin on the ground. The murders had been forgotten almost immediately: the General Election had initially kept them off the front pages, and the nature of the crime didn't allow for any further developments.

Everyone knew whodunit, after all, and that he wouldn't strike again; there'd be no court case. There'd been no more news to break, and little enough to start with; the crime scene photos, gruesome as they were, only showed the end result.

She mulled potential titles. *The Other World's End Murders* was clunky and confusing; *The Mathias Family Murders* sounded like a copycat version of the Manson Family. In the end she settled on *The Eagle Mount Murders*: that had been the name of the caravan park outside Scorbridge, just north of Blackpool along Lancashire's Fylde Coast.

The second link in pete56283's email had connected Cally to an online archive containing scanned-in back issues of the long-defunct *Scorbridge Advertiser*, the only outlet to treat the killings as front-page news (tucking the election results in a box in the corner.) Below a picture of the burnt-out caravan, one of the bodies, covered by a blanket, lying in the foreground, was the headline WORLD'S END. On page 2, a photograph showed the blackened wall of a room inside the caravan, and the remains of the writing on it: *World's End* appeared at least twice.

Page 3 showed the family in life. The children got the most attention, depicted in a pair of school photographs: Alison, aged six, was angelically pretty, features still softened by a hint of puppy fat. Neal had been thirteen: thin and angular, facing the camera with a confident, shoulders-back stance and bright grin.

Lindsay Mathias, photographed in jeans and chunky sweater, was a tall woman with a pleasant smile, good shoulders and a no-nonsense air. Pretty, motherly, but capable, even tough.

Tony Mathias was the odd one out, with dark eyes and tangled black shoulder-length hair. *Mediterranean* was the word that sprang to mind: Spanish, Italian, maybe Greek.

He looked kind, Cally thought, but she knew, all too well, how appearances deceived. She wondered if the *Advertiser* reporter had known the family: the article's tone was of shock and bewildered grief rather than anything else.

The murders had seemingly come out of nowhere, but she knew crimes like that never did. There was always something. Long, simmering resentments. An escalating pattern of abuse. Untreated mental health issues. *Something.* Any number of horrors could happen behind closed doors, addiction and abuse in particular: people worked hardest to hide the things they were ashamed of but couldn't give up.

A psychotic episode, Cally told Iain, mainly as she'd found no evidence of any other root cause. But *He just went mad* was the kind of explanation that would satisfy Iain; it wouldn't do for her.

Which led to some extensive soul-searching as Cally sat alone amid the detritus of last night's pizza in the wee small hours. Much more research than usual, and every chance it would be more trouble than it was worth, especially given how meagre the podcast's financial rewards were. It was a labour of love as it was.

But this was the first time a fan had suggested a topic. She didn't want to blow that. More to the point, the case intrigued her.

When he died, Tony Mathias had been producing art for the

better part of twenty years, principally as a photographer. In the last half-decade of his life he'd attracted serious attention, with two high-profile exhibitions in London; not bad for a Northerner who'd remained stubbornly based in his native Lancashire. He'd been ranked alongside artists as diverse as Edward Woodman, Helen Chadwick and Robert Mapplethorpe.

He'd started out in glamour photography to pay the bills during the 1970s, leading to his first exhibition, a series of male and female nudes – hence the comparisons to Mapplethorpe – before progressing to landscapes and interiors, usually uninhabited. Bored with photographing the human form in various stages of undress, he'd turned instead to the places it lived in or built for itself. "I'm interested in what we do to the world, the tracks we leave behind," he said in one rare interview. "I like trying to capture the essence of a place on film, not just the image. The *feel* of it, the atmosphere, the history."

Examples of the art itself were fairly sparse online; all Cally could find were images from a retrospective held in 1998 at a gallery in his hometown, Rishcot, as part of a season of work celebrating local artists. It had been organised through Bernard Gowland, his agent, who still represented the estate.

Gowland was still both and working; the 'Contact Us' section of his agency website provided an email address, so he was one of three people Cally emailed before finally returning to bed. The others were the Lancashire Constabulary's enquiries team, and Dr Anand Sabharwal, a lecturer in Pathology at Nottingham University who – after some digging – Cally had identified as having carried out the Mathias family's post-mortems.

She woke to the sound of the shower in the en-suite bathroom, but kept her eyes shut and lay still. The water cut out, and eventually she heard Iain go downstairs.

"See you later, hun," he called, and the front door closed. She opened her eyes then, waited till his car started, then threw back the covers. She'd only returned to bed at three that morning – Iain had, thankfully, slept through – but wasn't tired at all.

Cally knew the power of denial well, and before coming back to bed had resolved, for the time being, not to think about Iain, Millicent, Dad, her finances, or anything else unrelated to the case. As a result, she felt better than she had in days.

She showered and dressed. Today might involve venturing outside, so better to be ready for that now. Depression had an infuriating habit of landing on you when you least expected it, making even simple tasks feel insanely difficult. In that frame of mind, showering, dressing *and* going out could be impossible. Better to get ready now.

Cally took her laptop downstairs, washed up and browned some frozen mince in a pan. She whizzed tinned tomatoes, garlic, onions and herbs in a blender, mixed them and the mince in the slow cooker and switched it on. A serviceable Bolognese sauce would be ready when Iain got home. That should keep the peace.

Then she grilled two pieces of toast, brewed coffee, carried both into the front room and powered up the laptop again. Her breath caught when she saw two new emails, but neither were of any interest and she shook her head. Silly to expect a reply so soon. Cally finished the toast and drained her coffee, and that was when her phone rang.

Probably Iain, calling from work. The best way to keep him happy would be to delay talking to him till the last possible moment, so she almost let it ring out. But she relented, and picked up the phone.

It wasn't Iain: it was a landline number, based in London. She'd have suspected a scam call, except that something about the number made her brain itch: she'd seen it somewhere before. She typed it into her browser quickly, stared at the search result, then reached for the phone, but the call had already gone to her answering service.

Cally had only noticed the Gowland Agency's office number because its last three digits were 666; being a long-time goth and heavy metal fan, that had amused her. It was also the number of the missed call.

New voicemail message, announced her phone.

She clicked the link, surprised to see her fingers tremble slightly.

The voice on the message was warm and deep and pleasantly rough, with the faintest of Geordie accents.

"I'm calling to leave a message for Cally Darker. This is Bernard Gowland. I'd like to have a chat about your email. Give me a call back when you can."

6.

"I saw your email when I came in the office this morning," Gowland said.

"Thanks for calling me back. Is it okay if I record this?"

"Absolutely, pet."

"Thanks."

Cally set her phone to record, set it down beside her laptop, then brought up the Gowland Agency's website.

"As you can imagine," Gowland said, "I've not heard Tony Mathias' name in some time."

"I'm guessing there's not much interest in his work these days." Cally clicked the *About Us* tab on the website and scrolled down to Gowland's biography. He'd been born in 1941, putting him in his early eighties now; his photograph showed a white-haired man with a strong-boned, craggy face that would have looked forbidding if he hadn't been smiling.

"Sadly, no," Gowland said. "And it's a bloody shame. I mean, he did genuinely extraordinary work that deserves to be remembered, and I honestly think his best was still ahead of him when he died. One thing you learn, in this game, is that so much of it's blind chance, be it financial success or being remembered."

He sighed, sounding infinitely melancholic; Cally's bright mood darkened slightly at the edges, but when he spoke again, he sounded cheerier. "Anyway, I had a listen to your podcast. The Miles Giffard one – very well-done, I thought."

"Thank you," she managed, wondering for a dizzy moment if he was about to offer to represent her.

"Tony Mathias could – *should*, in my admittedly biased opinion – have been one of the outstanding artists of his generation. But if he's remembered at all, it's as a nutcase who killed his family."

"I'm sorry," said Cally, unsure if he was reproaching her for snuffling round the carcasses.

"No, it's natural to be curious about these things. I wouldn't be calling you if I didn't think you were doing something worthwhile. You give an actual monkey's for the people you talk about. And you want to know *why*."

"Thank you," Cally mumbled again. When Gowland remained silent, she steeled herself and asked, "Do *you* have any idea?"

Gowland sighed again. "Bloody wish I did. Been trying to figure it out for years. He'd been working on an installation for the Whitworth in Manchester, and, far as I could tell, it was all going great guns. But four, five days before it happened – the Friday, I think, which would've been… what, the third of June? Murders were on the ninth, weren't they? It's not the kind of thing you forget. Anyway, that was when the gallery got in touch with me, damn near having a fit."

Cally cleared her throat. "How come?"

"Tony had decided he had to rip the whole thing up and start again from scratch. Completely different concept. A month before they were due to open, this was, so they were *not* happy. Can't say I was either – I was Tony's agent, so if there was a problem *I* should've been the first to hear. I was used to artistic temperament from some clients, but Tony was very professional. Certainly wasn't like him to dump a project, not when he'd signed everything and taken the brass. He took his time before starting anything. Notes – well, tapes, because he was dyslexic, had terrible handwriting – and sketches galore, though good luck seeing them before he'd set to work. He *hated* discussing works in progress. Getting material for a proposal out of him was like pulling bastard teeth." Gowland coughed. "Pardon my French."

"It's fine," said Cally, amused by the old-fashioned courtesy.

"Anyway, I rang the park manager at Eagle Mount, and she put him on. And I don't mind saying, I was worried, but not in that way."

"How do you mean?"

"He didn't sound himself. I mean, he didn't sound *well*. His voice was rough, like he'd been smoking heavily, or getting tanked up a lot. And he sounded... well, distracted. But all I thought at the time was he'd come down with some sort of bug. Anyway, he told me some unforeseen problems had come up with the project and he didn't see a way round them. *I know it's bloody unprofessional and what-have-you,* he told me, *but I've got to pull the plug on it and do something else.*"

Gowland's Newcastle accent, faint till now, had sharpened; he stopped speaking for a moment, then took a deep breath. "He promised me it would be all right," he said. "He'd something new in mind that he'd crack on with and have all ready for the agreed date. I tried to tell him I needed more information than that. Felt to me like he was just trying to get me off his back. He said he'd been under the weather last couple days, some sort of virus, needed to rest up over the weekend, then get back on the horse in the week. *It'll all be right, mate,* he told me, *honestly it will, but I've got to go for now.*"

The next silence was so long that Cally actually glanced at the phone to make sure Gowland was still there. "What happened then?"

"He hung up," said Gowland. "And that was the last time I spoke to him. In hindsight, it was bloody obvious the virus story was just an excuse to get out of the conversation: the real problem was in his head. Very sensitive bloke, Tony – but also very much a man's man, if you know what I mean. How he was brought up. His parents – his father, especially – thought all artists were, well..."

"Gay?"

"I'm afraid so. And it wasn't the best time to be that way in Britain. How old are you again?"

"Twenty-seven," she said, hoping the conversation wasn't about to take a lecherous turn.

"About what I thought." Gowland sighed. "Before your time, then. Count yourself lucky, is all I can say. A lot's changed, thank God, but it was an ugly bloody time. Thatcher was no friend to the gays, though she'd barely got started with her nastiness then. AIDS had just started making the news too, and there were all sorts of silly scare stories about it."

Being bi and a regular at Pride, Cally knew her queer history and didn't need any lessons, but Gowland sounded half-lost in his own memories. Best to let him carry on; if he came out of that reverie, he might not reveal so much.

"There *were* stories Tony had relationships with men before he met Lindsay," he went on. "No idea if there was any truth in them. Either way, he felt he had to be this old-fashioned bloke like his father – strong and silent, all that malarkey. The only place anything came out was in his work. Maybe that was why he became an artist in the first place. I did wonder if he'd hit some sort of block, if that was the problem. Happens to the best. But he'd been there before, and he'd got through it."

Gowland's voice had roughened, and he broke off. Cally heard running water, then a faint gulping sound. "Sorry about that, lass," he said. "Throat's always drying out these days. After… what he did… I wondered if Tony had hit a block he couldn't get through. Thought he was finished. If that was why. But that wouldn't explain Lindsay and the kids. He *adored* them, absolutely bloody adored them. I suppose it's natural, feeling guilty after the fact. Thinking there was something I should've seen. I wasn't just his agent, I was his *friend*, or thought I was." Gowland's voice became croaky again. "One sec."

She heard him gulping once more, then a sigh of satisfaction. "But as I say," he resumed, "at the time I thought he was just sick. Got back onto the Whitworth, assured them everything was under control. Then it was the weekend. I meant to give him a bell mid-week, but some other things came up and I hadn't time to call him. And then on the Friday I come into the office and my phone's ringing non-stop with reporters asking if I've any comment about my star client slaughtering his entire family."

"I'm sorry," said Cally.

"The rotten truth of it is I've no idea what he was going through, and believe me I wish I did. Might have been a clue in his tapes, but they all went up in smoke when he burned the caravan."

Cally tried not to sigh; ultimately all Gowland could tell her was *he went doolally*, and she'd need more than that to make the podcast work. "What about his neighbours? Did they say anything to the police?"

"Have to ask the police that, I'm afraid. Can't even remember their names now – the neighbours or the coppers."

"What about the park manager?"

"Edna something. Doubt she's still around: must have been seventy at least, and sounded like a chain-smoker into the bargain." A pause. "You spoken to the police?"

"I've emailed to ask if any of the investigating officers are still around. And I'm trying to get in touch with the pathologist who did the post-mortems. See if he found anything. You know. A brain tumour, something like that."

Although Cally doubted it, having seen the crime scene pictures of the blackened, curled-up things that had been Tony and Lindsay Mathias. Even before the fire, they'd both been practically headless. *What did he load the gun with? Bazooka shells?*

"I hope they can tell you more than me."

"You've been very helpful. Honestly."

"Have you tried Stella?"

"Stella?" said Cally.

"Tony's sister."

"I didn't know he had one. There wasn't much about his background online."

"He liked to preserve a certain mystery. Well, look, I've got your email: I'll send you what information I've got. I've some old promotional materials, and some hard information on his background written down somewhere. I'll get it scanned and sent. Wonders of modern technology."

"That would be amazing, if it's no hassle."

"None at all, pet. Glad to help."

"Thanks." It sounded like a hassle to Cally, but she wasn't going to question it. "You think his sister would know anything?"

"Might do. Police might have been more forthcoming with her than me. I wouldn't know, I'm afraid. I'm not the only one who thinks I should have seen it coming."

"Do you have any idea–"

"How to contact her?" Gowland chuckled. "Try her website. She's an actress. No megastar, but you'd recognise her. Done a lot of TV in her time. Mostly stage and voiceover work now, but she does all right. Stella Di Mauro, she calls herself. Her mother's maiden name. You're based in Manchester, aren't you?"

"Er, yeah."

"Well, so's she. That might help. Just don't tell her I sent you, whatever you do."

"Okay."

"I'll email you later today. I've some agency work to do first. I delegate most of it these days, but I like to keep my hand in. Probably go round the bend if I didn't have something to do." Gowland chuckled, then stopped, possibly realising that might not sound so funny in the light of Tony Mathias' fate.

"Thanks so much." Cally felt warm and a little teary. "You're really kind."

"Am I hell. Like I said, it'd be good to see Tony getting remembered – his work, not just the bad stuff. And I reckon you'd do that, if you talked about him. So keep me posted, and if I can be any further help, get in touch. I'll send you my mobile number." Another chuckle. "Just don't give it out."

"I won't." She felt a little dizzy.

"Best of luck, then. Nice talking to you, pet."

Cally rocked back on the sofa. "Whew."

It was the biggest boost her self-esteem had had in weeks, and gave her sufficient energy to spring-clean the house and even go for a short walk in the nearby park afterwards. It was barely dented even by the brusque email she received that afternoon, informing her that Lancashire Constabulary were unable to assist her with any enquiries into the case in question.

7.

Stella Di Mauro liked her coffee black, strong, and with more sugar than Cally had seen anyone take in her life.

A pile of empty sachets lay beside the saucer; Stella finally took a sip, head cocked to one side, then wrinkled her nose and tore open one more. She stirred, tapped the spoon on the rim of the cup, sipped again, nodded, took a longer swallow and finally sighed in satisfaction. She looked at Cally and grinned. "Wondering how I stay so thin? Me too. No idea whatsoever, but I'm very fucking glad."

Cally hadn't really been thinking at all, more gazing in rapt fascination. Stella di Mauro was tall, lean, and gym-toned, with thick gunmetal hair, a high-cheekboned face and her brother's olive complexion, which made her bright blue eyes look more vivid still. She'd certainly taken exceptional care of herself: no one in their seventies looked – and moved – like that by luck alone. If she'd dyed her hair black she'd have easily looked twenty years younger.

"Spoken to Gowland yet?" Stella asked. "I see you have. Don't be fooled, darling, that's all I'll say. He can lay that rough-diamond Geordie charm of his on all he likes, but believe you me, he's a mercenary little cunt."

Her voice was throaty, with aristocratic, cut-glass vowels that gave her liberal use of obscenities a particular ring. That was what RADA did for you, presumably. (According to her website, she'd graduated from there in 1975.)

Cally made a non-committal noise and checked her phone was still recording, wondering if she'd ever get to ask the questions she'd jotted down earlier. She hadn't so much lost control of the interview as never had it in the first place. Stella Di Mauro was a force of nature: all you could do was bear mute awed witness to her.

Cally should have known it had been too easy. Once she'd found Stella's website yesterday and sent an email, she'd been surprised how quickly the actress had replied to suggest meeting for coffee in the Java Bar, a small café on the Station Approach at Oxford Road.

Eleven o'clock sharp, Stella's email had said; Cally had arrived early and found a corner table but yesterday's energy and confidence had seeped steadily away as she sat alone amid black-painted walls, wood-panelled floor and low lighting, nursing a cup of herbal tea so as not to exacerbate her jitters with caffeine, and the appointed time came and went.

By quarter past she'd half-convinced herself the meeting had been a cruel prank to punish her for daring to exploit Tony Mathias for her grubby little podcast, but then Stella had come striding in, waving imperiously to the barista. *Bloody bus got caught in traffic. My usual, please, Tim, darling. Cally, isn't it? What's that you're drinking? Let me get you another. Least I can do.*

And now Cally perched on a backless stool resembling an upholstered cube as Stella, draped regally across the bench seat, held forth. Beyond fumblingly asking permission to record the conversation, Cally had barely got a word in.

"Seriously." Stella wagged a finger. "*Don't* be fooled by Gowland. He's a manipulative sod. It's how he's done so well – fair play in that sense, I suppose. But the man cares about money and nothing else. It was his sole interest when Tonio died and you can bet it's the same now: wring a few more dollars out of the carcass. The bitterest disappointment of his career was not making a fortune out of what happened."

"Because of the election, right?" said Cally. "It kind of overshadowed–"

"Election my very-well-toned-for-seventy-four-years-old

bottom, my dear. I'm not a fool. I know how it goes in the arts world – soon as you die, up goes your value, and Gowland thought it was Christmas come early when Tonio died. Maybe that's why he put so much snow up his nose."

"Cocaine?"

"Oh, he had quite a problem with the old Bolivian marching powder back in the early '80s, did our Bernard. Mind you, so did half of London. Never my stimulant of choice" – Stella raised her coffee cup – "but *chacun à son goût.*"

She sipped her coffee again, and Cally took the chance to speak. "What did he do?"

"Oh, 'twas priceless. Gowland barged into gallery after gallery, completely hammered on the devil's dandruff and Teacher's Highland Cream, rattling on to anyone who'd listen and several who wouldn't about the great lost genius of Tony Mathias and demanding exorbitant fees for them to show a retrospective of his work."

Perhaps genuine grief had played a role in such bad judgement. Cally didn't know if cocaine made you maudlin, but Scotch definitely could.

"All of which, of course, scuppered any chance of a posthumous retrospective and damn near sank the Gowland Agency into the bargain. Reputation counts for a lot, and once word got around half his clients were set to jump ship. Luckily for him, Jane Mulryan had just parted ways with Saatchi and Saatchi, and he took her on as a partner. She kept the agency afloat while he dried out. Kept his clients on board, smoothed all the ruffled feathers – of which there were plenty – and explained it all as grief for a star client and close friend. Laid it on with a trowel. Made her want to throw up, she told me years later. Unfortunately Tonio's will made Gowland his artistic executor in perpetuity. Did my best to fight it, but our parents were gone by then and I was but a struggling actress. Couldn't afford the legal fees. So," Stella raised her coffee cup again in a mock toast, "the Gowland Agency represents the Tony Mathias estate even to this day."

Stella fell silent at last, and Cally cleared her throat. "What was he like? Tony, I mean?"

"Toni*o*," Stella smiled. "That was his real name – Antonio Mathias – but only Momma and I called him that. Even Lindsay called him Tony. Dad fought in Italy during the War – got wounded in Sicily, met Momma in the hospital there. She'd lost most of her family and the rest were diehard *Fascisti* who thought the sun shone out of Mussolini's arse and that she was an out-and-out traitor for fraternising with the enemy."

"So they didn't want anything to do with her?"

"They wanted to do plenty of things with her," Stella said grimly. "Which was why she and Dad left Sicily and never went back. Tonio and I grew up in Jerusalem Heights in Rishcot. Ever been to Rishcot? If not, don't bother. Miserable, benighted place, and Jerusalem Heights was the arsehole of it. And from all I've heard, it hasn't improved. We got the lot growing up. Eyetie, wop, gyppo – not that we were Roma that I know of, but we looked different and Momma had an accent you could blunt an axe on and still lapsed into Sicilian whenever she got emotional. Which was often. No barrel of laughs, as you can imagine, but a lot harder on Tonio than on me."

"How come?"

"I could fight. He couldn't. I've never gone *looking* for trouble, but I know it when I see it. And you can often walk away or talk your way out, but some people will follow you if you walk away, and whatever you say, they'll twist. Because they just want to hurt you. As I think you know very well, dear."

Cally certainly did, both from her schooldays and growing up with Millicent. "You've listened to the podcast?"

"Well, obviously. If you intend to record one about my darling brother, I'm doing my fucking homework. Wasn't any hardship. Don't start rehearsing the new play till next week, so I rather binged it. You do a good job, or I wouldn't be here. Anyway, yes – some people are just cunts, and all you can do is ensure they don't come after you. Hit them first, hit hard, and keep hitting them till you're sure they won't get back up again. Unfortunately Tonio never accepted that. Hated violence of any kind. Dad was convinced he was gay, though I'm afraid those weren't the words he used."

"Was he?"

"Bisexual," said Stella, after a pause. "I didn't give a shit. So he liked both boys and girls – so what? Far more important things in life to be bothered about. Besides, by the time I worked it out – which was before *Tonio* did – I'd caught the acting bug. And believe you me, darling, the performing arts are no place for the homophobic."

"Glad he had you in his corner," Cally said. Dad and Lucy had been more than accepting when she'd come out, but Millicent had nearly had an embolism. An ugly scenario suggested itself to her. "Did his wife know?"

Stella snorted. "I insisted he tell her. Lindsay took it all very much in her stride. Completely different background to us – very middle-class, very Bohemian. Nothing shocked her. I should add, his sexual orientation had nothing to do with his distaste for violence. That was just who Tonio was. Gentlest man I ever knew. Dad taught him how to shoot when we were little, with a .22 rifle. And he was an excellent shot, if he was aiming at a paper target. Even enjoyed himself, under those circumstances. But when Dad took him out to bag rabbits for the pot, it was no soap." Stella shook her head, emphatically. "He could never have harmed a living thing. Let alone a person, let alone–"

She broke off. Cally took a deep breath. "And yet he did."

She immediately regretted saying so, especially when Stella pinned her in that bright blue stare. But eventually the older woman nodded. "Yes. He did. And that's the big mystery."

Cally felt a rush of disappointment. "You've no idea why?"

"I have a theory of sorts, but no proof. I don't know what made him do what he did, but I do know when and where.

He went to that place, and barely a fortnight afterwards…"
Stella made a brief, stiff gesture with one hand, unable to say
the rest.

Cally's heart thumped, fast and hard. "What place?"

Stella swirled her cup's contents, downed them at a gulp
and signalled the barista. "Another, please, Tim."

Neither of them spoke for a few seconds. Then Stella replaced
the cup carefully in its saucer, and said: "Warden Fell."

8.

"It was in Lancashire," Stella said. "About thirty miles from Eagle Mount. Never understood why Tonio lived there. He could easily have afforded a proper house, but he said he liked the freedom to move anywhere they liked. Even though they'd lived there five years when–" She stopped.

Cally waited. The barista brought another coffee and a fistful of sugar sachets. Stella smiled up at him. "Thank you, darling. How well you know me."

The barista blushed slightly, and walked back to the bar. Stella watched him go.

"Think he's got a bit of a thing for you," Cally whispered. It felt strangely intimate, as if she and Stella had somehow become closer.

Stella snorted. "Fancies me rotten, dear. Not that he'll get anywhere. I'd break the poor little chap."

Cally laughed out loud. Stella chuckled, too, but her eyes glistened. She dabbed them carefully with a napkin, then ripped open a sugar sachet. "So, Warden Fell. An RAF base of some kind, during the War. Afterwards, most of it was shut down, with a few parts remaining operational into the fifties or sixties. After that, it was abandoned."

"Why did he go there?" Cally asked.

Stella began sugaring her coffee once more. "He'd heard – no idea where – that the buildings were exactly as they'd been left. That is, the ones from the War still had old propaganda posters and gramophone records lying around, and the same sort of memorabilia in the later ones. Supposedly, there was even a building dating back to the *First* World War, similarly frozen in time. He became obsessed with the place; couldn't stop talking about it."

Cally could understand the appeal; old, abandoned places fascinated her too. She'd never forget seeing inside the old lunatic asylums – long torn down now but preserved on online 'urbex' forums – like Hellingly, Menston and Cane Hill; haunting in their vast decay, echoing with ghosts.

People had spent their lives in places like that, some just for falling pregnant out of wedlock or some equally minor deviation from the norm. Half a century ago, Cally might have too.

She shuddered, but Stella didn't notice. "He said it was a sort of time capsule – one where everything was perfectly preserved and falling apart at the same time. The ideal metaphor for modern Britain, he said – endlessly reliving its lost glory days as it rotted away. He was a cheery bugger."

Cally remembered her conversation with Gowland. "He was doing a commission for the Whitworth, when he died. Was that about Warden Fell?"

Stella Di Mauro chuckled. "No flies on you, dear, are there? Yes, that's right. It played right into Tonio's pet obsessions. He was always on about how superficial society had become – only caring about the surface of things. Images. Gloss. Nothing of depth. And of course, photography was part of the problem, because it only ever captured the surface. The image instead of what was behind it. He was obsessed with the idea of showing the skull beneath the skin, to borrow a line from Auden. Warden Fell was perfect. Layers of time. Layers of history. That's what he said, anyway."

Stella added the last two sugar-sachets to her coffee and gave it a final stir. "*The Ghosts of Warden Fell*. That's what he was going to call it. An installation: he'd gravitated towards those, and to multi-media work. Felt he needed more than flat images on their own. He intended to photograph different rooms at the station from every possible angle – walls, floors, ceilings – blow up the pictures to life-size, laminate and mount them and – well, *assemble* each room in the gallery space. Recreate each incarnation of Warden Fell in the Whitworth Gallery, so you'd walk in and be surrounded by, say, this decaying RAF officer's lounge from World War Two. He'd record new footage on an old Super 8 camera – actors playing the officers and airmen, and project that onto the walls. So you'd literally be seeing..." Stella gestured, inviting Cally to fill in the blank.

"The Ghosts of Warden Fell."

"Exactly. He was going to record ambient sound and local radio traffic there – scroll back and forth through the various frequencies, picking up scraps of static, news broadcasts, aircraft pilots, the police – and that would play on a loop, non-stop, until someone entered the room. Movement-activated, you see. Then it would fade into the background and the other recordings would start playing, as these projected, ghostly images flickered and moved through the abandoned rooms."

"Other recordings?"

"It would vary, depending on the room. If it was this airmen's lounge from World War Two, you'd hear snippets of Vera Lynn and Glenn Miller, old news broadcasts, Churchill's speeches. As if someone had tuned the radio dial to 1940 for a moment. And then that and the projected images would fade out, and you'd be alone in the room again as the static and background noise faded back up."

"Wow." Cally wasn't feigning enthusiasm: she'd genuinely have loved to have seen that. "And then you'd go into the next room, and that would be the fifties?"

"Exactly. He planned four rooms – one for each World War, one for the fifties, one for the sixties. The rub was actually getting into Warden Fell. The station was off-limits to the general public. He wrote to the MOD, requesting access, and was turned down flat." Stella sipped her coffee again. "But Tonio always preferred begging forgiveness to asking permission anyway."

"He broke in?"

"Obviously."

"Couldn't he have got shot?"

"He always said if you wouldn't take risks for your art, you weren't much of an artist."

Cally tried and failed to visualise doing that for the podcast. "Risks are one thing. Getting killed for it, though…"

"He'd set his heart on it, darling. And once Tonio had the bit between his teeth, good luck stopping him. People never understood that. Because he was gentle, they thought he was soft. Because of his sexuality, they thought he was weak. Because he loathed violence, they thought him a coward. And he was none of those things. Couldn't have achieved all he did if he had been." Stella's voice cracked slightly; she took a deep breath.

"So you think something happened to him then?" said Cally, as the other woman recomposed herself.

"Certain of it," Stella said. "The question is *what*. We were very close, but we both had active careers. Mine took me all over the country, and he had a young family to care for. Even so we spoke, normally, several times a week. He liked me to keep in touch. I didn't really have anyone else, you see, and I'd had a few bad years before getting my act together and focusing on my work. Never been particularly lucky when it came to men. No shortage of offers over the years, but a distinct lack of people I'd give my heart for safe-keeping, if you know what I mean."

Cally thought of Iain. "Yeah."

Stella smiled sadly. "Well, may you have better luck than I in that department. It hasn't been a bad life, all told, but it would have been a sight easier with a partner I could rely on. Someone who sees who you are and accepts it, wants it to grow – a price above rubies, dear, to use a Biblical phrase. Believe you me." She waved her relationship woes away. "Tonio had that with Lindsay. And he and his family were in turn a rock for me. I'd ring two or three times a week. Call the payphone at the caravan park outside the old girl's office–"

"Edna somebody?"

"Sorry, darling?"

"The woman at the caravan park. Edna someone or other? That's what–" Cally stopped before she uttered Bernard Gowland's name.

Stella nodded and cocked her head. "Edna... what was it? Welthorpe? Winterborne? Began with W, I remember *that*. Unusual name. What *was* it? It'll bother me all day now if I don't – ah." Stella clicked her fingers. "Woodwiss. That was it. Edna Woodwiss. Can't be many of those to the pound. Doubt it'll do you much good, though. Be astonished if she was still alive. Pretty sure she was tea-lady on the Ark. Decent old girl. She was very kind to me, afterwards."

Stella swirled her coffee moodily in its cup. "Anyway, I'd ring the payphone, which she'd usually answer. She'd shout Tonio, and we'd chat. As I say, she was a good old thing. Tonio, of course, had told me all about his plans to sneak into Warden Fell – yes, I know, over the phone. A brave and gifted artist, but the brains of a wet tea-bag when it came to common sense."

"Could somebody have found out what he was going to do?" said Cally. "Been waiting for him when he went in?"

"Unlikely. When I first spoke to him after his visit, he was very chipper. But perhaps the authorities *became* aware of what he'd done. Particularly as–"

Cally hadn't missed the aborted sentence. "Particularly as?"

"There was interference on the line when I spoke to him that day, and whenever we talked after that."

"What kind of interference?"

"Like a crossed line – does that still happen? I know it's all different now. Digital. When did telephone exchanges stop being a thing? The nineties? Anyway, the telephone system was still very much an analogue affair in those days. Sometimes you'd be talking to one person, but you'd hear a completely different conversation going on in the background. Or now and again, the foreground. It had never happened before with the phone at Eagle Mount, but it was constant after Warden Fell. Had trouble hearing him a couple of times. It only occurred to me in retrospect that his phone might have been bugged."

"But he didn't seem worried?"

"Certainly not that first time. A little gruff, as if he was coming down with a cold – I didn't think anything of that at the time, though later... but no, he was in good spirits. Said he'd hit some problems with the current project, but nothing he couldn't handle. I suspect he was deliberately playing down his concerns for my benefit, but even so, he didn't seem particularly worried. This would have been the Thursday. Exactly two weeks before the General Election. At that point, he was entirely normal. Entirely his usual self."

Stella signalled the barista for another coffee. "In the meantime I'd had news of my own. Earlier that year I'd auditioned for Birmingham Rep – didn't quite make the cut, but one of the directors really liked my work and when one of the regular company fell ill, he offered me a place. Guaranteed employment for the rest of the summer season, and a good chance of work over autumn and winter; naturally I jumped at the chance. Tonio was delighted when I told him. He was, at that moment, as untroubled as I'd ever known him. I want to make that absolutely clear."

"So what happened to him wasn't connected with Warden Fell?" Cally felt disappointed: the abandoned base, the secrecy, the potentially bugged phones had all suggested some suitably juicy intrigue, but she couldn't build the podcast around a red herring.

"I never said *that*." Stella sounded quite severe. "Pay attention, darling. You're the first person I've told of this."

"Oh."

"Don't look so surprised. There were journalists sniffing round afterwards, but they wanted stuff about sex and drugs, to make Tonio look like some sort of degenerate monster, not loony-left ramblings about military bases and tapped phones. I didn't hide my politics – CND, Anti-Apartheid – and I was no doubt listed somewhere as a dangerous subversive. Tonio, too. Certainly the impression I got when the police interviewed me, along with another gentleman who seemed very much cut from a different cloth. Public-school accent, Savile Row suit. Didn't say much, except at the end, to tell me to forget anything I thought I knew about Warden Fell. Draw from that what you will. It's possible there was no connection, and they just didn't want the place getting any unwanted attention. But I think that Mr Savile Row, whoever he was, knew exactly what had happened to my brother. I've my suspicions, which we'll come to, but for now I'll stick to the facts so I don't sound deranged. And yes, I'm telling tales out of school, but I doubt Mr Savile Row would be particularly bothered now. All sorts of nasty business from the eighties has come out in the wash – Hillsborough, Orgreave and so on. It's ancient history, done and dusted. No one cares. A footnote. Like the murders themselves, pushed into the background by that wretched Thatcher woman."

Cally couldn't help laughing at the arch disdain in Stella's tone. The older woman chuckled. "I suppose that did sound a bit lady-of-the-manor. Ironic when you consider I'm about as upper-class as Bernard Manning."

"Who?"

"Count yourself lucky you don't know. Anyway, back to my brother. As I said, we normally spoke three times a week – Monday, Wednesday or Thursday and the weekend. He'd bounce ideas off me and I'd let off steam either about my lack of work or the people I was working with. Joys of showbiz for you there. However, my first few days in Birmingham were rather hectic – learning lines and blocking, sorting out digs – so it wasn't till the following Wednesday that we spoke again, and by *then*, there'd been a very noticeable change."

The barista brought Stella another coffee and set it before her. "Thank you, darling," she said, but left it untouched. "You know, my dear," she told Cally, "I know it's early, but I think I could use something stronger."

9.

Cally was almost Stella's height, but had to run across Whitworth Street West, then Oxford Street, to keep up with her long-legged stride. Her eyes watered, despite the Clarityn she'd taken before leaving the house; the pollen count was particularly high today.

Stella strutted past the square off-white edifice of the Palace Theatre, beneath banners advertising *Greatest Days* and *Dirty Dancing*, halted as though snapping to attention and nodding towards a plain wooden entrance beneath the sign of *The Stage Door*. "Opens at nine sharp," she said. "They know us actors well."

The bar was quiet and low-lit, with wooden tables, comfortable-looking padded chairs and bench seating; Stella ordered a double brandy and sought out a quiet corner; Cally bought a diet cola, trying not to flinch at the prices, then joined her, setting her phone to record once more.

Stella downed half the brandy at a gulp, then launched back into her story. "What happened in that intervening week, I've no idea, and believe me, darling, I tried to find out. If the police learned anything, I never heard about it; Edna Woodwiss, as I said, was very helpful and kind, but she couldn't tell me much about the period leading up to the murders."

"She didn't notice anything unusual?" said Cally.

"I didn't say *that*. Two days after I first spoke to him, Tonio stopped leaving the caravan. Soon after that, so did Lindsay. So, more to the point, did Neal and Alison, and it normally took a ball and chain to keep them inside. Those two were out in all weathers, unless there was a full-blown monsoon going. Edna

56

only saw them outside once, on the Monday evening after I called, playing on the grass outside. But only for a moment, before Tonio started bellowing at them to get back in. I had to ask her to repeat herself, because Tonio never raised his voice to the children. Made a point of it. Our father had been like that, you see, and Tonio was determined to be nothing like him. Edna had been genuinely shocked as well. She didn't see the children clearly with the sun going down. They were in silhouette, but she said Neal was ... limping."

"An accident?" suggested Cally. "Maybe that was why they were keeping him indoors?"

"I very much wanted to believe that," said Stella. "My brother wasn't a flawless parent, or a flawless anything else. I'm sure he sometimes fell short of the standards he set himself. But what parent *doesn't*? Shouting at the children once, in isolation, wouldn't mean anything. But even if Neal was temporarily disabled, that wouldn't stop Alison going outside. Or Lindsay. And then there's... how it ended."

She drained the last of her brandy, staring silently down into the glass. "Another?" said Cally at last.

"Just a single this time, please." Stella didn't look up. "Don't want to get completely hammered."

Cally went and got the brandy, wincing at the bar tab again. Still, along with bus fare to Manchester, one herbal tea and one diet cola, it was the only actual expense she'd incurred all morning, Stella having insisted on paying for her own drinks till now. Cheap at the price, for what Cally was getting in return.

Stella gazed into space, picking at her lip. "Wish I still smoked, sometimes. Not that you can in a bar any longer. Ah. Thank you, my dear."

"You're welcome." Cally checked the phone was still recording; the last thing she wanted was to lose some essential information to a technical fault. Everything remained in working order.

Stella took a fortifying sip. "When I spoke to my brother the following Wednesday, something felt wrong from the very start: Edna actually seemed reluctant to fetch him, and he took so long to show up I thought we'd been cut off, but just I was about to put the phone down, someone picked up the handset and said '*Hello?*'"

She took another, deeper sip. "I said '*Tonio?*' because I was far from certain it was him. It certainly didn't *sound* like him. It was a hoarse, rasping voice, thick and sort of slurred, as if he was drunk. Or sick. Tonio drank very sparingly; another way he avoided emulating our father."

"'*Who's this?*' The voice said. And then: '*Spingula?*'"

"Spingula?"

"'Pin,' darling, in Sicilian. Momma called me it, when we were very young, because I was so bloody thin – it became Tonio's pet name for me. only he used it. Then he said '*What do you want?*' And, well, what did you say to that? I didn't *want* anything, other than to talk to my brother. That's supposed to be what family *do*. But I pulled myself together and asked him how he was."

"And how was he?" Cally prompted again. Stella's speech had grown halting, as if running out of steam.

"Not *good*, obviously. He was normally quite the motor-mouth, at least with me. Runs in the family, I suppose."

Stella's eyes were glistening again; surprising even herself, Cally touched her hand. "Are you okay talking about this?"

Stella snorted. "I doubt it, darling. I mean, you'd worry about me if I *was*. Both our parents were dead, remember. Tonio, Lindsay, the children were the only blood family I had. And suddenly they were gone. That was bad enough, but then there was *how*. My sweet, gentle brother, who hated violence, took a rifle and shot his own children." Her voice cracked, but she waved Cally back. "No, keep recording. It needs to be said. Never told my side of it, other than to the police. And the odd therapist. But I've run ahead of myself. You want to know about those last conversations, before the end."

"If that's okay." Even as she spoke, Cally was angry with herself; she sounded as though she were asking Stella to stand her the price of a drink.

"Of course it's 'okay,' darling. I knew what we'd be discussing. It's just not easy. Nor should it be. Anyway, I said I was just calling, as usual, and gabbled the latest news from the glamorous world of theatre – which normally got a laugh, or at least a chuckle, but he just grunted. So I asked him how they all were, and he said *Not too clever*. Something our grandfather used to say during his last illness, which wasn't reassuring. He said they were all down with a virus of some kind – flu, probably – so they were staying in the caravan and sweating it out. It'd be done in a week or so. Edna was very kindly going to the shops for them in the meantime. And I almost believed him."

"But not quite?"

"No, but I didn't realise exactly why till later. It was how he'd said it: *It'll be done in a week or so*. I think that was the closest he came to telling me what was really going on. He knew it wasn't the flu, and that it wasn't getting better."

Stella drained the rest of her brandy. "We last spoke on the following Tuesday. Two days before the end. According to Edna they hadn't left the caravan in that time. I started to tell her I'd try again in a couple of days, but she'd already gone to fetch him – she was worried too, you see. She came back a minute or so later. *He's just coming*, was all she said."

Stella looked down; Cally thought she was about to request another brandy, but she pushed it away and leant back, fingers steepled at her lips. "Edna told me later that when he came out, Tonio was muffled up from head to foot. A heavy parka with the hood up, a scarf over his face, sunglasses, gloves. Not an inch of skin exposed. When he finally came to the phone, he said he felt better, and did sound a little more *compos mentis*, but it just didn't sound like him anymore."

"How do you mean?"

"I mean it didn't *sound* like my brother. Oh, it was a bad line – crossed lines again, half a dozen other conversations going on in the background – but that voice. Rasping, thick – but above all, cold."

"Cold?" said Cally.

Stella nodded. "Tonio was *warm*. He was kind. There was none of that in the voice I heard. I could almost believe someone was impersonating him, but whoever it was talked like Tonio. Even called me *spingula*. Said they were all on the mend, the sprogs would love to see their Aunty Stella, and when could I come up? But – cold. I told him I'd be very tied up in Brum for the foreseeable, and he started trying to talk me into getting time off – even call in sick myself. And then suddenly – I've never forgotten this – his voice changed. Still rasping, still hoarse, but *now*, finally, it was warm again. *Now* it sounded like him. And he said *No*, spingula, *don't come. Honestly. Stay put.* And then he put the phone down. I would have thought he was angry with me, but–"

"But he sounded warm," said Cally.

Stella nodded. "I don't know what would have happened had I gone up there, but I've no doubt I'd also be dead. Shot, or infected."

"Infected?"

"I'll come to that. But something like the brother I knew re-emerged at the end of that phone call, quite possibly for the last time ever. He made sure, at least, that I wasn't a victim too. Two days later, he and his family were dead."

10.

At last, Cally cleared her throat. "Can I get you another brandy?"

Stella considered, then nodded. "Another double, if I may."

When she came back from the bar, Cally checked again she was still recording, then asked: "What did you mean by *infected*?"

"A theory, nothing more." Stella shrugged. "You can't go forty years without an answer, even if you have to invent one. I've no evidence to support it, and I'm fully aware it sounds like the rantings of someone who makes hats from Bacofoil, so I'd appreciate it if you didn't make your podcast some lurid conspiracy theory affair."

"That's not my thing."

"No. We wouldn't be talking otherwise. My theory, for what it's worth, is that Warden Fell had been used to manufacture, test or store chemical or biological weapons. This *was* during the Cold War, after all – most major governments experimented with them, if only to perfect counter-measures. When Tonio broke in there, he became infected and he in turn he, unwittingly, infected his family. Their isolation was to protect themselves and others, and to hide his own shame at contaminating them too. Killing them was an act of mercy, the fire at attempt to destroy the evidence. But there's no proof, as I said; it's all a guess, although given how I was not-so-subtly warned to forget Warden Fell, perhaps not entirely a wild one. Might explain why he scrawled *World's End* all over the walls. No doubt it all felt quite apocalyptic. So that's that. Don't break out the straitjackets. Anything else?"

"You said he hated violence of any kind."

"Always did."

"But he had a rifle."

"I know. That almost astonished me more than the murders themselves. The police solved that mystery, at least. It seems he got it via the local paper."

"The *Scorbridge Advertiser*?"

A nod. "The classified ads had a shooting and fishing section. This was before Hungerford and Dunblane; firearms legislation wasn't as tight as it is now. A local farmer advertised an old gun for sale; Tonio arranged to buy it, the day after I spoke to him for the last time. Apparently they met that evening on some benighted country lane. All very cloak and dagger. Tonio didn't even have a licence, of course, but he'd offered the seller two or three times the asking price, and I don't believe the other chap was particularly scrupulous. Or bright, for that matter." Stella emptied her glass in a single swallow. "Anyway, he sold Tonio the rifle and a box of ammunition, and the next day my brother used them. Is that all?"

It sounded like a warning that she'd reached her limit, and Cally shook her head. "Thank you." She wanted to say more, but could think of nothing that wouldn't have sounded trite or patronising.

Stella took out a small notepad, wrote in it with a fountain pen, then tore out the page. "My email, telephone number, and home address." She drew the paper back as Cally reached for it. "I'm trusting you with this. I don't just give this information to anyone. It's not to be shared with others."

"I understand."

A grim smile. "I hoped you would. This is for ease of contact, in case of any further questions, or new evidence. If you *do* learn anything, I expect to be told before you make it public. Are we clear?"

It was more a royal command than a request. Cally nodded.

"All right," said Stella Di Mauro and walked stiffly out, leaving Cally nursing the dregs of her cola.

She uploaded the recordings to her Google Drive before heading home; once home, she downloaded the audio files to her laptop and played them back, skipping through them to ensure the sound quality was constant throughout. It did; Stella Di Mauro's voice rang from the speakers, crisp and clear.

She'd listen to them properly later, but that could wait. She was still no closer to a reason, aside from Stella's theory, which the woman herself admitted sounded downright crackpot. On the other hand, there was no denying Tony's visit to Warden Fell had coincided with the onset of his breakdown.

But even if he'd changed *after* Warden Fell, that didn't mean he'd done so *because* of it. The real cause could have been something else entirely.

To hide his shame, Stella had said; perhaps she'd got the motive right, but not the cause. She'd called her brother gentle, incapable of harm, but however well you thought you knew someone, parts were always off-limits and secret; you never knew what went on there. Just as things went on behind closed doors that the outside world couldn't guess at. Like addiction. Or abuse.

Stella wouldn't have entertained the possibility of her brother molesting his children even for a second – would probably have scratched Cally's eyes out for suggesting it – but it was impossible not to consider the possibility, at least Lindsay Mathias had been described as a strong and capable woman. If she'd discovered evidence of abuse and tried to leave, taking them with her – especially if she'd intended to expose him, too – that probably would have felt like the *World's End* to Tony. Even Stella might have turned her back on him. Death, and murder, might seem preferable to that kind of shame.

But that was pure speculation too. Cally couldn't accuse anyone of something like that without evidence, alive or dead. She didn't want a furious Stella coming after her. Bernard Gowland wouldn't want that kind of publicity for his late client, either, and despite what Stella had said, Cally had liked him too. She'd liked them both.

Truth's true whether people like it or not.

But while it sounded far more plausible than Tony Mathias accidentally contracting the Black Death at Warden Fell, it didn't explain why he'd wrapped himself up the way he had.

And it didn't explain the rifle. That wasn't just brutally violent in a way Tony had supposedly never been: he'd found the advert, called the seller, arranged to meet and bought the gun. Planned, premeditated, cold-blooded.?

What didn't he want people to know?

Another reason it was easier piecing this kind of thing together second-hand, from existing sources: you didn't have to deal with grieving loved ones, or juggle their feelings against the questions that needed asking.

Who says they need asking anyway? You're not the police, or even a proper journalist.

But ordinary folk like Cally *did* solve cases, old and new, sometimes.

To Stella Di Mauro, her brother had been a good man who, out of nowhere, had done something horribly aberrant and wrong. But when someone snapped like that, there was usually a trail that, at least in retrospect, proved horribly clear.

It might be better to ask Gowland; he had a soft spot for Tony, but whatever Stella's opinion of him, he hadn't made his living by being overly sentimental.

But that wasn't a conversation Cally wanted to have now. Instead, perhaps, she could look into the background. Cally opened a browser window, and typed in *Warden Fell*.

11.

Warden Fell was in the Forest of Bowland in north-west Lancashire, a few miles from Pendle Hill. Cally knew the area; she'd stayed at the Pendle Inn one Halloween weekend five years ago with Stevie, her then-partner.

They'd driven up on a Friday evening, after work. Only twenty miles from Manchester, but another world. Brickwork, concrete and neatly-tailored parks had given way to hills, woods and moorlands, broken up by scattered, stone-built villages that formed little clusters of light after dark.

Here and there were bigger settlements: the old mill-towns like Burnley and Rishcot, grown in the 1800s and still clinging on despite the deaths of the industries that had built them. But for long stretches she'd seen only occasional road-lamps and distant pylons, faint, easily-erased pencil-marks against the grey, rainy sky. A rugged, isolated environment, demanding self-reliance and independence from those it bred, regarding outsiders with suspicion.

Pendle Hill had been home to the legendary Pendle Witches; Stevie had guessed – rightly – that a weekend spent hiking over hill and dale, followed by pub grub, whisky and a side order of ghost stories, would be Cally's ideal romantic getaway. She'd understood Cally, better than poor Iain ever would. They'd climbed Pendle Hill; maybe they'd glimpsed Warden Fell from its summit.

Cally didn't believe in the supernatural – despite the Catholicism Millicent had tried ramming down her throat – but loved a ghost story, especially in surroundings like that, where such things seemed almost possible, giving the nights at the Pendle Inn a delicious thrill of unease once the lights were out and the village outside silent. She and Stevie had snuggled a little bit closer, and their lovemaking had gained extra spice and urgency.

Warden Fell's Wikipedia page was a stub giving only the hill's height and location. Cally searched patiently as the afternoon wore on, bookmarking webpage after webpage and gathering information scrap by scrap.

Ninety percent of what she found was irrelevant. There was plenty of folklore about Warden Fell, but that'd be a footnote to the episodes at most. Probably not even that. The podcast was about human beings like Cally herself; she always tried to remember that, but after interviewing Gowland and Stella she was particularly aware of it, and didn't want to appear to take the topic lightly in any way. Likewise, Neolithic settlements, Iron Age earthworks and the hill being one of the likeliest locations of Greston Castle wouldn't explain what Tony Mathias had done. Assuming anything would.

Still, slowly but surely she assembled a history of Warden Fell from 1911, when one of Britain's first Aero Clubs had been founded there. Little more than a field, hut and hangar, but the fledgeling Royal Flying Corps had nonetheless commandeered it for pilot training after the outbreak of the First World War.

Cally loved the little detours her research so often led her down: history was her favourite subject precisely because no other topic revealed so much about what had driven people or what drove them still. And she always found a particular fascination in cul-de-sacs and roads not taken – what-ifs, could-have-beens and buried things that came to light long after the events were forgotten and the protagonists dead.

A case in point: today she learned that the earliest unmanned aerial vehicles had flown during the First World War. Dubbed 'ATs' or 'Aerial Targets' to conceal their true purpose, none had ever been used in combat, and for years had been assumed to have been failures. Records showing how successful the designs had really been were only declassified in 2016.

According to the same records, most AT designs were developed and built at the Royal Aircraft Factory in Farnborough, but two smaller aerodromes were selected as secondary sites: Chillingholme on Tyneside, and Warden Fell in Lancashire.

The ATs built at Warden Fell, however, were plagued with technical issues. Designers and engineers blamed 'atmospheric anomalies'; the same machines flew successfully at Farnborough and Chillingholme. By early 1918, Warden Fell had resumed its earlier function as a training field.

During the 1920s it fell into disuse, but was revived on a 'care and maintenance' basis by the RAF as World War Two approached. It briefly served as a training station again, until the 'atmospheric anomalies' resurfaced, disrupting radio communications between pilots and the control tower and causing three fatal crashes.

In spite of that, Warden Fell served as part of the Chain Home early warning network during the Battle of Britain, then as a relay station and listening post. As far as Cally could tell, the mysterious anomalies proved less of an issue during that period; one article claimed the station gained a reputation as an unlucky or jinxed posting, but gave no further details.

With the advent of the Cold War, Warden Fell was incorporated into Chain Home's successor, ROTOR, but by the end of the 1950s the threat was from missiles, not bombers, and it reverted to its former role of listening post and transmitter relay before being declared surplus to requirements in 1966. It had stood empty ever since but remained Ministry of Defence property, despite lacking any strategic value that Cally could discover. A private buyer made an offer for the site in 1981, hoping to re-establish the old Aero Club, but the MOD had refused to sell.

And so Warden Fell had been left to decay, off-limits, unused and unwanted, until Tony Mathias had come along in 1983.

Cally found no evidence there to support Stella's theory that Warden Fell had ever been more than an airfield or radio station. But, to paraphrase Mandy Rice-Davies, *they would say that, wouldn't they?* The government would hardly admit to stockpiling nerve gas or weaponised anthrax in an Area of Outstanding Natural Beauty.

Rabbit-hole thinking. You can't prove they didn't have the Ark of the Covenant or a giant pink giraffe called Edwin either. What can you prove?

Cally only found one picture of Warden Fell after its shutdown, on an aviation website called *The Drome*. Dated 2015, it showed the station from some distance outside the chain-link fence surrounding it. The buildings looked pretty dilapidated; it didn't look as if anyone had been inside in years, even the MOD.

Urbex, she thought.

Warden Fell would certainly appeal to anyone who liked poking around abandoned, disused places. For hard-core urban explorers, its being strictly off-limits would only have heightened the attraction.

Cally reached for the laptop to bring up an urbex site, but as she did the front door opened: "I'm home!"

"Hey." She gave Iain her brightest smile. It wasn't hard: the day had put her in an upbeat mood.

"Had a good day?"

"Very." She started telling him – the meeting with Stella, the afternoon's research – but tailed off as his smile faded. "What?"

"I thought we agreed last night you were going to look for a job."

Cally vaguely recalled Iain droning on about how she needed to pull herself together or some similar platitude (yet again.) Tuning him out and agreeing intermittently with whatever he said had been the least painful option at the time.

"Did we? I don't remember – I can't–"

He sighed and shook his head.

"For Christ's sake," she said. "I'm signed off sick, Iain. Can't you get that through your head?"

He snorted. "Cally, you're just making excuses."

"Iain, look, I'm sorry. I'm not capable of holding down a job right now–"

"You've no trouble spending all day digging up useless, sick stuff on the internet. That's all computer work, isn't it? No difference."

"Iain–"

"No, Cally. It's time I put my foot down. Do you seriously think you're going to make your fortune or something, with this morbid crap? You need to grow up and take responsibility for yourself, as I keep saying. How do you ever expect to form a proper relationship and start a family?"

"A *what*?" Cally had no intention of starting a family, ever. No doubt Iain had just decided not to hear it; like the podcast, like her depression, it was all just part of her refusal to grow up. She couldn't handle the full-blown row this was set to turn into; grabbing the laptop, she stormed upstairs.

"I don't suppose you sorted dinner out?" he yelled.

"It's in the fucking slow cooker," she shouted back, but Iain followed her up the stairs. "Cally, don't run away," he said. "We need to talk about this."

What she needed, right now, was to be away from him; in the end she had to lock herself in the upstairs bathroom, fingers in her ears while he shouted through the door, trying and failing not to cry. Biting her wrist so he didn't hear.

Finally, he gave up and went downstairs. Eventually Cally tiptoed to the bedroom, undressed and crawled into bed. Later still, she heard the TV, turned up aggressively loud. She pulled the covers over her head, crying quietly, and finally slept.

12.

She woke in the middle of the night; Iain lay snoring beside her, a few inches and an eternity away.

After several long minutes Cally uncurled herself, very slowly, from the foetal position she'd fallen asleep in and slid – very slowly, once again – out of bed. Iain wasn't likely to wake – once he started snoring, he could usually sleep through an artillery bombardment – but she wouldn't take the chance. With her luck, this would be the night she'd breathe too hard and wake him up.

She picked up her phone, laptop and clothes; got dressed on the landing and crept downstairs. For now, at least, she was calm, and knew what she had to do.

But you'll have to pack your stuff, and talk to Dad, and–

Except she wouldn't: Dad and Lucy would always welcome her, their spare room ready and waiting. How did the Robert Frost poem go? Home was the place where, when you went there, they had to take you in? That was Dad and Lucy: hugs, hot chocolate, and *take all the time you need*. She even kept some spare clothes there.

As for packing, she already had all she'd need tonight. She'd brought the phone and laptop with her. Her shoulder-bag was beside the sofa, where she'd left it after coming back from meeting Stella, which now seemed years ago.

Phone, laptop, chargers, meds, keys; everything else she could come back for.

Cally consulted her phone. It was two a.m.; Dad and Lucy's place was perhaps two hours' drive away. *Showing up without warning at four in the morning*; she almost laughed. But she still had her own key; she could tiptoe in, leave a note. The important thing was to leave while she'd still the will to do so.

Cally faltered; she began the ritual of checking her email and socials, but didn't get past her inbox: there was a message from Lucy, no subject, sent at seven p.m.

Oh Christ. Dad. He's had a stroke, a heart attack, an accident, while you were lying in bed feeling sorry for yourself.

Cally clicked on the message.

> Hi Cally. Lucy here! Hope you and Iain are well. Just to let you know your Dad and I are going away tonight for a fortnight in Crete – little surprise I arranged for our anniversary. SO SORRY not to have told you but completely forgot. Off to John Lennon airport in half an hour! Here's a link to the place we're staying.
>
> Love to both of you. Lucy xxx

Cally breathed out in relief, then put a hand to her mouth to muffle laughter. She jabbed the link in the text message and found herself studying a picture of a rented villa in Elounda. They'd be there now; probably lying in bed, recovering from the jet lag.

Their house in Bala would be empty. There'd be food in the freezer, and a bed to sleep in. No awkward explanations, no creeping in on tiptoe. Just get in the car, and drive.

Could it really be that simple?

Cally decided that it could, and the thought made her happier than she'd felt in months. Tonight, at least, life was simple and straightforward, its problems easily solved. That wouldn't last, but it should be enough to get her home.

She stuffed the phone and laptop into her shoulder-bag, pulled on her boots, then scribbled a quick note on a post-it. *Iain, this isn't working. I've gone back to my Dad's. Will be in touch about my stuff. Cally x.* She wasn't sure about the *x*, but it seemed to say *No hard feelings*, which seemed a good idea. She stuck the note on the coffee-table, stood up and went to the front door.

Sure about this?

For a moment she hesitated: the leaden weight of her depression threatened to flatten her, her anxiety to paralyse her. But then she'd unlocked the door and stepped through, easing it shut behind her and relocked it with a slow, slow turn of the key.

The air outside was fresh and cool. She looked up at the bedroom window, afraid she'd see the light come on, but it stayed dark. Beyond the roof, stars glittered in the sky, through rags of cloud glowing dull orange from reflected streetlight.

The skies above her father's house would be far clearer, and far more alive with stars.

She went down the drive, past Iain's car to the kerb where her battered green Punto was parked, and realised she was smiling. She considered letting the handbrake off and wheeling the car along the street before starting it, in case the engine woke Iain, then laughed. She wasn't breaking out of prison. Iain couldn't stop her going. No one could. Nothing.

Cally unlocked the car and got behind the wheel. For a second the long drive to Bala stretched dauntingly ahead, and fear and paralysis threatened to settle on her again. But only for a second. The engine coughed and growled, then purred; she typed Dad's postcode into the sat-nav. She knew the way, but it broke the journey down into simple steps, easy to focus on and follow if her nerve flagged. But she didn't think it would.

And then she could give all the attention she wanted to the Eagle Mount Murders, to Tony Mathias, and to Warden Fell.

Cally glanced one last time at the bedroom window: still dark, unlit and unaware. Then she put the Punto into first and drove.

Part Two
I Know A Dark Much Blacker Than Night

13.

Cally drove through Bala around five a.m., then followed a road leading up into the hills above the lake. She'd driven slowly and steadily, but her earlier energy had dissipated over the journey; when she finally reached Dad's converted farmhouse, it took nearly half an hour to chivvy herself out of the car and in through the front door.

She was hungry, but thankfully there was a block of cheese in the fridge, and half a sliced loaf. Making a sandwich exhausted the last of her energy; after another half-hour she crawled upstairs to the spare room, undressed, slid under the covers and slept.

Karl – the ex Cally had fled without her pills – had revered Charles Bukowski, and modelled himself on the man in all the worst ways possible. Largely thanks to that, Cally wasn't a Bukowski fan, but she'd never forgotten an interview with him she'd seen, where he'd talked about his remedy for depression.

It was simplicity itself; he went to bed for a couple of days, getting up only to eat, drink, or answer the call of nature; within two or three days, he felt rejuvenated. It wasn't hard to understand: no work, no pressure, no people. That last was easiest if you lived alone, so Cally decided to try it now.

It worked, too. She woke or half-woke several times when her mobile rang, but ignored it. Probably only Iain anyway. She slept almost continuously through her first day at the farmhouse, and finally woke up ravenous.

A couple of takeaways in Bala delivered, but Cally resisted the temptation. There were eggs in the kitchen, and a fully-stocked chest freezer in the basement. She retrieved a fresh loaf of bread, a packet of bacon and a cottage pie from there, defrosted a few bread slices in the microwave and made another cheese and pickle sandwich. Appetite sated, she crawled back up to bed.

Cally often thought of her depression as a tide, sometimes sweeping in, sometimes receding. By the following afternoon the tide was finally going out. She'd sweated copiously through the hot day and night before and both she and the room stank, but it was another beautiful day outside and when she opened the bedroom window the air was fresh and clean, and Cally wanted to be out in it, even though it would play hell with her hay fever. Thankfully there was a nearly-full packet of Clarityn in the bathroom cabinet, so she took a dose, before showering.

She soaped and scrubbed and shampooed herself till it felt like she was cocooned in lather, then let the water rinse it away. Sitting in front of the bedroom mirror in a towelling robe, hair wrapped turban-like in a towel, she felt almost normal again. She dabbed on a little light make-up, just for fun.

And then the doorbell rang.

When she looked out of the window, she saw a police car in the yard outside.

The two officers were about Cally's age. A trim but solid-looking woman with short chestnut hair and a round face, a lean man with dark hair and eyes. Mediterranean-looking, like Tony Mathias. Both were unsmiling.

Iain was her first thought, and then another, deeper dread: something had happened to Lucy and Dad. Cally's hand went up to her mouth.

"What's happened?" she said. "Are they okay?"

The woman frowned; the man cleared his throat. "I'm

sorry?" he said. He had a strong Welsh accent. "Is who okay?"

The policewoman recovered the initiative first. "Miss Darker?"

"Ms," Cally said automatically. "But yeah."

"Cally Darker?" The woman had very little accent; a hint of Scouse, nothing more. There was a funny look on her face; she looked shocked, somehow, as if she'd seen someone or something she hadn't expected to. But only briefly; then it was gone. "Is that right?"

"Yes." Cally looked from her to the man. "What's happened?"

"I'm Police Constable Rooke." The policewoman's face was composed again, giving nothing away. "This is Constable Greene. Can we come in?"

Cally wanted to fold her arms and say *not until you tell me what this is about,* but a superstitious part of her feared it would be bad news about Dad or Lucy after all if she antagonised these two. Besides, it was hard to be confrontational in a robe, towel-turban and bunny slippers, so she nodded and invited them in.

Rooke came in first, Greene following. The door clicked shut behind him. "Are you on your own here, love?"

If not for the *love,* and Greene's gentle Welsh accent, Cally might have been nervous, but those, along with Rooke's presence, calmed her somewhat. "Yeah," she said. "This is my dad's place. Owen Darker. Him and his partner are away at the moment. Flew out to Crete last night."

Rooke nodded. "Do you know an Iain West?"

Cally's imagination took another, uglier turn: something had happened to Iain, and she was a suspect. "My boyfriend. Ex."

"That's why we're here."

"Sorry?"

"Mr West contacted us," Rooke explained. "He was concerned about you."

"Concerned?"

"He said you had a history of mental health problems and you'd suddenly run off."

"Oh, for God's sake." Cally burst out laughing. "Bloody hell, he needs to get over himself."

"Sorry?" Greene looked lost.

She motioned to the kitchen. "Please, come on through. Cup of tea?"

She started filling the kettle. "I'm okay, thanks," said Greene.

"I'll have one," said Rooke. "Bloody parched. It's lethal out there."

"Regular? Decaf? Herbal? We've got" – Cally inspected the various jars and packets – "camomile, peppermint and Turkish Apple."

"Camomile, thanks."

"Good choice."

Rooke flashed a small, oddly shy grin. "Just what you need on a hot day."

"Yup. Sure you don't want one?" Cally asked Greene.

"Oh, um, go on, then. Just builder's tea for me, thanks."

"So why does Mr West need to get over himself?" said Rooke.

Cally felt almost light-headed – Dad and Lucy were okay, and Iain was just being ridiculous. They'd expected to find her rocking in a corner or dead in the bathtub: as long as she acted normal she should be fine. Whatever *normal* was. Functional, anyway.

She decided the truth would do, more or less. "I have depression and anxiety. Never made any secret of that. Unfortunately Iain doesn't understand those things. If you're not bouncing off the walls in a padded cell you just need a better attitude and to pull your socks up. We really shouldn't have moved in together – he's a nice guy, but we're just not suited." She realised she was repeating Millicent's assessment verbatim. Ugh.

The kettle boiled, and she turned to fill the cups. "I'd just lost my job and I didn't want to leave Manchester. As you can see, Dad's all the way out here, which is lovely, but…"

Out in the sticks, she managed not to say, but Rooke just grinned again. "Bit of a way from the bright lights of the city, eh?"

Cally grinned back and handed her the mug of camomile. "Basically."

There was milk in the fridge; like the bread, Dad had forgotten to bin it before leaving for the airport. Cally sniffed it to check it was still fresh, then added it to Greene's cup.

"Ta very much," he said as she handed it over. "Just one thing, though. You said you wanted to stay in Manchester, but we, er, understand your mother lives in the area."

"Have you *met* my mother?" Shit. A rant about Millicent might have them doubting Cally's stability after all.

"You don't get on?" said Rooke.

"No one does. She's a bloody nightmare. Pity Dad's not here. He could back me up on this. Ever heard of NPD?"

"They a band?" said Greene.

Rooke gave him a look. "Narcissistic Personality Disorder, you mushroom."

"I was joking."

"Uh-huh."

Greene rolled his eyes; Rooke gave Cally a *See what I have to deal with?* look. She wondered if the two officers were a couple. Probably not, or they wouldn't be allowed to work together.

Rooke seemed familiar; Cally couldn't shake the feeling they'd met before. Maybe that was what the expression on Rooke's face had been; perhaps she'd recognised Cally too. Maybe they'd crossed paths in Bala; easily done in so small a town.

"Mind if I, er, use the facilities?" said Greene.

"Up the stairs, second on the right."

"So," said Rook, as Greene slipped out. "NPD, you said?"

"Don't take my word, just ask anyone who knows her. I've

not been in a great place the last few weeks, but there wasn't any suicidal ideation or self-harm" – she pulled up her sleeves to expose her unmarked forearms – "just the depression crap. And the relationship wasn't exactly helping. I'd been thinking of leaving for a while, but I didn't want to ring Dad and worry him. Then Lucy messaged to say they'd be away for a couple of weeks, and–"

"And you took the opportunity," said Rooke.

"Yeah. I've got my meds – show you if you want – and I'm still taking them. I just wanted to stay up here for a bit, work on my podcast till Dad gets home."

"Yeah, this podcast," said Rooke. "One of things Mr West was worried about."

Cally rolled her eyes. "It bloody would be. It's a true crime podcast. *You Want It Darker*."

"Leonard Cohen fan, huh?"

"I've been known to give him a spin. I know, no wonder I'm depressed, right?"

Rooke laughed. "You said that, not me."

"I started doing it a while back because I've always liked true crime. One of my listeners emailed me some links about a murder case he thought might interest me. Iain took one look at them and freaked, and now he thinks that's why I'm depressed."

"And it's not?" said Rooke.

"Nah. Chemical imbalance, that's all." Or a reaction to the state of the world, a struggle to fit into the society around her, or a lack of congruence between her core self and self-concept; depended who you asked.

Rooke smiled. "Have to give it a listen."

Cally smiled back. "Let me know what you think."

"We might need to pop back. You know, just to look in and–"

"Make sure I haven't slit my wrists?"

Rooke shrugged. "Gotta be on the safe side."

"I'll put the kettle on."

"I'll look forward to it."

Greene came back in. "Thanks for that, Miss Darker."

She realised she hadn't heard the toilet flush. He'd been poking around upstairs, while Rooke had kept her talking. Cally felt her mood darken, and folded her arms. "Anything else I can do for you both?"

Rooke looked embarrassed, maybe even hurt. Or that might have been wishful thinking; Cally had been starting to like the policewoman.

"I think that's everything." Rooke took another gulp from her mug and put it down. "We'll be on our way, Ms Darker. Come on, Dave."

Cally closed the front door behind them, more firmly than she'd intended. She laid her forehead against it for a moment, then watched them through the spyhole, returning to their car. Rooke said something; Cally couldn't tell what. *She was a right nutter*, probably.

They didn't get back in the vehicle immediately; maybe they were fetching a door ram and a team of men with butterfly nets. Cally snorted: now she *was* being paranoid. Even so, she kept watch till they'd driven away.

Shaken now, she felt an urge to retreat to her bedroom again, which made her angry: she'd been planning to go outside, take a walk. She shouldn't let this stop her. But fighting the anxiety only made it worse, and soon it was all she could do to make it up the stairs. She crawled back into bed, hid under the covers and curled into a foetal position; despite the stifling heat, she drifted quickly off.

She woke an hour later, slick with perspiration and desperately thirsty but with the fear and the dark mood gone as if sweated out. She showered again, quickly, then towelled herself dry and dressed, lathering her exposed skin with the suncream she took everywhere. Dad might be Welsh, but Cally had Millicent's Irish red hair and milky skin, which burned in sunlight like griddled steak.

She spent the rest of the afternoon walking in the hills, as if she could outpace the low mood and anxiety. It seemed to work; she lost herself both in the exercise and in the pauses where she drank in her surroundings, with no thought of past or future, of Millicent or Iain. She was in a beautiful and peaceful part of the world and should appreciate it while she could.

Eventually she strolled along the lake shore and rested on a bench. The only sound the restful lapping of the water on the shore. Llyn Tegid was nearly three and three-quarter miles long and half a mile across, bracketed by hills on either side, and its name meant 'lake of beauty.' The sight of it and the sound of the waters soothed and relaxed her; by the time she plodded, aching, back to the farmhouse, Cally was at peace again, and ready to delve further into Warden Fell.

14.

The cottage pie was still half-frozen, but the bacon had thawed; Cally grilled three rashers for a sandwich. She'd go into Bala tomorrow, buy some groceries; she didn't have much money left in her account, but rent wasn't an issue for the immediate future, and Dad and Lucy always kept a cash reserve in the kitchen, stored in a blue-and-white jar. They wouldn't mind her dipping into it; she'd make a note of the amount and pay them back when flush. Meanwhile, she had all she needed – including, most importantly, wi-fi.

Her favourite urbex site was *Desuetude.com* – she'd always loved the name – but entering *Warden Fell* its search field yielded no results. Given the sparse pickings she'd found on Google, that wasn't a surprise. Cally tried various keywords: *airfield, airbase, aerodrome and Lancashire*; finally, *Forest of Bowland* brought up a thread by a user called CORRAN.

The first pictures showed a bramble-covered chain-link fence and a cluster of overgrown, tumbledown buildings. Any identifying signage had been removed, but it was identical to the picture from *The Drome*.

Heard about this place from a local bird, but she didn't know what it was, CORRAN had written, and no one else on *Desuetude* seemed to know either. The thread had been posted in 2014, before the information about the AT programme had been declassified.

Plenty of pictures, CORRAN said, *posted below*.

Cally scrolled through them. Old corridors and old rooms, floors littered with dust, broken concrete and flaky paint. Here and there were scraps of décor and equipment, but only scraps. If they had been perfectly preserved in Tony Mathias' day, they no longer were. The military, ordinary thieves or simply time had cleared it out.

Either way, there was nothing to show what purpose Warden Fell had served; certainly no evidence of chemical or biological weapons. There were a couple of old signs that had escaped removal, some lettering that hadn't been completely painted over; Cally magnified them as fully as she could, but found nothing.

Of course, nothing short of a skull and crossbones would be any help to her, but there might be details in these photos that would be as good as a signed confession to someone with a military background, plus the time and inclination to go over these pictures with a magnifying glass.

And she knew someone fitting that description, barely three miles from here.

Unfortunately.

Cally only used Facebook intermittently; she logged in to see a few unimportant notifications and half a dozen messages from Iain, sent the morning she'd left.

Hopefully the police had at least told him she hadn't hung herself from a rafter; she'd no intention of replying as she'd only get dragged into a conversation she'd neither the energy nor desire for. She was here for one reason alone. But as Cally scrolled down her friends list, she was briefly distracted by Donna's profile.

She and Donna had dated, a few years ago; it had ended badly, but they'd reestablished contact in the past year and exchanged a few tentative messages on a 'let's be friends' basis. Donna had been a tall, athletic blonde with a flat-top haircut and a love of 'adventures,' which had usually involved dashing off to foreign countries at short notice for weekends of clubbing, drinking and anything else she could think of. When not doing that, she'd enjoyed hiking in the Peaks and all-night clubbing sessions in Manchester's Gay Village. Sometimes on the same day.

They'd spent countless nights in Vanilla, the Village's main lesbian club, and the relationship had been fun while it lasted. Cally had envied Donna's fearlessness and full-on hedonism, but ultimately her possessiveness had undermined the relationship. Part of her all-or-nothing nature, maybe. But trust mattered in any relationship, and ultimately, Donna hadn't trusted her.

Cally had never cheated on Donna, or any other partner: if you wanted to be with someone else, you ended the relationship and moved on. Nonetheless, on several occasions, there'd been confrontations between Donna and other women; once it had nearly become an actual fight and Donna had been ejected from the club, with Cally trailing after.

And *that* was when Cally realised where she'd seen Constable Rooke before. The other woman had been out of uniform, dressed up for going out, her hair hadn't been as short and of course, they'd both been a few years younger. But it had been the same woman.

They'd both been waiting at the bar, and got to chatting. Cally couldn't remember what they'd discussed, only that they'd fallen into conversation easily and naturally and it had been very pleasant. She'd had a nice smile, Cally remembered that. If they'd got to know each other better that night, they might have kept in touch.

Instead, Donna had come steaming in and had almost punched the other woman. She'd been marched out, and Cally had dashed after her with one shamefaced, apologetic backward glance. Donna was still her partner; besides if Cally had stayed on at the club there'd have been hell to pay. As it was, they'd had a blazing row that night, and the relationship had ended shortly after.

Small world, Cally thought, followed by *Trust Donna to try and deck a policewoman*. Cally chuckled, and kept scrolling. Finally, she found Griff Parry's profile.

She didn't have Griff's email, so a direct message here was the best way to reach him. He didn't seem to be online at that moment, so he'd hopefully reply when she wasn't either. She had his phone number, but speaking to him would be awkward at best.

And whose fault's that?

She typed, quickly:

> Hi Griff,
>   Hope you're okay. Any chance I could pick your brains about something Army-related?
>   Cally x

For the second time in as many days, she regretted the *x* instantly, and thought of unsending the message and trying again. But before she could, it registered as 'seen.'

"I thought he wasn't bloody online?" she demanded, but Facebook hadn't yet reached the level of sentience required to answer her back. Which was probably for the best.

The laptop emitted a ringtone and a screen came up. *video call requested.*

"Oh, shit," she muttered. She was tempted to decline the call; Griff would probably still fall over himself to help her out. But she felt guilty enough as it was.

No reason you should. You're both adults, and you've told him often enough it was a mistake.

True, but it didn't help.

She clicked *accept* and gave him her brightest smile. "Hey, Griff."

"Hello there, *cariad*." He still had a nice voice, rendered almost musical by his Welsh accent, so like yet unlike Dad's. "How's my girl?"

"I'm not your girl, Griff, but I'm okay."

He peered out of the screen at her. "That your Da's kitchen?"

Bugger. But as he'd told her once, the Army trained you to be observant, and he'd never been slow on the uptake to begin with. "Yeah. Staying here for a bit."

"You and the fella?"

He couldn't avoid sounding hopeful; it would have been easier to lie, but she hadn't the energy. "No."

"Oh."

He probably thought he was being subtle. Cally sighed. "We split up."

"Oh. Brilliant." He coughed. "I mean, sorry."

Cally nearly laughed out loud. Griff had the lolloping, clumsy good nature of a giant puppy. It still surfaced sometimes, making his present state all the more painful to see.

Six years younger than Cally, the son of her 'Aunty' Gwen (in reality no relation), Griff had joined the Army at eighteen and returned from Afghanistan the week after his nineteenth birthday with a prosthetic leg and an intermittent thousand-yard-stare from PTSD. Sometimes he was lost in dark reveries, back in Helmand or Kabul, or sunk in depression. Occasionally, he was the boy she remembered, trapped in a maimed body and peering out at the world from behind a gaunt, prematurely lined face.

He lived in a small bungalow in nearby Fron-Goch and made the best of things he could. He could still drive and kept active; last year he'd sent her a selfie from the summit of Cadair Idris, with the Mawddach Estuary and Cardigan Bay behind him. At least some of the time, he seemed happy.

The reason Cally had hesitated to call him was very simple, and all her fault. Griff had had a crush on her since the age of twelve. Last year, while visiting Dad and wallowing in yet another spell of depression, she'd gone drinking with Griff and – after far too many whiskies – they'd ended up on the back seat of his car.

It thankfully went no further than some furious snogging

and wandering hands, and she'd felt thoroughly ashamed of herself the next morning, but Griff, despite Cally repeatedly trying to let him down as gently as she could, still hoped they might pick up where they'd left off.

He'd always been shy around girls, and the Army hadn't changed that. He'd had few actual relationships and the isolated location wasn't teeming with potential partners, especially when you factored in the disability and war trauma. In a city, he'd have stood a better chance, but he'd told Cally more than once he could never live in one. Whenever they spoke, Griff could never conceal his hope they'd someday become an item. Cally was already regretting calling him: it felt too much like trading on his feelings for her.

Damaged or not, he's an adult with his own mind. He can always say no.

True, but Cally was fairly certain he wouldn't. She shook her head and managed a smile. "Honestly. What are you like?"

"Hopelessly devoted, like the song says." He grinned. Yellow teeth: he still smoked too much.

"If you're quoting Olivia Newton-John, something's badly wrong."

"I can control it. I listen to Slayer the rest of the time, honest."

That must amuse the neighbours. "Seriously, how've you been?"

He shrugged. "Up and down. You know what it's like."

"Yeah." Well, she did and she didn't. Anxiety attacks, yes; PTSD, no. Speaking to Griff often made Cally feel ashamed for not coping with her own issues better. "Been seeing anyone?"

"Just the occasional sheep." Griff occasionally made such jokes at his own expense, although God help any bloody *Saesneg* who did the same. "So yes, I'm still available."

"Dear God. Give up."

"Never."

We need to find you a nice girl, Cally wanted to say. But as far Griff was concerned, he already had. "Anyway–"

"Anyway, yeah," said Griff, trying to sound nonchalant. "You wanted to pick my brains, right?"

"Yeah." She outlined the basics – the murder-suicide, Warden Fell, the theory Tony Mathias might have carried some kind of contamination back to his family. "Couldn't find any evidence online, but then I wouldn't know what to look for."

"So you thought you'd ask an ex-squaddie?" he said. "Always a smart move. Not been there yourself, have you?"

"Just some pictures from an urbex site."

"Pop us the link and I'll take a shufti." He gave what he no doubt hoped was a roguish grin. "We can discuss it over dinner."

"We can go for a drink," said Cally, "and *maybe* have a bite afterwards."

"That's all I'm asking for," he said, wide-eyed.

"It's also all you're getting."

They chatted for a couple more minutes; Cally ended the call, pasted the link to *Desuetude.com* into Messenger, hit *Send* and logged out.

It was only then she thought of something which, she realised with a mixture of annoyance and dismay, should have been obvious. She logged back on to Duesuetude.com and viewed CORRAN's profile: he'd last posted there in 2019, half a decade since exploring Warden Fell. Which rather put paid to the idea that the place was lethal to all who went there. Unless CORRAN had just been lucky. Or Warden Fell was no longer contaminated, if it ever had been; it might have been disinfected, or the contaminant might have lost its potency.

Cally turned back to her notes. There was another lead she could pursue, and it was better than brooding on her mistakes; once she started down that road she could end up on it for a long time, travelling ever deeper into her own personal Slough of Despond. *Sod that for a game of soldiers.*

So she picked up her phone, and made another call.

15.

Cally followed the A584 northward out of Blackpool, then the A587 across the Wyre to Scorbridge.

The small village had been almost swallowed up by newer residential properties for those who could afford a comfortable seaside retirement; even the road leading out of it was lined with bungalows against a backdrop of fields. A private road branched off to Cally's left; down it was a gate bearing the sign *Eagle Mount Caravan Park*, beside a small cottage.

Here we go.

There was a window with a protruding wooden sill on Cally's side of the gate, an electric doorbell and a PLEASE RING FOR ATTENTION notice. She pressed the bell; a blurred figure moved behind the frosted glass, and the window opened.

Behind it was a man in his late forties with blue eyes, chestnut-brown hair lightly threaded with grey, sideburns and a flushed-looking face that suggested high blood pressure. He smiled; his lips were almost girlishly red and full. "Hello, there! What can I do for you?"

"Roland?" she asked.

"That's me. And you are?"

"Cally Darker. We spoke last night?"

"Of course. Lovely to meet you. One second." Roland pulled the window down and emerged from a wooden door just inside the gate to open it. "Just go through. Park in front of the office."

The 'office' was the other side of the house; a Land Rover was parked on the gravelled, sandy ground in front of it, but there was enough space for two other vehicles. Cally pulled in as Roland Woodwiss came round the corner.

He was broad-shouldered, and very tall: six foot four or five, with a spare frame and only a slight paunch. He wore a light blue cotton shirt, chinos and loafers and was putting on a peaked cap; his hair was thinning across his pink scalp. Cally shook his hand, and immediately regretted it. He looked and sounded pleasant enough, but there was something *greasy* about him. Nothing she could have put into words, but something about Roland Woodwiss repelled Cally on a level that surprised her.

"Welcome to Eagle Mount." He leant in as if to kiss her on the cheek, but thankfully didn't, then motioned to the fields behind the house as Cally wiped her hand as surreptitiously as she could on the leg of her jeans. "Here it is."

The park covered several acres, ending at the fence on the bluffs where the land gave way to the grey-brown expanse of the Irish Sea. She couldn't smell the sea itself, only the scent of various flowers, and was glad she'd her Clarityn.

"Bit of a different operation these days," said Roland. "Back in the 'eighties, some people came in their own caravans, for a few weeks or long-term, like the Mathiases. Now they're all statics, rented out. Without wanting to sound prejudiced, you get a better class of customer."

He had a smooth, posh voice – not quite in Stella Di Mauro's league, but close – and carried himself with a confidence bordering on arrogance, as if expecting a confrontation at any moment. He looked and sounded a high-level executive; Cally suspected something had gone badly wrong for Roland Woodwiss to end up here, something that went far beyond mere bad luck.

Are you psychic now? Focus on the job in bloody hand.

"Don't get me wrong," he said, "we're still something of a budget option, but we try to provide quality over quantity. Nice, roomy units, all mod cons. The lockdown was a bit of a squeaky bum time, but…"

Cally looked over the grounds, trying to overlay them with the images from 1983. The caravans were laid out in neat rows, except for a sandy area just right of centre fitted with a slide, swings and climbing frame. She pointed. "Is that where...?"

"Er," said Roland; she realised she'd interrupted him in mid-speech. She was about to apologise, but he was already nodding. "Yes. Mumsy left it empty. Wouldn't rent the space out afterwards."

Cally took out her phone. "Okay if I record?"

"Sure. Testing, testing, one two three, eh?"

Cally gave him a polite smile. "You said your Mum wouldn't rent the space out again?"

He shook his head. "She said it would've felt like building a house on a graveyard. Believe it or not, some people specifically wanted to rent that plot. Bit ghoulish" – he glanced sidelong at Cally and cleared his throat – "but it takes all types, and money's money. If people want that sort of thing, well – why not? Of course, nobody remembers the whole business now, so that ship's sailed."

He beamed at her. His small blue eyes were narrow, unblinking slits; Cally thought of a predatory reptile disguising itself as something harmless or benign. "You're the first person I've spoken to, outside the local community, who'd ever heard of it. Well done you."

Greasy, she thought again, but she smiled back and resisted the urge to move a couple of steps away. "So when did it become a playground?"

"Oh, that was when I took over, back in the Noughties. Got to use every bit of space, somewhere like this, but Mumsy didn't want anyone else living on top of it, so I compromised. She still wasn't happy, of course. But she knew the family well."

"Did you?"

"I was only nine," he reminded her, "but I used to play with Neal and Alison." A sullen expression flickered over his face;

Cally would have missed it if she'd blinked. "I didn't really have any friends at school. The only children I could play with were the ones here. Sort of captive audience." He sniggered – a snorting sound, three short breaths expelled through his nose, *thn-thn-thn*. "The Mathiases were the only ones with children my age here all year round. Nice kids. Alison especially." His eyes turned distant. "She was lovely."

The way he said it, and how he smiled when he did, made the hairs on Cally's forearms rise. "Were you here when it happened?"

"Mm?" he blinked. "No, no. They hadn't really left the caravan since the weekend before, you see. Mumsy said they had the flu and not to go near. *Leave them alone for the time being*, she said. And the night it happened, I was at a birthday party."

Thought you didn't have any friends, Cally almost said; perhaps recognising the inconsistency in his own account, Roland added, "Richard Turner, he was called. New boy. Only been at school a few days, so he invited the whole class. I wasn't missing *that*."

Roland's gaze grew distant again. "The Turners lived on the other side of Scorbridge. We heard sirens – fire engines, police cars – but didn't realise where they were going at the time. Everything carried on as normal. Except that Mumsy didn't come to pick me up."

He turned abruptly and stepped away; Cally thought he was ending the interview, but instead he motioned her to follow. Just past the Land Rover, a metal bench rested against the wall of the house; Roland sat down with a sigh, patting the seat beside him. Reluctantly, Cally joined him, although she didn't sit as close as he'd apparently hoped.

"I was in the living room on my own," Roland said. "All the other children had gone home except Richard and his big sister, who didn't want anything to do with her brother's friends." His red lips formed a sour smile. "And Richard had already decided he didn't like me, just like everyone else, so he was in his room playing with his new toys. Probably my strongest memory of the night – sitting on their sofa in corduroy trousers and a *Star Wars* t-shirt, a half-empty glass of flat own-brand cola in front of me, listening to the birthday boy playing with his Millennium Falcon – not a euphemism," he added, sniggering. *Thn-thn-thn.* "His parents were in the kitchen, and they kept looking at me and muttering to each other. Sorry, I know that's not very helpful to you."

"It's okay," she said, but Roland Woodwiss had already sunk back into his reverie, gazing seaward but towards a vanishing point forty years in the past. The sullen expression she'd glimpsed had returned; his lower lip stuck out. "I was embarrassed," he said. "Fed up, too. All the other children had been horrible, even then. Especially the *girls*," he added with a mixture of dull, sulky anger and the tone of a gluttonous child discussing cakes and chocolate, before licking his red lips. "Turned Richard against me too. Wouldn't even let me have *one* friend."

His right hand became a fist, then reopened, fingers wriggling, as if to shake the tension out. He seemed suddenly childlike, and in the most grotesque way. Cally looked around, but only two caravans had vehicles parked outside and there was no sign of movement inside them.

Eagle Mount abruptly felt very isolated, and she felt herself shrinking away from Roland Woodwiss, trying to make herself invisible. If he noticed, he gave no sign. "And now Mumsy couldn't even be bothered to come and get me. Perfect rotten ending to the day. I just wanted to go home to bed, not talk to anybody else."

Cally could relate to that feeling at least.

Roland smiled tightly. "Off I go feeling sorry for myself. The Turners' phone rang, and Mrs Turner went and answered it. She was trying to sound cheerful, but I could tell she was annoyed. Not because I'd *done* anything," he added hurriedly, "but it'd been a long day. I expect she wanted to go to bed, too, but here I still was. But then she said 'what?' then went very quiet, almost whispering. She called for Mr Turner. They talked for a bit. Then Mr Turner came through and told me there'd been an accident at the park. He said not to worry, Mumsy was okay, but she'd asked if I could stay the night."

He snorted again. *Thn-thn-thn.* "Only sleepover I had in school, not that it was any fun. There was no spare room and Richard wouldn't let me sleep in his. Had to sleep on the sofa. Took ages to get to sleep. Very lonely. Kept thinking they were lying about Mumsy and in the morning I'd find out she was dead. But next morning she turned up in the Land Rover. She and the Turners talked a bit, but, again, very quietly. She only told me what had happened on the way home."

He puffed his cheeks out and blew. "Sorry. Still get a bit emotional, thinking about it now. I cried my eyes out over Alison. Mumsy didn't tell me everything, just that there'd been an accident and they were all dead. I didn't realise it was worse than that till later. There were police cars parked outside the park. Mumsy parked in front of the house instead of out back, so I wouldn't see. My bedroom window looked out over here," he motioned, "but Mumsy pulled the curtains so I couldn't see out. I lay on my bed crying for ages. In the end I opened the curtains, though. They'd taken the bodies away by then, so there was just the burned-out caravan." Roland stared at the play area. "And the stains on the grass."

Maybe he'd meant the playground as a sort of memorial to Alison Mathias; even so, when Cally pictured Roland Woodwiss watching children play there, the hairs on her arms rose again.

"That's all I can really tell you about the murders," he said. "I was very upset, of course. Mumsy kept me home from school for a few days. She was devastated, too. Sometimes think she liked those kids more than me." He shook his head as though to dislodge the unwelcome thought. "That's it."

"What about Tony Mathias?" Cally asked.

"What about him?"

"How well did you know him?"

"We had tea and scones every Thursday afternoon." *Thn-thn-thn*. "He was a grown-up; I was a small boy. I saw him once or twice most days. I spent a lot of time with the children."

"What was he like?"

"I didn't like him."

"Why not?"

"*He* didn't like *me*. I don't know why."

Cally could make an educated guess.

"He was always polite. Had to be, when Mumsy owned all this. But you can tell, can't you? I always felt he looked down his nose at me. His bitch of a wife was the same." Roland's mouth tightened. Again, his fist opened and closed. "Neal was no better, I'm afraid. That's why I cried about Alison. She was special, Miss Darker. I mean that. She really was a lovely person. Almost the only one at all, when I was growing up, who treated me with any..."

For a moment, Cally felt a degree of sympathy for him. To be rejected, loathed, despised as a freak; she knew that feeling all too well. But then it was gone, leaving her feeling more uncomfortable in his presence than before. She cleared her throat and stood. "Thanks, Mr Woodwiss. You've been a big help."

He hadn't, really; she might get more out of him given time to think of the right questions, but Cally felt too alone and isolated here with him to think of any.

"Of course," he said as she picked up her phone, "you should really talk to my mother."

"What?"

"Mumsy," he said. "*She* knew Tony Mathias *very* well. *And* his wife. *She* could tell you *much* more about him than me."

"But I thought she was..."

"Mm?" Roland raised his eyebrows.

Gowland and Stella had both assumed Edna Woodwiss must be dead by now; Cally realised she'd done the same. And what was the old saying? *When you assume, you make an ASS of U and ME both.* "She's still alive?"

Roland smirked. "I wasn't going to suggest you use a Ouija board."

His snide, mocking tone made her even more uncomfortable than before. "Do you think she'd talk to me?"

Roland's smile widened. "Well, she said she would when I told her about you. I thought I'd make it a surprise. You like surprises, don't you? Most girls do." He rooted in his pockets. "I wrote down her address. Where is it? Oh, yes."

He held out a folded piece of paper, but snatched it back when she reached for it. "I've been helpful, haven't I?"

He leant forward, almost close enough to kiss. With an effort, Cally stood her ground. "Yes."

"Oh, goody," he said. "I should really ask for something in return, shouldn't I?"

He was looking straight in her eyes, unblinking. His tongue flickered across his lips. Cally fought the urge to slap his face; play along, and he'd give her what she wanted. But that thought was sickening, too, or rather that of what he'd want in return.

But Roland Woodwiss sniggered again. *Thn-thn-thn.* "Only messing," he said, and held out the paper again. He let a thick fingertip brush her knuckles, then raised his eyebrows. "What do we say?"

"Thank you," she managed, then moved towards the car. She was afraid he'd bar her way, but then, still smiling, he stepped aside. Cally rushed to the Punto and started the engine, engaged the locks, then reversed into the drive, but the gate was closed and locked.

Ram the gate, she thought, but her hands and feet wouldn't move. Roland moved up the drive, not even glancing at her, then unlocked the gate and motioned her mockingly through. Cally drove; when she looked up, Roland Woodwiss was receding in the rearview, waving goodbye.

16.

"Bet you were surprised to find me still alive, eh?" Edna Woodwiss sounded slightly out of breath; Cally made to get up, but the old woman pointed an arthritic finger. "Sit! The day I can no longer make a pot of tea unassisted, then by all means cart me out back of here and humanely destroy me."

Here was a sheltered accommodation unit in Lytham St Annes. The flats permitted independent living, but most of the residents were either physically or mentally incapable of it, so Cally had been relieved to find Edna apparently *compos mentis*.

The air was stale and thick with *pot-pourri* – flies swarmed in, Edna declared, when the windows were opened – but Cally made herself comfortable in the armchair and set her phone to record as Edna bustled about the small kitchenette.

Edna Woodwiss was a small woman, once plump but thinner in old age, her still-round face haloed by frizzy white hair. Her eyes were the same blue as her son's, but had a warmth and openness they'd utterly lacked. She was very well-spoken, but her voice was a gravelly caw that had made Cally jump when she'd first heard it. Luckily Edna had been less offended than amused; she was used to it by now.

"People always thought I was older," she said, returning with the tea-tray mounted on the front of her rollator frame. "Of course, I *am* now. Ninety-four, would you believe? Fifty-four at the time you're talking about. I've one of those faces, I suppose. But most of all, of course, it's my voice."

Settling on the sofa, she lifted the tea-tray from the rollator onto the coffee-table; pot, mugs and silverware rattled. Edna lifted her head, displaying a white scar on one side of her wattled throat. "Car accident, when I was twelve. Very traumatic – that's when I went grey, practically overnight. But otherwise, no permanent damage, except that I sound as though I should be flying around on a broomstick."

Cally laughed, then covered her mouth. Edna chuckled. "Don't worry about it, dear. We all need a sense of humour. And if you've been dealing with Roland, you're definitely in need of a laugh."

Cally shifted uncomfortably in the armchair.

Edna sighed. "I made excuses for Roland when he was younger. He'd grown up without a father, and he was always a child with his own peculiar interests. Being different from the norm doesn't make you wicked, as I'm sure you know yourself, dear."

Cally laughed again, but more nervously. "I'm not sure how to take that."

Edna gestured airily. "Only an observation, although it's really a compliment, given the rubbish most people seem interested in these days. There's a Japanese saying: 'the nail that sticks up gets hammered down.' I was one such child; I pride myself that I can usually recognise another. Those who differ from the herd rarely an easy ride, especially in childhood. Children's innocence is a two-edged sword. Not having learned the rules of adult behaviour, they can be refreshingly honest, with a greater capacity for joy, but they can also be outstandingly cruel. Which I certainly think you've experienced your share of. No?"

Edna's gaze was uncomfortably direct. Cally felt as though she were being X-rayed, all her inner workings exposed. The old woman smiled gently. "For a very long time I assumed any difficulties Roland suffered were wholly due to other people's prejudices. I was even, God help me, *proud* to have a child with a will of his own. An act of hubris on my part, perhaps, but when your child's all you have..." She shrugged. "And I suppose guilt came into it, too."

"Guilt?"

Edna Woodwiss sighed. "Roland was the one thing to come out of my marriage to his useless father. All I had, as I said. He was something outside myself to care for, tend, protect. And so I gave him everything I was capable of giving him. But not love." She looked up at Cally. "I couldn't, you see. It's a terrible thing to confess, but I have never known a moment's affection for my son, and believe me, I wanted to. But there's something about Roland – always has been – that repels not only me, but almost everyone he's ever encountered. You must have noticed yourself."

Cally had no idea what to say. Edna smiled. "Be honest, dear. You've met him. He is repellent, isn't he? That is the only word that fits?"

At last, Cally nodded.

"I didn't neglect or mistreat him," said Edna. "I did all any mother could be expected to do for a child, except in that one respect. You can't force yourself to feel what you don't. I did my best to hide it, but I don't think I succeeded. Children aren't stupid, and Roland certainly wasn't. Tea?"

"Please."

Edna filled their cups, nodding approval when Cally took hers with only a dash of milk. "Excellent. That's how tea should be drunk. Though I never bother with sugar myself," she added, as Cally stirred her second teaspoonful of it into her cup. Edna added an even tinier dash of milk to her own brew and stirring.

"In the summer of 1987," she said at last, "there was an – *incident* – involving Roland and another child. He was very fortunate not to face criminal charges; the girl's family decided she'd already suffered enough, and didn't want to put her through the misery of a police investigation. Thankfully, they moved away from the area, in the hope she'd forget what had happened. Or I doubt I'd have been able to stay, and Eagle Mount would be long gone."

Cally thought of Roland Woodwiss' slitted narrow eyes, the reptile flicker of his tongue across his plump red lips.

"Roland had been all I'd had at the start, but by the time we're talking about I had Eagle Mount as well. Built it up from almost nothing, and perhaps, I cared about it more." Edna shook her head. "I'm not sure what the correct term for my son is. As I said, I think virtually everyone he's ever met finds him repulsive. And make no mistake, my dear, he knows it, and so, under that smiling surface, he's full of rage. He hides it, because he knows he must, but I doubt any woman or girl or any age would be safe from him if his appetites weren't more than matched by his fear of punishment. That's held him in check." Edna sighed, suddenly weary. "Or so I tell myself. Perhaps I'm just salving my conscience."

"Has he always lived in Scorbridge?"

Edna shook her head. "He still lived here when he studied law at Lancashire Polytechnic. It was within commuting distance. I insisted on that, so I could keep an eye on him. To the best of my knowledge, he never behaved improperly. He did very well, and was offered a position with a solicitor's firm in London. I actually dared hope something had changed for the better."

She was silent, brooding, till Cally cleared her throat. "And it hadn't?"

Edna snorted like an angry horse. "Of course not. Once again, Roland avoided any police involvement – I suspect money changed hands, as he certainly had very little left when he moved back here. No doubt his employers wanted to protect *their* reputation, if not his. After that he worked for me, and I made sure he was never alone or unsupervised with anyone vulnerable."

"But now he runs the place?"

"Time takes its toll, dear. I was ill a few years ago; he managed to get power of attorney. And now I'm here."

"So why's he letting me talk to you? Doesn't he know you'd tell me–"

Edna's gaze was pitying and sad. "I'm officially gaga, my dear, however well I can still string a sentence together. Whenever anyone in authority hears the story, they go *Oh, it's batty old Edna again*. Rather neat, when you think about it. Every time I tell the truth, I confirm the lie. But don't waste any tears. I haven't long left, this cage isn't too uncomfortable, and perhaps it's no more than I deserve."

"Deserve?"

"Child of mine or not, I should have had the courage to face the truth about Roland. I should have ensured he was locked away where he could pose no threat to women or girls. That or put him down as you would a rabid dog."

"Jesus," said Cally, unable to hold back.

Edna sighed. "All too often people know what they should do, but don't dare. Instead, they invent excuses for doing something less personally inconvenient. I would, if I believed in any deity, simply pray that he doesn't act on his compulsions. But you're not here to discuss my son. You want to know about Tony Mathias, and what he did. No?"

"Yes," Cally said at last.

"And most of all, why. But then, we'd all like to." Edna saw Cally's expression and snorted again. "You didn't think *I'd* have the answers, did you? Why would I keep them to myself?"

"Because nobody was interested in finding out?" said Cally.

"Well, this is true. There was no crime to solve. No case to bring to court. Even so, the police lost interest with astonishing speed. They didn't even–" She stopped.

"Didn't even what?"

"We'll get to that. Perhaps. But first, I'll tell you what you came to hear."

"Why would you do that?"

"Why not?"

"Roland practically keeps you prisoner here. And then he just says that he's sending someone over and you just do as he tells you?"

"Oh, I could clam up to spite him, I know. But he'd find some suitably petty revenge to take, and I've precious little company these days. Besides, I liked Tony, and I liked his family. I believed them all to be genuinely good people, and never saw anything to suggest otherwise until that last terrible day. So, either Tony Mathias was a violent and abusive man whose character I profoundly misjudged, or he was a kind and loving father, husband and friend who for some reason committed a dreadful act. I'd dearly love, before I die, to know which it was. And whether I could have prevented it. I know that's probably too much to expect, but if nothing else I'd like them to be remembered, as they were. Is that what you intend?"

"Yes," said Cally.

"Then I'll begin."

17.

"The Mathiases first came to Eagle Mount in 1977," Edna Woodwiss said. "It was the Queen's Silver Jubilee. Strange to think the old girl's gone – I'm on my fifth monarch now. Anyway, they stayed for a fortnight, then moved on. Alison, the little one, was barely a year old; Roland was enraptured. I genuinely think she was the only person he ever had real feelings for, and I include myself in that, I'm afraid. Probably because – uniquely – she seemed to genuinely like him."

She was lovely, Roland Woodwiss had said; Cally supposed there'd been something like tenderness in his voice, even if it had made her skin horripilate.

Edna cleared her throat violently, spat into a tissue and sipped her tea. "When they came back, the following year, it was to stay. A quiet spot on the coast, close enough to Blackpool, where they could get any mod cons they required. And because I had the ideal studio for Tony."

"Studio?" But of course he'd have needed somewhere to work in. He wouldn't have had that in the caravan.

"Back then, the caravan park itself occupied a single two-acre field, but I also owned the adjoining one, which was full of dilapidated farm buildings and equipment. It's part of the caravan park now, but back then the only thing of use there was an old potting shed, which proved ideal for Tony's purposes. Much of it was glass, giving him plenty of natural light, but it also had electricity. So I rented it to him, and he used it as a studio and darkroom. He worked on a succession of projects there. The last of which, of course, was for the Whitworth Gallery in Manchester."

Cally nodded.

"He was very enthusiastic about it," Edna went on. "Couldn't wait to begin, and was positively cock-a-hoop when he got back from Warden Fell. Over the next few days, however, his behaviour began to change."

"He told you about Warden Fell?"

"No, dear. *I* told *him*. Do close your mouth, you'll catch flies."

Cally did so.

"You seem surprised," said Edna.

"Sorry. I knew he must have found out about the place from somewhere. I just hadn't thought about where."

"And you certainly didn't think it was from his croaky old bat of a landlady," said Edna, clearly amused. "But it was. Roland's father served there. His stories about Warden Fell were pretty much all he left me, other than Roland himself and a dose of the clap from some German floozy shortly before he buggered off, and quite frankly good riddance to him."

She knocked back the last of her tea much as Stella Di Mauro had disposed of that last double brandy, then refilled her cup. Cally sipped quietly at hers.

"He was full of stories about Warden Fell," said Edna. "But Adrian Woodwiss was always full of stories, although one had to take them all with a pinch of salt."

"What kind of stories?"

"Other than his own hi-jinks and escapades, which Adrian always found infinitely more fascinating than everyone else did, they mainly concerned the history of Warden Fell itself. Supposedly witches had held Sabbats and Black Masses there. Supposedly it had been the site of a mediaeval castle, remnants of which survived in certain restricted areas below-ground – which, of course, Adrian had gained access to. And, supposedly, the hill was haunted. *You mean ghosts?* I asked him once. *Worse than ghosts, darling*, he told me." Edna Woodwiss pursed her lips. "He never explained what he meant by that. Normally I'd think it was just Adrian being Adrian, trying to make himself sound more interesting, but I remember his expression at that moment. He'd seen something up there, or *thought* he had. That said, Adrian did like a drink, even on duty, just to keep out the cold. How much do you already know about the place, dear? You seem to have some foreknowledge."

"Just bits and pieces from the internet," said Cally. "I know it got used a few times over the years – both World Wars, and after–"

"All the way through to the '60s, when Adrian was there. The station performed various different roles over the decades, and for some reason – Adrian never understood why – each successive incarnation of Warden Fell avoided using the previous ones' buildings if they could help it. You'd think they'd repurpose and occupy them, or failing that pull them down, but they just left them as they were, and built new ones. The old buildings were out of bounds, but airmen would go in on a dare, retrieving some small item as proof. Schoolboy stuff. Adrian had an old cigarette tin he'd pinched from the old Royal Flying Corps station's ready room. That was the thing about those abandoned sections, you see: they'd all be full of posters, pin-ups and other ephemera of their time, albeit covered in dust and what have you."

"Did he ever say anything about poison gas, or germ warfare?"

"Who on earth do you think he was, dear? Adrian never rose above the rank of an ordinary Aircraftman – although he'd have you believe otherwise – a radio operator. About as pedestrian a military career as one could get. What brought that on?"

Cally decided not to mention Stella Di Mauro yet. "There's a theory there might have chemical or biological weapons at Warden Fell. When Tony broke in, he got infected–"

"And went murderously insane?"

It sounded even stupider than ever, said like that. "Or infected his family," Cally said, "and it was a mercy killing."

Edna pursed her lips. "If Warden Fell *had* ever been used for such purposes, I doubt Adrian could have kept his big mouth shut. Of course, it could have happened after his time, when it was officially shut down, but according to Tony, security around the station was non-existent, which you'd hardly expect if it was full of radioactive leprosy. Heaven knows I'm no fan of the military, but if they were *that* incompetent the Red Army would have been goose-stepping along the Thames Embankment decades ago. Still, for all I tell myself there can't be a connection, it's the one thing that does stand out. I wonder sometimes if Roland inherited something twisted from his father that made him what he is; if I was fanciful, I might almost believe something at Warden Fell contaminated Adrian and was passed onto Roland in the womb. Corrupted him. Or perhaps I'm just trying to absolve myself of responsibility for what he's become."

Edna trailed off, lost in thought. "Did you tell the police?" Cally asked. "About Tony and Warden Fell, I mean?"

"They already knew, my dear. They had a particularly charming gentleman with them who, although we were never formally introduced, was clearly someone of importance. Looked at me as though I were a laboratory specimen awaiting dissection."

"Did he wear a Savile Row suit?" said Cally.

Edna's eyebrows rose. "I see you've spoken to dear Stella. Yes, she encountered that frustrated vivisectionist too."

"He told Stella to forget she'd ever heard of Warden Fell."

"So was I, which would suggest there was something of importance there. In which case, I'm partly responsible for Tony his family's deaths."

Cally could think of nothing to say. She wasn't sure how long the silence lasted, but just as she'd begun to despair of it ever ending, Edna continued.

"After he returned, Tony seemed slightly unwell. A cough, a few sniffles: his voice was a little croaky. A summer cold, I thought, or hay fever. But it worsened, progressively, and over the weekend Lindsay and the children all developed the same symptoms."

She described what had followed just as Stella had: the family retreating to the caravan, with Tony occasionally emerging muffled in layers of clothing. "I now wonder if they were disfigured somehow. Certain kinds of disease would do that, wouldn't they?"

"I suppose." Cally thought of smallpox, or the effects of mustard gas.

"No one but Tony left the caravan in that final week, and his face was always concealed. Even his eyes."

Cally thought of Tony and Lindsay's incinerated remains. If the children hadn't fled the caravan, he'd presumably have burned them too. Fire purified; that was the saying, wasn't it? It might have seemed logical: burn away the contamination, and his guilt. "I still don't get it, though."

"What don't you get, dear?"

"If he *did* pick something up at Warden Fell, why didn't he call somebody?"

"Who? The authorities? If your theory's correct, dear, he'd stumbled across a state secret, and plenty of people have been killed to protect those. Perhaps he thought that at best his family would be used as human guinea pigs to observe the effects of whatever it was they had. This was during the Cold War, remember; there was justifiable suspicion about what even supposedly democratic governments might do in the name of national security, and in some cases outright paranoia. Tony himself was suffering, too, which wouldn't have helped his judgement either. Either way, if he didn't trust the proper authorities even to grant his loved ones a painless death... well. A dreadful business, anyway. Awful to have to witness. Poor Leonard."

"Leonard?"

"Leonard Bainbridge. He and his wife Irene were the

Mathias' neighbours. Retired couple. No children of their own; doted on Alison and Neal. So what happened was a terrible blow. Leonard saw the whole thing, you see. No one else did."

18.

"No one?" Cally was thrown. "Weren't you there?"

"Astonishingly, Miss Darker, even I once had a personal life. I couldn't be there every minute of every day. Besides, it was election night, remember? I'd walked to the church hall in Scorbridge to vote."

"Sorry. I didn't mean any offence."

The old woman chuckled. "You didn't cause any, my dear. I'm just teasing you. Once I'd voted, I walked out of the town and back towards Eagle Mount. That was when I heard the first shot, which I initially assumed was a car backfiring. There were two more a few seconds later, one after the other, then nothing for about a minute. I'd almost put it out of my mind by the time the corner of my lane came in sight, but then there were two more. I realised then that they were gunshots, but not – until Leonard came stumbling out of the lane – that they were coming from my property. Even from a distance, I could see the poor man was utterly distraught."

Edna took another sip of tea. "These days the bus stop on our corner is just a steel post, but back then, there was a proper shelter with a bench seat – and beside it, a telephone box. Good luck finding one these days, especially in working order, but this was long before the days of those gadgets." She nodded in the direction of Cally's smartphone. "Back then, to make a call when you were out of doors, you found a payphone. Poor Leonard almost fell into that telephone box. I kept walking at my normal pace – sort of automatic pilot, I suppose – but it was dawning that something terrible had happened. And that it involved Tony and his family."

She shook her head. "I started to run when Leonard came out of the phone box. His face was grey, he was swaying – he looked as though he were about to have a heart attack. He did, eventually, about a year later. It killed him. But I learned about that second-hand from Irene. They moved away within a fortnight of the killings. Impossible for them to stay. Irene later said Tony Mathias had killed Leonard as surely as he had his own loved ones. As Leonard made it to the bus stand I heard the sound of police sirens approaching – and then, one final gunshot. By now I could see smoke rising from the caravan site, but first of all I went to Leonard. He was shivering terribly, and shaking his head from side to side. Not surprising, really."

After a long pause, Edna went on. "The police arrived, and parked at the top of the lane. Astonishingly, none of them were armed. They made their way down, went over the gate, and that was when the explosion happened."

"Explosion?"

"Oh, yes. The potting shed. Tony's studio, remember? Turned out he'd set a fire there before returning to the caravan with the rifle."

"I didn't know it *exploded*."

"Well, you wouldn't, dear. There wasn't much left to photograph, and it didn't look anywhere near as arresting as the remains of the caravan. Nowhere as good a picture for the front cover of the *Advertiser*, and for the interior spread, they had all those lovely pictures of the dead, beautiful wife and children."

Cally supposed a heap of ash and charcoal wouldn't have greatly interested *gore.net's* viewers either, not when there were mangled children and charred corpses to feast on. No surprise that Cally hadn't heard of it before: she'd been equally ignorant Tony Mathias had had a studio, even if a moment's logical thought should have told her he must have had one.

"Besides," Edna added, "the police kept that out of the paper."

"What? How come?"

"They were playing things close to the chest, in case it turned out there was an IRA connection. Those chaps had a rather unfortunate tendency to blow things up on the British mainland at the time. I think the police hoped that treating it as an ordinary murder for as long as possible would make it less likely that any accomplices would panic and go to ground." Edna drained her tea. "Could I trouble you for another drink, my dear? My throat, you know."

"Sure." Cally moved towards the glass-fronted drinks cabinet. "Brandy? Sherry?"

"What sort of raging alcoholic do you take me for? This isn't a Jack Higgins novel. It's far too early for that sort of thing. I meant to ask if you'd mind making another pot of tea."

"Sorry." Her face burning, Cally grabbed the pot and dashed into the kitchenette. "So the studio actually blew up?"

"Tony made a very hit and miss arsonist. Lack of practice, I suppose." Edna Woodwiss gave a grim, reedy chuckle. "Only one room in the caravan suffered serious fire damage, but where the studio had been was a hole in the ground. Luckily most of the debris came down in the empty field or on the beach."

The kettle began to boil. "Poor Leonard was taken away in an ambulance – Irene came back at some juncture, and they took her to see him. But by then, I was busy getting the third-degree down at Scorbridge police station."

"You?" Cally spooned tea into the pot.

"Well, it *was* my caravan park, and with the Mathiases dead I was the closest they had to a living suspect. One of life's occasional reminders that you're still regarded as 'a bit odd,' and that things haven't changed much since your schooldays." Edna shrugged. "In olden times they'd have burned me as a witch. Thankfully, the local plod weren't as thuggish as their big-city contemporaries, or I'd have ended up confessing to the Hyde Park Bombing and Lord Mountbatten. Mind you, the investigating officer was bad enough. A woman – unusual at the time – and therefore determined to show she was as ruthless as any man. And her sergeant wouldn't have been out of place in the Gestapo. Luckily, I knew one of the other officers slightly, which probably helped. A young detective. Peter Culleton."

"Peter?" said Cally, remembering that initial email.

"That's right, dear." Edna sighed and shook her head. "He died not long afterwards too, sadly. House fire. A nice young man – only a boy, really. Very sweet, but I believe he had something of a drinking problem."

Not Cally's mysterious correspondent, then. Maybe a family member. But why would they, or anyone else, want this business reopened?

And why choose you?

Because she was thorough, conscientious, did a good job? Or because she was so desperate for validation she'd easily be manipulated into digging on their behalf?

"Are you all right, Miss Darker?"

"Sorry. I'm okay."

Edna regarded her sceptically, then went on. "They finally let me go that evening, and I called the Turner family, as Roland's doubtless told you. He likes to give his account of that night, despite having witnessed nothing of note."

The kettle boiled; Cally refilled the pot. "You asked them to let him sleep over."

Edna nodded. "I didn't know what awaited me at the caravan park, but that wretched policewoman – what *was* her name? – ensured I saw the crime scene photographs, and I shall never forget them. Grim viewing at the best of times; even less so when the victims are – just – recognisable as people you knew. The children, at least. The other remains could have been anybody."

"You think they faked their deaths?" said Cally, setting the pot down on the table.

"Don't be ridiculous, dear. Why on earth would they? But then, that's the question, isn't it? what we keep coming back to: *why?* The most obvious explanation is that Tony Mathias was controlling and abusive, and killed his family rather than lose them. All I can say is that, even in those benighted days, I had some idea of the warning signs and saw none. Nor were they in financial trouble – the opposite, in fact. Hard to believe some sort of Plus X wasn't involved."

"Some sort of what?"

"From a science-fiction novel I read years ago. That unknown factor which makes something otherwise impossible, possible – be it physical, psychological, a truth, a lie. In this case, X is whatever turned Tony Mathias from a sweet, gentle man into a family annihilator. Perhaps, for instance, he and Lindsay *did* fake their deaths because they were Russian spies, and are living out their twilight years in St Petersburg as we speak. But I doubt it. Have you considered a brain tumour, my dear?"

"What as, a fashion accessory?"

"Very droll. But have you?"

"In Tony's case? Yeah, of course. But…"

"Difficult to prove. Given the condition of the… remains."

For the first time Edna Woodwiss' composure faltered, and she drew a deep, shuddering breath before taking a long draught of her tea.

Cally nodded, remembering the blackened remains of Tony and Lindsay, Alison's headless corpse and Neal, with his torso almost flattened by multiple hits, a crushed and broken rag of cloth, skin and bone. The top of the boy's head had been blown away, but the rest had seemed intact; mercifully his face had been buried in the grass. She tried to focus. "Didn't anything happen around that time that was out of the ordinary, or…"

"The police interrogated me quite thoroughly on that point;

moreover, I've done the same to myself over the years. There was nothing."

"Except Warden Fell," said Cally.

Edna bit her lip. "Turn that thing off, dear."

"Sorry?"

"That." Edna motioned to the phone. "Please. Turn it off."

Shit. Perhaps she'd offended Edna, or the memories had proven too painful.

Edna drew herself up, as if steeling herself. "I can't shed any further light on events," she said at last. "But, just possibly, Tony Mathias himself can."

19.

Her mobile rang as Cally drove back towards Wales, but she ignored it; she recognised the number as Roland Woodwiss', and had no desire to talk to him – ever, if she could help it, but definitely not now.

The phone rang unanswered on the Punto's passenger seat, beside an old carrier bag. She didn't look at the bag either; didn't want to think about it till she was back in Bala. It was the one place she felt secure.

And when you are? Do you really want to bring that into Dad's house?

Cally drove, concentrating on the road ahead; the tension eased as she crossed the Welsh border, as if entering another country finally put her at a safe distance from Eagle Mount.

Edna had directed Cally to the bookcase, and an old hardback of de Beauvoir's *The Second Sex*. "One book of mine I can be sure Roland wouldn't go near," she'd chuckled grimly. "Well, open it, dear."

A hole the size of Cally's thumb had been cut out of the pages; there was something stuffed into it, wrapped in tissue.

"Go on," said Edna.

Cally had unwrapped the tissue; inside was a small steel key.

"That will open a storage crate at a facility in Blackpool. Inside that is a carrier bag, containing a plastic case full of cassette tapes. You know what those are, I hope?"

"I'm not *that* young."

"Take it as a compliment, dear. At the time of the killings there was an old boundary hedge around the field containing the potting shed. I found the case caught in it about a fortnight afterwards – blown there by the explosion, I presume. I informed the police, of course, but they never came for it."

"What's on the tapes?" Cally asked.

"According to the labels, some are recordings made at Warden Fell. Others are journal entries. Tony didn't keep a written diary, because he was dyslexic."

Gowland had mentioned that, too. "According to the labels?" said Cally. "Haven't you listened to them?"

"Why would I want to, dear? Do I want to know why Tony did what he did? Yes. Do I want to hear him going out of his mind? No. As for the Warden Fell recordings, what could *I* have made of them?"

"Why not tell Stella, though? Or his agent?"

"That Gowland person?" Edna snorted. "I wanted nothing to do with *him*."

That Gowland person. Even though Cally had liked Bernard Gowland, she couldn't help but grin.

"All he'd see is a chance to profit by selling the tapes to the highest bidder," Edna went on. "The same as Roland, if he knew of their existence. I'd burn them before allowing that."

"Why not Stella, though? I thought you got on with her."

"Stella Di Mauro is a very dear woman. And there's the rub. If I hesitated to listen to the tapes myself, I could hardly expose Stella to them. Better she think of the whole tragedy as the equivalent of a lightning strike – blind chance, a calamity from above – than realise her beloved brother was never who she thought he was."

"Huh? But I thought you said–"

"That I always thought Tony Mathias a good and decent man? That what he did was utterly out of character? Yes. But he still did it. That kind and decent man shot his wife and children down like animals before blowing out his own brains.

That's plain fact. Ultimately, Miss Darker, nobody really knows anybody. So while I *say* I want to know why, I'm also afraid to. Nor did I want to be responsible for destroying Stella's memories of her brother. But now, I have you."

Cally felt downright dazed: she'd hoped to find something of interest, but hadn't expected the potential answers to the case to fall so readily into her lap. "But we've only just met. I'm nobody."

"It's pure selfishness on my part, Miss Darker. I couldn't bring myself to listen to them. But I can put the facts before a trustworthy third party. And in due course you can tell me – and Stella, of course – what you've learned, if you see fit."

Cally still hadn't looked inside the carrier bag; she'd been tempted to pull over en route and do so but resisted; she'd wait till she was safely home in Bala with a square meal inside her.

All she'd eaten today was a piece of toast at breakfast and a ham sandwich before her visit to Edna, forced down between gulps of water while vainly trying to banish the image of Roland Woodwiss' smirking face and slitted lizard eyes. Now Cally's hands shook with hunger.

Afraid of wreaking havoc on her bank balance, she'd dipped into Dad's kitchen cash-jar to cover her fuel costs; there was enough left over for some groceries. She stopped in Corwen to buy milk, bread, bacon, a carton of cream and a bar of chocolate, which she nibbled as she drove home. She felt steadier after that, but it still seemed far too long before the green hills around Bala rose protectively about her.

Cally drove up to the house, let herself in and ate the crust of the bread-loaf straight out of the packet, then put the cottage pie in the oven and stretched out on the living-room sofa, setting her phone alarm to alert her when it was ready.

She ate a portion of cottage pie, put the remainder in the fridge and washed up before putting the percolator on. In the living room, she prepared a mug of coffee almost strong and sweet enough to satisfy Stella Di Mauro, then added a rich, decadent glug of cream.

Only a couple of days earlier she'd been having coffee with Stella in the bustling centre of Manchester; now here she was. Swings and roundabouts: hills and lakes, peace and beauty on the one hand, restaurants, nightlife, bars and live music on the other. The Village. Which made her think of Donna, and then about whether Constable Rooke, with her rather lovely smile, really had been the same woman she'd been talking to the night they'd been kicked out of Vanilla.

Cally sighed and took a fortifying swallow from her coffee-mug, then laid the carrying case down on the coffee table. It was about a foot square and made of moulded, bright-yellow plastic. The tip of one corner was slightly melted and a hairline crack ran along one side, but otherwise it was intact. Even the colours were bright. It fastened with a simple catch, and when she pushed it, the case hinged open with a click.

Inside the case was a rack of cassette cartridges, arranged in two neat rows of ten. Each bore a liner card with crude, spidery block-capital writing on its spine. The ones in the left-hand row had titles like WADEN FELL AMBINT SOUND 4, WARDEN FELL RADIO TRAFFIC 3, and WAARDEN FELL SOND 6; nine of those on the right were titled JOURNAL, followed by dates.

The cassettes were C90s, meaning an hour and a half of total recording time. The first nine JOURNAL tapes each covered a three-day period, from late April through May 1983, making the average journal entry about half an hour.

The ninth cassette covered the 22nd, 23rd and 24th May – the period immediately before he'd gone to Warden Fell. The tenth had no writing on it at all. Maybe it was blank; maybe Tony simply hadn't bothered to date it because he'd been busy descending into psychosis.

Even if the Warden Fell material proved irrelevant, the

journals were the best chance anyone had ever had of knowing Tony Mathias' state of mind in his final days. It could be all she'd hoped, and more besides.

Assuming the tapes weren't degraded beyond use; heat from the explosion, exposure to the elements or the simple passage of forty years could have rendered them useless. All the answers on a silver platter, only to turn to dust when touched.

Cally felt strangely reluctant to begin. In part, at least, it was for Stella Di Mauro's sake. Cally had liked and admired her, and wanted to believe Tony Mathias had been the complicated but gentle man his sister remembered. Part of an equation with an unknown factor: loving family man plus X equals killer. Because the alternative was that he'd always been a monster-in-waiting, and what had happened on 9th June, 1983 had only ever been a matter of time.

Maybe there were no answers here either; maybe everything seemed normal, right up until the end.

You don't believe that. You're just afraid.

Dad's stereo system was just across the room. LP turntable, CD player, and tape deck, with hi-fi and surround sound.

Hear a man go murderously insane in glorious stereo.

Cally shook her head. The tapes mightn't even play. No point agonising until that was settled. She reached for the first cassette in the left-hand row. WADEN FELL AMBINT SOUND 4. Background noise, basically, rather than Tony Mathias in full diary-of-a-madman mode.

Well, as she'd once heard an old man say, *faint heart never fucked a donkey.*

She switched the stereo on, opened the cartridge, took out the cassette and looked through the roller openings at the exposed tape. It was dull brown, smooth and glossy; from what she remembered, that was how it was meant to look. She thought of comparing it to one of Dad's cassettes, but decided against it.

Just get it done.

Cally popped open one of the tape decks, inserted the cassette, then closed it. After a moment, she pressed *Play.*

20.

A long, whispering hiss issued from the surround speakers, so abruptly Cally jumped and let out a very undignified squeak of fright before realising it was the background noise cassettes always made when recording live.

Just as her heart-rate was returning to normal, a voice boomed out of the speakers, and made her jump again.

"Okay. Warden Fell, Ambient Sound Recording Number Four."

"Bloody hell," Cally muttered, and turned the volume down.

"We're in the oldest surviving building," Tony Mathias said. "This would have housed the old Aero Club before World War One."

Like Stella, he spoke in crisp, Received Pronunciation English, but a Lancashire burr showed through here and there. He had a low, rich baritone, velvety and warm. A voice for reading bedtime stories, or murmuring sweet nothings in your ear at night. It went with everything she'd heard about the man: kind, gentle, warm. Except that the kind and gentle didn't murder their loved ones.

Didn't they? Parents killed their children in the Holocaust, to avoid the horror of the camps. Murder and suicide could seem like lesser evils compared to watching your family die slow, agonising deaths. There was a rationality to that, however grim.

But Neal and Alison had fled him, run out of the caravan. How did that square with people in debilitating pain?

You'd run if someone came to shoot you, pain or not. Painkillers could dull the suffering of even fatal illness. And radiation sickness had the 'walking ghost' stage, where the worst symptoms abated before the final terminal decline.

So now they're storing nuclear bombs at Warden Fell? Listen to yourself.

"During the Great War," Tony went on, "it housed the Royal Flying Corps training squadron. This was the briefing room." A cough. "Anyway. Recording."

Footsteps scuffed, then silence. Cally turned the volume up a little. The tape hissed. Water dripped. Wind blew, then faded. Something skittered briefly: a small animal, or detritus blown across the floor.

But as the minutes went by, Cally thought she could hear something else. There seemed to be something *under* the hiss: faint rhythms and patterns of sound, like submerged rocks in a stream that made its surface eddy and swirl.

She turned the volume further up; it was very faint, more a rhythm than anything else, like a drumbeat, except the instrument, she was sure, was some sort of voice. Something about it stirred a faint sense of unease in her. Nonetheless, if she could just hear a little better, filter out that staticky hiss, she might make out the details. She thought she'd begun to till she heard a faint shiver of metal on glass from the coffee table and realised the tea-tray was vibrating from the high volume.

A sudden, violent hiss and crackle, like water hitting hot fat, making her jump once more. "Red Three to Tower. Red Three to Tower. Tower, respond. Tower respond."

It was a thin, nasal voice, with the kind of clipped, half-strangled vowels Cally associated with the Royal Family, or politicians and soldiers in old newsreels. It certainly wasn't Tony Mathias.

The crackle faded, and all that remained was the dripping – and that low, rhythmic undersound, now louder than before.

It was definitely a voice; Cally could make out words of some kind, although they weren't English nor any other language she knew. A refrain, repeated over and over. *Angana sor varalakh kai torja,* it sounded like; *angana sor varalakh cha voran.* It wasn't just one voice, either, but a chorus, and they all somehow sounded *wrong*, as though their mouths were damaged or malformed. A choir of wounded airmen, perhaps, all horribly disfigured from accidents.

Even so, the more she listened the closer she felt to grasping some part of its meaning. And the closer she came to *that*, the worse the unease the sound instilled became. And not just unease: queasiness, too, and a kind of disorientation.

Switch it off, then.

She would, in just a moment, but not quite yet. If she only listened a little longer, she might understand. She only had to listen a little longer. A little more.

But then the tape crackled, and the sound began to cut in and out. It crackled more loudly, and Cally realised was coming from the stereo itself.

"Shit," she almost shouted, and lunged for the Stop button. The tape-hiss and water-drip cut out, and the abrupt silence was uncomfortable and oppressive.

"Shit, shit, shit." Cally reached for the Eject button, dreading to see the damage to the tape. Or the player, come to that. The stereo system was Dad's pride and joy, and obsolete technology like the tape deck was hard to fix or replace. He'd be devastated if it had suffered serious damage.

Child of the digital generation or not, Cally was familiar enough with the old technology to know she'd only see the problem when she tried to remove the cassette. When she did – slowly, carefully – the shiny brown tape hung down from either side of the cassette's undercarriage, into a dreadful rat's-nest tangle wound around the deck's spindles. The smooth tape was horribly crumpled, but it didn't, at least, seem broken.

"Fuck. Fuck." Cally took a deep breath. "Okay. Don't panic."

Worst case scenario, she'd lost a tape of ordinary background noise – that, and whatever the hell that chant or song had been.

And that other voice. *Red Three to Tower*. It had sounded like an old-school fighter pilot, but World War One pilots hadn't had radios. World War Two, yes, but not the first one.

None of those sounds belonged on that tape anyway, but for now. All that mattered was getting the tape out of the machine, without damaging either.

"Don't panic," she muttered, again. "Don't panic."

Funnily enough, she wasn't. Despite being prey to generalised, reasonless terror at random intervals, in the face of an actual crisis Cally felt remarkably calm. This was a straightforward problem she could address with skill, work and patience, and by focusing on it to the exclusion of all else. That was her comfort zone; it was the world's myriad competing demands on her attention and resources Cally couldn't bear.

She laid the cassette flat, slid an ordinary Bic pen through the left-hand reel and slowly wound the loose tape in. She left some slack to work with, then set about working the snarled tape free of the spindles.

Little by little it came loose; little by little it was unravelled and wound back into the cassette, till finally Cally was done. She returned the cassette to its cartridge and the cartridge to its row, then closed the deck and switched off the stereo with a deep, relieved sigh.

At least the tape hadn't been Tony's journal. Cally gnawed a hangnail for a couple of minutes, then returned to the sofa, drank the last of her lukewarm coffee, then poured a fresh cup.

Caffeine, really? Last thing you need right now.

Probably true, but what the hell. She stirred in cream and sugar, then looked at her phone. Eight missed calls; two messages.

Six of the missed calls and one voice message were from Roland Woodwiss; she didn't want that smooth, greasy voice in her ear this late at night. She could delete his message without listening, but then she'd always worry it had been something important.

But two of the missed calls weren't from Roland, and nor was the other message. It was Griff, and the prospect of talking to him was nowhere near as uncomfortable, misguided amorousness or no.

"All right, Cally my love? I've gone through all those pictures you sent me. Now, how about that drink?"

"Fuck it," she muttered, and called him back. It would be a friendly voice, at least, and any kind of company was appealing right now. However annoying his crush, Griff still understood the meaning of the word *no*.

21.

For once Griff was otherwise engaged that night, off to meet two other ex-squaddies in Aberystwyth. He'd be staying overnight, but would be back in Fron-Goch by mid-morning tomorrow, so Cally agreed to a drink and pub lunch in Bala at noon.

She wished she could have met with him that evening. It would be far too easy tonight to imagine every creaking floorboard or breath of wind as Roland Woodwiss, having trailed her home to claim the kiss – or more – he felt entitled to for his help.

She shuddered. Then again, despite the coffee, Cally now felt shockingly tired, so she'd probably have invited Griff up to the house. He'd have interpreted that entirely the wrong way. Worse, she couldn't guarantee she wouldn't have ended up snogging him again after a couple of drinks. Or worse. If she ever slept with Griff, the poor sod would take it as a marriage proposal. She felt guilty enough when it came to him as it was.

She decided to turn in. She switched all the lights on before going upstairs: a terrible waste of electricity, but just for tonight, forgivable.

Not just because of Roland Woodwiss; the Warden Fell cassette had unsettled her too. *Red Three to Tower*. Cally would have liked to believe that'd just been Tony Mathias practising the period sound he'd wanted to add for the installation, but the voice had sounded too different, and where had the accompanying crackle of radio static come from? And then there was the chant.

Angana sor varalakh kai torja, angana sor varalakh cha voran. Cally could still feel its rhythm inside her head; as she climbed the stairs, her fingers tapped it out on her thigh. It conjured visions of the deserted rooms and corridors on *Desuetude.com*, and made the isolation and the darkness in them seem very real and present.

The thought came seemingly from nowhere: *it's an emptiness that isn't empty*. That was they hadn't reused buildings at Warden Fell, but built new ones instead. The old buildings were populated with echoes from the past.

Nonsense thoughts, born out of a long and trying day. A good ghost story, nothing more.

Even so, she left the bedroom lights on too, pulling the sheets over her head despite the heat, with a breathing-gap for her nose and mouth. Just enough darkness to sleep in.

Despite Cally's exhaustion, sleep seemed to take forever to claim her, and was fitful and restless when it did; she surfaced at odd intervals, knowing each time she'd emerged from a nightmare, but unable to remember its details.

Her dreams, good or bad, were almost always like that: pictures made of smoke, crumbling into wisps and tatters on waking, leaving only their mood behind.

Which, in this case, was one of unease, breathlessness and dread. Cally flung the damp cocoon of sheets back, but the night air was warm and thick, despite the open window; it was like trying to inhale cotton wool. That was the first thing she registered.

The second was that the room was now completely dark. The bedroom light and the one on the landing had both gone out, and she couldn't even see a glimmer from downstairs through the open bedroom door.

The third thing she registered was that parts of this darkness were blacker than the rest. There were shapes in the dark, one of which was standing beside the bed. It was leaning over Cally: in a moment, she'd see its face.

Later, she'd wonder if her scream if people had looked out of their windows in Bala, trying to pinpoint the source of her scream. Probably not: she couldn't tell what time it was, but the night was black and still and she could hear nothing. No whisper of cars along the A494 on the opposing shore of Llyn Tegid, no far-off laughter from the town's pubs. She'd heard both more than once in the past, but not tonight. Tonight, everyone was safe in their beds. Everyone but her.

She lashed out at the figure with her fists, kicked with her feet, flung herself out of bed and rolled across the floor. She had to keep moving, so that it, or they – because there might have been other intruders present too – couldn't get hold of her. But then she hit the wall, and there was nowhere left to go.

Cally pushed herself to her feet, back against the wall, and raised her fists, looking for the intruders. But the darkness was now a thick and swirling soup; even the bed's white sheets and mattress were only a dull-grey blur. The dark thinned and thickened again in arbitrary patterns. Some seemed vaguely humanoid; others didn't. Cally thought she saw one that was far too short to be a person, and far too broad, like a huge toad. There was no furniture in the part of the room it occupied, nothing she might have mistaken for something else. In another empty corner was a shape so tall its head brushed the ceiling; it seemed to spread stiff, ragged wings, like a huge cormorant. But when she tried to make either out in detail, they dissolved back into the general darkness.

Which actually helped; the more Cally thought about it, the less likely it seemed anything had been there to begin with. Gigantic toads? Enormous birds? Such things didn't exist in this part of the world; even if they did, they'd have better things to do than break into her bedroom in the middle of the night.

Cally managed a weak, breathless laugh, but it was far too

thin, breathless and lonely to be any comfort. Even so, she grew slowly calmer. The shapes weren't real, just her mind attempting to find patterns in the darkness. No one other than her had made any movement or sound; any intruders in the house – toad, cormorant or burglar – would surely have done so by now.

There was no one here but her, and never had been: that was the likeliest explanation. Optical illusions; nothing more.

But why had the lights gone out?

A power cut, she told herself. But when she opened the curtain there were lights gleaming along the A494, and when she craned her neck she could see the town's.

Which meant nothing. The power line supplying the house could have come down. Likelier still, a fuse had blown, or circuit breaker tripped, here in the house.

But it would have had to be more than one circuit breaker, because the lights were out downstairs too.

Someone had cut the power; Roland Woodwiss, maybe, armed with night-vision goggles, come to torment her with impunity now she was alone in the dark and far from help.

No. That was her anxiety talking, threatening to become full-blown panic. There were explanations, *rational* explanations. Not knowing was the hard part.

Cally couldn't make the bedside table out in the thick gloom, but the bed itself still remained faintly visible. She shuffled along the wall towards it. Her phone was on the bedside table: whatever the blackout's cause, her phone would provide a source of light.

Cally shuffled forward, arms outstretched; a moment later she shattered the Bala night a second time when she stubbed her toes on the bedside table, she hopped on her uninjured foot, letting out an inventive selection of obscenities. Weirdly, she now felt better: this was a concrete hurt, instead of ghosts and shadows, and besides, the image of herself hopping around in her knickers was so absurd she couldn't help but laugh.

Cally fumbled across the table till she found the hard, comforting outline of her phone. She pushed the button on its side, but the screen stayed blank.

"Oh come the fuck on," she muttered, pushing the button again and again. "This is not a good time." She didn't remember switching the phone off, but she must have done: a blown fuse or downed power-line wouldn't have made it go dead. If something else had, that raised the question of *what*, which Cally wouldn't be in any mood to consider before sunrise.

Thankfully, on the third or fourth attempt the phone buzzed and the screen lit up, albeit with a grey, lacklustre glow, far weaker than it should have been. But it a was light, nonetheless, and pushed, however feebly, at the encroaching darkness.

Cally advanced towards the bedroom door, trying not to hyperventilate. The shadows seemed peculiarly thick there, and as she raised her feeble light she bit her lips, convinced it was about to encounter something it couldn't dispel.

But there was only the half-ajar door and beyond that, the landing. She padded across it, then downstairs to the little pantry under the staircase, which housed the fuse box.

She was close to believing in rational explanations again – even a little light went a long way – but when she opened the box every circuit breaker had tripped. Which made no sense. Every fuse in the house would have to have blown together; that couldn't be right.

And yet, all the lights were out, and Cally had a horrible feeling the glow from her phone, already anaemic, was growing fainter.

Maybe one breaker had tripped and that had somehow set off the rest; if so, getting the lights back on should be easy enough. She reached out, and flicked the first breaker back on.

The lights in the hall flashed back into life, throwing a long black shadow across the floor; Cally spun round with a gasp, but there was nothing there. When she turned back to the circuit breakers, she realised the shadow that had startled her had been her own.

Probably something symbolic there. She flicked the next breaker, then the next, working her way along the row. They all stayed in position; all the lights in the house came back on, and stayed on.

Cally was shaking. The smell of her own sour sweat filled the pantry, but the muggy night felt far colder than it should.

She went into the front room and found a blanket to wrap herself in; she didn't want to go back upstairs. The lights might go out again; she'd rather be near the fuse box if that happened.

She needed bright lights and loud noises to distract her from how isolated she was here, and Dad had finally signed up to Disney Plus. Cally found *Buffy the Vampire Slayer,* selected a random episode and started watching. There were seven seasons of the show; more than enough to last her till morning, or till she fell asleep. Whichever came first.

22.

When Cally woke she ached in a dozen places from sleeping on the sofa, her mouth tasted foul, and she felt greasy with night-sweat, but it was daylight again. No shadows other than the neat, clearly-defined ones cast by the sun; the previous night's fears now seemed as ridiculous as they deserved to be.

Unfortunately, the onset of day had brought fresh waves of pollen, and obviously a lot of it; her nose was blocked and her throat sore, and there was a rash on her forearms. More Clarityn was clearly called for.

Her phone stayed dark; she guessed the battery had died, and plugged it in to recharge, then focused blearily on the mantelpiece carriage-clock and saw it was almost eleven-thirty.

Bloody hell, you needed that.

She needed something by way of breakfast, first of all. Except there wasn't time; she had about half an hour before she was due to meet Griff.

Which, she reminded herself as she blundered upstairs; would involve a pub lunch. That was an incentive, at least.

She showered and dressed, then slathered herself with sunblock to avoid being incinerated. Her hair was still wet, but would dry out naturally. She'd had no time to apply make-up, but that couldn't do any harm. It wasn't as if Griff needed any encouragement to moon over her.

Luckily, it only took five minutes to drive into Bala and a couple more to find a parking spot; the White Lion, a one-time coaching inn dating back to the 1700s, was only a short stroll away. She reached it almost on the stroke of noon, the bag containing Tony Mathias' carry-case hanging at her side.

It was cool inside the pub, with whitewashed plaster walls and wooden beams.

"*Bore da!*" called Griff. Bala was, after all, a predominantly Welsh-speaking town. And why not? As Dad had said more than once, it was their bloody country.

He was at a table in a little nook, tucked away from the rest of the pub, with the words *Cwtch Gwyniad* lettered on the wall beside it. Griff liked to find out-of-the-way corners to situate himself when in public, drawing attention to himself only when he chose.

"*Prynhawn da,*" Cally corrected, since it was after midday. She'd wanted Dad to teach her Welsh when she was little, but her mother had vetoed the idea. Millicent was a massive snob; more importantly, Cally suspected, she'd been afraid of Cally and Dad being able to have conversations she couldn't eavesdrop on.

Cally had begun learning the language since Dad and Lucy had moved here, albeit on an on-again-off-again basis. She knew enough to scrape by, but it was probably time to download the Duolingo app again. *Cwtch* meant *hug* or *cuddle*, or alternatively *cupboard* or *cubbyhole*; a *gwyniad* was a freshwater whitefish unique to Llyn Tegid.

She squeezed into the nook, holding a diet lemonade with ice; Griff, already halfway through a pint of bitter, raised his eyebrows. "Not drinking?"

"I'm driving," she said, setting the carry-case down beside her chair.

"So am I," he grinned.

Cally managed not to groan aloud. With luck, he wouldn't drink too much or failing that she could persuade him to get a taxi home, although that was easier said than done around here. In a major city you took being able to summon a taxi,

Uber or Lyft within minutes for granted; the sparser service in rural areas could be a real culture shock. For Griff, it was all too often a choice between driving drunk or walking home, which was hard work with one leg.

"I'll be fine with this for now," she said. "How you doing?"

"All the better for seeing you, *cariad*. What about you? You're looking a bit rough."

"Oh, thanks."

"I mean, like you've been crying or something. You all right?"

"Hay fever." She showed him the rash on her arms, which had at least faded a little. "Anti-histamines are kicking in, thank fuck."

"As long as that's all."

There were stuffed fish mounted in cases on the walls of the *cwtch*: the long green-gold torpedo of a pike with its hooked and grinning jaw; a trio of spiny-crested perch; a long, spotted trout. There'd once been three *gwyniad* in a jar of formaldehyde, but they'd begun to decay and as *gwyniad* couldn't legally be removed from the lake now, they hadn't been replaced.

Griff rubbed his hands together. "So, what do you fancy? My treat."

"I can buy my own dinner, Griff," she said gently. If anything, lunch should be on her. "Besides, I missed breakfast, so you'd need a bloody bank loan. *No*," she added sharply, before he could volunteer to take one out.

She chose the vegan burger with chunky chips; Griff plumped for bangers and mash, and Cally immediately wished she'd ordered that herself as it might actually have been the healthier option. It would take more hill-walking than she liked to think of to burn this little lot off. She was going to have to start watching what she ate again.

"So," she said, once they'd resupplied themselves with drinks, "anything to tell me?"

"Other than my undying love for you?"

"Bloody hell, Griff, give it a rest."

He laughed. "All right, all right. I looked over all the pictures you sent. All those different buildings. Bloody weird, I call it, even by military standards. Normally they'd either use 'em or knock 'em down."

Cally told him how, according to Adrian Woodwiss, the old buildings were left empty and out of bounds instead of being repurposed. "What if the buildings were contaminated somehow?" she said.

Griff frowned and shook his head. "If it was that bad, they'd have bulldozed the lot and probably concreted it over."

Cally sighed. "Bang goes that theory, then."

"Only thing I can think of," Griff said, "is if they had something stored underground, somewhere like that. If that leaked, it could've contaminated the other buildings."

"Really? That's possible?"

"Course it's *possible*. Anything's *possible*. It's even possible you might never come to your senses and marry me, but is it *likely*?"

"Oink, flap," said Cally. "Oink, flap."

Griff blew a raspberry, and Cally laughed despite herself. It was hard to stay angry with him. "Look," he said, more seriously, "they *could* have been storing the Ebola virus or a nuke or enough nerve gas to wipe out the North of England under the place, but that doesn't mean they *were*. Without proof one way or the other, they could have a bloody *dragon* under there for all I know. But I can only go off what I see. And from what you've shown me, apart from there being so many bloody buildings, there's bugger-all unusual there." He drained his pint and blinked at the empty glass. "How'd that happen?"

Cally took the hint and went to the bar; another diet lemonade felt quite appealing anyway. When she came back, Griff was leaning over the table, peering down at the bag. "So what's this? Little thank-you present or something?"

"I'll get you a bottle of Penderyn later," she promised. "This is more of 'another mission, should you choose to accept it,' kind of thing."

"Oh aye?" But then Griff looked past her and beamed happily. "Heads up," he said, "it's time for din-dins."

After they'd eaten, Cally tried to resist the dessert menu's siren song, while Griff browsed it with fascination and delight. "Reckon I'll go for the chocolate brownie," he said. "You?"

"Apple tart, maybe, with vegan cream."

"What in God's name is vegan cream? No, don't tell me. I want to sleep tonight."

Just a joke, but it brought back unwelcome recollections of last night, which presumably showed in Cally's face, as Griff looked genuinely concerned. "Bloody hell, love, you all right?"

"Bit of a crap night," she said. "Just some bad dreams."

A lie, but one she'd very much like to believe. It would have been nice to dismiss last night as the result of eating too much cheese.

"Sorry to hear that, chuck." Griff's gaze shifted to the carry-case. "So what *is* that, then?"

"Half of it's recordings Tony Mathias made at Warden Fell – background noise and radio traffic."

"At an abandoned airbase? Bloody weirdos, these artists."

"And what's wrong with being a weirdo?"

"Nothing at all, if it's one like you."

"If you were a dog, I'd have you neutered."

He responded with a faint, mournful growl and whine, accompanied by far-too-convincing puppy-dog eyes. Cally tossed a scrunched-up paper napkin at him. "The other half's his diary."

"On *tape*?"

"He was dyslexic."

"Ah, right. So you want me to digitise this little lot?"

"Think you can? I tried to play one of them last night, but the bloody machine chewed it up."

"That's cassette for you," Griff picked up the carry-case. "Right, let the dog see the rabbit here. I'll take a look, you order dessert."

"What *did* your last slave die of again?"

"Not getting me a chocolate brownie with ice cream when told to. Off you go, woman, chop-chop."

"You want that cake as an enema?"

By the time Cally returned, Griff had stacked the used plates and cutlery and shifted them aside. The carry-case was open in front of him, and he was inspecting a cassette; as she sat down, he replaced it and reached for another, and carried on until his dessert arrived, along with a pot of camomile tea for Cally, who'd managed to resist the apple tart in the end.

He put the case aside, grinned at her and set to work on the brownie. "Cheers me dear."

"Well?"

"Mm?" He glanced at the carry-case. "I'll have a crack."

"Thanks."

"No promises until I've actually had a proper listen, but I think I can manage something."

"The one I'd really like to hear is that." Cally tapped the final cassette, the unmarked one. "If there's actually anything on it."

"Noted. I'll start on that, then." Griff slid the case into its bag, set it down beside him and patted it. "Now then," he said, and returned to the brownie.

They walked back to the car park at the north-east end of Bala. Griff moved with an easy, natural stride, sometimes almost outpacing Cally, prosthetic leg or no.

He'd sunk several pints, but to no visible effect; he might as well have been drinking lemonade too. Even so, Cally thought *friends don't let friends drive drunk*, over and over, as he unlocked his Land Rover Defender's door.

"All right, *cariad*." He swept her into a brief, clumsy hug that reeked of stale beer. "Give you a shout tomorrow."

"Okay."

"Love ya."

She patted his back and told herself that was the beer talking, which made her feel guiltier for not stopping him. "Drive carefully, for God's sake. And text me when you're back safe."

"Yes, Mother."

"Make your bloody mind up."

"Yes'm." He gave her a surprisingly crisp salute, then got behind the wheel. Cally watched him drive away, then eyed her own car. She thought of going back home, but after last night, the house's solitude wasn't the comfort it normally was. For now, she wanted to be among people a little while longer. Not to *talk* to them or anything; just not to feel alone.

She went to the pharmacy first, to stock up on Clarityn, since her hay fever was seemingly in overdrive; that done, she pottered around antique and charity shops and the local bookstore before her earlier resolve over the apple tart gave out. She queued for a caramel latte and cinnamon roll at Ty Coffi, keeping her eye on a table in a shady corner of the café throughout. To her relief it was still unoccupied by the time she'd been served: the outside tables were the ones in demand right now.

She sipped her latte and dug a chunk out of her sweet roll. Retail therapy and comfort-eating weren't a long-term fix, but they'd do for now. Hopefully she'd feel better with the tapes out of the house.

No one's making you play them.

True, but if she didn't listen to them, she wouldn't get any answers, although that no longer seemed the worst thing imaginable. She could apologise to Edna Woodwiss and return the tapes; if she hadn't the stomach for it, so be it. Edna had taken the same approach for the past forty years, after all.

Because the Mathias family were her friends. What's your excuse?

She didn't *need* one, for Christ's sake. The podcast was supposed to be something that *didn't* fuck up her mental health.

Anyway, there was no rush; she could forget the tapes for a day or two, let Griff do his thing. Spend some time walking around the hills and lake, reading or working on her Welsh.

That inspired Cally to take out her phone, which she'd left charging till the last minute before going to meet Griff; it was only at thirty percent, but that should be ample to run through a lesson on Duolingo.

"Cally? I mean, Ms Darker?"

Cally didn't recognise her at first: she wore a sundress and sandals instead of boots and uniform, and was a Danish pastry and a glass mug of herbal tea on a tray. Amazing the difference such small things made.

"Mind if I join you?" said Constable Rooke.

23.

Rooke set her tray down on the table. "I wanted to say sorry."

"What about?" Cally winced internally; it came out harsher than she'd meant.

"The other day." Rooke pulled back the opposite chair. "I'm not apologising for doing my job, Ms Darker. We'd had a report. You were alone in the house. Dave looked the place over to see there was nothing indicating you were–"

"A danger to myself or others?" Cally knew the phrasing.

"Yeah. And I stayed with you because we seemed to have a bit more of a connection. Two birds, one stone."

"Thought you'd see what you could get out of me, you mean?"

"I get why you were pissed off, and I *am* sorry for that." Rooke paused, suddenly awkward. "I actually *did* enjoy talking to you."

She had blue eyes, with a pale butterfly of freckles across the bridge of her nose and thin red lips. "Glad you had fun," said Cally. "Does everybody you check up on get this?"

"No, just the–" Rooke broke off. "Just the nice ones."

Cally laughed. "I'm not nice."

"I wouldn't have said that."

"Ask my exes. I'm evil incarnate."

Rooke snorted. "I've seen more evil ducks."

"Ducks can be evil bastards."

"You're thinking of geese. *They're* scary buggers."

Cally laughed again, relaxing a little. The affinity with Rooke she'd felt the other day had returned, stronger than ever. She'd needed someone she could talk to without judgements or criticism – which certainly hadn't described Iain – and despite what had happened before, she felt she'd finally found one.

"Or swans," Rooke added. "They're the drag queen version. Like a goose went into Paddy's Goose and got a makeover."

"Paddy's Goose?" Cally knew the place: a deceptively traditional-looking pub on Bloom Street at the edge of the Gay Village, one of the city's oldest gay-friendly bars, and particularly popular with crossdressers and trans people. She'd once seen two lads in smart suits, obviously new in town, stride in only to freeze like rabbits in the headlights when a six-foot drag queen with ice-sculpture hair and tattooed forearms materialised to take their orders. They'd gulped their pints and fled, the pub erupting in laughter behind them:

Then Cally remembered where she thought she'd seen Rooke before. "You know Manchester?

"Bloody should," said Rooke. "Lived there four years. Try being a Scouse copper in Manchester on a Saturday night."

"Are you into pain or something?" Disparaging comments about all things Liverpudlian was virtually a national pastime in Manchester. It was usually good-humoured, (although not all Scousers would've agreed,) but when dealing with an ugly drunk, the humour quickly turned sour.

"Not like that I'm not. I liked Manchester, especially the scene there. You used to go to Vanilla, didn't you?"

So she'd been right. "Yeah."

"Thought so. Think I remember talking to you one time – well, you or your twin."

Cally laughed yet again; it felt good to do so. "It was bugging me yesterday, where I'd seen you before, and then I remembered the same thing. I thought no, it can't be, but–"

"Yup, it was."

"Surprised you remember it."

"You're not easy to forget."

"Thanks, I think."

"It's a compliment, trust me." Rooke grinned.

Neither of them mentioned the Donna incident.

"What's your name, anyway?" Cally said. "Can't keep calling you Constable."

"Ellen."

"Nice to meet you, Ellen."

"It is, isn't it?"

All too often Cally felt constrained on more fronts than she could even articulate – pinned down by low mood and anxiety, the succession of shitty jobs and failed relationships – but just now the world felt far bigger, and more full of possibility. It might not last, but she'd enjoy it while she could.

And anxiety or not, depression or not, she was lucky: she could stay here as long as she needed, and beyond that, it was a big world, full of places to be and things to do. It shouldn't be hard to find *something* that would make her content. The podcast felt distant and unimportant: so, more to the point, did the whole business of Tony Mathias and Eagle Mount.

"You okay?" said Ellen.

"I am, actually." There was a dreg of latte left; Cally drained it. "You know what I could go for right now? A proper drink. Nice cold glass of white wine."

Ellen grinned. "That *does* sound nice. Trouble is, I'm driving."

"Me too. Of course, I'm not far from here."

Ellen nodded. "And a bottle from the Spar or Co-op'd be a sight cheaper than down the pub."

"If you fancy it, I'll even cook. I make a decent spag bol." Cally had meant to make today a Meatless Monday, but sod it.

"I could live with that."

"Back to mine, then?"

"Okay."

24.

Ellen picked up two bottles of Hock, another of Tempranillo and a bag of ice; Cally bought mince and parmesan, plus a blackcurrant cheesecake for dessert (having cast all good intentions to the wind; she told herself she'd start being good tomorrow.) Ellen followed her into the hills in a Nissan Juke with blue paintwork half-hidden under splatters of hard-baked mud.

In the house, Cally directed Ellen to the living-room sofa. "Make yourself comfy," she said.

"Can I help with anything?"

"I'll be fine. Just chill."

"Chance would be a fine thing." Cally knew what Ellen meant. Both cars had grown baking hot while parked; winding down the windows hadn't helped.

"Try this," she said, and switched on one of the ceiling fans

"Oh my God," said Ellen, stretching out on the sofa beneath the current of cold air. She was compact rather than petite, sturdy rather than slender; at first glance she looked soft, but her build owed more to muscle than fat.

Cally emptied the ice into a plastic bucket and shoved the bottles of Hock into it, then poured in a carafe of cold water. "That'll be nice and chilled in a few minutes."

Ellen gave her a weary thumbs-up. "I had a listen to your podcast," she called after her.

"Oh?"

Cally filled a carafe of water and took it through with a pair of tumblers, then went back for wineglasses.

Ellen slipped off her sandals and rubbed her feet. "Liked it, especially the Miles Giffard one."

"Quite a few people seem to."

Ellen shuffled up on the sofa to make room. "Listened to that one, the Haw Bridge Torso Case, and the World's End Murders. Saved that for last because it was a big bugger."

"Yeah." Cally had split it into two parts: one covered the killings themselves and the families' decades-long wait for answers; the second explored the killer's arrest and background before returning the focus to the two young women whose lives he'd cut so brutally short. "I wanted to do justice to it."

"You did." Ellen drank off a tumbler of water and eyed the bucket. "Think that's cold enough yet?"

Cally took out a bottle. "Feels like it." There was a foot of space between them: a short distance and a huge, aching gap.

Ellen smiled. "Then let's get started."

They drank, and talked; one of those long, everything-and-nothing conversations you occasionally fell into with someone else and found yourself feeling as though you'd always known them.

At least until Ellen swayed and Cally reached out to steady her. "You okay?" she asked, feeling a little guilty; the ingredients for the meal were still in the fridge, and the second bottle of Hock was almost empty.

Ellen nodded. "Sorry – lost track of how much I'd had," she said. "Reacts with my meds."

"You too, huh?" It happened to a lot of people on antidepressants. Cally was one of the lucky ones who were more or less unaffected. Same story with antihistamines, more was the pity; her hay fever always played havoc with her sleep.

Ellen nodded, and seemed on the point of saying more, before shifting the conversation to another topic. Cally sipped her wine, drifting slightly.

"...on now?"

Cally blinked. "Sorry?"

Ellen laughed. "What I was asking, Buggerlugs, was what you were working on now?"

"Apart from this?" Cally picked up the Hock bottle.

Ellen swatted her on the shoulder. "Come on, spill the beans." Her eyes were heavy-lidded. Too much wine.

"The Eagle Mount Murders."

"Don't know 'em."

"It's a pretty obscure case. One of my listeners called them 'the other World's End Murders,' but I didn't want to use that."

"How come?"

"Would've sounded too much like cashing in on the real World's End Murders, trying to make out there was a link–"

"Not that, you mushroom. Why did this fanboy of yours call them that?"

Cally explained about what Tony Mathias had scrawled on the caravan wall. She touched on the topic of Warden Fell, but stopped when Ellen's eyelids drooped: it might have just been the wine, but why chance it? "Anyway, that's the story so far. The bit that's missing is why he did it."

Ellen leant back on the sofa. "Hate to tell you, but sometimes the reason why is... there isn't one."

"How'd you mean?"

Ellen's eyes had were drooping again; she blinked and sat up straight. "I mean that sometimes people do horrible things for no real reason. They just decide they want to. Or that they like it."

"There wasn't any history of it with Tony."

"None you could *find*. People can have all sorts going on, bottled up, that no one else even guesses about till suddenly – ping. Or he just got up one morning, a little switch went click in here" – Ellen touched her forehead – "and killing everybody suddenly seemed like this great idea. Only one who could tell you was him."

Cally realised she hadn't mentioned the tapes; before she could, Ellen said: "What did the police reckon?"

"Just got an email back saying they couldn't help. Very brusque, now I think of it."

Ellen frowned. "That doesn't sound right. I think my old sergeant transferred to Lancashire Constabulary – that's who it'd be, wouldn't it?"

"Yeah."

"Still got his email somewhere," said Ellen. "I'll drop him a line. See if he can help."

"Really?"

"Why not?"

Ellen swayed, putting a hand to her forehead. "Whoa," she said, "Ooh."

"You okay?"

"Yeah, just a little... bit dizzy, there. Give me a moment." Ellen put a hand over her mouth. "Oh, God, I'm going to – where's the–"

Thankfully, she bolted for the kitchen, reaching the sink just in time. She threw up, loudly and abundantly, then turned on the taps and rinsed her mouth. She stumbled back to the sofa, face red with embarrassment. "Sorry"

"It's okay." Cally put a tentative arm around her shoulders. "We've all been there."

"Thanks." Ellen rested her head on Cally's shoulder for a moment, then lurched upright. Cally thought she was about to make another dash for the sink, but instead she lay back and shut her eyes. "So sorry."

"It's okay, honestly."

"Just give me a minute," Ellen said. "I'll be all right."

She'd clearly had enough wine for one evening. "I'll make a brew," said Cally. She went into the kitchen, put the kettle on to boil, and called: "Tea or coffee?". In answer, Ellen began to snore.

Sighing, Cally laid Ellen on her side, head pillowed on

cushions against the sofa-arm, then covered her with a thin blanket and placed Ellen's shoes together at one end of the sofa. She emptied the melted ice down the kitchen sink and positioned the empty bucket by Ellen's head, just in case. She felt very tired, too, she realised. *A quick nap, then cook dinner and stick to soft drinks for the rest of the night.* She made her way to the stairs and stumbled up to her room to undress.

25.

The screaming tore Cally awake.

She'd been dreaming, or rather nightmaring. At least not that she remembered: as ever, all memory of it disappeared on waking, except for a few fragmentary sounds and images. Jagged stone walls on every side, rearing up into infinity. The flap of huge, ragged wings. And a chant or song she couldn't comprehend but with a rhythm. And something long and thick and eel-like that swam impossibly through the air towards her.

The blackness around her was total and she didn't know where she was. Iain's house. Donna's old flat. Dad and Millicent's old house in Sale–

No, none of the above. It was Dad and Lucy's house in Bala, and someone was screaming downstairs.

Ellen.

Cally switched on the bedside lamp, but nothing happened. She grabbed her phone, but the screen didn't light up. The battery was dead again.

The charge had already been low, she told herself, and the bedside light's bulb must have blown. This wasn't a repetition of last night. It wasn't.

Cally stumbled through bedroom door, flicking the switches for the bedroom and landing lights in turn, but neither came on.

The screams from below became whooping gasps of fright. She groped along the landing to the top of the stairs.

The enclosed staircase was more cut off from any vestigial light, of course, but even so it was choked with a smoke-dense blackness deeper than the one she'd woken in. Cally was certain of that, even before it moved.

Something floated as if in water, several feet above the steps. It was huge, stretching from the bottom of the stairs almost to the top, bigger than either of the things she'd seen last night.

Hallucinated, not seen. There was nothing there then. There's nothing here now.

Logic and good sense told her that, but they belonged to the light; in the dark, they were meaningless.

Just behind the thing's heavy, bulbous head, two fins – or tiny hands? – moved. Its body was long and tapering, like a huge eel or tadpole. Like the thing in her dream, undulating towards her, through the air.

Shadows. Darkness. An absence of light. Your brain's looking for patterns, that's all. There's nothing there, but something is *happening to Ellen. So for Christ's sake* move.

But Cally still saw it nonetheless, maddeningly vague and yet substantial. A ripple moved slowly through it, from head to tail. The 'hands' kneaded the air, but it moved neither towards her nor away. Just hung there, stationary. Daring her to approach.

The whooping cries from downstairs grew faster, higher and fainter. Ellen was hyperventilating so fast she might pass out. "Fuck," said Cally, then, grabbing the banister as an anchor, started down.

The eel-shape swam to meet her. There was a momentary impression of a dank chill against her exposed skin, but so briefly she could only have imagined it. Cally swayed, disorientated, but pressed on, down the stairs.

The blackness swirled thick around her, only clearing as she reached the bottom. "Ellen?" she called, entering the living room. "Ellen!"

"Who's that?" Ellen's voice was high and tearful; Cally barely recognised it.

"It's me." Cally flicked the light-switch; nothing happened. "Cally."

"Cally?" The name seemingly meant nothing to Ellen; perhaps she was as lost as Cally had been on first waking. But then she said it again – "Cally" – and this time there was recognition in her voice.

"Right here." Cally picked her way towards the sofa, aided by the thin moonlight through the patio doors and the pale blur of Ellen's face. "On my way."

"I can see." Ellen managed a shaky laugh. "You practically glow in the dark."

She'd forgotten she was in her underwear. "Goes with being a natural redhead," she said, and extended a hand; the shape up ahead did the same, like a mirror-image. What if it wasn't Ellen? A silly idea, but somehow still a frightening one, even when a small hot hand gripped hers.

Ellen was trembling; Cally put an arm around her and guided her to the sofa. "Just wait here. Be right back."

"Don't." Ellen's arms tightened around her. "Please."

"Ow! Okay. What happened?"

Ellen was silent a moment, then whispered: "Night terrors. I get 'em sometimes. You know, like you wake up and think someone's there? It's fucking horrible."

"Yeah." Cally had experienced it herself, though thankfully only once or twice, not counting last night and tonight. "Sounded bad."

"It was a doozy, even for me." Another shaky laugh. "You're not the only basket-case here, remember? Normally I don't see anything. Just *feels* like someone's there. This time, though – actually thought I saw it for a second."

"It?" Not *him, her* or *them. It.*

"Like a big fucking bird." Ellen spread her arms out, almost dead straight. Like a cormorant, unfolding its wings. "The lights out?"

"Yeah. Something's on the fritz somewhere. Happened last night too. I was gonna check, if–"

"Yeah. I'm all right now."

After a couple of attempts Cally's phone came on. Only a fraction of battery power remained, but its thin watery glow was enough to check the breakers by.

None of the lights had been on when Cally had gone to bed but, as before, all the breakers had tripped; once again they all clicked back into their original positions without a hitch, and when she emerged from the cupboard, the landing and front-room lights were on.

Ellen had wrapped herself in the blanket, despite the heat; and her face was a copper's impassive mask again. "Sorry about that," she said. "Acted like a right wuss."

"You said yourself, these things just happen sometimes." Cally indicated herself. "I'm not exactly a mental health poster child myself, am I? It's–"

"Yeah," said Ellen, cutting her off. "I should go,"

Shit. "You don't have to–"

"I should, anyway." Ellen began folding the blanket. Her hands shook. "Got work in the morning."

"You could stay till it's light. Get a bit more sleep."

"I couldn't," said Ellen, but gestured towards the couch, which didn't escape Cally's notice.

"You don't have to sleep *there*," Cally said. "I've a bed. We can share. Just share it, nothing else."

The corner of Ellen's mouth twitched in a smile. *Careful, love, the mask's slipping.* "Wouldn't want to put you out."

"Wouldn't have offered if you were."

"If you're sure?" The mask slipped entirely; Ellen couldn't hide her relief, or gratitude, at being asked to stay.

She doesn't want to be alone tonight either.

"I'm sure," said Cally, and took Ellen's hand; Ellen didn't pull away, but squeezed back, then gathered her shoes and handbag. Still clutching Cally's hand, she let herself be led upstairs.

"Do you want the lights left on?" said Cally, fingers resting on the wall switch.

"Nah." Ellen sat on the edge of the bed, looking strangely small and vulnerable in one of Cally's spare t-shirts. "Well, maybe just the little one."

"No problem," said Cally, secretly relieved.

She turned on the bedside lamp and lay down; she kept to her side and Ellen to hers. A little awkward, but it felt safer. Soon Ellen was snoring again, but Cally didn't mind. The rhythm of it was almost soothing, and helped her slide quickly into sleep as well.

26.

When Cally woke, her phone – now fully recharged – gave the time as six-thirty, and she was alone in the bed. Even Ellen's clothes had gone.

Maybe she'd been a hallucination too. Maybe the tapes and case Edna had gifted Cally had been contaminated with some residue of whatever had killed Tony and his family. That would explain, after all, why Ellen had also seen *a big fucking bird*, as she'd put it, looming over her.

If she'd been there at all.

"Ellen?" Cally called, and groaned: her head pounded and her mouth tasted foul. The wine, plus the hay fever. Her nose was blocked solid, her eyes stung and her arms were covered in hives. She fumbled in her shoulder-bag for the Clarityn.

"Kitchen," Ellen shouted back. Cally grabbed her towelling rob and tramped downstairs.

Ellen was at the breakfast table with a mug of camomile and a half-eaten piece of toast. "Hope you don't mind," she said, "I was starving."

"No problem." Cally went to the sink for a glass of water. "Never did make dinner, did I?"

"No. Want one of these?" Ellen held up a packet of ibuprofen. "Had a head like Birkenhead when I woke up."

Cally's mouth was so dry the painkillers stuck to her tongue, and it took almost the full glass of water to dislodge them. "Sorry about dinner."

"Too much wine on an empty stomach," said Ellen.

Cally cleared her throat. "Do you want to try again?"

"Can't, sorry. My shift starts at eight."

The brush-off. "Oh, okay."

"But we could get together again later, if you want? I'm off at six." Ellen grinned. "You can make that spag bol. Nice home-cooked meal at the end of a hard day."

"Seriously?"

"Seriously. Come over to mine if you want. I'm just down the road in Llanuwchllyn."

Meaning: *I'd rather it wasn't here next time.* Which was understandable enough; after the past couple of nights Cally wouldn't mind a change of scene herself. "Sounds good."

"Coolio." Ellen scribbled in a notepad. "Here's the address. And my number."

"Okay."

They faced one another for a moment; then Ellen smiled. "See you later, then."

Cally watched her get into the Juke, waved as she drove off. She'd forgotten to ask what time, but that was a good excuse to call later.

A shower, coffee and breakfast, along with the ibuprofen and several glasses of water, banished the worst of the ill-effects Cally had woken with. That done, she dressed, covered up with sun-block, and went walking in the hills.

Exercise, minimal thought, time alone in nature and a break from the house. After the past two nights, the prospect of being alone there felt oppressive, which Cally hated; it had always been a sanctuary for her.

Clear your head. Sweat all the crap out.

Despite the antihistamines her nose was alternately stuffed and streaming, her eyes watering and she still felt run-down, but Cally kept walking in the hope the exercise would help and that the Clarityn would eventually kick in. Around midday, she sat down and opened the salad box she'd packed; her stomach was growling. She ate slowly, gazing out across blue water and green hills. Distant traffic purred, grazing sheep bleated, a bird flickered across the sun.

Cally thought of cormorants again, recalling the shape she'd glimpsed – but a bright clear day like this drove shadows away, and that was all it had been. The toad-thing, too, and the eel-thing. None of them had actually existed.

Ellen saw it too.

No. Ellen had *thought* she'd seen something. *Almost* thought it. She suffered from night terrors; imagining such things went with the territory. Ghosts didn't exist: the only real monsters were human. As for the Warden Fell cassettes being somehow toxic, Edna Woodwiss had handled them on first finding the things, and remained alive and well today. Even if they could still have been dangerous forty years later, they hadn't been *then*.

Cally packed away the salad box and munched an apple, nodding to herself. It was paranoia on her part, nothing more. She and Ellen had both suffered an attack of night terrors last night – probably not helped, in Cally's case, by listening to the Warden Fell tapes.

Maybe she'd immersed herself too deeply in Eagle Mount and suchlike cases, descending into world after world poisoned or destroyed by sickness, resentment and violence. Perhaps she should take a break from the podcast. Focus on something else for a while.

Like what? Fluffy bunnies? Cat pictures?

The water-bottle was almost empty; the hot sun continued to blaze, and her hay fever wouldn't abate. Today's pollen count must be through the roof. Probably something to do with global warming, she told herself, then shook her head. Contemplating the climate crisis was the last thing her depression needed.

She plodded back to the house, drank more water, pulled the bedroom curtains and lay down, setting her alarm half an hour ahead. When it shrilled, she showered again, then texted Ellen: *What time's good for you? 7? 8?*

She stayed off the internet and away from anything podcast- or true-crime-related. She read, or tried: most of her books were still at Iain's, and she'd never got into eBooks so she only had what was in the house, none of which seemed to hold her attention. The hay fever again, or perhaps she was coming down with a summer cold. She made camomile tea with honey for her throat and took a couple of paracetamol; that seemed to help.

Around four o'clock she finally fired up the laptop and went online. On Facebook there were two new messages from Iain, demanding to know when she was picking up her things. The first was full of false bonhomie, the second so formal it resembled a solicitor's letter.

At least he isn't worried about you now.

She'd have to reply, and more importantly make a return trip to Manchester before Iain donated her belongings to charity, but she'd message him later; she'd no time for his bullshit now.

She had two new emails, too, both from Griff. One was direct from him; the other via WeTransfer.

All right *cariad*, the first began.

Well, I've been slaving away all night. Think the tape you played first was the best quality one, the others are in a right state. But I managed to get all of the tape for 22nd-24th May digitised, and some of that last tape. Only some, because that one was *really* fritzed. Needed a lot of work to clean it up so you can actually hear it! Just call me your pet genius.☺

Speaking of background sound, though, there's some really weird noise on it – you'll see what I meant when you play it. Very like the stuff on that chewed-up tape (I had a listen to make sure it'd still play.) Buggered if I know what it is. I'll see if I can isolate the sound and clear it up. Never know, it might solve the mystery! ☺

Anyway: have a listen, see what you think. Give us a call
after if you like.

Griff xxxxxx

"Bless." Cally felt guilty again. *Slaving away through the night*,
he'd said, although Griff being Griff, he'd probably exaggerated
for effect.

*He's a grown-up. You've never led him on or given him cause to
think anything's going to happen. You asked for help, he said yes.
Anything else is his problem.*

All true, but despite her best efforts part of Cally wouldn't
accept it. Ever since The Incident In The Back Of Griff's Car,
she'd been careful not to be at all ambiguous about any
prospect of a relationship (i.e. none,) but still struggled not
to feel manipulatory where he was concerned. Now she was
seeing Ellen, she felt guiltier than ever.

"Sod it," she muttered, and clicked the WeTransfer link. She
downloaded the recordings, plugged a pair of Dad's headphones
into the laptop, and opened the first file.

27.

Tony Mathias' diary depicted the same man Gowland, Stella and Edna Woodwiss had described: good-humoured, kindly, and intelligent. If he sometimes struggled to balance his work's demands with those of his marriage and family, he displayed no resentment, more a rueful *Oh well, that's life* attitude which was rather sweet, albeit a bit cloying after a while. Either he'd hidden his psychosis perfectly, or something at Warden Fell had triggered it.

Where did you study psychology again?

Maybe she should run the recordings by someone with that kind of background, see if they spotted any red flags. Or maybe she wouldn't need to: the next entry might reveal all.

"All right," Tony Mathias said, concluding his entry for 24th May 1983, "that's all for tonight. Got to do the washing-up, and then read Alison's bedtime story. Glamorous life of an artist, eh?" He chuckled. "And tomorrow, Warden Fell."

There was a loud sharp click, then silence; the recording had ended. Cally rubbed the backs of her arms; the fine hairs there were bristling.

She returned to the folder where she'd saved the recordings, moving the cursor arrow to TONY MATHIAS JOURNAL 25TH/26TH MAY, finger resting on the mousepad.

One click, and you'll have your answers.

Or not. Maybe she'd have to look further back for evidence of his madness. Or maybe there was none to find; maybe Ellen was right, and there was no better reason than *shit happens*.

Cally opened a can of Pepsi Max and stared at the screen

again. Her dilemma hadn't changed: whatever she learned, even if it revealed Tony Mathias as a monster, she'd have to tell Stella Di Mauro.

No law says you've got to play it.

But she *did*, even so. That'd been true the second Edna had given her the key, maybe even before.

The tape crackled and hissed, and there was a rough sawing noise that Cally eventually recognised as ragged breathing. And in the background, a half-familiar rhythm of some kind. A radio or another tape, possibly, playing nearby.

"A slurping sound, a gulp, and a half-contented sigh. "Right. Not sure where to start. First things first, I suppose. This is my journal entry for 25th May, 1983, but I'm actually recording on the morning of the 26th. Normally I record last thing at night before turning in, but one thing I can definitely say about yesterday is that it wasn't bloody normal."

His crisp RP diction had lapsed into broad Lancashire; he took a deep breath and paused. When he continued, his voice was smooth once more. "Yesterday was a long day. Had to drive out to the Forest of Bowland, and then there was the small matter of gaining access to Warden Fell. I wanted to get everything I needed in a single go if at all possible – didn't want to run the risk of being caught more than once – but I hope the MOD has better security around the airbases they're still using. Nobody on site, no cameras, just some old fencing that must have been there twenty years, apparently without a lick of maintenance. Even if they're determined to hang onto the place, they're clearly buggered if they can find a use for it."

Another slurp, then a racking cough. "Sorry for all the sound effects. Think I'm coming down with something. Surprisingly cold out there, despite the time of year. Damp, too. Could be the trees. The hilltop's so heavily overgrown with them, most of it's in perpetual shadow. Microclimate, I think they call it."

He cleared his throat again. "That aside, I couldn't have asked for better working conditions. No one around. Even the First World War buildings are weirdly well-preserved. Maybe the tree cover gives some sort of protection? I don't know. Or particularly care: it's the results I'm interested in."

Cally sipped her Pepsi Max.

"The old RFC aerodrome's noticeboards are still there, complete with postcards, posters, aircraft identification charts – bit faded, but otherwise intact after sixty bloody years. Cigarette packets, ashtrays, lighters, newspapers, magazines – things that should have rotted or rusted years ago, or been shredded by rats for their nests. Anyway. I set up my trusty cassette recorder, then took my pictures. Lots of different angles. Just hope they've turned out all right. Haven't even looked yet. To be honest, I'm a little nervous about doing so. And I'm not sure there's much point."

Cally leant forward.

"I might have to drop the whole project," said Tony. "Or radically rethink it. Neither of which will go down well with the Whitworth, or Bernard. But as it stands, the concept's – well, buggered."

A pause; the tape crackled.

"I played the ambient sound tapes back last night. It was getting late – wouldn't have been dark for hours yet, but it *felt* darker than it should. If that makes sense. Probably those bloody trees again. Besides, now I knew how easily I could get in and out, I felt happier about making a second trip if necessary."

Another gulp. Cally wondered what he was drinking. Long since brewed and drunk and gone, whatever it was, and the kettle buried in some landfill, but hearing him drink – such an ordinary, day-to-day activity – made Cally feel as though Tony Mathias were in the room, as if she could turn and ask him what had happened.

But you can't.

Even so, she hesitated before looking up, and was relieved to find herself alone.

"It *was* dark when I got back home," he went on. "Lights were all off in the caravan, so I knew everyone was in bed. I wasn't tired – in fact, I was pretty jazzed up – so I went to the studio to listen to the tapes properly. Now when I was recording at Warden Fell all I heard was wind, some leaves blowing around, a pipe dripping somewhere. Nothing else. *Nothing*. But when I play the tapes back... Some of them sound like old radio transmissions. I swear one sounds like a World War Two pilot on manoeuvres, trying to get through to the control tower. Right up to the moment he ploughs into a hillside."

Red Three to Tower. Red Three to Tower.

"I've heard stories about people picking up old radio signals from years ago, but some of the voices I've picked up – there's some seventeenth century stuff, all *thees* and *thous* and '*Sblood*s, some that sounds mediaeval, maybe even older. And then there's that *song*, or chant. Whatever it us. God knows how old that is. Or what language."

Another slurp. "The same stuff turns up on the radio traffic, too. I suppose it could be a very clever hoax; I could see some too-clever-by-half artist type – yes, all right, like me – setting something like this up, but what'd be the point? So what does that leave? Some sort of bizarre natural phenomenon that turns the hill into a gigantic bloody tape-machine – or..."

A long silence. The tape hissing. And, in the background, that maddeningly familiar chant.

"Or I've actually captured a ghost on tape. Which is a rather disconcerting thought."

"No shit." Cally didn't believe in ghosts, and really didn't want to start now.

"Either way," said Tony, "I'm not sure what that means for the planned installation. I could look at changing the format. Artist's impressions of whatever settlements existed on Warden Fell in the past – Greston Castle for example, if it really *was* there. *I* didn't put those sounds on the tape, but no one'll believe that if I use them in the installation. And it's fair to say they could be significant. Ghosts on tape – you'd think that would be one for the books, wouldn't you? Should probably tell somebody about it, but who? I suppose a real artist wouldn't think twice about using them – whatever it takes to make the show work, all grist to the mill, et cetera."

A grunt. "After all, the show's *called The Ghosts of Warden Fell.* Ghosts of the past; echoes, imprints. But that was a *metaphor.* This is something else."

He snorted. "Not making much sense, am I? So, what are my alternatives? Adapt the concept to fit with this stuff, somehow? Alternatively, junk the whole project and start again from scratch, which should give everyone at the Whitworth a collective embolism and send poor Bernard into a nervous breakdown."

Tony sounded amused, but then he gave a tired, dusty sigh. "I'd better come up with an alternative, and sooner rather than later. Not today, though. Still feeling wiped out. Nothing too bad. Touch of the sniffles. Probably picked it up from all that cold and damp. No fun in summertime."

"Try hay fever, mush," Cally muttered, sounding almost as rough and croaky as him.

"Not today, but soon," he sighed. "I need something concrete in place if I'm to stand a chance of their scrapping *The Ghosts of Warden Fell.* Need to get Bernard on-side at the very least. All right. Anyway. Quick precis of some of the sounds I've picked up."

Cally fumbled for pen and paper. She'd read most cases of so-called Electronic Voice Phenomena were down to the human brain's need to seek patterns, finding them where none existed. Seeing a face on Mars, or hearing the dead in radio static.

Some of the things Tony Mathias thought he'd heard might

have been nothing more than that; others still might have been symptoms of psychosis. But the sounds she'd heard on that first, chewed-up tape had been clear and unambiguous. *Red Three to Tower. Red Three to Tower.* And that strange chanting–

The chanting.

That naggingly familiar song Cally had assumed was playing elsewhere in Tony's studio: she recognised it now. It had been on that first tape from Warden Fell. *Angana sor varalakh kai torja, angana sor varalakh cha voran.*

She'd typed the words into Google, trying a few alternate spellings – all she had was the phonetic pronunciation – but nothing had come up. If it *was* a language, it wasn't one she could identify online.

If it had a melody, it was atonal or off-key. But it was infectious nonetheless; she was tapping out its rhythm on her thigh. Another moment and she might have begun humming it: it was getting louder, and clearer.

Cally's stomach had tightened; her breathing had speeded up. She pulled off the headphones, fumbled at the laptop till the recording stopped, then slammed the computer shut.

28.

Several minutes of deep breathing and running a meditation app on her phone staved off what had almost become a full-blown panic attack; Cally had found it useful in the past, and was glad she'd remembered to use it this time.

One of the recordings from Warden Fell playing in the background. That was the logical explanation, wasn't it? It was definitely the one Cally wanted to believe.

Then believe it. There aren't any ghosts. The electrics in the house are playing up; you and Ellen both had night terrors. That's all. You never believed in that crap before: why start now?

Besides, she'd things to do, like cooking dinner for Ellen tonight. Cally checked her phone, but she still hadn't replied.

She's a serving police officer. Maybe text messages from a not-even-girlfriend aren't her top priority right now. Or maybe she'll just call you at the end of her shift.

That made sense, especially if Ellen wanted time to decompress before dealing with company. An hour alone with a good book, or playing Tetris on your phone, could work wonders after a tough day. Another thing Iain had never understood. Early in their relationship, when she'd still had a job, he'd driven her to and from work. As always, he'd meant well, but eventually Cally had insisted on driving herself as he'd been incapable of giving her an hour's quiet.

Talking of which, she saw he'd texted her a couple of times, demanding to know when she was picking up her. again, Cally decided to ignore him for now.

The unwelcome prospect of a day alone with her thoughts

stretched ahead. *Give us a call after if you like*, Griff had said; even his flirting would be a pleasant distraction right now.

The living room felt uncomfortably close; Cally opened the patio doors and wandered over to the bench and sun umbrella in back garden to phone Griff. The phone rang for a while without going to voicemail; she was about to hang up when a thick, slurred voice said: "Hello?"

"Griff?"

"Who's this?"

"It's me. Cally."

"All right, *cariad*. How you doing?"

"I'm okay, what about you? You sound terrible."

"I'm all right. Too many late nights, that's all. Rat-arsed in Aber, then burning the midnight oil with this little lot." Griff coughed. "Christ. Probably caught some sort of lurgy off one of the lads. Long as it's not Covid I'll be all right."

"You sure you're okay? You got any testing kits in the house? Need anything bringing over?"

"Yes, yes and no. Other than yourself in a nurse's outfit, obviously."

"In your dreams, Parry."

"Oh, it is. Regularly."

"And I definitely don't need to know about *that*. So, what do you know?"

"Not a great deal. My undying love for you, obviously. So, you had a listen yet?"

"Up to the one after he got back from Warden Fell."

"That's as far as I've got. Interesting, isn't it? The background noise on that last one?"

"What *is* it? How did it get there?"

"Buggered if I know. Don't recognise the language, but then I'm not exactly a cunning linguist. Although–"

"For the sake of your genitals, Griff, do *not* finish that sentence."

"Sorry. You'll need someone who knows their languages to

have a listen. Expect one of the eggheads at Aber Uni could tell you something."

"Thanks, Griff. Seriously, you need me to pick anything up in Bala for you? Soup? Cough medicine?"

"You're a treasure, *cariad*, but I've plenty of cans of Heinz here. Anything else, I'll let you know – if that's okay?"

"Sure. But I'm not wearing the nurse's outfit."

"Spoilsport."

"Any idea how it got on the tape?"

"You've got me there too, I'm afraid." A pause. "You heard what he said? About recording a ghost?"

"I don't believe in ghosts, Griff."

"Doesn't mean they're not there. What was it you used to say? Great thing about facts is that they're true whether you like it or not."

Cally knew Griff was vaguely religious, though not in a fire-and-brimstone way. Her New Atheist phase was thankfully far behind her, so she no longer went around telling anyone with any spiritual belief they were stupid or insane, something she cringed to remember now.

"Anyway, I'm not done yet. I'll figure something out." Griff broke into a brief coughing fit, followed by some gruesome hacking sounds. "Uck. Sorry about that."

"Just take care of yourself, okay?"

"As you wish, *cariad*."

"I never should have shown you *The Princess Bride*."

"Least it wasn't *Krull*."

"I like *Krull*," said Cally, miffed.

"I know. You'd think they'd have treatment for that by now."

"Seriously, Griff. Take care, okay?"

"All right." A hint of mischief crept into his voice. "Gonna punish me if I don't?"

"Yes. I'll make you watch *Hawk the Slayer* again."

"That kind of suffering I can do without. All right, *cariad*, I'm off for a lie-down. If I'm up to it later I'll get back to this little lot. Hopefully get the rest of the diary stuff sorted today."

"Okay, just don't kill yourself on my account."

"Don't worry about me. To be honest, it's rather tickled *my* curiosity, too. Wouldn't mind getting to the bottom of it myself. All right, my love. Speak to you later."

All right, my love: trust Griff to get that one in at the end. Again Cally felt a pang of guilt over involving him, but told herself once more that he was an adult and responsible for himself. As usual, it didn't help.

Glancing at the phone, she noticed two things: it was now after six o'clock and the end of Ellen's shift, and she'd received a text message.

8pm ok? Want to have a bath and chill first. xx

Sure x, she texted back. That done, she went upstairs, showered, dressed and gathered her ingredients for the evening meal, then sat watching the clock till it was time to set off for Llanuwchllyn.

29.

Llyn Tegid runs north-east to south-west, with Bala at the north end. The village of Llanuwchllyn is in the hills above the south end; the name means 'the church above the lake.' It's nothing if not accurate: the church of St Deiniol dates back to 1291.

The village itself is among the most sparsely-populated in Wales, mostly consisting of small stone cottages, but Ellen lived in a block of low-rise flats along a side-street on the outskirts. Cally pulled up outside almost on the dot of eight o'clock; the door buzzed open before she'd even taken her finger off the bell-push.

The flat was single-bedroomed, with thin blue-grey carpet and magnolia-painted walls. "Here's the kitchen," Ellen said; Cally put the makings of the Bolognese on the counter. The small kitchen window looked out over the evening hills.

She held up two bottles: the unopened Tempranillo from last night, and one of Pepsi Max. "In case you wanted to lay off the sauce this evening."

"Sod that. It's been a day and a half, I can tell you."

There was a moment of awkward silence; they stood a couple of feet apart, neither certain what came next. *Fuck it*, thought Cally, and stepped forward to give Ellen a quick hug. Her hair was still damp from her bath, grapefruit-scented from whatever shampoo she'd used, a fresh, clean smell.

They ate, sipped red wine and snuggled on the couch to watch a cheesy horror film, wooden acting, over-the-top gore effects and all. For someone whose day job traded in life's uglier aspects, Ellen was surprisingly fond of watching people being eaten by zombies.

"I've always loved a good horror movie," she said. "Just not slashers or things like *Saw* or *Hostel*. That shit happens in real life." She nodded at the TV. "This doesn't."

Cally thought of Tony Mathias saying *I've actually captured a ghost on tape,* but said nothing, having no desire to kill the mood. Even so, Ellen seemed suddenly withdrawn and preoccupied. "You see a lot of stuff like that?" Cally asked. "Around here?"

"Not quite that bad. But you still see some shit. Not like Manchester, though."

"I bet." Cally could feel Ellen wanted to tell her something, so she kept quiet and waited.

"I saw some pretty horrible stuff on the job there," Ellen said. Suicides, overdoses – especially when you find them a week later – and then there's all the stupid fucking fights on a Saturday night in the city centre. People beating shit out of each other, glassing each other, and sometimes they can't even remember over what. I've been at a couple of murder scenes, but mostly it was just ordinary stuff like that. Worst part is, most of the time, we're too late. Just turn up afterwards to clear all the shit up. Makes you wish you had time travel so you could pop back and show up before it happened. Did I mention I love *Dr Who*?"

"Classic or new?"

"Oh, classic. Can't beat Tom Baker."

"Amen, sister."

Ellen laughed briefly, but it faded. Cally squeezed her hand; Ellen squeezed back. "You remember I said last night, you're not the only basket-case here?" She held up her free hand. "Had a full-scale nervous breakdown back in Manchester. Off work for six months. When I was ready to go back, they… politely encouraged… me to put in for a transfer somewhere quieter."

"For your own good? Or did they just not want to deal with it?"

"Bit of both, maybe. But it was probably the right choice, if I'm honest. The job's different out here. Sometimes you actually feel you're doing something useful. When you aren't trying stay awake, anyway."

Cally squeezed her hand again. "Thanks for telling me."

Ellen put her head on Cally's shoulder. "You showed me yours, thought I should show you mine."

Cally smiled. "I like the sound of that."

"Thought you would."

They'd shared a bed the night before, but they'd both been badly shaken and needing comfort. This time it was a simple matter of choice.

Ellen soon drifted off, but Cally didn't mind; she felt a peace and comfort she hadn't known in some time, although she had to bite back giggles when Ellen started snoring; she'd been quite indignant when Cally had mentioned it over dinner, insisting she did no such thing.

In sleep Ellen's face lost its hardness; she looked ridiculously young, bringing out every protective instinct Cally had. Ironic, given that in a crisis Ellen would almost certainly be the one to act.

She wasn't last night.

Even the strongest people had weak points. What mattered was that Ellen had been through the same mill as her; probably one reason Cally felt so at ease in her company. After Iain, it was a joy to spend time with someone who actually *got it*.

Cally lay back, more at ease that she remembered being in months, and shut her eyes.

30.

She wasn't sure if she'd slept or not, let alone how long for. If she'd dreamt she had no memory of it, but the near-panic she felt was unpleasantly familiar.

The room was pitch-black, and it hadn't been before. There'd been streetlights outside, shining hazily through the drawn curtains: that was gone now. The window was two or three paces from the bed; Cally could easily have crossed to it and pulled the curtains back, but there'd be nothing but a black, empty void.

Or maybe it's just a power-cut.

Cally's gaze shifted to the bedside lamp. An easy theory to test. But it hadn't been a power-cut last night, or the night before. And maybe the electrics at Dad's house were on the fritz, but at Ellen's flat too?

Might be a local issue.

The dark was very thick. Blacker than night. And it was moving.

She gasped; Ellen grunted and stirred, thankfully without waking. Cally sat up, pushing herself back against the headboard. Beneath the window, the blackness seemed somehow even thicker: something broad and flabby hunched there.

The Toad.

Cally looked up: something long and tapering hovered, undulating, in the darkness that swathed the ceiling.

The Eel.

When she looked towards the bedroom door, its pale

rectangle was hidden by something with a bottle-shaped body and long, slender neck, which as if to display itself to her, slowly spread its long, ragged wings.

The Cormorant.

Cally had once worked in a call centre beside an old wharf; cormorants had been a common sight there, cruising over the still waters before diving from view, resurfacing far away. They took off from the water, long wings stiffly extended and beating fast, skimming low across the surface before slowly gaining height. Once or twice she'd seen one on the bank, spreading its wings to dry them, and that had fascinated her most of all.

But this shape evoked only dread, and was no more a cormorant than the Eel was an eel or the Toad a toad. She was just giving the shapes the most familiar names she could. She attempted to tell herself there *were* no shapes at all, that once again her brain was seeking patterns in the patternless, but none of it convinced her, and the shapes seemed more substantial than before.

Cally forced herself to shut her eyes. Maybe if she did that, she'd only see darkness on opening them again. Or better still, the very ordinary outlines of Ellen Rooke's bedroom.

Or you might see something that's moved closer to you, and in far more detail. Right before it bites off your face.

She summoned all her rationality to dismiss that idea; that was a child's thinking, fear of the dark. She was a long way from childhood now.

But the dark makes children of us all.

When she finally managed to open her eyes, the shapes were no closer, but seemed no less real; if anything, they stood out more distinctly than ever from the surrounding darkness. And then Cormorant craned forward, its neck extending towards her.

Overhead, the Eel undulated frantically, as if battling a torrent, its head angling downwards – again, towards Cally. And when she finally dragged her gaze from the ceiling to the window, the Toad seemed lower and flatter, as though compressed. Gathering itself to spring.

Last night, on the stairs, the Eel had proven as insubstantial as smoke, but all three figures appeared very solid now. By the same token, all three seemed to be struggling to reach Cally, as though, in achieving a more substantial presence in the world, they'd sacrificed some freedom of movement.

The first night they were just shadows; the second, they were thicker ones. Tonight, they're almost real. What happens tomorrow?

Cally fumbled for the bedside lamp. The Cormorant's head, now inches from her outstretched legs, split open, yawning wide. There was no sound, but Cally imagined a goose-like hiss of rage.

But impotent rage; the Cormorant didn't want her to touch the lamp, but couldn't stop her. The light might banish the spectres; it had to be worth a try.

And if it doesn't come on? Or it does, and they're still here?

Cally shut her eyes and, had Millicent's attempts at religious indoctrination been more successful, might even have been desperate enough to pray. Then she found the lamp's switch, and pushed it.

The inside of her eyelids glowed orange. Beside her, Ellen mumbled. Cally didn't want to look, but if she didn't, Ellen might open her eyes first. What would happen then, if the Cormorant, Eel or Toad were still there? If Ellen cried out first, would they attack her instead?

Keep your eyes shut, then, a part of Cally urged: *do it to her, not me.* But she was immediately disgusted with herself. If these things were anybody's problem, they were hers.

She opened her eyes, and the room was empty. Drawn curtains, a wardrobe. A desk, chair, laptop. Their discarded, jumbled clothes. No Eel, no Toad, no Cormorant. They'd only been shadows, and the light had driven them away.

Only shadows? You weren't so sure a few seconds ago. What a difference an energy-saving bulb makes.

"Whassup? Cally? Whass going on?" Ellen stared blearily at her, face puffy, with half-open eyes.

"Bad dream, that's all." Cally hesitated. "Okay if I leave the light on? I'm just a bit…"

"No problem." Ellen patted her arm. "Been there, done that. Now go back to sleep."

Cally tried, but the morning light was filtering through the curtains before she did.

31.

Once again, Cally woke to an empty bed after a few hours' sleep. The shower hissed in the bathroom next door. Another early shift for Ellen; Cally had better be up and about too.

She ached all over, and her eyes felt full of salt. There were painkillers and antihistamines in her shoulder-bag – taking them was becoming a regular morning routine – but her throat was sore and dry. First order of business, then, was finding water.

The bedside light had been switched off; remembering her earlier panic was embarrassing, despite knowing Ellen suffered from night terrors too, which was still the likeliest explanation for last night's episode – far more likely, after all, than the Cormorant, Toad and Eel being actual creatures trying to get at her.

Cally chuckled to herself, though it sounded more forced than she'd have liked. The realer such an experience seemed, the greater the need to disbelieve in it afterwards. Depressive episodes and anxiety attacks were unpleasant, but at least you knew what you saw and heard were real; the problem was how you reacted.

Seeing and hearing things that *didn't* exist – that *couldn't*, without rearranging your very conception of reality – didn't allow that luxury. If you couldn't trust your own five senses, you could think you were having a perfectly normal conversation in a flat in Llanuwchllyn, while you were actually sitting on the bus to Wrexham covered in your own excrement.

Cally shuddered and rubbed her arms. More than anything

now she wanted a shower, but that would wait till she got home.

Having packed a change of clothes, she wriggled gratefully into clean underwear, t-shirt and gold harem pants, stuffing last night's outfit into her shoulder-bag, then slipped her flats on and went into the kitchen. She made toast and coffee for herself and a camomile tea for Ellen, then rooted in her shoulder-bag again for her various pills, swallowing them with tap water as the shower stopped.

Cally put two more slices of bread in the toaster. They popped up as Ellen came in, buttoning her uniform shirt; Cally offered them to her on a sideplate. "Here you go, milady."

"Ta."

"Did I mention?" said Cally. "I've got a terrible thing for women in uniform."

"Ha ha. You okay?"

"Yeah. Sorry about last night."

"Say what?"

"I woke you up."

"Oh, yeah. The bedside lamp?"

"Yeah." Cally reached for the camomile tea. "Here. Made you a brew."

"You little star," said Ellen, which was funny coming from a woman a good head shorter; she took a sip and smiled. "Brill. Just cool enough to actually drink before I go. What was it, a nightmare?"

"More of a night terror, like you had. Felt bloody real, anyway."

Ellen gave her a hug, and Cally squeezed her back, although the uniform and utility belt got in the way. She wasn't sure how long it lasted before Ellen whispered. "Sorry. Gotta go now."

"Walk you out?"

"That was the general idea."

In the car park, Ellen took Cally's hand. "Thanks for last

night," she almost whispered, as if afraid of being overheard. "Had a lovely time."

"You and me both."

"Want to… do this again? Tonight, maybe?" Ellen didn't meet Cally's eyes; her face turned pink. "Or, you know, some other time. Doesn't have to be–"

"Hey." Cally's eyes were stinging, but that was just her hay fever. "Love to. Tonight would be great." The house felt far too big and empty for her alone just now.

Ellen grinned. "Brilliant. Give you a shout later, yeah?"

"You bet."

Ellen pecked her on the lips and ran to the Juke. Cally walked to the Punto; they waved to one another as the Ellen drove away.

Back home, Cally soaked in a hot bath; by the time she got out, her hives had faded and her eyes had stopped streaming, though despite the antihistamines, her throat was still sore and her nose blocked.

She lay on her bed, browsing on her phone as the morning passed. She decided a day off was in order: she'd try to simply read, and watch TV. Take it easy. It would do her good.

Griff texted her just before midday – *You have mail!* – but she ignored it; anything Griff-related made her feel even guiltier than usual right now. Cally paced around the house; she opened and discarded several books and channel-hopped without finding anything to hold her interest, tossing the TV remote away in disgust. She considered a walk, but the pollen count must be through the ceiling today: her nose and throat were *still* blocked and sore, and she'd no desire to make them worse.

She might be coming down with a summer cold, which seemed ever more likely over the next couple of hours, as muscle pain, chills and headaches set in. Cally retreated to her bedroom with bottled water, hot tea, paracetamol and her laptop. She napped for an hour and woke feeling mildly better. By then it was four o'clock, and boredom was her main problem again.

And so she accessed her emails, to find another WeTransfer link from Griff. Two more files: TONY MATHIAS DIARY 2ND JUNE, and TONY MATHIAS DIARY 8TH JUNE. The day before the killings. *That's everything from that tape,* said the accompanying message. No jokes or flirting: Griff must be feeling rough. She'd have to call him. Later.

She downloaded the files, with much the same self-disgust as when she ordered takeout despite her bank balance and waistline. She reminded herself she could still shut the computer off and leave the files unopened.

And do what instead?

"Bollocks," she muttered, with considerable feeling. "Okay. Fine."

Cally sighed and put on her headphones and rested the cursor on the file for the 8th June, then moved it away. She wasn't sure she wanted to hear it yet. And it might only make sense in the context of what came before. She clicked on TONY MATHIAS DIARY 2ND JUNE, and waited for the dead to speak again.

32.

The tape hissed and crackled; a faint noise sounded in the background, continuous and repetitive, which Cally soon identified as the chant.

Angana sor varalakh kai torja, angana sor varalakh cha voran.

Other than that, silence. When Tony Mathias finally spoke, she almost cried out.

"All right." His voice was so hoarse and gravelly it was barely recognisable. "This is my journal entry for... er... Thursday, second of June. Sorry. I've lost track a little. Normally I record every night. But the last few days, I've been really fucking rough. Pardon my French. I don't know what's wrong. When Stella called yesterday, I realised how out of it I've been. Thought I should try and keep a record. But... oh, bloody hell."

Cally realised he was close to tears.

"First, one small detail. *The Ghosts of Warden Fell* isn't happening. This isn't about art. It's much more fucking important." No *Pardon my French* this time, and the Lancashire accent came through in almost every syllable.

"I played a couple of the tapes in the caravan. God, I wish I hadn't." A match scraped, followed by an outburst of coughing. "Shouldn't be smoking, but fuck it. I'd more or less quit – can't do that around the kids – but good luck staying on the wagon right now. Where was I? Oh, yes. I played one of the tapes to Lindsay and the kids. Just wanted to be sure I wasn't hearing things. Going doolally. Wish I had been."

More coughing. "They all heard it, anyway. We listened a few times. Something about that chant – even Alison thought she'd heard it somewhere. Oh God, Alison. She's been in fits ever since. Lindsay's furious, and I don't blame her."

More coughing. "Sod this. All right, put the fag out, Tony. Stick to tea. Better for you. Still got this bloody cold, and now Lindsay and the kids have it too. Another reason she's pissed off with me."

He slurped his tea. "I'll detail this as best as I can. Facts and figures. Need plenty of those, because it's going to sound insane. Now: I'd considered playing the tapes to Lindsay before. Get a second opinion – hopefully she'd tell me I was imagining it all. I was still in two minds about scrapping the project because of the amount of grief that'd cause, and still drawing a blank about what to do instead."

A sigh. "What forced my hand was the power cut. The power in the studio's died on me a few times since I got back from Warden Fell. No idea why. I'm no electrician, but everything in the studio's in perfect working order, far as I can tell, except when it decides not to be."

Tony cleared his throat. His voice became brusque and clipped, the Lancashire accent disappearing. "Whole thing was becoming very irritating, so I decided to work on it in the caravan instead."

Cally had to wonder if that had been the only reason, or if the darkness in the studio had seemed unusually oppressive, or less empty than it should.

That's your problem, not his.

"That bloody chant," he said. "Ear worm, the Germans call it. Gets stuck in your head. That's why I played it. Hoped Lindsay might recognise it and maybe I'd stop thinking about it. It half-worked; they all thought they knew it, even the kids. Just couldn't put a name to it. And then–"

Hoarse breathing; the tape's crackle, and the chant. *Angana sor varalakh–*

"I've not been sleeping well. Haven't, really, since I went there. This cold or whatever it is. Thought I was getting feverish; I kept waking at odd hours, thinking someone was in the bedroom with us. Hallucination. Only now it's not just me. And–"

Another slurp of tea. "Power in the caravan's been on the blink for the past night or so as well. Never any problem with it before. Hadn't been in the studio, either, till just lately. No one else at Eagle Mount's having any problems I know of. Just us. For now, anyway. It's been spreading, after all. The studio, then the caravan. And not just the lights." Tony Mathias' voice cracked briefly. "My children wake up screaming. My little girl. My little boy. I've no idea what I've done or how this is happening. But Alison was in absolute hysterics earlier. Screaming about a huge bird standing over her bed.

"That's bad enough, but it's not the worst. I think I've seen it, too, sometimes. When I've woken up at night. Lindsay won't talk about it, but I think she has as well. I've seen other things too. Last night I thought I heard something slithering round the caravan. Like a big snake."

Or an Eel? Cally's hand went to her mouth.

"So I'm scrapping the project. To hell with the consequences. I'll call the Whitworth tomorrow. If they blacklist me or Bernard drops me, we'll cope, we always have. Maybe I should burn the tapes, but – I've no idea what I'm dealing with. For all I know, that'll make it worse–"

He broke off. Ragged breathing, the crackling tape; that low, familiar chant.

Cally checked the timeline she'd established from her interviews with Gowland, Stella and Edna Woodwiss. The following day had been Friday third of June; Tony had called the Whitworth, who'd rung Bernard Gowland in a panic. That was when Gowland had called Eagle Mount, and spoken to Tony for the last time.

"There were years when Warden Fell operated with no problems," Tony said. "The end of the war, through to the sixties. So whatever it is must come and go. Wax and wane, like the moon. Some sort of cycle–"He broke off again. "God, listen to me. I'm not playing the tapes again. I'm boxing up all the Warden Fell stuff, and maybe it'll pass. Fade. We can go about our lives. Please God. But I can't burn them yet. If this doesn't stop on its own, I'll have to find help. A priest, maybe? Not that I'm any kind of believer. An occultist? Aren't there scientists who study stuff like this? Parapsychologists? Like that film last year? *Ghostbusters*. The kids enjoyed that one. Silly, but fun. Maybe not so silly now. God knows where one finds such people. If it comes to that, then the more I can show them, the better the chances they can help us. I *cannot* believe I'm seriously talking like this. But, for now, I'm going to try to forget about Warden Fell and concentrate on a new project. And hopefully that'll be enough. If not – well. We'll see."

The tape ran on in silence, except for the chant. Cally switched it off. Her hands shook, and when she shut the laptop and tried to stand, her legs buckled. She sat back down on the bed. "Oh Jesus. Oh Jesus." Her voice had the same rough, gravelly quality as Tony Mathias'.

Tony Mathias killed his family because something went wrong with him. Nothing to do with ghosts or curses.

But he'd seen the Cormorant, and heard what might have been the Eel. Maybe he'd seen the Toad too.

You haven't seen anything. Just bad dreams.

Bad dreams, yes: ever since playing the tapes. And power cuts. Dreams Ellen had experienced too.

Cally went out into the garden. Hay fever or no, she wanted natural light and fresh air. She stretched out on the bench, sun on her face, drifting.

Her phone rang. Griff? Ellen? Cally grabbed it and swiped the *Accept* option, but could already see the number wasn't either of theirs. Not Dad's or Lucy's either. A landline number, with a Peterborough area code.

"Hello?" she said. Probably a marketing call. She'd cut them off as soon as the sales pitch started.

"Hello?" A lilting, sing-song accent; South Asian, she guessed. "Is this Miss Darker?"

"Yes." Her thumb inched towards the *End Call* button.

"Of the podcast called *You Want It Darker*?"

Her thumb stopped. "That's right," she said at last.

"This is Dr Anand Sabharwal. You emailed me about the Tony Mathias case. Is this a good time?"

33.

Fifteen minutes later Cally was at the kitchen table, a large coffee at hand, connecting her laptop's webcam and mic. She'd hurriedly herself presentable; tying her hair back, dabbing on some light make-up and, as she had no clean t-shirt, borrowing a short-sleeved check shirt from Lucy's wardrobe. She thought it rather suited her.

As she uncapped her biro, the Skype tone sounded. She checked the picture and sound quality, gave her hair a final primp, then answered the call. "Hello–"

"Good aftern–" The voice from the phone overlapped with hers, then broke off. A second's awkward silence, then her caller gave her a small, tight smile. "Good afternoon, Miss Darker."

Anand Sabharwal was thin and white-haired, with light brown skin drawn tightly over a fine-boned face, and sat in a high-backed chair in front of a patio window, polishing a pair of half-moon reading glasses that hung around his neck on a cord. "You wish to discuss the Tony Mathias case. Are you recording this call?"

"If that's okay."

"I've no objection." He donned the glasses; the lenses glinted with reflected screen-light.

Cally clicked RECORD CALL. "First of all, thanks for getting in touch with me."

"Being useful is a habit I've found rather hard to get rid of." He smiled again; there was something strained about it. "What do you wish to know?"

"Anything you can tell me would be useful," she said. "There's hardly anything in the public domain, but I've spoken to Edna Woodwiss–"

"Good grief. Is she still alive?"

"She is, yes."

"Goodness. And the police?"

"They just said, straight off, that they couldn't help."

Sabharwal nodded. "I'm not entirely surprised. It wasn't something anybody wished to dwell on."

"Including you?"

His gaze shifted; he wouldn't meet her eyes. "I've always found it a hard case *not* to think about. On one level, it's the kind of mystery that's both profound and horribly banal. Outwardly sane people commit such acts far more often than we like to admit. And more often than not, there is no explanation. All you can do is tend to the survivors. But there were none, in this instance. But the reason my police colleagues don't want to discuss the case – why even I hesitated to contact you – is that there *are* explanations, of sorts. The trouble is, they raise more questions than they answer. What do you know so far?"

"Tony Mathias had been working on an art installation, based on an old airbase in Lancashire called Warden Fell. A few days after he broke in there, he and his family more or less confined themselves to their caravan. The few times he went outside, he was muffled up in heavy clothes, in the middle of summer. And then he bought a rifle and–"

"Shotgun," said Sabharwal. "Bolt-action, which is more commonly seen on rifles. Hence Mr Bainbridge misidentified it as such. And then Mr Mathias shot his wife in the head, then followed his children outside and shot them both down in front of Mr Bainbridge before going back inside the caravan. Then came back outside and shot his son again. Repeatedly. Now, why do you suppose he did that?"

He's asking you? This is going to be helpful.

Cally shrugged. "My best guess was that he'd become contaminated in some way."

"Contaminated?"

"Something that made him and his family ill, possibly caused a psychotic break."

"An interesting theory," said Sabharwal. "But I found no evidence of any infection or toxic substance – with one exception. Both children had been given barbiturates – partially metabolised, but more than double the lethal dose for an adult male."

"What? Sorry, I'm not sure I…"

Dr Sabharwal sighed. "Like so much else about this case, it's both simple and impossible. Alison and Neal Mathias had both been given massive overdoses of barbiturates about forty-eight hours earlier. They should already have been dead, Miss Darker, yet the drugs, seemingly, had no effect upon them whatsoever."

Dr Sabharwal patiently awaited her response. "How?" Cally said at last.

"You see what I mean about the answers only raising further questions, Miss Darker? As I've said, there was no indication of any bacteriological, viral, toxicological or radiological contamination in the children's remains. Other than the overdose presumably administered by Mr Mathias."

Goodbye to the idea of Warden Fell as a dumping ground for bioweapons or poison gas, then – but what did that put in its place? Sabharwal went on: "I suspect he administered similar overdoses to his wife, to as little effect, but as their remains were almost completely carbonised, it was impossible to be sure. No doubt, he intended to set a fire when the others were dead"

"You mean, he originally wanted it look like an accident?"

"I don't believe he cared about that by the end. Let's return to my earlier question. He shot his daughter once, directly in the head, but shot the boy a total of three times. Why do you suppose he did that?"

"Make sure he was dead?"

"The boy survived the first gunshot wound, although it shattered his spine, but the second discharge, which penetrated his heart, killed him instantly. Nonetheless, a third shot was fired, into the head."

"Again, couldn't he have just been making sure?"

"So I initially thought," said Sabharwal. "Tony Mathias also killed his wife with a shotgun blast to the head, probably at point-blank range, so that her corpse was virtually headless, and at the end he did the same to himself. Yes, it ensured instant death, but his real motive was concealment."

"Concealment?" Cally visualised Lindsay Mathias' face, with its bright no-nonsense smile, disintegrating as the blast struck it; the blonde hair vanishing in smoke and blood. *He was a very good shot*, Stella Di Mauro had said, *if he was aiming at a paper target. But he could never have harmed a living thing. Let alone a person, let alone–*

Except he had. He'd shot his son in the back and his daughter in the face, obliterating her head in a single instant. Then Neal again. One in the torso, finishing him off, then again in the head, decapitating him like his sister and his mother.

Except he hadn't. Cally remembered the crime scene pictures. The top of Neal Mathias' head had been sheared away, but the rest had survived. Perhaps his aim had been slightly off.

"Concealment," Sabharwal repeated. "Better to be thought a madman than a monster. He was trying to hide what his family had become."

34.

"As I said," Sabharwal went on, "I found no evidence of contamination in the conventional sense. But some form of contamination certainly took place, Miss Darker. I just have no idea what kind. Physiological changes had taken place in both children. *Extreme* physiological changes. In normal circumstances I would have assumed them to be severe birth defects, but school photographs showed two quite ordinary, even beautiful children."

He licked his lips, clasping his hands before him. "Neal Mathias' leg was deformed," he said at last. "It was covered in coarse grey fur, completely unlike the boy's normal hair in either colour or texture, and it bent backwards at the knee. A split had formed in the soft tissue between the second and third toes of his foot, extending all the way back to the ankle joint."

"You mean they'd been mutilated somehow?"

Sabharwal shook his head. "I hesitate to use the term 'naturally', but the division had occurred without any form of surgery. The foot had divided into two sections. On one, the big and second toe had begun to fuse together; on the second, the three small toes had done the same. And the skin around them was hardening. Some form of keratinous material had accumulated in it."

"Like a hoof?" Cally expected Sabharwal to shake his head again, but he nodded.

"Exactly. His entire leg was coming to resemble the hind leg of an ungulate mammal. Specifically, I think, that of a goat."

"A goat's leg," Cally repeated.

"I'm more than aware how absurd it sounds. But I assure you it's true, although good luck finding a copy of my report or the post-mortem photographs. The visible defects on the daughter, Alison, were more minor – at first glance."

"Meaning?"

"At first I thought she'd developed body hair, unusual in a child so young but far from impossible. However, under closer examination the 'hairs' proved to be the tips of feathers. They had formed under the skin, and were in the process of being extruded."

"She was growing feathers," Cally repeated, as flatly as she could. Sabharwal nodded placidly. "Jesus, did she have a beak as well?"

A wintry smile. "Impossible to say, though no less unbelievable than what we *did* find. Her skull was totally destroyed, as I said, and we couldn't reconstruct it. There were far fewer bone fragments than there should have been, but we found a great deal of cartilaginous tissue. And another substance – semi-solid to begin with, but it broke down very quickly. We never identified it. As it was scattered around Alison Mathias' body along with the bone and cartilage, it was presumably part of her cranial structure, but as it liquefied so rapidly, we couldn't work out how. Or what the poor child might have looked like immediately before her death. There wasn't enough solid material left to piece together."

Cally looked at her notepad, realising she hadn't written anything, then at the laptop screen to confirm it was still recording.

"I suspect Mr Bainbridge was fortunate the setting sun was behind the children as they ran towards him: it meant he never saw their faces. God knows the poor man was traumatised enough by what he *did* see."

Sabharwal picked up a glass of water and sipped it. His hand trembled slightly. He set the glass down and took a deep breath.

"Tony Mathias had loaded the shotgun with rifled slugs – a single, solid projectile in each cartridge, instead of clusters of pellets. Such rounds have a devastating effect on the human body. Not, however, to the degree I observed. Alison Mathias' skull wasn't just shattered, it was... *obliterated*, because almost none of the bone structure was still, in fact, bone, just cartilage and... jelly. The rifled slug quite simply blew her head apart."

Cally tried and failed to formulate a response several times.

Sabharwal gave another wintry smile. "You see why the report wasn't published. The one thing we never want to say, in my profession, is that we have no answers. And as well as being most insistent we didn't release the post-mortem results or discuss the case with anyone, the Ministry of Defence was also very unforthcoming about the purpose Warden Fell was being put to."

"So there *was* a connection?"

"As I said, there's no direct physical evidence of a link. But something triggered those changes, and the only unusual event in any of their lives, immediately prior to the murders, is the airbase. Of course, there's another possibility, even more frightening."

"There is?"

"That the reason for it was the same reason that some children develop incurable cancers, or, indeed, that loving parents get up one day and slaughter their families." His smile this time was full of some unrevealed pain of his own. "Sometimes – as the Americans say – shit happens."

The sudden use of profanity made Cally blink. Sabharwal polished his spectacle lenses again. "I'm fairly certain similar physical changes were taking place in Tony and Lindsay Mathias. And while I can't say for certain, I believe profound psychological changes occurred too. And that those, most of all, led Tony Mathias to do what he did."

"Why do you think that, Dr Sabharwal?" Cally managed at last. Her throat was very dry. The coffee was lukewarm now; she gulped down half of it in one go.

"First, circumstantial evidence. He confined his family to the caravan, hardly went out at all. I think he and Lindsay grew afraid of what they might do – the children especially. Being young and immature, I suspect they were particularly susceptible. Of course, that evidence is open to interpretation: they may simply have acted out of shame, or a fear their condition might be infectious."

Cally realised she'd begun doodling in the notepad. A spiral, turning and turning. "But there was something else?"

"Very much so. When Tony Mathias shot the boy in the head, he didn't cause the same degree of catastrophic damage as to himself, Lindsay or Alison. The top of the cranium was blown away, but the rest of the skull remained intact."

Dr Sabharwal sipped his water.

"To identify Neal Mathias, we had to find items he'd handled at school and match fingerprints from them to the corpse's, because his face, what remained of it, no longer bore any resemblance to the child in his school photographs. The ears were pointed. Scales had begun developed on the skin. The right pupil was a vertical slit, like a snake's. And the brain…"

"What about it?" Cally realised she wasn't doodling spirals anymore: dominating the page, ragged wings outspread, was a sketch of a cormorant. She dropped the pen, and wiped her fingers on her jeans.

Dr Sabharwal sucked his teeth. "What remained of it no longer bore any structural resemblance to a human brain at all. Which might explain the changes to the skull. The process wasn't as advanced as in Alison's case, but the bones had grown thinner, parts of it had been replaced with cartilage and in other places there were holes, and quantities of the same rapidly-liquefying gelatine. I think at a later stage, it might have re-ossified. The skull was changing shape to accommodate the metamorphosis the brain was undergoing. If you imagine a normal human brain as roughly football-shaped, this was more like a rugby ball. Neal Mathias' brain wasn't that of a human anymore, or any animal species I know."

"What, then?"

"I don't know. Perhaps we're into the realm of flying saucers and little green men, or witches and devils. Unfortunately, I don't believe in either. As I said, every answer only deepens the mystery." He spread his hands. "And that, I'm afraid, is all I can tell you. Not much help, is it?"

Cally made a non-committal sound, thinking of her interview with Edna Woodwiss. "Thanks for your time, doctor," she said at last. "I really appreciate it. I hope you're not going to get into any trouble."

Sabharwal shrugged. "I strongly doubt anyone would care anymore. Warden Fell's secrets, whatever they were, are yesterday's news."

"Thanks all the same."

Sabharwal hesitated and looked away. "I assure you my motives were entirely selfish."

"Oh?" said Cally.

"The whole business has never left me, Ms Darker. I dream about them, you see. Every single night."

"*Every* night? For forty years?"

Sabharwal shrugged. "Often, they aren't too bad. I'm just clearing up, doing the autopsies, seeing the wounds and deformities all over again. But sometimes I'm there: as Leonard Bainbridge, or one of the children, or as Tony Mathias himself. It destroyed my marriage. Since I received your email, I've had some of the worst I've ever experienced."

"I'm sorry." What else could she say?

"My initial reaction was to ignore your message, but two nights ago it occurred to me that if disregarding you made things worse, aiding you might have the opposite effect. I thought quite seriously about calling you then. That night, my dreams were very mild. Yesterday, I decided to contact you. And for the first time in years, I didn't dream at all. So you see, entirely selfish. Now, if you've no further questions–"

"No," said Cally. "Nothing right now."

"Feel free to contact me should you think of any. And if you *do* happen to uncover any answers, I'd love to know them."

"I'll be in touch if I do." Perhaps they'd buy him a few more quiet nights.

Sabharwal smiled. "Then good day, Miss Darker."

The screen went blank.

35.

Cally was still trying to digest it all when Ellen rang; she was shocked to see it was half-past six already.

Time flies when you're having fun.

"Hi, lovely," she said.

"Yo. Fancy eating out tonight?"

"Well," said Cally. "I've had worse chat-up lines."

"God, you've a mind like a sewer. I meant dinner! I thought Bala Spice, maybe?"

"Ah." Cally hesitated. "Think I'm coming down with something. Might be flu."

"Oh, poppet. Okay – I'll bring a takeout. Can't beat a curry when you've got the plague."

Cally winced at that phrase. "I don't want to give this to you."

"Think that ship's sailed, after last night."

Fair point. Besides, seeing ghosts was one thing; letting them rule your life was quite another. "Okay."

Cally took paracetamol and researched Dr Sabharwal; everything indicated he was well-respected, with no time for fringe science or conspiracy theories. Which only made what he'd told her more worrying.

Don't give way to your anxieties. Consider the facts rationally.

Whatever had infected Tony Mathias couldn't spread to her. Edna Woodwiss had handled the tapes, and was unaffected forty years on. The dreams or hallucinations she'd had were only that; anything similar the Mathiases had experienced was a coincidence.

That was logic. That was reason. She almost believed it by the time Ellen arrived.

"Who else is coming?" said Cally, watching Ellen open cartons of chicken korma, lamb madras, pilau rice, and multiple side dishes on the kitchen table.

Ellen produced two huge garlic naan breads and shrugged. "Feed a cold, starve a fever."

Cally fetched plates and cutlery, shaking her head. So much for eating healthily; still, there'd be plenty left over for tomorrow, with any luck.

In the event, they ate quite sparingly, but the heat and spice unblocked Cally's sinuses. "I almost feel normal again," she admitted. Even her voice sounded less rough.

Ellen grinned. "Garlic's nature's antibiotic. Least, that's what Rav always says."

"Who?"

"Ravi Parekh. My old sergeant. Which reminds me."

"What?"

Ellen waved a fork over the table. "You done?"

"Think so."

Ellen began putting the lids back onto the foil cartons. "Remember me telling you Rav transferred to Lancashire Constabulary?"

"Vaguely."

"I gave him a bell. Just a friendly call. But the Eagle Mount Murders happened to come up in conversation."

"Oh, did they?"

"It was all very natural."

"Uh-huh."

"*Anyway*, I segued smoothly into how you did a pretty good podcast–"

"Only pretty good?"

Ellen blew a raspberry "– You were covering the case, and

had he any idea why they'd want to avoid discussing it?"

"Oh, *very* smooth."

"Don't knock it. It worked."

"Seriously?"

"Rav not only looked into it, he came back quicker than I thought. Apparently the case files were all lost. House-fire, or something."

"Oh." Something about that sounded familiar, but Cally couldn't remember from where.

"That'll be why they said they couldn't help you. Unless, of course–" Ellen raised her hands dramatically – "the powers that be are covering it up."

"Really?"

"Don't be daft. Let's just say it's a good job Joe Public don't realise how often documents go AWOL."

"I feel *so* much safer now. Is that the big news?"

"Wind your neck in, grumpy-knickers. The big news is Rav tracked down one of the original investigating officers, and he said he'd talk to you." When Cally failed to answer, Ellen added: "I think the words you're looking for are *thank* and *you*, followed by *truly, Mistress Rooke, thou art amazeballs*."

Cally laughed. "Seriously, Ellen, thank you. That's amazing."

Ellen pretended to examine her fingernails. "All in a day's work."

"How did he manage that so fast?"

"Just called a friend in Records. Case files might have gone up in smoke, but there was of the investigating officers, and one of them's still knocking around." Ellen held out a written note. "DCI Graham Harrower, retired. Seventy-odd, but far as I know he's still got most of his marbles."

"Most?"

Ellen pulled a face. "Only snag is he won't talk on the phone."

"You've literally just given me his number."

"That's to arrange time and place," Ellen said. "He won't

discuss Eagle Mount over phone, Skype, email, anything that could be monitored. It's face to face or nothing."

"Paranoid, much?" said Cally. Then again, both Edna and Sabharwal had hinted at some form of cover-up. Sabharwal had thought Warden Fell would be old news by now; by the sound of it, Harrower disagreed. "Where's he live, anyway?"

"You'll love this – Manchester. Anyway, never mind him." Ellen pinned the note to the fridge with a magnet. "How about a movie?"

"If you can manage not to fart the Hallelujah Chorus throughout, okay."

"I'll do my best."

They watched two films back to back, till neither could keep their eyes open, then went upstairs, turning out the lights as they went. Darkness flooded into the house behind them.

36.

Cally fell, but slowly; the darkness was absolute, but she could see.

It was a pit of some sort, between fifty and a hundred feet across; with uneven, jagged, blackish-grey rock walls glistening with moss and slime, scored with ledges, pitted with caves.

A few creatures huddled on ledges, too hunched to be clearly seen, but fighting to maintain their grip: everything here was constantly battling the relentless force trying to drag them deeper into the Pit. Other shapes screamed above and below her; a couple tumbled past, but too quickly for Cally to make them out.

The sound of the Pit was deafening: a constant, echoing din that didn't end. Like waves on a sea, different sounds rose and became clear, then subsided into the general clamour. It drove painfully into her ears, shook her till she felt physically sick.

And through it all, she fell.

Cally twisted her body as she plummeted, straining towards the walls of the shaft in search of a handhold. She couldn't see the entrance to the Pit, or a bottom to the shaft: no beginning and no end. Maybe if she couldn't arrest her descent she'd fall forever. Would that be worse than something lying in wait for her below/ Both seemed equally plausible, and equally appalling.

She veered towards the rock-face, but horribly slowly. Maybe she'd never reach it and she'd fall forever, tormented throughout by false hope.

Cally lunged, and caught hold of a ledge; she was relieved,

till she saw her arm seemed impossibly long, and far thinner than a human arm should be. the colour was wrong; too: a livid purple. And it had no hand.

Another arm shot out and secured a grip: she saw the rows of suckers on its pallid underside and tried to scream, but no sound emerged as she was pulled slowly in towards the wall.

None she could hear, anyway; the din around her could have drowned it out. Most of the sounds were screams of agony, terror, or revulsion. But as a third octopus-like tentacle uncoiled from her to fasten on the Pit's wall, Cally realised others were fragments of speech, often a single phrase, repeating over and over again:

In nominee patri, et filii, et Spiritu Sancti.

Red Three to Tower. Red Three to Tower.

'Sblood, man, make an end of this!

She thought she heard what sounded like French, another language that sounded vaguely Germanic, even a snatch of the Latin drummed into her at school. And there were other voices still, that spoke no language she recognised at all, that might have been the grunting and howling of beasts.

Most of the sounds faded in and out, but one remained constant, providing an underlying rhythm to it all and growing clearer and clearer as she listened. Another language Cally didn't know, but familiar nonetheless: *Angana sor varalakh kai torja, angana sor varalakh cha voran.*

Cally's tentacles pulled tight; their grip held, and she was drawn up against the Pit's wall. She clutched for handholds with what she saw with relief were her own, still-human arms, even as more tentacles unfurled from her body and splayed out across the rock, anchoring her with their suckers.

Her arms had altered too, though; thin wiry black fur bristled along them from her wrists to her shoulders. She found footholds, but didn't look down; fearing both the drop below, and seeing what her legs might have become. She didn't dare look closely at her hands.

This was a dream. She tried to tell herself that, over and over again. A dream. It had to be a dream.

"No."

Griff clung naked to the rock beside her. His arms and legs had become long, jointed chitinous limbs ending in scissor-like pincers. A smaller pair of segmented legs had forced themselves out of his ribcage; between them and his hipbones the skin bulged outwards, stretched tight. The skin was bleeding where serrated pincer-tips had broken through from within.

Griff's claws were wedged into cracks in the rock but even so, his wasted body was being dragged downwards, and the limbs pulled taut. The Pit tried to pull Cally down too but for now, at least, her tentacles held her fast.

Her tentacles. The idea made her dizzy and sick, but she'd no time to contemplate that; Griff was talking to her.

Griff was talking to her, and he had no eyes, just two perfect round holes that trickled blood. Things crawled and moved in them.

"No, *cariad*, it's not a dream." His voice cracked. "I keep trying to wake up and I can't."

He opened his mouth to say more, but one of his 'arms' slipped free of its ledge and swung out wildly, narrowly missing Cally's head. Griff's body peeled away from the wall of the Pit and his other 'arm' also came free; the rest of his claws slipped from their anchorages and he fell away, dwindling to a tumbling speck amongst the others below, his screams fading into the rest.

Something crawled out of a cave below; a huge toad the size of a cow. Like Griff, it had no eyes. A thin white arm protruded from each socket, hands groping at the air. When it opened its mouth, pale eyes blinked inside its throat.

Wind blew past Cally and there was thunder overhead; and then something was above her, beating its ragged wings. It alighted on a ledge above her.

Clawed, webbed feet. Black, oily feathers.

The Cormorant.

When it spread its wings, she saw a face, not quite human, in the middle of its chest: low-browed and snout-nosed, with a grinning mouth full of teeth. There were no eyes on the end of its snaky neck as it drew back to strike, only a long sharp beak that slowly came to bear on her.

A scream blasted through the pit; it came from somewhere outside, from the waking world outside this dream that was not a dream. The Pit's walls flew apart, and she woke.

Into another bad dream.

37.

The scream went on, and something grabbed Cally's arm. She screamed too, but it was a human hand; Ellen's hand. Ellen was sitting up beside her in the bed, staring towards the door and shouting: "What the fuck – Jesus Christ – what the fuck–"

It wasn't dark this time: the bedroom light flickered like a strobe, which meant there was no dismissing the thing beside the bedroom door as shadows. It was very solid: Cally's first impression was of a vaguely humanoid shape, wearing what looked like a bulky coat of glossy black fur, its face hunched down far between raised shoulders. But it was impossibly broad and squat and its pallid, snouty, stupidly grinning face was set far lower than any person's could have been.

There was a stench of decay and excrement, sulphur and dead fish and bitter metal, and the shape moved. The flickering light gave it a horribly jerky quality, like stop motion photography, as it rose on thin legs, balanced on clawed, webbed black feet.

It couldn't be, but was.

The Cormorant spread its ragged wings, and Cally clutched Ellen tight, as if that would protect her.

"No no no," said Ellen. "No no no no no–"

The serpentine neck uncoiled. The 'head' rose into the air; the beak's needle tip swivelled to and fro, like a missile seeking its target, then became still. Cally wasn't sure if it was aimed at her or Ellen, but pressed together as they were, it hardly mattered.

The beak hinged open into four separate sections like an unholy flower in bloom, each lined with row on row of thin hooked fangs. In its centre, instead of a throat, was raw flesh with ring on ring of rasping teeth, like a lamprey's mouth, ringed with root-like tendrils that whipped at the air.

"Fuck *that*," yelled Ellen, and threw herself sideways as the beak lunged. She was still hanging onto Cally, so they both tumbled out of bed onto the floor.

The beak snapped shut on the air they'd just occupied, then swung back and forth, searching. The face in the Cormorant's chest snarled and dribbled.

The lights kept flickering, and the Cormorant's beak reared up again. Ellen scrambled to her feet and lunged for the standing lamp in the corner of the room. It was unplugged, the power cord looped around a hook halfway down its length, and stood on a heavy round base. Ellen grabbed it, then leapt back behind the bed as the beak made a stabbing motion in her direction.

"Yeah?" she shouted. Cally loved her in that moment: she looked magnificent, taking on a monster with a lampstand. "Come on then, you beaky twat!"

The beak jabbed at Ellen again, and she swiped at it with the lamp. It clanged loudly off the beak and the neck whipped back.

She knocked aside another lunge and yelled: "Come on!" again, but wasn't causing it any real damage; she was focusing on the beak. If the Cormorant had a brain, it was behind the leering idiot face in its torso, and that face didn't look at all distressed. If anything, its grin was wider than ever now, a long tongue hanging from its mouth, thick with drool. The lips peeled back and the nostrils flared; Cally realised it was laughing, and her stomach clenched cold with dread.

The Cormorant's beak jabbed at Ellen again, but they weren't serious blows, just feints; it was toying with her. The neck stretched out to Ellen's right and the beak lunged. Ellen swung at it and her balance went; she swayed, arms pinwheeling, fighting to stay upright.

The Cormorant reared back, the neck seeming almost to fold

in on itself as it drew back through the bedroom door onto the landing. It wasn't toying now, and off-balance as she was Ellen would never avoid the next strike. It would either skewer her with its closed beak, or the jaws would snap shut on her face and crush her skull.

Cally wasn't quick to act in a crisis on her own account, but when someone else's safety was concerned she often surprised herself, and did so now. Her paralysis broke and she lunged forward, grabbing Ellen around the knees and yanking hard. Ellen crashed full-length to the carpet with a squawk of alarm as the Cormorant's beak shot forward, through the space where her head had been, and punched through one of the windows.

The Cormorant tried to pull its beak back, but the broken glass had snagged its neck. As it struggled, Cally slammed the lamp's heavy base down on the back of the 'head,' forcing the jagged glass into its throat; when she turned, the face in its chest was grimacing in pain.

She'd hurt it, but not enough. The real target was the face. Cally scrambled onto the bed, kneeling on the mattress and swinging the lamp back over her shoulder. The Cormorant's neck pulled taut as it tried to free itself. In another second it might have managed, but Cally swung the lamp again before it could try.

The heavy base smashed into the leering features in its chest, the impact almost jolting the lamp from Cally's grip. The Cormorant shrieked: a million fingernails scraping down a million blackboards and blasted out through the speakers at a stadium gig, so loud the cells of her body seemed to vibrate. Her hands opened and her balance went, and she fell back off the bed onto the floor.

The light's flickering grew so fast as to be undetectable. She was sure the light would explode; thought it had when she heard glass shatter, but when the Cormorant's beak whipped back into view, flailing from side to side, she realised it had been the remains of the window.

The shriek rang on, echoing and distorted. And then it stopped. The lights blinked once and came back on normally. And the Cormorant was gone.

Through the broken window she heard alarms shrilling. Her car, and Ellen's. Had to be. But other sounds, coming from within the house, all but drowned them out. Coming from downstairs.

38.

"The fuck?" demanded Ellen. "What the fuck? What the *fuck*?"

Cally got to her feet, not answering. What could she say, after all?

"What. The. Fuck?" Ellen demanded again, grabbing Cally's arm. Cally slid off the bed to grab her dressing gown and slippers. Not exactly dressing for battle, but preferable to charging sky-clad into the fray, however in keeping that might be with her Celtic heritage. She retrieved the standing lamp and advanced onto the landing.

"Cally? Cally, what the hell just... oi! Oh, Christ's sake..." Ellen's voice tailed off. "Wait up, will you? Jesus."

Cally reached the end of the landing. A loud blurred clamour boomed up the stairs. There was only darkness: they'd turned off all the lights other than the bedroom one. Half the fun of lovemaking was seeing what was going on.

Holding the lamp like a spear, Cally advanced down the stairs. She'd had cause to regret the house's isolated position over the past few days, but she was glad of it now: a house in a built-up area would already be getting swarmed by neighbours demanding explanations she'd be in no state to give.

As she reached the bottom of the stairs Cally began to make out individual parts of the din.

Red Three to Tower. Red Three to Tower. Tower, do you receive? Tower! Tower! This is Red Three! Please respond. Instruments not functioning. Visibility nil. Tower. Tower–

Then a scream, so loud and sudden Cally ducked as if from

an incoming blow. Then it began again, swimming in static: *Red Three to Tower. Red Three to Tower. Tower, do you receive?*

It came from ahead, from the front room. She prodded the door open with the lamp, and another voice shouted from the darkness.

'Sblood, man, make an end of this! Kill me now and toy with me not. A pox on thee and all traitors. I die a true soldier of the king.

The room wasn't completely dark. The TV screen was a blur of grey static. Cally thought she glimpsed something in it less random that the rest, but looked away. She didn't want to see.

Other lights gleamed: the stereo. Cally groped for the light switch, but couldn't find it. Maybe it had disappeared. An impossibility, but tonight seemed a night for them. The Cormorant had been impossibility incarnate, and she couldn't dismiss it as a nightmare or a fever dream. Even if she tried to rationalise away the broken window, Ellen had seen it too.

She found the light switch at last, but another voice burst from the stereo speakers, making her jump.

In God's name let us strike and make an end of this devilment! Show no quarter, lads; there'll be no mercy in Heaven for such as these, and therefore give them none here on Earth.

"Jesus," Cally muttered. She found the switch again, and she clicked on the lights.

Other voices, other loops, rose and fell, but too quickly to decipher. All but one, that throbbed under the rest like a low relentless pulse:

Angana sor varalakh kai torja, angana sor varalakh cha voran.

She had to switch it off, and now. She stepped forward, but someone grabbed her shoulder.

"Fuck!" She jumped, swinging the lamp, but it glanced off the edge of the door; a good thing too, as the hand was Ellen Rooke's.

"Jesus, Cally," said Ellen, just as Cally said "Jesus, Ellen." That made Ellen laugh shakily; Cally laughed too, but it quickly faded.

Ellen was very pale – Cally had never seen that butterfly of freckles standing out so starkly – and clutching one of the one-kilo exercise weights from Cally's bedside drawer. She was somehow fully dressed; how the hell had she done that so quickly? Something you learned in police training, maybe.

Cally put down the lamp and went to the stereo, jabbing the power button till it fell silent. The TV screen foamed with static; and the chant continued coming from it, now on its own.

Cally stabbed the TV remote's power button. At first nothing happened and she felt panic stirring, but finally the sound cut out; the screen faded to black.

Inside the house was silence. Outside, the car alarms continued shrilling. Ellen ran to the front door. "Cally, can you open this please? *Now*?"

"Sure. Sure. Gimme a second. Wait." She'd left her shoulder-bag downstairs, pills and all. She'd thought she could at least feel safe here.

She should have. Would have, if she hadn't dug into Eagle Mount and Warden Fell, hadn't brought Tony Mathias and his family's deaths into her father's home.

Stop panicking. Use your brain.

Was she still trying to tell herself there was a rational explanation for the Cormorant, the TV, the stereo, the shattered window, the blaring alarms? Especially now there was a witness?

"Cally!" shouted Ellen.

"All right! Okay!"

She found the keys and ran into the hall. Ellen stepped aside to let Cally unlock the door, but had shot past into the front yard as soon as the door opened.

"Ellen, wait. Ellen!" Cally stumbled after her, almost tripping over in her ludicrous slippers.

The two cars were parked side by side, their lights flashing; she was about halfway to Ellen when the Juke's lights went out and the noise of the alarms was reduced by half. Cally pointed her own key-fob in the Punto's general direction, and its alarm cut out too. Its lights stopped flashing, and there was silence. A dog barked somewhere, far away in the distance.

Cally wondered if they'd heard anything down in Bala. Sound travelled a long way on these clear, quiet nights. She shook her head; it didn't matter. They were both in one piece. That was what counted.

Her dressing-gown was flapping wide; Cally fastened it around herself and padded over. "Ellen? Are you okay?"

Cally put a hand on her shoulder, but Ellen squirmed away from her touch. "What the *fuck* was that?"

"I dunno," said Cally.

That earned her an angry glare. "Don't give me that."

Obviously, Ellen had been in the police long enough to spot an obvious lie. "I *don't* know," said Cally, "not *really*. It's the same sound as was on the tape. That's all I know."

"*Tape?*"

She realised she'd never told Ellen about the cassettes. "Tony Mathias," she explained. "He kept a diary on audiocassette. Managed to get hold of part of it. A friend of mine's been converting it to digital…"

She trailed off. Ellen was staring at her, the way people might have stared at Pandora after learning she'd opened the box.

The realm of flying saucers and little green men, Sabharwal had said. Or another realm, equally insane and impossible that didn't operate by science's rules, that moved through unguessable cycles so that at times some folk – urbexers called CORRAN, for example – could walk through Warden Fell untouched, while at others the simple act of playing a cassette might prove lethal to whoever heard it.

Madness, of course. Impossible. But then, were the events of the last few minutes.

Cally opened her mouth, trying to decide where to begin, but Ellen was already shaking her head. "Forget it," she said. "Nope."

Not only was she fully dressed, Cally saw; she was carrying her handbag too; everything gathered and ready for departure. "I'm sorry," said Ellen. "I'm out. I'm sorry, but nope. I'm out. I'm sorry."

"Ellen," Cally called out, but she was already weaving towards her car. "Ellen!"

"Nope." It took Ellen a couple of attempts to get the car door open; when Cally moved towards her, she raised a hand to ward her off. "I'm sorry. No."

She wouldn't even look at Cally. Her voice was flat and dead, her upraised hand formal and cold. *Halt. Stop. No entry.* Cally had no reply to it. Something broke inside her, seeping cold paralysis into her body; all she could do was watch Ellen get into the car. The driver's door slammed shut with the cold finality of a falling guillotine blade, the engine spluttered into life and the Juke reversed in a spray of gravel and accelerated towards the main road, leaving her alone in the night.

39.

Cally dressed, switched on every light in the house and taped a cardboard sheet over the shattered window. She didn't turn on the TV, afraid of what might appear on the screen or come out of the speakers. She stared at a book without taking in a word till it was light, then paced the garden until she knew Bala would be coming to life.

The summer cold seemed to have cleared up overnight, along with the worst of her hay fever symptoms. Small mercies, Cally supposed, although she'd rather still have them if she could have Ellen back too. She drove into Bala for a bacon roll and caramel latte at Ty Coffi, but almost instantly regretted it. Ellen would be on duty by now; what if she walked in?

Sod her. She ran a mile as soon as things turned weird.

Cally shook her head. Who wouldn't run from a gigantic bird with a half-human face in its chest? And if running kept Ellen safe, Cally could concentrate on her own well-being.

And Griff's. She'd rung him during the night, and again from the café, but there'd been no reply. By now it was after ten o'clock, and she felt calm enough to make some sort of plan.

She made one other call first, though, to the number Ellen had given her.

"Hello," said a gruff voice.

"Hi," she began, "is that–"

"This is Graham Harrower." The line wasn't good. There was static, and a faint ghost-voice muttering in the background. Part of someone else's call. "I'm not available at present, but leave your name, contact details and the reason for your call and I'll call you back if I want to talk to you. Thank you."

Cally cleared her throat, left what she hoped was a clear and concise message, and saved Harrower's number to her contacts. Then she drove out to Fron-Goch.

Griff's Land Rover was in the drive, but the curtains were drawn. No sound or movement. She rang the doorbell, rapped on the windows and shouted through the letterbox, but there was no answer. the neighbouring bungalows' curtains twitched; they probably thought this was a lover's tiff. Cally smiled despite herself; Griff would have found that hilarious.

Still would. You can't get hold of him. Doesn't mean he's dead.

He'd been sick; was probably still in bed. But he wasn't a deep sleeper, not since Afghanistan; loud bangs and sudden noises snapped him wide awake.

If you're that worried, call 999.

But that was the one thing that would have made Griff genuinely angry with her. He cherished his independence and Cally suspected there'd been at least one involuntary committal in his past; cops or paramedics kicking in his door would be the stuff of his nightmares. Although if his mental physical state was the issue, she might be doing him a worse turn by *not* calling someone.

Cally was still undecided when her phone rang. Relieved, she hit answer without looking at the screen. "Griff?"

"Hello?" She recognised the voice at the other end, despite the interference and ghostly mutters of other conversations, and yet she didn't. "Who am I speaking to?"

She looked at the caller ID: GRAHAM HARROWER. "Oh. Hi. This is Cally Darker. Mr Harrower?"

"Chief Inspector," he said, like a teacher addressing a slow pupil. "Retired, though, so I suppose *Mister* will do. So, we've something we want to talk about, don't we?"

"Er, yeah. I wanted to talk about–"

"I know," he interrupted. "Did your 'friend' explain I'll only discuss the matter in person?"

"She did." She didn't like the way he said 'friend', but attitudes weren't all they could be in the police even now; back in the '80s they'd been legendarily homophobic. Or biphobic, in her case, not that Harrower would care about the distinction. Besides, Ellen probably wasn't her friend any longer, with or without inverted commas. Cally could talk to a bigot for a few hours; she'd done worse. "Fine by me. When's good for you?"

"I'd say the sooner the better," he said. "Wouldn't you, Miss Darker?"

"Ms," she corrected automatically. "And yes. When's convenient?"

"How's today looking for you? It's only a couple of hours drive from sheep-shagger country."

Ah, homophobia *and* racism; still, hardly a surprise to find the two together. "I can do that."

"Very glad to hear it," he said, as if the very idea she couldn't was proof of her stupidity. "It's half-ten now. So, giving you a reasonable margin to get here, shall we say three p.m. today? I'd say that's ample time."

Assuming there were no traffic problems she could do it with time to spare. "Yes, that should be fine."

"Good. You'll want my address. Have you pen and paper?"

Cally took it down; he made her repeat it back to him. "All right, then. See you at three. *Ms* Darker," he added, emphasising the title with unmistakable scorn.

"Prick," she muttered, once the call was safely over. Then she returned the phone to her shoulder-bag, giving Griff's front door a last look. She'd call him again later. Before that, she had a long drive ahead.

She hadn't thought she'd return to Manchester so soon, far less that she'd be glad to do so, but after checking into the Premier

Inn on Chapel Street, Cally fell full-length onto her bed and nearly cried with relief. She couldn't face another night in Dad and Lucy's house right now, although the idea that her former sanctuary was now unsafe was so painful her throat closed up.

She showered and drank a cup of coffee by the window, looking out over the Manchester skyline. She'd never found the sight relaxing before, but did now; she was among people, in the heart of a major city, instead of alone somewhere anything could happen and no one would know. Maybe the Cormorant and its friends would leave her alone here. Events like that went with seclusion and isolation, to tiny numbers of witnesses who could safely be dismissed as delusional.

Even so, she couldn't bring herself to listen to any more of Tony Mathias' recordings, not even to prepare for talking to Harrower. She still felt frightened and lost. She wanted to go home, but *home* meant somewhere safe; if the farmhouse no longer was, she didn't know where to go.

She brought up Ellen's details, thumb hovering over the 'call' icon, but in the end closed the Contacts screen. The phone might ring unanswered or be cut off; Ellen might have call-blocked her, which would hurt too much right now, and if Ellen actually picked up the phone that would be worst of all: Cally had no idea what she'd say, or how.

Hopefully, Ellen was doing her best to forget Cally completely and convince herself she'd hallucinated the Cormorant and its companions. Maybe that would keep her safe.

She could see Sacred Trinity Church's clock-tower from her window, and realised it was after two o'clock. She dressed quickly: her clothes whiffed of sweat after the long hot drive, but she'd nothing else to wear. She should have stopped at Iain's to pick up her things. She'd better do that afterwards, before he gave them all to a charity shop.

Harrower lived in Stalybridge, on the edge of the Peak District, thirty-five minutes' drive away. It was quarter past two before Cally got back to the Punto, which was cutting it finer than she liked when driving to an unfamiliar address. She wasn't looking forward to meeting Harrower on any level; she'd need all her confidence and composure, which was little enough as it was, without her turning up late.

Luckily, traffic was light, and her sat-nav proved reliable. She pulled up on a pleasant suburban road in Buckton Vale with ten minutes to spare. Cally sat for a couple of minutes, enjoying the quiet, gazing out towards the distant slopes of Harridge Pike.

Harrower lived at number twelve. Another bungalow; Cally looked at its plain white frontage, trying not to think about Griff. A curtain twitched in the front room window, revealing a silhouetted figure gazing out at her, then fell back into place.

Cally took a deep breath, and got out of the car.

40.

"Ms Darker, I presume?" Harrower looked Cally up and down, and sniffed; she resisted the temptation to ask what his problem was. "Sit. I'll make tea."

"I'm more of a coffee-drinker..." she said to his retreating back, then subsided on the leather sofa he'd indicated.

Cally looked around the front room. Harrower's wedding photo was on the mantelpiece, alongside pictures of his children and grandchildren. On the walls were photographs of Harrower in uniform, some with public figures of the 1980s: James Anderton, Margaret Thatcher.

Bigots and homophobes and Tories, oh my.

It was a shrine to himself; even the family pictures seemed arranged to reflect his past glories back at him. Maybe when you were old and alone, wondering if it had all been worthwhile, you needed every possible reminder of what had been.

All was clean and polished, but empty, and reeking of stale smoke. Cally wondered when the children and grandchildren had last been here, if ever, and where Mrs Harrower had gone.

Harrower re-entered with a tray: teapot, milk jug, cups. He was still tall, though slightly stooped, and thinner than in the photographs. Despite the hot weather, he wore corduroy trousers, a lumberjack shirt and a brown cardigan with antler-horn buttons. All were pressed and creaseless; his brushed-steel hair was neatly cut and brushed, but his beard, nicotine-stained around the mouth, straggled messily to his chest.

The armchair one by the coffee table was clearly his: the leather bore the impressions of his shoulders and buttocks and was dark where his head had rested. When he sat, he sighed in satisfaction, fitting himself into the place shaped exactly for him.

Cally made no move towards the tea things, but Harrower raised a hand to ward her off nonetheless. The first and middle fingers were yellowed, like his beard, were yellowed from smoking. "Two minutes. Let it stew."

He took a packet of Silk Cut and a brass Zippo lighter from his cardigan and lit up, then offered her the packet. "Want one?"

"No, thanks. I don't."

"Not in fashion anymore, is it?" His voice sounded stronger than the rest of him – rich and deep, but with a bored, superior note, like the well-to-do customers she'd encountered in her call-centre days who'd talked to the advisers as if they were morons.

"So," he said. "You want to know about Eagle Mount."

Cally took her phone from her shoulder-bag. "Mind if I record this conversation?"

He smirked. His eyes were dark grey, with yellowed sclera: iron nailheads in old ivory. "God forbid you should have to rely on your memory, or have developed any shorthand skills. That's gone out of fashion too, hasn't it? Can't do anything without one of those wretched things anymore. Go on, then."

Cally's face felt hot. She'd forgotten how crushed and weak-willed her last call centre job had left her. Her confidence and sense of herself had only really returned in Wales; she felt both shrivelling in Harrower's presence, and had a brief but overwhelming urge to smash the heavy glass ashtray into his smug face. Instead she set the phone to record and put it on the sofa's arm.

"Ask your questions," Harrower said. "Or didn't you bother to prepare any?"

She hadn't. Yet another excuse for Harrower to demonstrate the contempt he clearly held her in. She'd thought she'd know what to ask, but now nothing would come.

He let out a long, loud sigh. "All right, I'll do your job for you. I assume what you want to know is why. Everyone else does."

"Do you have any idea?"

Harrower snorted. "People always want a reason. Daddy never loved me. Mummy locked me in the wardrobe. All excuses. All rubbish. There's good, there's evil, and the choice between them. But people don't like to hear that. Again, not *fashionable*. People choose to do terrible things, Ms Darker, every day, every week, every month, every year. Have done from the beginning of time. Always will. Usually because they think they're entitled to something they want, no matter the consequences. Sometimes just *because*."

How many times had she heard that one? If it was all Graham Harrower could tell her, Cally had come a long way for nothing.

He dragged so hard on his cigarette it burned down almost to the filter, then stubbed it out. "People see too many films. Think it's about us getting inside the criminals' heads and *understanding* them. But that's for social workers and other apologists. Cause and effect, Ms Darker, that's all that matters. What people *do*. Their pathetic, after-the-fact excuses are irrelevant."

He took out another cigarette, slowly and studiedly, as if to prove that he wasn't afraid of the memories he was revisiting.

"I wanted to make all that very clear up front, Ms Darker, for a very simple reason. I've seen a great deal of evil in my time, and almost all of it was explicable in those terms. People faced with a choice, and choosing wickedness, cruelty and chaos. Eagle Mount was, almost, the sole exception."

He puffed on his cigarette. "I lived near Scorbridge at the time. Mathias was a local celebrity of sorts. I knew of his degenerate past, but he was now married with a family, and by all accounts faithful to his wife, which raised him in my estimation. He didn't give way to his perversion and excuse it by calling it his *nature*. He made a *choice*, to lead a decent, wholesome life. I'd seen him with his family, the affection between them, and didn't believe that could have been faked. But no one likes admitting they've been fooled, and you can never be sure with an artist. So the killings weren't the shock to me they were to others. Such as Peter."

"Peter?" Again Cally remembered that initial email that had started it all. p56283. *Best, Pete*, it had ended.

"Detective Constable Peter Culleton." Harrower's voice softened for a moment. "A good lad. Decent. Conscientious. He knew the family – was more than a little in love with Lindsay Mathias, I think. He really shouldn't have worked on the investigation, but I'd every confidence in his professionalism. Rose Bennison was the senior investigating officer. There weren't many female Detective Chief Inspectors then. You didn't get automatically promoted for being a one-legged black lesbian."

He leant forward and poured two cups of tea. *The investigating officer was bad enough*, Edna Woodwiss had told her. *A woman – unusual at the time – and therefore determined to show she was as ruthless as any man. And her sergeant wouldn't have been out of place in the Gestapo.* But, like Harrower, she'd spoken kindly of Peter Culleton.

Cally poured as much milk into her own brew as she could, feeling Harrower's disapproving gaze on her.

"He died, didn't he?" she said. "Peter Culleton? A house fire?"

A note of anger entered Harrower's voice. "Rose Bennison slandered him as a drunk. I try not to hold that against her. When things go wrong, somebody has to carry the can. She was the officer in charge, and tried to shift the blame. Failed. That was the end of her career. Married a rich man, went to live in Spain. But he wasn't a drunk. I almost wish he had been. Might have been better. She's dead too now. Bennison. Cancer, back in '07." He shrugged. "She's irrelevant, anyway. It was Peter who mattered."

Cally waited. Harrower raised his eyebrows. "Aren't you going to ask how?"

"I thought you were about to tell me."

She couldn't see much of the thin mouth under his drooping, stained moustache, but she saw the lips tighten. Then he smiled slightly. "Fair. I *have* drawn things out a little. It's not an easy topic to discuss. Not because Peter was a friend. I've no problem sharing memories of a good man. Or telling the truth, even when it's unflattering. But it's one thing when people don't like what you say. Another when they refuse to even believe it. When they think you're mad."

He drained his tea at a gulp, then refilled it, adding splash of milk. "But I don't think you will, somehow, Ms Darker. I think you'll believe me. You're aware Mathias was dyslexic?"

She nodded.

Harrower grunted. "Handwriting like a bloody spastic. But like so many artists, he had to share his oh-so-precious thoughts with the world. Kept a diary on cassette tape – you're aware of this?"

"Yes."

"Destroyed in the fire, of course," said Harrower. Cally said nothing. "The only clue, after the fire, was what he'd scrawled on one wall."

"World's End," said Cally.

Harrower nodded. "He wouldn't have been the first to convince himself Judgement Day was imminent, or to send himself and his family on ahead. But Peter was adamant neither of them had been at all religious. And then, under the caravan, we found a few surviving fragments – they'd fallen through the floor where it had burned away. Balls of paper – abandoned drafts he'd crumpled up and discarded – and a tape. He'd made multiple attempts at some sort of suicide note. Peter volunteered to transcribe them. He wanted answers more than anyone. He did his best to decipher Mathias' scrawls, but even typed up, they made little sense. Kept breaking off into nonsense phrases.

Foreign languages. French, something Peter thought might have been Anglo-Saxon – don't ask me how he knew that – even bits that read like a pilot talking to a control tower."

Red Three to Tower. Red Three to Tower. Tower, respond. Tower respond.

Harrower was watching Cally beadily. She wondered if anything resembling *Angana sor varalakh kai torja, angana sor varalakh cha voran* had cropped up amid the fragments. "You mentioned a tape," she said. "Was that part of his suicide note?"

"An attempt at one. It'd been damaged by the heat, plus the foam the fire brigade sprayed all over the wreckage. Miracle Peter got it to play at all, but he was a very clever lad. Not the most physical – rather thin and pale. Limp blond hair. Glasses. Not a complete drip – people learned that the hard way – but his brain was his real strength. Had a very good brain, Peter Culleton. A very fine young man, Ms Darker. Very fine police officer, but most of all a very fine young man. Grammar-school boy, scholarship. Intelligent. Well-read. Could do pretty much anything he put his mind to. He was my friend, and I genuinely believe, given time, I'd have been taking orders from *him*, and I wouldn't have had a problem with that."

The cigarette had burned down between his fingers. Harrower stubbed it out, then lit another. "He put a great deal of work into fixing that tape, even after our resident technical bods gave up. Cloak and dagger squad from the MOD didn't care – if it hadn't been for Peter the tape would've been destroyed anyway. Although that might not have been the worst thing."

"What was the MOD's involvement, exactly?" said Cally. "Dr Sabharwal said–"

"Oh, old Ali Baba?" Harrower snorted. "That was what we called him. We assumed they were MOD. They weren't big on showing identification. What *was* made very clear was that if they told us to jump our only question should be how high. Very secretive bunch in very nice suits. They sat in on some of the interviews, but their principal concern was ensuring the whole affair was quickly forgotten, mostly by putting the fear of God into all involved."

He shrugged. "Made no odds to us. Case had closed itself. But Peter was determined to understand what'd happened to Lindsay Mathias, and he was convinced the cassette was the key. So he took it home with him – quite irregular, of course. And somehow, he got it to play."

Harrower puffed on his cigarette. "Bennison didn't care. Just wanted the whole business done and dusted. So he confided in me. Said the tape reminded him of a Pentecostal service he'd seen. People speaking in tongues. You understand the term?"

"People talking in an unknown language, or one they couldn't know. Tony Mathias was doing that?"

"Part of his breakdown, I assumed. But according to Peter, there were background sounds too – *intrusions*, he called them. He didn't think Mathias had been aware of them. Some of them resembled the bits of crazy-talk on the paper fragments. Peter was convinced it all meant something. He wanted to know why, but that's a fool's errand, Ms Darker."

"Because sometimes there's no other reason than *because*."

"That's right. You've been paying attention to somebody with a brain."

Cally thought of Ellen. "I do my best."

"Peter was sure he could find an answer. I began to worry about him. He was getting obsessed. Came on shift a couple of times looking like a bloody tramp. Even smelled drink on him one morning, which was a shock. His physical health was suffering too. Had to send him home eventually – he was coughing and shaking, could barely stand. Flu, I assumed. Unseasonal, but it happens."

"But it wasn't?"

"No," he said. "No, it wasn't."

41.

Harrower's gaze shifted to the drinks cabinet in the corner. He took a deep breath and straightened in his chair, resisting temptation for now. Maybe he didn't want to show weakness in front of Cally. Or maybe he'd have felt obliged to offer her a drink and didn't want to waste good Scotch on her.

"Peter was off for about a week," he said. "I had to testify at a trial in Manchester. Armed robbery case. Spoke to Peter before I went. I don't mind admitting I was concerned. He wasn't making much sense. Feverish, maybe; flu can do that to you. When I got back..."

Harrower looked towards the drinks cabinet again. "Can I offer you a drop of something stronger, Ms Darker?"

"I love a good single malt," she said, "especially Cragganmore or Lagavulin. But I'm driving. Don't let me stop you, though."

For the first time he eyed her with something other than disdain. "Don't worry. I shan't."

He went to the cabinet and came back with a cut-glass tumbler half-full of Scotch. He took a deep sip, sighed and retrieved his cigarette from the ashtray. "I was in Manchester for two days. I came home to find several messages from Peter on my answering machine. Barely recognised his voice. He said he needed help, but was afraid to call the doctor." Harrower reached for the whisky again. "His last message begged me to come to him. He sounded terribly afraid, and while he wasn't the most *physical* of officers, Peter Culleton didn't frighten easily."

He ground his cigarette out, then toyed with the packet. "He might have been simply delirious, but I was worried he was suffering a breakdown. Such things happened. I'd thought Peter was stronger than that, but he'd become obsessed with the case. In the messages he'd left, he – broke off, several times, from the flow of whatever he was trying to say. He'd gabble, sometimes in foreign languages, sometimes in English, but very – *archaic* English. All thees and thous and whatnot."

'Sblood, man, make an end of this! Kill me now and toy with me not. A pox on thee and all traitors. I die a true soldier of the king.

"Like what was on Tony Mathias' tapes?" asked Cally.

"I couldn't say for certain, Ms Darker, since neither the answering-machine tapes nor Peter's transcripts still exist. I destroyed the tapes myself, afterwards. But I suspect so.

"Peter lived alone – fortunately, as it turned out. Some new-build Barratt Home. The doors and windows were all tightly shut. He didn't answer when I knocked. Then I felt the heat, realised I could smell smoke. I shouted his name and tried to break down the door. That was when he finally responded. Bellowing at me to go away, leave him alone. There was something dreadfully wrong with his voice." Harrower smiled, but his eyes glistened. "Seemed he'd changed his mind about wanting my help."

Cally said nothing. Harrower was painfully exposed now; the last thing a man like him would ever want to be. If she made a sound, he might clam up.

"I didn't listen, of course," he said. "I had to get him out of there. I couldn't break the front door down, I went into the garden. He had garden gnomes. God knows why. Stupid things. Anyway, I picked one up. Threw it at the front-room window, hard as I could." A brief, grim laugh. "Mistake."

He put down his glass and touched the rim lightly, as if telling a dog to stay. "He'd shut all the external doors and windows in the house, even put draught excluders across the bottom of the doors. Think he hoped he'd asphyxiate from the fumes – painless, comparatively. And the fire would destroy the evidence."

Cally almost asked *what evidence*, but after talking to Sabharwal, thought she could guess.

"But Peter was no better an arsonist than Tony Mathias," said Harrower. "With everything sealed, there wasn't enough oxygen. Till I broke the window, of course. Then the air from outside was sucked in. And when *that* hit the fire … boom. Every window exploded outwards"

He turned his head and touched his right cheek, just below the eye, leaning towards Cally. A curved scar, very thin. "Another quarter-inch, I'd have been blinded." He brushed the tip of his other finger over his left temple. "A few nicks there, too. Just tiny pieces of glass. Not even a scar, but a fraction of an inch the other way, and I'd need a guide dog. And I hate dogs."

Cally should have guessed.

"I *did* sustain severe facial injuries, mostly here." Harrower indicated his cheeks and chin. "No actual impairment, but messy, painful, and terribly unsightly. This whole area's a mass of scars. Can't shave without slicing myself up. Even when I trim it, I have to use a very light touch."

Harrower gazed at a photograph on the mantelpiece that Cally had only half-registered before. A piece of black ribbon was fixed across one corner, and it showed a younger Harrower – clean-shaven and unscarred – beside a bespectacled, blond-haired man. They held cigars and grinned at the camera, arms were around one another's shoulders.

Cally didn't need to ask to know who the blond man was, any more than she needed to say *You loved him, didn't you?* Either question would end the interview here and now. The second one most of all, as it was one she suspected Harrower refused to answer even to himself.

Harrower's eyes were moist with pain; the rest of his face was like iron. He blinked repeatedly, till his eyes were dry, then continued.

"Peter was screaming inside the house. Terrible pain. I

thought I heard other voices, too. I tried to go towards the house, but the heat was unbelievable. Bright orange flames, roaring out of every window and from the doorway, which the blast had blown off its hinges. If *that* had hit me instead of the glass, Ms Darker, we'd be having this conversation through a Ouija board."

Harrower reached for his glass again, then stopped himself. "The hallway was on fire. Like the mouth of a furnace. But then I saw movement. Somebody walked down the hall, through the fire, and then out into the front garden."

He touched his upper lip with the tip of his tongue again, looked longingly at the remains of his whisky, then composed himself once more. "Was it Peter Culleton? That's what you want to ask, Ms Darker. But it's a question I still struggle to answer."

Harrower lit another cigarette. "Yes, I was injured, bleeding badly and in shock. However, I was not only an experienced police officer, but a detective. I was required to observe facts and record details, be they mundane or outlandish. What I'm about to tell you isn't in the official report on the fire, the records of the coroner's inquest, nor those of the internal police enquiry. I didn't even tell the Mysterious Men In The Very Nice Suits, when they interviewed me afterwards. Although they might have believed me. I'd have found myself pensioned off, or reassigned to the kind of duty they give officers they wish to forget about. It is, however, what I saw."

Harrower ground his cigarette out in the ashtray. "He was badly burned all over his body, but the right side of his face, his head, remained as I had known it. The left side, however, had altered completely. It had grown huge. Distended. I didn't understand what I was seeing to begin with. I'd seen severe swelling as a result of head injuries, but that side of his head was now three or four times the length and height of the other. Then he moved forward, and I saw."

Harrower took a deep breath. Cally waited.

"The left side of Peter's head," said Harrower, "was that of a gigantic insect." He looked at her, daring her to mock or disbelieve. "The biggest feature was a huge compound eye, like a horrible jewel with countless bright facets, glittering in the firelight. The eye was housed in a shiny black shiny black... shell? Armour? Like an insect's, or a spider's. *Chitin*. That's the word. There was a sort of mandible at what should have been the corner of his mouth, and a blurred, smeary line where it merged with Peter's face. His arms were covered in dry, brownish-coloured scales. His hands were now, basically, claws, and instead of nails ended in what I can only describe as talons – curved, thick, very sharp. Grey-black colour, like pencil-lead. Another pair of arms had sprouted from the centre of his abdomen – very small and white, like a baby's. Some sort of bristly black hair covered him from the waist down. His torso was a sort of hotch-potch of scales, fur, chitin and skin. But *this* part..." Harrower touched the right side of his face. "... was still unmistakably him."

He looked at the whisky once more, then forced himself to continue, lighting another cigarette instead. Cally managed not to cough. Her clothes and hair would stink of smoke by the time she left. "This wasn't, I should add, a fleeting glimpse. He stood there twenty, maybe thirty seconds, swaying. I just stared, trying to make sense of what I was seeing. Failing completely, of course. The more you looked, the more impossible it became.

"His right eye, the human one – I've never seen such anguish. I don't know what he wanted. A witness? Help? Or just to know another human still–" Harrower broke off. "I don't know if he'd always intended to do what he did next, or if it was a reaction to something he saw or didn't see in my face. I can't even be sure how much of him was still Peter by then. He'd set the fire, like Mathias, to destroy what he was becoming, the evidence of what he'd become, and the source of the contamination."

"Contamination?" said Cally, unable to stop herself.

Harrower looked at her, annoyed; for a horrible moment she thought she'd lost him. But he nodded.

"We'll come to that," he said. "Perhaps the thing he was becoming was trying to escape; I like to think that whatever was left of him reasserted himself at that point. Gave me one last look, then turned and walked back into the house, hunched over against the heat. He broke into a sort of staggering run. And then he was gone." His face trembled for a moment, then set hard again. "He was twenty-seven years old."

I'm sorry, Cally almost said, but didn't. She suspected any display of sympathy would enrage him.

"I passed out then," he said. "Mental shock, as much as physical injury – I'd seen some appalling things during my career, but *that*, as you can imagine, was in a class by itself."

Harrower's head went back as he drained his whisky in one gulp. The beard was thinner on his throat, exposing the white scars criss-crossing his neck.

"As I said," he went on, setting the glass back down, "I've normally no truck with excuses. Crime is almost always about people without the moral fibre to resist their baser impulses, or who actively embrace them. But on a tiny number of occasions, I've seen exceptions to that rule, and this was one. Peter Culleton was destroyed, ultimately, by the same thing that destroyed the Mathias family. Or rather, they destroyed themselves because it was the only moral option. I've no doubt that what they'd have become would have presented a lethal danger to others, and spread the same contamination wherever it went. But you want to know what the contamination was, don't you, Ms Darker? Well, so did I. I needed to understand the most – why the best – why Peter Culleton became that thing. And that, ultimately, meant understanding Warden Fell."

42.

Harrower refilled his glass; he didn't offer Cally any this time. "How much do you know about that place?"

Cally began describing the airbase's various incarnations, but Harrower shook his head. "That's just the surface. You've got to go further back than that, Ms Darker. Much further. Allow me to educate you."

He sipped his whisky. "There's been human activity around Warden Fell for thousands of years. Along with several attempts to erase all evidence of it – most notably, and successfully, in the case of Greston Castle. Ah, I see that name rings a bell."

"I came across the name," said Cally, "but it didn't seem relevant to–"

"Oh, it's relevant, Ms Darker. I can assure you of *that*. Greston Castle was slighted during the English Civil Wars. That means that after the castle fell, its captors didn't want it, so they made sure no one else could use it. But Greston Castle wasn't just slighted, it was *obliterated* – so thoroughly nobody now knows the exact site, only the general area. Warden Fell is considered to be only one of several possible locations, but I've no doubt it's the right one." Harrower swirled the whisky in his glass. "There's evidence of human habitation – flints, arrowheads, midden-heaps – on and around the hill dating back to the Palaeolithic Era. It may have been a holy site in pagan times – Warden Fell was a notorious meeting-place for witches in later years. Greston Castle's owners, the de Braceys, clamped down on such practices so ruthlessly that nearby Pendle Hill became the preferred destination. There are countless myths, legends and folk-tales of creatures being sighted on or near the hill. Vampires, werewolves, demons. That'll support the case for Warden Fell as the site of Greston Castle before we're done, too."

Harrower drank. "While no trace of the castle remains, there are earthworks indicating a possible hill-fort in Celtic times, plus coins and potsherds implying a continuous presence through the Roman and Anglo-Saxon periods. After the Norman Conquest, the land became the property of the de Braceys, where it remained until their extinction in the seventeenth century. The de Braceys built a stone keep that became known as Greston Castle during the reign of William II, but no one knows why."

"How do you mean?" Away from the painful topic of Peter Culleton, Cally felt safer prompting Harrower.

"Building a castle was a major task; it took years. They were built for a *reason*, not on a whim. But that area had no strategic importance. And then there was its design. A castle's battlements face outwards, Ms Darker, towards the enemy. Greston Castle's faced *inwards*. I don't know of another such structure in Britain. There *is*, however, one in Northern Bohemia, in the present-day Czech Republic. Castle Houska. Unlike Greston Castle, it's still standing – something of a tourist attraction, in fact. Like Greston Castle, it stands at a location of no apparent strategic value. But Castle Houska wasn't built to guard against an ordinary invader. It's not designed to repel an external attack–"

"–but to keep something in," said Cally. "Right?"

Harrower mimed applause. "Clever Ms Darker. The tradition is that Castle Houska was built over a deep pit from which, supposedly, demons emerged to terrorise the surrounding area. It was, in fact, said to go all the way down to Hell. Are you all right, Ms Darker?"

The bottomless pit. The endless falling. The screams. The Cormorant. The Toad. "I'm fine."

Harrower looked amused. *Well, fuck you too, dipshit.* "Which brings us back to Lancashire. Does the name 'Hogge's Pit' mean anything to you, Ms Darker?"

Cally shook her head.

"Unlike Greston Castle, there's no doubt about *its* location. All accounts agree there was once a deep pit at the summit of Warden Fell – but, like Greston Castle, no trace of it remains today. Like its counterpart at Castle Houska, Hogge's Pit was said to go all the way down to Hell, from which creatures crawled up to wreak havoc – hence all the lurid tales of werewolves and suchlike bogeys."

If they had something stored underground, Griff had said. *If that leaked, it could've contaminated the other buildings.* Just not the kind of contamination that showed up on Geiger counters, or in blood tests. *They could have a bloody* dragon *under there for all I know.* He'd been joking, but might have been more accurate than he'd realised.

Come on. You can't believe that.

She shouldn't, any more than she should believe Harrower's story, or Sabharwal's. But the Cormorant couldn't have been real, either, and Ellen had seen it too.

Harrower ground out his cigarette, slowly and deliberately. "The Celts, Romans and Saxons all built forts on the hill to contain the threat, with mixed success, but the Normans? Oh, they could build a fortress, those men. Very little escaped from Hogge's Pit after that."

He lit yet another Silk Cut, savoured the first puff, then reached for the whisky.

"Even so, it's said there were nights when a chorus of wailing, anguished voices could be heard from the hill where Greston Castle stood. The song of the damned, Ms Darker, of all the souls in Hell. If you heard it, and didn't immediately stop up your ears, you'd go mad or, worse, be carried off to Hell yourself. I wonder how such songs might sound, Ms Darker? Perhaps like someone speaking in tongues?"

Or, perhaps, like a certain chant.

"Sir Philip de Bracey was killed at the Battle of Marston Moor in 1644. His wife died giving birth to a stillborn child, and the de Bracey line became extinct. Greston Castle fell into disuse until 1648, when the Royalist Duke of Hamilton attempted to invade England from Scotland. One of his officers, Sir Bevil Wintringham, seized the castle. Both sides during the Civil Wars frequently accused one another of being in league with Satan, but Wintringham had a genuine reputation for practising Black Magic; he was popularly known known as 'Devil Wintringham.' Possibly just wartime propaganda, but there's a local tradition that Wintringham meant to raise the Devil to ensure a Royalist victory. It *is* a matter of historical record that the local population, who'd always been pro-Royalist, appealed to the Parliament forces for help and assisted them in taking the castle."

In God's name let us strike and make an end of this devilment! Show no quarter, lads; there'll be no mercy in Heaven for such as these, and therefore give them none here on Earth.

"Wintringham escaped," said Harrower, "but his men weren't so lucky. Pretty brutal business, by all accounts. Some of them were allegedly burned at the stake, and one was even said to have been flayed alive."

'Sblood, man, make an end of this! Kill me now and toy with me not. A pox on thee and all traitors. I die a true soldier of the king.

"The Castle itself, as I've said, was utterly destroyed, down to the foundations, every trace of it erased. Hogge's Pit was, presumably, filled in or at least sealed around the same time. There've been intermittent reports of what might be called paranormal activity in the area ever since, but if there's any pattern to it, no one's ever been able to determine what."

Harrower blew a stream of smoke in Cally's direction. "I think Warden Fell's like a volcano, myself," he said. "Sometimes it's dormant for a time, at others lethal. I can't pretend to be an expert when it comes to that. A vulcanologist could tell you what makes a volcano grow quiescent or more active. But if there *are* any experts on what's at Warden Fell, I wouldn't know where to find them. What I *do* know is that decades have passed without incident – the period from the end of World War Two to the 1960s, for instance."

Another period, no doubt, would have included 2014, the year of CORRAN'S visit to the place. Which was why all he'd seen or photographed were a few abandoned, decaying buildings. Lucky bastard.

"At other times, of course," said Harrower, "you can barely move for strange creatures, lights in the sky, ghostly voices and apparitions – the usual hocus pocus. Except it doesn't sound quite so silly to us, does it, Ms Darker?"

He was studying Cally with a beady, unblinking gaze. "Does it?" he repeated.

Cally tried to keep her voice level. "What's that supposed to mean?"

"Credit me with a little intelligence, Ms Darker. Why do you think I was so willing, even eager, to talk to you? I spent years trying to convince myself I couldn't have seen what I did the night Peter died – yet here I am, confiding in a pagan trollop who drools over old murders. Did you really think that was down to your devastating personal charm? I wanted to see you because I knew it was happening again."

Cally stood, her face burning. Harrower looked more amused than anything. "It is, isn't it?" he said.

She wanted to laugh in his face. Call him a madman, senile, an embittered old closet-case whose brains had curdled, anything that might hurt and wipe that smug smile away.

"It's confined to the hill, whatever it is," he said, "except when some fool like Mathias goes there and gets infected. And that infection can linger for years. Who was it? The sister? Or that old bag Woodwiss? One of them gave you something to listen to, didn't they? And now you've heard them sing. Been sleeping well, Ms Darker? Any bad dreams?"

She felt like a child in front of her mother again, helpless. She tried imagining Harrower in Millicent's dress and bouffant Thatcher perm; that should have rendered him absurd, but it didn't. "So what do I do?" she said at last.

"Do?" Harrower laughed. "Nothing you *can* do, Ms Darker. It was too late for Mathias after he went to Warden Fell. Too late for his family after he played his tapes to them. It was too late for poor Peter Culleton when he listened to Mathias' suicide note, and he was worth a dozen sluts like you. You know what's coming, Ms Darker. You know how your story ends."

"Fuck you, you old prick."

Cally remembered, just, to grab her phone from the sofa-arm and the shoulder-bag from the floor. She stumbled down the hallway; her hands shook so badly she could barely fumble at the Chubb lock on the front door. The stink of old man, furniture polish and stale smoke was choking, and all the while she could hear Graham Harrower laugh. It seemed to follow her all the way back to the car; she could still hear it as she drove away.

43.

Cally cried as she drove; her hands were shaking. She could barely see the road ahead and struggled to breathe. She should have pulled over to let the worst pass, but she needed shelter, sanctuary, a place of safety, if such a thing still existed now.

That infection can linger for years, Harrower had said. Where did it linger now? Would the chant start playing from the stereo and television speakers when Dad and Lucy got home?

No. Let it be in Cally and the files on her laptop. Nowhere else.

What about Ellen? She was in the house when the song played too. And what do you think's happened to Griff?

Cally dragged her sleeve across her eyes.

She managed to get back to the hotel without crashing or being pulled over, now on the verge of an all-out panic attack beyond any meditation app's capacity to ease. She somehow parked the car and walked through the lobby, clutching her wrist tightly so the pain would anchor her to reality; she felt as though she were spinning in space.

The lift pinged; the doors slid open. Cally wove down the corridor to her room, resisting the urge to hold onto the walls for support. She'd look drunk; even if no one was watching she wanted to retain some dignity.

Her key-card didn't work when she first put it in the lock; a scream of panic and rage built in Cally's throat, but she clenched her teeth and bit her lips. *Not in public. People will think you're mad.*

She almost hoped she was: better that than anything Harrower had said being true. But if she could at least maintain an appearance of normality she might still be able to function. If she ended up being sectioned, she'd lose what little control she had.

The door opened on the second try; Cally stumbled through. Outside her window were the city's roofs and towers, but they were no comfort now.

She pulled the curtains shut and fell onto the bed, pulling the covers over her like a cocoon. She curled up. Foetal position. *Back to the womb.* Alone and comfortless. She wished Ellen was there, and at the same time she was glad to be alone. *Even if I'm screwed, let Ellen be okay.*

The room spun. The mattress was a raft in a rough sea. Peter Culleton with half a fly's head. Neal Mathias sprouting feathers, and whatever little Alison had been becoming. Cally bit her lips again, this time so as not to laugh at the absurdity of it. What had Tony and Lindsay Mathias been turning into? What would *she* become?

Breathe.

She remembered her nightmare, the octopus tentacles anchoring her to the rock wall. Griff hanging on beside her with his pincer-limbs and empty bleeding eyes. *No,* cariad, *it's not a dream. I keep trying to wake up and I can't.*

"Oh, fucking hell. Griff..."

Breathe. Shut everything out. Try to rest.

Sometimes it was the only option. Take shelter, and weather the storm.

Cally shut her eyes, breathed deeply, and let the dark and silence take her.

Wind howled. A hurricane roared through into the Pit (Hogge's Pit?), trying to peel her off the wall.

She was exactly as she'd been at the end of the last

nightmare, clinging spreadeagled to the wall, secured by the tentacles sprouting from her body, and her black-furred arms. The hair on them already seemed thicker, the limbs themselves scrawnier, the nails and fingers longer. On the ledge above her was the Cormorant, the moronic face in its chest leering down at her, its sightless razor beak swaying on its serpent neck.

Screaming voices. Snatches of song and fractured speech in a Babel of tongues. And underlying it all like a drumbeat, coming from everywhere and nowhere at once: *Angana sor varalakh kai torja, anganaq sor varalakh cha voran.*

Below Cally, the Toad squatted on its ledge, the eyes in its throat staring up at her. Its black hide was leather, studded with warts.

Further down still, something swam up through the howling depths, as if the wind was stagnant water, its long body undulating to that endless chant.

The Eel had no eyes of its own, just a small white face, a baby's, set into its skull. The face's eyelids were stitched shut, but an eye, slit-pupiled and redly luminescent, burned in the centre of its forehead. A pair of stubby, spatulate-fingered hands protruded from behind the gills in its neck, and hundreds of tiny writhing scorpions' tails covered its skin.

The Eel's mouth yawned open, level with Cally's face, and even the hurricane couldn't sweep away its stinking breath. Stagnant water, dog piss, excrement, infected wounds. The mouth was huge and toothless, but yellow-nailed human hands filled the throat, clasping and unclasping. In its forehead, the baby's face, hitherto blank, screwed up in idiot laughter.

The Eel coiled upon itself; then flattened its tail against the wall and slid it towards Cally, trying to prise her loose.

From above, the Cormorant's beak suddenly stabbed down towards her face. Cally ducked at the last second and the blow missed, but it struck again, and again. The Toad leapt and capered on its ledge, seemingly unable to do more than encourage its companions.

The Eel's toothless mouth gaped; the infant face in its forehead cackled and drooled.

And then the rhythmic chanting that echoed through the Pit faltered; another voice, similar to the chanting one but subtly different, was repeating a refrain of its own, one that clashed and jarred with the other.

Mantakha sa niroleph chir karagh, it said. The Eel's baby-face screwed up, as if in pain. *Insapa veir bereloth. Insapa*, it continued, and the squirming of the Eel's tail grew weaker. *Maengrepa gir trequefa gla detiresh meirka*, the voice continued, and the tail went limp and pulled away from her.

As the Eel writhed in the air, the new voice began again. *Mantakha sa niroleph chir karagh. Insapa veir bereloth. Insapa. Maengrepa gir trequefa gla detiresh meirka.*

Above Cally, the Cormorant's beak recoiled, the serpentine neck retracting; it folded its ragged wings around itself, and the Toad crawled back into its cave, the arms protruding from its eye-sockets waving like a snail's eye-stalks.

The Eel plunged downwards, back into the Pit's depths. The Cormorant's wings flared outwards and, with a final squawk of rage, it flapped away.

Cally sagged against the rock-face. The stone was rough and jagged, cold and damp, and felt too horribly real to be part of any dream. Let her wake up now. Let this end.

But she didn't; she remained pressed flat against the wall, and the chanting went on. *Angana sor varalakh kai torja* – but for now, at least, that had faded into the background, eclipsed by the new refrain.

Which now grew louder still; it was coming from directly above her. Slowly she raised her head, and looked up.

A figure squatted on the Cormorant's former perch. It had two arms and two legs, a head on its shoulders with two eyes, two ears, a mouth, a nose, even if none of them looked quite human under the red ochre, chalk and charcoal that daubed its face. It wore animal skins and held a thighbone in each hand; as it chanted, it lowered them both to point at Cally.

And she wasn't afraid, that was the strangest thing; for the first time in her dreams of the Pit, she wasn't frightened.

And then she woke, tangled in damp sheets rank with sweat, in the hot and stifling dark.

The room lights came on when Cally pressed the switch, and there were no shadows that moved on their own. Another first: this time, nothing had followed her into the waking world from the Pit. She opened the curtains to let in the light, opened the window to let in the air.

Now what?

She glanced at her laptop, but looked away. She'd no desire to consult her notes, far less listen to the remainder of Tony Mathias' diary.

You know what's coming, Ms Darker.

The contamination, Harrower had implied, had spread from the tape itself. From it to Tony Mathias, to his family and to Peter Culleton, warping each of them into something other than human. She badly wanted to believe Harrower had lied – to torment her, maybe, as he'd obviously despised her sight unseen. A queer woman, fascinated by old crimes? Obviously a perverted degenerate. (*And proud of it, you bastard.*) But she couldn't see Sabharwal as a liar, and his account tallied with Harrower's.

And she hadn't imagined the Cormorant, or the voices coming out of the speakers in Dad's living room. Ellen had also witnessed both.

Cally realised she was rocking back and forth, gripping her head in her hands. She stood up. *Keep it together. Act normal if nothing else, so you aren't carted off and sectioned.*

And what then?

You know how your story ends.

She wouldn't accept that, but had no idea where to go, or to whom. Ellen was gone. Bala was no longer safe. Dad and Lucy were away.

For now. But what if the things Cally had encountered were still at the Bala house? Was it haunted, or only her? Or both?

How much did you have to hear before you were tainted too? If might already have spread to Ellen, dooming her as surely as the Mathias family, as Peter Culleton. As surely as Cally herself.

No. There had to be something. Warden Fell had limits. Whatever inhabited it was confined there, and even then went dormant for long periods. It could spread, but not easily. Not far.

Most importantly, Tony Mathias and Peter Culleton had never sought proper help; they'd been so appalled by what was happening they'd seen death as their only option. Cally had to be rational; it was her only chance. This was a phenomenon like any other, just not one she understood.

The Pit-nightmare still lingered vividly in Cally's memory; she scrabbled through her shoulder-bag for a cheap, battered pocket memo-book and a leaky biro, and wrote down the new incantation as best she could. *Mantakha sa niroleph chir karagh. Insapa veir bereloth. Insapa. Maengrepa gir trequefa gla detiresh meirka.* Maybe she could find something about it online.

But that would mean opening up her computer, and Cally couldn't face that. She didn't want to listen to Tony Mathias' diary and, despite everything, she knew she'd be tempted to and might be unable to resist.

What, then?

Cally checked her phone. It was later than she'd thought; almost seven p.m. Iain would be home now. There were books and clothes and DVDs and CDs – real, concrete things – at his house that Cally wanted back. That was something she could do something about, here and now. Something not remotely related to Eagle Mount or Warden Fell.

Cally went into the bathroom and ran the shower. Iain would expect her to be a mess, the madwoman in the attic. She wouldn't give him that satisfaction.

Whatever the truth of the matter.

44.

When she phoned Iain, the line wasn't great; again, there was static on the line, cross-talk in the background.

Iain clearly hadn't expected her to call, still less to announce she was coming over right now, which gave Cally a certain mean satisfaction. She was surprised how calm she sounded, but after the last few days, this was a comparatively minor challenge.

She spritzed her jeans and shirt with Febreze, applied a little light make-up, and studied her reflection. Hopefully she'd look as though she was doing just fine without him. She knew she wasn't, but it would be nice to make him think so.

Iain didn't live far from the city centre, so Cally was there within half an hour. She was wearing a couple of nice chunky pewter rings as well, so her knock on his door was suitably thunderous.

"Coming," he shouted from inside. Cally put her hands on her hips, striking the most assured pose she could manage, then smiled as the door opened. "What kept you?"

"Ha ha." Iain was still in his work clothes; his face was flushed. "Only just got home. Don't arrange my whole life around *you* anymore." He went back into the house, leaving the door open for her to follow. Cally didn't bother closing it; once she'd carried her belongings to the car she'd no desire to prolong the meeting.

Iain clearly felt the same; there were three clear plastic crates in the living room, inside which Cally could identify various DVDs, CDs, books, clothes and ornaments of hers. "Oh," she said, "thanks."

"Comes from being organised."

"Fair enough," she said; she wasn't here for a fight.

She carried the crates out to the Punto, putting two in the boot and one on the backseat, refusing his offers of help. She really *had* moved on from Iain; she'd hardly given him a thought since leaving, but then, the relationship had really been over for her long before she'd left. She was the one who'd kept things going long past that point.

By the time she'd finished she was feeling downright guilty. She didn't know if they could part as friends, but she should at least try: he'd done his best, by his own lights, to support her; it wasn't his fault he hadn't known how.

Cally went back into the hallway, and met Iain coming back to shut the door; he hadn't expected her to come back in. Hadn't thought they'd anything left to say.

"Look," she said, "I'm sorry about–"

"What the *fuck*?"

She'd more or less automatically held her arms out to him as she spoke. An open gesture, welcoming; it might even have become a hug. But he was staring at her left arm as though she'd offered him a dog-turd.

The short-sleeved shirt left her forearms bare; had the day been colder she'd have worn a sweatshirt or a hoodie, and Iain wouldn't have seen anything. But that would only have delayed the revelation.

A tapering growth about seven inches long sprouted from Cally's inner arm, just below the elbow, its livid purple colour shading into the white of her skin where they joined.

She thought at first – or tried to convince herself – that she'd developed some sort of freakish skin-tag, but then it moved, its tip swaying to and fro before lunging towards Iain. He stumbled back, tripped and fell; Cally tried to grab the growth, but it writhed free, exposing an underside even whiter than her skin, lined with rows of suckers.

"Jesus Christ." Iain scooted back down the hallway on his arse. "Jesus *Christ*."

"Iain," she said.

"Get out." There was an ugly, near-hysterical note of panic in his voice as he scrambled to his feet. *What are you scared of, dipshit? You're not the one with a tentacle growing out of her arm.* "Get the fuck out of my house."

He stepped towards her, fists clenched, then drew back. Afraid he'd touch the tentacle, or it would touch him. Instead, he snatched the mop in its bucket at the foot of the stairs.

Cally burst out laughing. *Hysteria*. From the Greek *hystera*, meaning *womb*, because people used to believe it was caused by women's wombs wandering around their bodies. *That's what happens when you let men practice medicine*, she thought, which made her laugh again.

But it was definitely time to leave. However ludicrous a spectacle Iain presented, he might still injure her or worse. And under the laughter, the panic was mounting, driving the self-possession she'd so briefly felt away.

The world spun. Only God or the Devil knew how she'd get back to the hotel. Not that she believed in either. Or Hell. Or so she told herself. She stumbled as she backed out of the doorway, but managed not to fall, although she practically collapsed against the Punto, tumbling inside once she opened the door.

Iain emerged from the house, still clutching the mop. Cally started the engine and watched him recede in the rearview mirror.

Before getting out of the car, Cally retrieved a black New Model Army hoodie from the backseat crate and pulled it on to conceal the growth. As on her return from Harrower's bungalow, she made her way through the lobby and back to her room with an effort, shaking badly, but on getting there resisted the urge to crawl into bed and hide. She couldn't afford that now, and sleep would be no refuge. She'd find herself in the Pit again, and when or if she woke there was no telling what she'd have become.

Hanging a DO NOT DISTURB sign on her door, Cally turned on the lights and pulled the curtains, then sat on the end of the bed, hands over her mouth, trying not to sob too loudly. Finally, steeling herself, she peeled off the hoodie and forced herself to study her arm.

The tentacle had twined itself around her forearm; when exposed, it stirred and swayed back and forth, as if tasting the air. It looked longer than before; Cally hoped that was her imagination. When had it appeared? How had she not noticed?

Gingerly she touched it; it recoiled, then wrapped itself about her fingers. She pulled free and rubbed her hand convulsively against her thigh, trying to wipe the rubbery, faintly slimy feel of it away.

It was growing out of a white, stretched swelling on her arm. The join between the two was a smeared jumble of purple and white; it was impossible to see exactly where one became the other.

When she ran her fingers down her other arm from elbow to wrist, she found a smooth, raised bump, like the hives from a nettle-sting but wider, and perfectly round. When she held it close to her face, she saw a purple speck at the centre.

No more pretending, then. Harrower wasn't lying, or Sabharwal. Tony Mathias wasn't insane – or if he was, it was because of a strain nobody could have borne. He and his family started changing. So did Peter Culleton.

And so, now, was she.

It must have started when she listened to the first recordings. The Mathiases, and Culleton, had all thought they'd had a virus: runny nose and streaming eyes, sore throat, general debility. Like a cold, or flu. Or the hay fever Cally had already been suffering from; she wouldn't have even noticed when the change began.

No more denial; she had to know the worst. Cally undressed and went to the full-length bathroom mirror. She was haggard and shaking, teary-eyed, her hair in disarray. But none of that mattered now.

She found more bumps like the one on her right arm. Many were mottled and purple in the centre; several were swelling. From one, a few inches above her hip, the tip of a tentacle and three or four suckers protruded.

The fire had destroyed all evidence of whatever Tony and Lindsay had been becoming, but Peter Culleton had been turning into a hybrid of fly and lizard; Alison Mathias had sprouted feathers, Neal had had scales and pointed ears. Griff, at least in her nightmare, had developed segmented, chitinous limbs.

Hybrids. Chimeras. Like the Cormorant, the Toad, and the Eel. Maybe they'd been people too, once, until they'd heard the song of the damned.

Cally checked her arms for black fur, but to her relief there was no sign of any, at least for now.

Her tangled hair fell over one eye. When she raised a hand to push it back, her elbow caught her left breast; a sharp pain went through her.

"Fuck." Cally cupped her breast and leant closer to the mirror. A dried, yellowish substance crusted her nipple. She swallowed hard; her aunt had died of breast cancer when Cally was thirteen, so she was always alert for warning signs.

She moistened a towel and cleaned the dried matter away, but what she saw resembled no cancer symptoms she'd heard of. The nipple itself had disappeared; in its place was a dry horizontal slit like a bloodless half-healed cut. And then it opened. There was no pain, but when the cut's edges peeled back, they revealed a yellow eye with a horizontally-slitted pupil, like a goat's.

There was no holding back a scream this time, although Cally managed to clap both hands over her mouth in time to muffle it. the yellow eye stared back at her unblinkingly, then slowly closed again.

For the first time in her life, Cally thought she might faint; she ran water from the cold tap over her wrists. Millicent had taught her that; Cally had never expected the advice to be of any use.

When she was sure she wasn't going to pass out she went back into the bedroom and put her clothes back on, then sat at the dressing-table in front of the laptop.

She cried for some time. What else could she do? This was the end of everything. All that remained was the same choice Tony Mathias and Peter Culleton had faced: become a monster, or die human.

And use fire, so no one will know.

But even changed, wouldn't she still be Cally Darker? People everywhere lived with disfigurement and deformity.

You think that's all this is? Her nightmares, and everything Harrower had told her, suggested otherwise. But Graham Harrower was a narrow-minded bigot who saw everything unlike himself as evil. And Cally wasn't going to let dreams and folktales dictate her actions.

Who says you'll still be you? Remember Neal Mathias and what was happening to his brain.

Cally doubted any doctor had seen a case like hers before. But if the alternative was suicide, she should at least try.

Get dressed, then, and head to A&E.

Cally started to get up, then stopped. Time was running short – it might already be too late – but any information she could glean would be useful, and better she listen to the recording than others do so and risk contamination themselves.

You know how your story ends.

No. She knew how stories *like* hers had ended. But there

were still gaps, and one of them might hide a chance of survival. If nothing else, she'd know the worst.

Cally opened her laptop, and clicked on Tony Mathias' final diary entry.

Part Three

Trinity

45.

Edna Woodwiss hardly slept anymore, as if her body, realising how little time remained, sought to experience every possible moment. As a result she often read late into the night, dozing off in a nest of cushions on the sofa. It made her ache in the mornings, of course, but most things did these days.

Her sleep was fitful; she'd often surface, rising to answer the call of nature or brew a pot of tea. But she knew as soon as she woke this time, blinking and squinting, that something was different now.

When she realised what it was she was unable – much to her own annoyance – to hold back a gasp.

A man was sitting in the armchair opposite her. his upper body was in shadow – the only light in the room was from the lamp beside her – so she could only see one long, trousered leg crossed over another. Edna opened her mouth to cry out, but he raised a finger to his lips and breathed, "Sh," one soft sibilant sound carrying such an infinity of menace Edna immediately closed her mouth again.

He uncrossed his legs and put his hands on the arms of the chair. Recognition began to dawn, but it wasn't until he sniggered that Edna knew. That rapid triple snort through his nose: *thn-thn-thn.*

"Roland?" Fresh from sleep, her voice was more of a grating croak than ever.

"Hello, Mumsy." Roland leant into the light. His red, happily smiling face; his beady little blue eyes. Edna had accepted years ago she loathed her only child, but never so much as now. She feared him as well, but then she'd been afraid of Roland for a long time now.

"I thought it was time we had a little chat," he said.

"Did you, indeed?" Edna shuffled upright, clenching her arthritic hands. "You picked your time for it."

"Needs must."

"I'm surprised they let you in this late."

Thn-thn-thn. "I didn't have to ask. I have ways and means now, Mumsy. A lot's changed for me lately. Things are looking up, you might say. I'm going to have some fun at long last. Lots and lots of fun."

Edna swallowed hard, knowing as she did what Roland called *fun*. "Not afraid of the police anymore, then?"

"No," he said, simply. "After tomorrow night, no one will be. And it's all thanks to you, Mumsy."

He'd finally gone completely mad, all his lust and hatred, bottled up so long, boiling over at last. But madmen should be humoured, or so Edna had always heard. "Oh? What is it I've done?"

Roland pretended to look surprised. "Don't you know? Pretty Cally Darker, Mumsy. You talked to her, didn't you, Mumsy? Told her secrets? Gave her secret things you wouldn't give to me."

Edna's throat felt very tight.

Roland shook his head. "Mumsy thought she was so clever, didn't she? Mumsy thought Roland didn't know knew about Mr Tony Mathias' tapes. But I did. I just didn't know what you'd done with them."

"Can we not just get on with this?" another voice, with a faint Geordie accent. Further back, in the deeper shadows of the room, Edna now saw two more men. One stood straight and soldier-like; the one who'd spoken leant on a cane. *I know that voice*, thought Edna. "Just do what you've got to do. I'm tired, I just want to go home–"

"Shut up!" The words *reverberated*, as if blasted through

a speaker system, which Edna was sure would rouse the neighbours, but there was only silence. The man with the cane shrank back; Edna found she was glad she couldn't see Roland's expression.

Roland turned back to her. A smile now stretched across his face, exposing his white teeth. His little blue eyes gleamed, and Edna Woodwiss thought her son might be the most terrible thing she'd seen. All the times she'd thought him corrupted somehow, tainted in her womb; she knew now at last that it hadn't been fanciful at all. And neither her nor Adrian Woodwiss' genes had been responsible, but something else entirely.

"I didn't know what you'd done with them," he repeated. "But I realised I didn't *have* to. Because *I* didn't need to listen to them. Someone else had to do that. Someone very special, and they had to do it in all innocence, of their own free will. And all of a sudden, there she was. Pretty Cally Darker. And you were so lonely, so desperate for a little company. Someone to talk to. So you gave them to her, didn't you? And pretty Cally Darker listened. And now, it's going to be Tony Mathias and 1983 all over again."

Oh, God. Edna had liked the Darker girl; the thought of any harm coming to her, especially a repetition of *that*, was appalling.

"Only," said Roland, "much, much *better*. Things are going to change, and I'm going to have lots and lots of fun. All thanks to you, Mumsy. You thought you were so clever, but in the end you gave me exactly what I needed. It's going to be very special. I'm sorry you won't see it. But I wanted you to know."

Edna straightened up as far as she could. She wouldn't show fear. She would *not*. "So you've come to kill me."

He beamed and nodded.

"Won't that look a bit suspicious, right after your visit?"

He shook his head. "You don't *listen*, Mumsy. You *never* listen. I told you: after tomorrow night, the police won't matter.

But no one knows I'm here anyway. Besides, there won't be a single mark on you. See?"

He lifted a hand, and Edna felt a terrible pressure around her heart. The tired old muscle struggled to beat, but the pressure grew and grew; there could be only one ending.

"I'm just sorry it has to be so *quick*," Roland said. "I'd much rather have made this *last*. But I've things to attend to, places to be." His teeth glinted, and his eyes. "People to do. Still, as I said, I wanted you to know."

Edna tried to reply. One last comeback. But the pressure in her chest grew intolerable, and she felt her heart collapse like an empty beer-can. She couldn't breathe. The room darkened.

"Goodbye, Mumsy," said her son.

Roland Woodwiss sat and watched his mother die. Her eyes roved helplessly in their sockets, became fixed and unblinking, then slowly began to glaze. He'd always known she wouldn't suffer long enough, but he'd still hoped it wouldn't be quite so fast.

"Well?" said the third man. "That it? Had your fun?"

He didn't even bother to hide his disgust. He didn't respect Roland. Neither of them did. But he'd let it go for now. They didn't know who was in charge just yet. But they would.

He'd thought he'd feel better when he saw his mother die. After all, she'd always hated him. He'd disgusted her, just by *existing*, and that had hurt terribly. People had always flinched away from him as if he was unclean, however polite or helpful he was, however hard he worked. He'd done all the things a good boy was supposed to do, but other children, work colleagues, and most of all girls like pretty Cally Darker had all turned away. But all that might have been supportable, if his mother hadn't shown the same revulsion.

He'd never say so out loud: *Mummy didn't love me* was a pathetic excuse for anything. But he had loved her once, and she'd hurt him terribly with the disgust she'd been increasingly unable to hide. He'd thought seeing her die – alone, afraid, in pain – would be satisfying. But it wasn't.

Instead, he felt something stir in him that felt disgustingly like grief.

I don't feel sad, Roland Woodwiss told himself. *I don't feel bad. I don't.*

"Yes," he said at last. "I'm finished."

He kept his eyes fixed on the third man's, trying to stare him down, but couldn't, quite. In the end it was Roland who looked away. But that would change as well.

All that and more.

"Let's be on our way," he said. "We've work to do."

A pale light began to shine. It quickly grew too bright for the naked eye to bear; then, with a sound like a long deep sigh, it faded, and the room was empty. Only Edna Woodwiss remained, growing cold among her cushions, waiting to be found.

46.

There was no missing it this time; when the final file began to play, over the hiss and crackle and Tony Mathias' heavy breathing, the murmured refrain was loud and clear.

"Wednesday," Tony said. "Eighth of June, 1983."

The tape stopped – a second of silence – then played again. He sighed.

"No," he said. "Just played this back. It's still there. No getting rid of it. , wherever I go. I'm recording this in my car, halfway up the motorway from home, but it's still there. Bet if I turn on the radio, it'll come out of that too." A pause. "May as well test the theory."

A click, a burst of static, then music. Cally recognised the song: Echo and the Bunnymen. *The Killing Moon.* The volume rose till the sound distorted, she heard the now-familiar chant being spoken over the song as well, overlapping with the main background sound.

The radio snapped off. "So it isn't just the tapes anymore," said Tony, profound weariness in his voice. "Same as it's not just Warden Fell that's haunted now. It's me. It's *us.*"

His voice cracked; Cally felt the anguish in it. "If I'd known, I'd never have… but it doesn't matter now, does it? Too late."

A few seconds' silence.

"Not much point recording this, really. I want people to *know*, but the sound will pass it on. Warden Fell's tainted, and now so am I, and Lindsay, and Neal. Even Alison. Oh, God." A shuddering breath. "Irony is, of course, that no one'd believe it, but if they listen to this they'll get concrete fucking proof."

The tentacle on Cally's left arm was still again, fastened around her wrist. She told herself, once more, it hadn't grown.

"I could put it in writing," Tony said. "Even *that* might not be safe, but... Okay. I'm going to run through it. If I *can* get away with writing it down, I can refer to this." A grim laugh. "I'll be busy enough trying to make it legible."

Cally paused the recording and made coffee, adding milk and every sugar sachet. She knew she was wasting time, but she needed sweetness and comfort, and they were nowhere else to be found.

"I stopped playing the tapes, but the sound followed me. When I switched on the radio, played a record or cassette, it came out of the speakers. All the little bits and pieces from Warden Fell, but most of all that chant. For the purposes of any future transcript, it's *Angana sor varalakh kai torja, angana sor varalakh cha voran*. Although I probably shouldn't write that down. No idea what it means. I don't recognise the language, but there's a lot of languages out there. Living and dead. I suspect this is the second kind."

Silence. Ragged breathing. Very faintly, in the background, the swoosh and hiss of passing traffic. But most of all, the chant.

"Started getting bad static on the TV, as well. Could barely get a picture. And I started worrying about what I *might* see. Especially when the sounds started coming out the speakers there too. I thought about burning the tapes, but they were my only proof. Back when I thought someone might be able to help. We're past that now. It's affecting us all, and not just physically. I'm afraid of my own children. The things they're starting to say. I suppose it's because they're young. Kids are more vulnerable to disease of every kind; if you're still growing and developing the taint must corrupt the process. I hardly know them anymore. Nor does Lindsay – she's told me. We can both feel things changing inside us. In our heads. Wanting to do cruel things, ugly things. People would be horrified if they saw what we're becoming, but part of me's starting to *want* that. See the terror on their faces. Spread the taint. See them start to change, too. I want to hurt people. To destroy. I have never, *ever* wanted that. It's not just corrupting my body. It's corrupting my mind. Maybe even my soul, if there's such a thing. Stella called last night. I tried talk her into coming up. And yet it wasn't me doing it. It was, and it wasn't. As if I was no longer in control. I managed to come back to myself in time, told her to stay away. But that was when I realised – what's happening isn't going to stop. And so, last night..."

He'd begun to cry. "Last night, Lindsay and I did a terrible thing. Or rather, I did, but she agreed. We both agreed it was the only way. There's no stopping this. Nothing any doctor can do, but at least we're still ourselves right now. Or Lindsay and I are, anyway. The children..." A shuddering breath. "Oh Christ, if there's an afterlife, and we carry *this* into it with us. No. It's got to end when we die. Please God, let it end then."

The tape crackled. The traffic swished. The chant murmured on. When he finally spoke again, Tony sounded horribly calm.

"We had sleeping pills. Barbiturates. A lot of them. I saw a television play where a mother killed herself and her kids – made them all cocoa and ground up all her pills into it. Thought I'd do the same. The gentle sleep. But we all woke up the next morning. Maybe there weren't enough."

Both children had been given barbiturates, Sabharwal had told Cally; *more than double the lethal dose for an adult male. They should already have been dead.*

"But I'm pretty sure there were," said Tony. "I think what we're becoming takes an awful lot of killing. It's going to take a lot more than drugs."

A rustle of paper. "I've never used a gun on a living creature. Ever. Couldn't. Not even rats. But I *can* use a gun, and I used to be a very good shot. At least with paper and cardboard. So *can* I do this, now? I've no idea. But if I don't... I don't think Lindsay could. She couldn't give them the pills, last night. Besides, it *should* be me. I started this. I've made it happen. But killing anything's hard enough – never mind your own wife, your own kids. But I don't see any other choice. If I don't stop this, it'll *spread*. And it *is* my fault. I didn't know, but I still went to Warden Fell. I still brought the taint home with me. I'm the one who's got to end it."

Another rustle. "There's an ad in the local rag. A shotgun for sale. I can do it quickly with something like that. I'm going to ring him after this. I know the guy – if I offer more money, he won't ask questions or want to see a licence. Lindsay, first, so she doesn't have to see. She might try and stop me, if she did. Knowing it's necessary isn't the same as being able to do it. Then the children. Then burn everything. The tapes. Everything. Us. Nothing left to spread the taint."

A lighter clicked; even the chanting seemed to fade. Cally heard him draw forty-year old smoke into long-dead lungs. "This recording's probably pointless. Same with trying to write it up. I think either will spread the taint. Worst thing is, I'm doing this because I love my family. I love my wife, I love my daughter, I love my son. I can't let this happen to us. Or anyone else. But if I do the job right, no one will ever understand that. At best, I'll be remembered as a madman. Murdered his family, killed himself."

The chant began to rise again.

"Well," said Tony Mathias at last, "so be it."

And that was the end.

Well, now you know it all. Feel any better?

Cally didn't dare look at herself, afraid her own change might have progressed further.

You know how your story ends.

No. A long succession of people, from Millicent on, had done their best to convince Cally she was in some way irremediably defective. Too loud, too opinionated, too disrespectful; not thin enough, not ladylike enough, not normal enough. Mad or a loser, a fuck-up or a failure. That she was, simply, *wrong*, and the world would be better for her absence. To kill herself would be to prove them right: that had become one of Cally's weapons against suicidal thoughts. But now she couldn't even tell if she was resisting the idea because of her own will to survive, or the influence of the taint.

Again, she remembered what Sabharwal had told her: *Neal Mathias' brain wasn't that of a human anymore, or even any animal species I know. Perhaps we're into the realm of flying saucers and little green men, or witches and devils.*

The mirror above the dressing-table showed Cally her old familiar face; unchanged, but only for now. No telling what she might become tomorrow, or the day after.

There's no stopping this. Nothing any doctor can do.

Except Tony Mathias couldn't have known that for sure. He'd just assumed it. Cally shut the laptop and stood up. If nothing else, she'd try.

47.

They'd put her in a single room; Cally hadn't thought hospitals still had those. Then again, hers weren't the usual issues people found in a Manchester A&E on Friday night: no stab wounds, no broken bones, no foreign objects stuck in her back passage.

I fell on it, I swear. Cally managed a weak laugh. She sat on the edge of the bed in a hospital gown, clothes folded on the chair by the bed, shoulder-bag on the floor by the chair. The hoodie had covered her forearm, but the gown left it exposed. When she hugged herself the tentacle stirred, trying to twine around her fingers again. She couldn't bear to touch it; looking at it was bad enough.

The hospital receptionist had seemingly felt the same way; her eyes had widened, the blood visibly draining from her florid face. Dr Mansaray, a small, gentle man who spoke with a soothing West African accent and insisted she call him Joseph, had been no less shocked. He'd fetched a porter and wheelchair and rushed her here, telling her to change into the hospital gown and wait; he'd be back shortly to conduct a proper examination.

That had been half an hour ago.

They were probably trying to decide what tests to run. Blood tests, tissue samples, X-rays, MRIs. No point cutting off the tentacles or gouging out the eye without seeing what they were connected to, and how far they extended under the skin.

Maybe Tony Mathias had been right and this was beyond any doctor's help; maybe he and Peter Culleton had made the only decision possible. But Cally still had that option, and her

263

laptop was in her shoulder-bag so she could destroy it along with herself, leaving no clues for others to investigate and contaminate themselves with.

What about Griff?

That had to be faced as well; if she was contaminated, so was he – possibly even worse than her Cally had to make sure he couldn't spread the taint either.

So, suicide and murder?

She laughed again. Full circle: in seeking to understand Tony Mathias' actions, she'd condemned herself to reenact them.

Not necessarily. Give the doctors a chance.

Voices outside. She couldn't make out the words, but one was Dr Mansaray's, raised in protest. The other had clipped, upper-class vowels, and a decidedly steely tone. Dr Mansaray fell silent; seconds later, footsteps approached the door.

This doesn't feel good.

Four men came in. Two paramedics, one blond-haired, one brown, pushing a hospital gurney; a male nurse in blue scrubs, with red hair and a round, blotchy face. The fourth man, fair-haired and blue-eyed, had a white coat and a stethoscope. "Good evening, Ms Darker. I'm Dr Maxfield."

He didn't sound like a medical man or look like one, despite the coat and stethoscope. None of them did; all four men had lean, hard physiques, hard faces and implacable eyes. Soldiers, whatever clothes they wore.

MOD. Warden Fell.

Maxfield had obviously expected more of a response from Cally, and his thin smile faded when none came. He motioned to the gurney. "If you'll just hop aboard, we'll take you somewhere we can help you."

People like this had shown up after the Eagle Mount killings, making sure that the whole affair was quickly buried and any documentation disappeared, and after Peter Culleton's demise too. They must receive an alert when a hospital registered a patient with certain symptoms. What you couldn't prevent, you could cover up. Stella and Sabharwal were wrong: Warden Fell wasn't yesterday's news at all.

You really screwed up this time.

They probably expected Cally to be so scared she'd obey without question. Part of her wanted to. *Believe and obey*: life was so much simpler when you did.

But she'd never been good at that. "Where, exactly?" she said.

"I'm sorry?" Maxfield clearly didn't like that; his smile had disappeared completely.

"Where are you taking me?"

"I've already told you."

"No, you haven't. What's this place called? Whereabouts in the country is it? What sort of treatments does it specialise in? Do you have a diagnosis yet? Or a prognosis?"

"What?" He wasn't used to having his orders questioned, this one. Which was something doctors handled every day. They dealt with far worse than Cally – people who were terrified, angry, even violent – and had to keep their cool. Maxfield didn't, and it showed.

She'd never know, now, if Dr Mansaray could have helped her or not; she'd no doubt Maxfield only cared about keeping the lid on Warden Fell. She might as well resist however she could; she wouldn't get a better chance.

"Prognosis," she repeated. "What have I got, and what's going to happen to me? Is there a treatment? What are my chances of survival?"

"Everything will be made clear once we get where we're going," said Maxfield, with what was obviously the last of his patience. The nurse looked impassive; the two paramedics watched with faint smiles and darting, watchful eyes.

They don't see their commanding officer being told to get stuffed often; that's why they're smiling. But they also know it won't end well; that's why their eyes are all over the place. They're waiting for it to kick off.

"There's no reason you can't tell me where we're going," said Cally. "I've a right to know that."

The blond paramedic flinched; the brown-haired one looked down. Maxfield, on the other hand, smiled: a genuine one this time. "You have no rights any longer, Ms Darker. No one does when Department Nine's involved. Allow me to illustrate. Gullis? Level One."

The nurse was already moving towards Cally. He held something flat and black in one hand: blue sparks flickered around the twin prongs at one end.

Cattle-prod, she realised, but before she could react the muscles of her body were wrenched violently; she wasn't sure if she cried out or not, but she tumbled off the bed, landing painfully on the floor.

Gullis picked up Cally's shoulder-bag and clothes, stuffed them into a compartment under the gurney, then folded a hatch shut. *Click*. The paramedics lifted her onto the trolley, then helped Gullis strap her down. Something cold and hard touched her neck.

Maxfield smiled down at her. "That, Ms Darker, is the business end of a silencer. The pistol it's attached to isn't very powerful, but at this range it doesn't *have* to be. you'll still be very, very dead. The bullet will sever your spinal cord, so there'll be hardly any blood. We'll just arrange your hair to cover any awkward red stains, wheel you out and no one will be any the wiser. I make myself clear? Nod, Ms Darker. Don't speak. I've heard *quite* enough of your voice for one day."

Cally visualised Maxfield hanging upside down from a tree, legs tied wide apart, while she took a handsaw to his groin. Then nodded.

"If you're a good little girl, you stand a chance of survival. Not a great one, admittedly, but a chance nonetheless. So will you be a good little girl, Ms Darker?"

Cally nodded again, and even managed a smile, largely because she'd now decided the handsaw would be a blunt one.

"Excellent," repeated Maxfield. "Gentlemen?"

Gullis opened the door, and the paramedics wheeled Cally through.

48.

The ceiling glided over Cally's head: fluorescent lights, grey-black speckled tiles. She glimpsed Dr Mansaray, mouth open as if to protest. But Gullis pushed him back; the gurney kept rolling, and he was gone.

Cattle-prods and silenced guns in a city-centre hospital; whatever she'd expected, it hadn't been that.

But it made sense, however brutal. If Maxfield *was* connected to Warden Fell, he'd know about the Mathiases, including the massive drug overdoses that had utterly failed to affect them. Even if Cally wasn't currently immune to sedatives or poison – not a theory she could easily test – chances were, she would be soon. Maxfield clearly didn't want to gamble. A shot to the head had been enough for the Mathiases; fire alone had sufficed for Culleton.

The gurney rolled into a lift. Steel doors closed with a soft chime, cutting off the hospital's hubbub. Maxfield and the others loomed over Cally, gazing down at her as though she were a laboratory specimen.

She looked straight up, avoiding their cold, empty stares, to see her own pale, frightened face, staring back at her from the lift's reflective ceiling.

In researching the podcast, Cally had seen several YouTube videos about firearms, enough to know that silencers – or *sound suppressors*, as you were apparently supposed to call them – were nowhere near as quiet as Hollywood portrayed them. Maxfield had probably feared drawing unwanted attention if he'd shot her in the hospital, silencer or no.

Maybe they'll kill you if necessary, but treat you if they can.

Or use her as a lab-rat, ending up dead and dissected.

The back of Maxfield's head was reflected in the ceiling. He had a large bald spot with strands of hair combed over it, like Cally's old maths teacher. He'd been completely bald on top; when he went outside on a windy day the swatch of hair he'd combed across his bare scalp would billow out to the side, like a windsock. Cally couldn't hold back a giggle at the memory.

"Something amusing, Ms Darker?" There was a faint smile on Maxfield's lips again.

"*We shall overcomb,*" Cally sang, still giggling, before she could stop herself. Maxfield's hand went up to his bald patch and he glared up at the ceiling. When he looked back down, he wasn't smiling anymore, and his face was brick-red.

A soft chime; the lift had arrived. Maxfield turned and pushed a button, and the doors stayed shut. "Very droll, Ms Darker. Gullis? Level One."

Gullis actually hesitated for a second, but Maxfield's eyebrows rose a fraction of an inch, daring him to disobey. Blue sparks flickered around the end of the prod.

"Please," Cally heard herself say, and immediately despised herself, knowing pleading wouldn't help. Another convulsion wrenched her; after that she was only vaguely aware of the doors opening and the gurney rolling through more corridors.

Then they were outside. Night sky. Neon light. Cool air, surprisingly fresh. Traffic sounds. Sirens. Voices.

Barked instructions. Doors opening. The gurney went up a ramp. Doors slammed, shutting out the night sounds.

Inside a vehicle. Metal walls painted sickly green. Strip lights in the ceiling, harsh and bright. An ambulance, she guessed, or something that resembled one from outside. Maxfield, Gullis and the paramedics sat along a bench seat opposite Cally. Maxfield's face was still red.

Worth it, she decided.

See if you still think so when we get where we're going.

The engine growled into life. The ambulance lumbered through the car park, then turned onto an open road, gathering speed as it wove through traffic. Maxfield gazed down at her; the flush had faded from his blank, empty face. She was a thing in a lab once more.

She couldn't tell how long they drove, as there was no clock. The ambulance rolled smoothly along. No stopping and starting, so they weren't trying to negotiate the city centre streets anymore. A motorway? Cally doubted it; they'd be going faster.

Maxfield smiled down at her. She craned her neck, pulling her head back to see the driver's compartment. She made out the driver in the front seat, and beyond that, the windscreen.

Or the upper part of it, anyway; to see more she'd need extendable eye-stalks she could extrude into the driver's compartment. She regretted that thought immediately; it was nowhere near as ludicrous as it would have been yesterday.

She couldn't see any details of the road itself, only the glare of the ambulance's headlights. No streetlights, no other lighting of any kind. She thought she glimpsed trees, or hedges, skimming by. A country lane; somewhere far from other people. No houses, no other cars.

Where no one can hear you scream.

"This will do," said Maxfield. "Pull over, Hotchkiss."

The ambulance veered left and halted. The engine's growl died. Silence.

"Oh, Ms Darker?"

Maxfield had removed his white coat; now he drew the silenced pistol from his waistband. It was tiny, almost a toy: the silencer was longer than the gun. It looked ridiculous.

A fist closed round Cally's stomach and another round her throat. "What happened to that chance of survival?"

"I *lied*, Ms Darker. We have one job, and that job is Warden Fell. We take it seriously, and we don't take chances."

Maxfield raised the gun. The hole at the end of the silencer must be tiny, but from Cally's vantage point it looked enormous. Maxfield's mouth opened, doubtless to deliver some final *bon mot*. One cheap quip, then a bullet between the eyes.

"Sir!"

Maxfield looked annoyed. "What is it, Hotchkiss?"

"Company, sir. Road ahead."

Maxfield lowered the gun, face cold and blank. "What are we looking at?"

"Three men, on foot, spread out across the road. Still coming."

Maxfield peered ahead through the windscreen. "Drunks walking home," he said, but didn't sound convinced. He motioned to the blond-haired paramedic. "Let them pass, watch them go, tell me when we're clear. Then we can finish this and enjoy what's left of our weekend."

"Sir?" said Hotchkiss. "They've stopped. 'Bout fifteen yards ahead."

"What are they doing?"

"Nothing. Just… standing there."

The strip lights flickered.

"Playing silly buggers, eh?" Maxfield said. "All right, drive on. We'll finish this somewhere else."

"They're spread out across the road, sir. Want me to–"

Maxfield sighed. "No. Just turn us round, back the way we came."

"Sir."

The engine groaned and sputtered, without turning over. Once, twice, three times.

"Hotchkiss," said Maxfield, in a velvety, threatening tone.

"It's the engine, sir. I don't know what–"

The lights flickered again.

"Shit," said the brown-haired paramedic.

"Let's keep it together, shall we, Rossner?" Maxfield murmured. "Deal with it, Gullis. Take Marsan with you. You're both cleared for Level Four."

"Understood, sir." Gullis reached under his scrubs again, but this time drew a Glock automatic and pulled back the slide to chamber a round.

No prizes for guessing what Level Four was, then. What were Levels Two and Three? Drugs? A beating? Maybe just the threat of using the gun.

The blond paramedic – Marsan –drew another Glock and racked the slide. Gullis opened the rear doors and stepped out. Marsan followed.

"Get that engine started, Hotchkiss," Maxfield said. "Now. No excuses."

Hotchkiss clearly tried, because the engine sputtered again, and again, but with no more success than before. The striplights blinked on and off.

"Shit," said Rossner again.

"Moderate your language, Rossner," said Maxfield. "And exercise a little more self-control."

"Sir."

Maxfield stood and waited. He ignored Cally. She was irrelevant, after all, securely strapped down and awaiting execution. She doubtless wasn't the first. The Mathiases and Culleton were only the deaths she knew about. No telling how many more had been required to keep Warden Fell's secrets. She remembered CORRAN, the urbexer who'd explored the airbase – how had they missed him? Maybe they hadn't. If, as Harrower had said, the place was like a volcano – sometimes lethal, sometimes dormant – and CORRAN had stumbled across it during one of those quiescent periods, seeing, doing and most importantly becoming nothing of interest. Department Nine might have merely taken note of him, then done no more.

Cally guessed she was destined for a crematorium somewhere, to simultaneously destroy the contamination and make her disappear without trace. If so, the fire could handle four bodies as easily as one; Maxfield wouldn't trouble himself over three drunks who refused to get out of his way.

But these aren't drunks rolling home from the pub. The flickering lights, the stalling engine. This is something else.

Voices from the road outside. "All right, fellas?" said Gullis. "What's up?"

Their reply was a whisper at first; Cally couldn't hear what they were saying, but realised it was three voices, all speaking in unison.

"Lads?" Gullis said again.

The strip lights flickered faster. With a faint, soft 'ting,' one went out.

The whispers became louder, clearer, and Cally made out the words.

"Angana sor varalakh kai torja. Angana sor varalakh cha voran."

"Oh shit," she said. "Oh, *shit.*"

It wasn't just the chant; she could feel things move inside her. In her guts; under her skin. Things that weren't part of any normal human anatomy. Something else was growing there, rooted in her flesh.

Cally felt a tearing sensation as something buried under the skin of her arm ripped free; it didn't hurt, but the absence of pain only made it more terrifying.

Maxfield glanced at her, then looked through the windscreen again. He'd grown very pale: "Level Four!" he shouted. "Gullis! Level Four, *now!*"

Gunshots rang out: loud, violent cracks. Maxfield turned back to Cally, raising his pistol. No parting words this time, it seemed.

Something whipped across her field of vision, fast and blurred; Maxfield cried out in pain and his gun-hand was jerked aside. There was a loud, metallic *snap*, then a crack of metal hitting metal. A faintly sulphurous smell; a puff of thin grey smoke. Another *snap*; this time she saw the little gun twitch, an empty cartridge jumping from the breech, but once again the shot smacked into the floor, because the pistol was pointing down and away.

Outside, there was more gunfire, but the chanting didn't stop, or even falter.

There was a cracking sound, and Maxfield screamed. Something was wrapped around his wrist, pulling ever tighter, like a noose. It was purple-coloured, with a white, suckered underside, and led from his arm to Cally.

Someone screamed outside, too, and there were wet, ugly sounds of things tearing like wallpaper and snapping like brittle wood. Another scream, and the gunfire cut out altogether, but the chant went on.

"Jesus Christ!" Hotchkiss shouted.

Maxfield dropped the pistol. His hand was dark and swollen and hung askew like an empty glove from a stick. "Rossner!"

Rossner had been gawping at the windscreen, mesmerised by whatever was happening up ahead, but now spun round; he stared at Cally, then reached under his hi-vis jacket and drew an automatic, racking the slide.

The tentacle released its hold, sending Maxfield tumbling backwards. It flew up, now so long it almost reached the ceiling, then sliced downwards to coil around Rossner's neck. A violent movement whiplashed along it, snapping Rossner's head askew on his shoulders: Cally both heard and felt the broomstick crack as his neck broke.

Maxfield tried to get up, but the tentacle let Rossner's body drop, then caught him around the neck as well. Cally shut her eyes, but heard and felt his spine break too.

The chanting from the road rose to a thunderous pitch, almost but not quite drowning out the screams.

"Fuck," shouted Hotchkiss. "*Fuck–*"

Something slammed into the front of the ambulance. Glass shattered, glittering fragments spraying the interior; Hotchkiss' scream was abruptly cut off, and the ambulance was shunted backward. It lurched abruptly, down and to the side; *off the road and into a ditch*, Cally realised as the gurney careered towards the open doors.

It slewed out through them, with her still tied helpless to it, then flipped over and crashed to the ground.

Then there was only darkness, the chanting, and the screams.

49.

Cally's face was buried in earth and grass; she could smell damp soil and stagnant water. The gurney pinned her down; she struggled, but couldn't lift her face to breathe.

Just when she was sure she'd suffocate, the gurney rolled off her. Only her feet were still immobilised; a strap around her ankles.

The screams went on and on, and the chanting. *"Angana sor varalakh kai torja. Angana sor varalakh–"*

"Oh, for Christ's sake!"

The chanting faltered and stopped. The screams went on.

"Just put an end to it, man! We needed them dealt with, they're dealt with. For Christ's sake just finish them!"

I know that voice, she thought.

"Shut up!" another man's voice: sulky. Petulant. Like a cruel child. "We've got to complete the incantation. We've got to finish things with her."

He means me. And I know his voice.

"So finish it!" the first voice snapped. "Kill the poor bastards and be done! Bad enough I have to do this at all."

"Look, lads, you're both right." The third voice was that of an old man, with an accent – Geordie, maybe Sunderland. *I know him, too. I know them all.* "Sooner we get this done, sooner we can all go home. Finish them off and do what we have to with the girl."

A heavy breath. "Fine," said the sullen voice. There was a sudden wet crunch and a splattering sound, and cries of disgust from the other two, but the screaming stopped. "Now, can we get on?"

276

Mutters of assent. And the chant began again.

"Angana sor varalakh kai torja. Angana sor varalakh cha voran."

Cally rolled onto her back. The stars wheeled above her; the air was clean and fresh. She kicked and struggled, and got one foot free; the other was now only loosely held, and she tugged that clear as well.

The gurney rocked onto its side next to her. Nearby the ambulance lay half-in and half-out of the ditch. The engine and driver's cabin had been crushed to barely a foot's thickness. Dark, sludgy matter resembling blackcurrant jam oozed out; all that remained of Hotchkiss.

Maxfield lay across the ditch, Rossner a few feet away. Both their heads were twisted at appalling angles; their dead faces stared sightlessly at Cally. She looked away. The ambulance's lights were out, the lane completely dark, but she could see far more clearly than should have been possible.

"Angana sor varalakh kai torja. Angana sor varalakh cha voran."

Another side-effect of her ongoing change, perhaps. What else might have altered? Cally forced herself to look at the tentacle; it was longer and thicker now, no longer emerging above her elbow but from somewhere near her shoulder under the torn, muddy hospital gown. She remembered feeling it tear free of her.

No guessing where the real root of the tentacle was. The men from Department Nine had robbed her of any chance to find out.

The doctors couldn't have helped you anyway. Nobody could.

She'd never know now.

"Angana sor varalakh kai torja. Angana–"

"Shup *up!*" she screamed aloud. There might have been the tiniest pause, but then three men moved out from behind the ambulance towards her and it began again.

She'd half-expected them to be robed and hooded, but they wore quite ordinary clothes. Only the chanting seemed otherworldly; that, and their presence here.

They arranged themselves in a line. The tallest, in the centre, faced Cally directly; the others stood a few yards away on each side. The base of a triangle, with her at its apex.

To her right stood Graham Harrower, dressed exactly as he'd been that afternoon. His had been the first voice she'd heard.

The man on the left wore a suit and leant on a stick. The oldest among them, with silvery-white hair and a deeply lined face. Bernard Gowland: his expression was as blank and empty as that of Maxfield's men, only his lips moving, framing and reframing that unending chant.

The third member of the unholy trinity gazed at her with his unblinking, piggy little eyes, fleshy lips pursed in a smile that could only be called gloating. Roland Woodwiss: another man, like Harrower and Gowland, who'd been so strangely willing to help. Smiling as always now, but with fury in his eyes. At Harrower, for berating him? At Cally? He repelled everyone, Edna had said. In which case, his rage might be against the whole world.

There was movement around her; things whipping through the grass. The tentacle. No: *tentacles*. One glance was all it took to confirm that there were several now, lashing about her. But that wasn't the worst thing; the worst was the movement *inside* her. There were things in motion under her skin. And deeper down, in the guts of her.

They kept repeating those same phrases in unison, and with each repetition the movement inside Cally grew stronger. They were feeding whatever Warden Fell was making her become; accelerating the process so she couldn't cut it short as the Mathiases and Peter Culleton had.

She looked for Rossner's pistol, or Maxfield's silenced pop-gun, but could find neither. Marsan and Gullis had fired dozens of rounds at the Trinity and achieved only their own deaths, but she could at least have turned the gun on herself. She could do nothing to them, while they, just by speaking, could turn her into whatever monstrosity she was fated to become.

"*Angana sor varalakh kai torja,*" the Trinity chorused again. "*Angana sor varalakh cha voran.*"

No stopping them chanting; no stopping the chant, no stopping what it did.

Isn't there?

She remembered. One thing. Maybe. No guarantee it would work; she'd ever only ever heard it used in a dream.

But those dreams weren't dreams. Aren't.

And she'd written it down.

She could still move of her own volition; they hadn't yet robbed Cally of that. She crawled towards the overturned gurney, fumbling at the hatch covering the compartment underneath. There must be a way to open it, but she couldn't find it.

Something unfolded in Cally's abdomen. She felt things tear. Her vision blurred and distorted. Maybe her eyes were stitching themselves closed, ready for new ones forming in her breasts to take over. Would she see through them, or would some other personality do that? Would whatever was essentially Cally herself be evicted from her body? Imprisoned in some tiny corner of it? Extinguished utterly? Or would it be warped into a parody of itself, like her physical form?

Oh God, oh Christ, please.

Her clawing fingers found a catch. She pushed and pressed and pulled. Something clicked. The hatch opened.

No. A new voice now, her own yet not her own. **Don't fight it. It's only change. Welcome it. Embrace.**

The contents of her bag spilled out. Cally pawed at them.

Embrace, said the new voice, almost drowning out even the chant. Then it wasn't an entreaty, but a command: **Embrace!**

Whatever was in her stomach began clawing the inside of Cally's throat. Blood spilled from her mouth.

There it was: her little Silvine memo book with its thin red cardboard cover. Cally fumbled at it, thick-fingered, and held it up in front of her – not looking down at it in case she coughed more blood and obliterated the words that were her last fading hope.

There is no hope. Embrace.

Her vision blurred. She squeezed her eyes shut; opened them. Managed, at last, to focus.

They can't help you. They'll only make it happen faster. Give up. Stop fighting. Embrace.

But why urge her to ignore the words if they'd truly spur this process on? And so Cally began reciting that other chant she'd heard in her last nightmare of the Pit.

"Mantakha sa niroleph chir karagh," she began, haltingly.

"Angana sor varalakh kai torja," chorused Gowland, Woodwiss and Harrower. Something kicked and writhed in her throat. Choking.

Not fair. Cheating.

She forced out the next line: *"Insapa veir bereloth. Insapa."*

"Angana sor varalakh cha voran."

You can't win. Embrace.

But the choking sensation had eased, a little. *"Maengrepa gir trequefa gla detiresh meirka,"* she said.

"Angana sor varalakh kai torja," the three men answered. Was it wishful thinking on Cally's part or did the chant sound a little strained?

"Mantakha sa niroleph chir karagh," she said again. *"Insapa veir bereloth. Insapa."*

You cannot win.

"Maengrepa gir trequefa gla detiresh meirka," she shouted, trying to drown that nagging voice and that chanting chorus.

Embrace. Embrace!

"Angana sor varalakh–"

They really *did* sound more strained now, as if they were having to force the words out. And Cally could speak more easily; her throat was clear. She risked looking up at them as she began the chant again.

"Mantakha sa niroleph chir karagh."

Bernard Gowland was leaning heavily on his stick, looking as though he might fall. Harrower was pale; he looked queasy and sick.

"Insapa veir bereloth. Insapa."

Roland Woodwiss' smile had vanished and his piggy eyes were a-boil with rage. *If looks could kill,* Cally thought. Although he was doing his best to accomplish that with words right now.

Embrace! cried the voice, but now shrill: pleading, almost hysterical. **Embrace! Embrace! Embrace!**

Fuck you too. Cally almost said it aloud but didn't, lest it break the spell. She just kept shouting the new chant, over and over again.

Harrower had vomited down himself. Gowland collapsed to his knees. Roland Woodwiss' lips peeled back from his teeth; little flashes of white light flitted between him and Cally. *"Angana,"* he began, then stopped; he was the only one speaking. *"Angana,"* he prompted again. *"Angana!"*

"Mantakha sa niroleph chir karagh," shouted Cally; Roland reared back, mouth open in pain. Bernard Gowland moaned and Graham Harrower almost fell. *"Insapa veir bereloth. Insapa. Maengrepa gir trequefa–"*

Roland Woodwiss roared, and his eyes turned black. The white flashes of light flurried faster and brighter between them. Cally forced herself to carry on. *"Gla detiresh meirka,"* she concluded, then began again. *"Mantakha–"*

The light became a dazzling, blinding flare, a soundless explosion. She covered her eyes and continued. *"– sa niroleph chir karagh."*

The glow dimmed. When Cally looked up, the road was empty, but she kept speaking. She still felt things moving inside her, but they were weaker now and each time she repeated the incantation, they diminished further. *"Insapa veir bereloth. Insapa."*

embrace, said that other voice, but it was fading. **embrace…**

"Maengrepa gir trequefa gla detiresh meirka," Cally concluded, then began again.

She repeated the incantation, over and over, till everything inside her was still. Finally she trailed off.

All was silent; any nocturnal creatures had long since fled, and who could blame them? The only sound was her own breath, fast and ragged; she forced herself to slow it down before it triggered a panic attack. She couldn't afford that now.

A faint, irregular 'ting' sounded; light flashed and flickered over grass, ditch and lane as the strip lights in the ambulance flickered back into life.

Cally retrieved her clothes from the gurney; once dressed, she stumbled past the wrecked ambulance into the lane. Gullis and Marsan were scattered across the road; she couldn't tell where one ended and the other began. A Glock pistol lay on the tarmac, surrounded by brass casings. An empty magazine lay beside it, and one full, where someone had tried to reload.

Cally picked up the Glock, clumsily inserted the magazine and pushed the weapon into her bag. She told herself it would at least be some defence against anyone else from Department Nine. But she knew who it was really for.

She could feel the tentacle wrapped around her arm, and other, newer growths under her clothing. The movement inside her had stopped for now, but she'd bought herself a reprieve, no more: the ultimate prognosis was the same. The only way to avoid it was the one Tony Mathias had chosen.

But not yet. First she had work to do.

Skirting Gullis and Marsan's remains, Cally took out her smartphone. Losing it would feel like losing a limb, but while she had it, it could be used to trace her. She flung it as far as she could, then took a deep breath of cool night air, and began to run.

50.

The Pit was black and thundering, all sounds blotted out except for the two chants, trying to overcome one another.

Above Cally, on the ledge where the Cormorant had been, squatted the skin-clad figure with the painted face. It extended its hands to her; when Cally reached to take them, she saw coarse black fur now covered her arms completely, and her fingers ended in curved black claws.

If she screamed, the Pit's clamour drowned it out. Peals of metallic laughter came from overhead: the Cormorant wheeled above her, holding something in its clawed feet. Its claws opened, and a wide, flat object plummeted towards her.

Cally flinched, but the object didn't strike the squatting figure or her; it landed flat against the rock-face, clinging to it as it slid down, between Cally and the rock-face.

Her grip on the rock broke; unable to gain any purchase on the flat object, she fell away from the wall of the Pit. But she hung suspended, defying both gravity and the wind.

The object the Cormorant had dropped was a mirror of black glass. Reflected in it was a creature with a goat's horned head and hooved legs and an octopus' bulbous purple sac and tentacles for the middle of its body. A lamprey-like mouth opened and closed in its belly. Its arms were covered in black fur, with long, taloned fingers. The goat's head jerked blindly to and fro; its mouth and eyes were stitched shut.

Above the octopus-body were two white human breasts, with yellow, horizontally-slitted eyes instead of nipples.

Cally screamed in pure revulsion. She wanted to claw at her

eyes with those black talons, but knew it would be futile. It wouldn't stop her seeing that vision. Or becoming it.

And then she began to plummet, and her scream became one of terror.

Broad thick hands seized her wrists.

Cally looked up into the Squatter's painted face. Its brow was a ridge beneath a seamed and sloping forehead, its nose broad and flat. The wide mouth smiled. In triumph, perhaps? Surely not in reassurance. You couldn't believe in hope or mercy here.

(There is no hope. You can't win. Embrace.)

Cally looked up, into its black, deep-set eyes–

And woke.

Cally sat upright on the metal bench seat, gasping in the cold morning air.

A car swept past the bus shelter; the driver, a young man in shirt and tie, barely glanced at her. No shrieks of revulsion, at least; she wasn't a goat-headed monster yet.

Yet.

Without her phone, she'd no idea how long she'd slept. She'd run, then slogged, through a maze of lanes, hopelessly lost. She'd thought she'd never escape, but around dawn the empty fields and coppices had given way to rows of semi-detached houses: she'd reached the outskirts of a town.

By then she'd been exhausted. When she'd found the bus shelter she'd gratefully collapsed onto the seat. She'd only meant to rest briefly before pressing on, but must have fallen almost instantly asleep.

The bus shelter's glass panels were missing and she couldn't find a hand mirror in her shoulder-bag. She shuffled stiffly up the road into the town centre, and finally nerved herself to stop at a shop window.

Her face and hands were still unmarked. The day was already

too warm for the hoodie, but she was afraid to see what was under it and couldn't afford to be noticed: the town was coming to life and there were pedestrians, cars and buses on the street.

In the shopping precinct, a Cash Generator was just opening; it had just turned nine a.m. Cally bought an old flip-phone and charger, and a top-up voucher from a nearby Post Office with her dwindling store of cash: any card transaction, like her discarded smartphone, would be a way to trace her.

She found a stop for a Manchester-bound bus and sat, waiting. She was going to die; that, or become the thing from her last nightmare. Not only her body, she was now sure, but her very *essence*, would be warped and twisted out of true. It would be the end of her, either way: better to die while there was something left.

Her depression might, for once, be her friend. She'd never actively wanted to kill herself, but hadn't always cared if she lived or died. More than once she'd have been content to simply go to sleep and never wake up. Maybe that was helping her face her end with something like equanimity, or perhaps some ancient reflex came into play in these situations. Either way, she had the gun. The way out was ready and prepared.

But first she had to arrange the fire, to destroy all trace of herself. And before that, she'd farewells to say, and a promise to keep.

It was nine-thirty a.m.

The last day of your life.

The bus arrived. She climbed aboard.

She got off on Deansgate. In the Starbucks on the corner of Queen Street, Cally found a quiet corner and plugged her little pay-as-you-go phone into a wall-socket.

She opened her laptop and pretended to work, nursing a latte. The podcast was irrelevant now, of course. Almost everything was.

According to the laptop's clock, the time was now 10.15.

Things to do; farewells to say.

First and foremost, Dad and Lucy. If she told the truth, they'd think she'd collapsed into full-blown psychosis and blame themselves for not seeing it in time. She'd tell them not to, but they still would – Dad especially, which was far more painful than the prospect of her own death.

Iain might actually come in useful for a change, having seen what had happened to her. Although knowing Iain, he was busily convincing himself it hadn't happened, not that Cally could blame him. She'd have done the same, if one look in a mirror wouldn't have prove her wrong.

Cally switched on the laptop's camera to inspect herself. Her face and hands remained unmarked. She was afraid to see what the rest of her looked like, but she'd have to. Find out how bad things were. How long she might have left. Her eyes were bloodshot and unpleasantly gummy; her vision blurred intermittently. She rubbed them; sooner or later they'd be sealed shut permanently, and she'd be seeing out of her breasts. The thought was as ridiculous as it was horrible and she almost laughed out loud.

An elegant thirty-something woman at a nearby table – probably a Yummy Mummy unwinding after the school run – was staring at her. Cally realised she'd been mumbling to herself. *Fuck off* and *who are you looking at*, the first responses that suggested themselves, would get her thrown out of here, and she needed time to gather herself and prepare. She gave the Yummy Mummy her warmest, most apologetic smile instead. "Sorry. Thinking aloud."

The Yummy Mummy looked away. She could feel the wrongness seeping out of Cally, the mark of Warden Fell.

No. Paranoia. Cally had been talking to herself, looked generally rough, and was wearing a black hooded top in mid-summer with the hood pulled up to conceal her red hair. She looked like an addict, or someone in the middle of a breakdown. That was all.

Even so, she peered out through the café's windows. She couldn't see any cause for concern, but then Department Nine were professionals and Cally an amateur. She probably wouldn't even notice them till they were upon her.

And what then?

But she knew already. That was what the Glock was really for. Put the barrel under her chin, and bang. She wouldn't be able to incinerate herself, but no doubt Department Nine would take care of that.

It was busy outside; there were kids who should have been in school. Then Cally remembered: today was Saturday. The Yummy Mummy couldn't have been on a school run. She looked at the woman again, who caught her eye and glanced away once more.

Paranoid again. She's out shopping, or she's dropped her kids off on a playdate. Don't overreact. You don't want to be noticed.

Cally switched the camera off: she didn't want to see herself anymore. She realised she was mumbling again, and almost stopped herself, till she registered what she was saying: *Mantakha sa niroleph chir karagh.*

Was that holding the changes at bay? She might as well check now; she shouldn't stay in the same place too long. As if in agreement, the flip-phone bleeped to signal it was fully charged. Cally set the time – eleven a.m, already – then unplugged and pocketed it before packing away the laptop.

She went into the disabled toilet; it was roomier than the others, and had a full-length mirror. Cally locked the door, then peeled off the hoodie and shirt and dropped her jeans.

She bit her lips, trying not to scream. The first tentacle, now almost two feet long, sprouted from her bicep. But it had been longer when the Trinity had attacked, and had emerged from her shoulder. So it had shrunk, and some of it had sunk back under her skin, at least for now.

However, it was still bigger, and the other white hives and welts were now extruding tentacles of their own, the shortest three inches long, the longest around six. The skin of her midriff remained unbroken, but there were irregular lumps under the surface, hard and bony to the touch. Cally snatched her hand away.

There was black hair now on her shoulders, upper arms and thighs. She didn't think her fingernails were any darker, or longer. She didn't remove her boots or unhook her bra. There was only so much she could bear to see.

Cally made her way down Queen Street to Lincoln Square. On a stone bench beneath the flat drab faces of the office blocks and the bronzed statue of Abraham Lincoln, she made a last effort to plan her final moves.

She'd still no idea what to tell Dad and Lucy; she hoped she'd think of something before the end. She'd had nothing to say to Millicent for years, and hadn't now. Millicent would no doubt feel vindicated by Cally's fate: *I did my best, but she went down the path of lust and wickedness.*

"*Insapa veir bereloth,*" Cally muttered, hoping to slow the sickness' progress a while longer. "*Insapa.*"

Who else?

Ellen. Yes, she'd run away, but Cally didn't hold that against her. And if she'd unknowingly spread the taint to her as well, Ellen deserved an apology from Cally , not vice versa.

She typed Ellen's number into the flip-phone from memory. Another legacy of her relationship with Karl. He'd take Cally's phone so she couldn't call anyone, so memorising numbers had become a reflex.

She didn't trust herself to call Ellen: there was no guessing what other voices might whisper in the background, spreading the taint. Instead she composed a text, rereading it constantly to ensure it only said what she wanted it to say. Tony Mathias' suicide notes, written and verbal, had been broken up by the voices from Hogge's Pit.

Having completed it, she saved the message to *Drafts*; she didn't want to believe Ellen would help the people who'd tried to murder Cally last night, but they were officials of some kind and Ellen *was* a copper. Even if she had any feelings left for Cally, they might tell Ellen she had to be found for her own safety. No; Cally would only send the text at the very end, when it wouldn't matter what Ellen did.

She had two things left to do. One was to compose a similar message for Dad and Lucy. The other would be hardest of all, because would have to be done face to face.

It was past midday. Maxfield and the others *must* have been found by now. Department Nine would be hunting Cally in earnest, and she'd wasted too much time already.

If the men in black don't get you, the Change will.

Or the Trinity: Gowland, Harrower and Roland Woodwiss. At least *they* hadn't reappeared yet. Maybe they were waiting till dark. Her deformities seemed less active in the daylight. Perhaps the Pit had less power then.

Cally shook her head, then stood and left the square.

She made her way slowly to Piccadilly Gardens and the bus station there, keeping to the backstreets because the city was full of CCTV cameras. Paranoid, maybe, but better that than caught.

Every minute mattered now, but when Cally had reached Piccadilly she'd just missed the bus she needed. The Metrolink didn't run to that destination and her remaining funds wouldn't stretch to a taxi there, leaving her no choice but to sit waiting helplessly for the next one an hour later.

Worse, the route was long and meandering: the journey took another hour and a half, during which she'd constantly expected the bus to be pulled over so that men in dark suits could frog-march her away. It was almost 3 p.m. when they finally reached Wagonfield, a suburban village about eight miles from the city, where South Manchester shaded into Cheshire.

By then she was dizzy, and sweating heavily. She wanted to believe it was from heat, exhaustion, stress, but she'd felt things stirring under her skin and inside her belly throughout the long bus ride. She muttered the incantation that had saved her before, (*Mantakha sa niroleph chir karagh*) but it no longer seemed to help.

Time's nearly up.

Cally knew Stella's address, but had no idea how to find it. But luck was finally with her here; as the bus went down Wagonfield's main road, it passed the entrance to Wakely Grove. Cally hit the bell, then shuffled down the aisle to the doors.

The bus pulled away. Behind her was a row of Victorian townhouses; across the road, a row of semis.

Seven, Wakely Grove. Seven, Wakely Grove.

Wakely Grove wasn't long, with half a dozen semi-detached houses on either side before another street cut it off. Cally stopped outside Number Seven, steadying herself against a lamppost. She'd no idea what to say, or how long she'd have to say it. If the *Mantakha* incantation no longer worked, the change might be all the more rapid for being held back so long. She might only have minutes to tell Stella what she'd learned. At least she'd be living proof of her own tale.

She still hadn't composed a message to Dad. Hadn't been able to find the words. No time now. Maybe she could give Stella a message, before the end. *I love you. This isn't your fault. I'm sorry.* Nowhere near enough, but it would have to do.

She'd probably end up blowing her brains out in Stella's front room. What would happen to Stella then, when the clean-up crew arrived? They might decide she'd seen too much; what was one more body?

But a gunshot suicide would get the police here first. It would be loud, and public. People would see Stella alive and well. That would keep her safe. Cally had to believe that.

She gasped as something moved inside her, like a long-legged crab scrabbling around in her guts. *Please don't let me infect Stella too*. She shouldn't risk it at all, but she'd promised. Tony's sister deserved to know.

She opened the flip-phone's *Drafts* folder and reviewed her message for Ellen one last time, ensuring it only said what she wanted it to, that she hadn't unwittingly added any words in an unknown tongue, then pressed *Send*.

Sending, said the flip-phone screen.

Sweat ran down Cally's face and back. Under the hoodie's sleeve, the tentacle coiled and uncoiled around her arm. Across the street, curtains twitched.

The phone beeped. *Message Sent*. Cally snapped the phone shut, went up the drive and rang the bell.

Silence. No movement behind the front door's frosted glass. Stella probably wasn't even home. It was a bright warm Saturday afternoon; why would she be waiting patiently for Cally to turn up with answers no one had been able to provide in forty years?

Maybe the door would open and someone like Maxfield would be standing there. But that had always been a risk.

The crab in her guts scrabbled harder. Its legs were serrated and blunt. They tore and gouged. Cally's laughter became a sob, and she pressed the doorbell again. This was her one chance to achieve something worthwhile. She couldn't just shoot herself, had to leave something more than that behind.

She held the doorbell down, wanting to cry, wanting to smash the door down, to find Stella and–

"All *right!*" A blurred shape appeared behind the frosted glass. "Take your finger off that bell before I cut it off and stick it up your–"

The front door opened. In the same moment the crab's movements became outright frenzied, and Cally doubled over at the pain, only remaining upright because she clung to the doorframe.

Stella Di Mauro stood there in sandals, shorts and halter

top, but still somehow looking as immaculate as she had back in the Java Bar. "Ms Darker? When I gave you my address–"

"I found out," Cally said.

"What?" Stella's expression was now equal parts puzzlement and concern. She could see Cally was in need of help, but didn't understand what she was saying. And she had to. She must.

"Tony," said Cally. "I found out what happened to him–"

And then her stomach burst open.

At least, that was how it felt, as if the crab had doubled or tripled in size and its limbs were sweeping through her in great scything blows, but when she fell through the doorway onto her hands and knees there was no blood. Yet. Something was in her throat, trying to choke her. She couldn't speak. She opened her mouth. Nothing came out.

Beaten at the last.

A final, obliterating spasm of pain, and Cally fell forward. Thick hallway carpet rushed up to meet her.

Then there was only blackness, and the falling.

51.

One long, hot summer, when Cally was fifteen, she'd stayed in Cumbria with Dad and Lucy, in a rented cottage beside a lake.

One afternoon, she'd peeled off her damp sundress, kicked off her sandals and run down the wooden landing stage in her underwear before jumping off. It had been a scorching day; all she'd been able to think of was the cool, soothing water, washing away the heat and sweat in a moment.

But water had been twelve, fifteen feet, deep. The surface had been almost tepid, but below that it had been so cold it had stopped her heart.

Literally. When the shock of it had hit her everything in her body had stopped – rigid, paralysed. She could neither swim nor breathe, and had begun sinking down, frozen in an untidy sprawl like a frog caught in mid-leap. It had been cold down there and terribly dark, the sunlight a distant glimmer on the water, impossibly far away and seemingly about to vanish altogether.

She could have died, but she'd been lucky. The paralysis had lasted only a second; when her right heel had jarred against the rocky lake floor, everything had restarted and she'd flailed upwards towards that distant light.

Nonetheless, that second had felt nightmarishly long. Her lungs had felt close to bursting: she'd been sure she'd never reach the surface and would drown after all. But then the light had brightened, the water had suddenly become warm and she'd burst through into the air before floundering towards the landing stage. She hadn't gone back in the water for the rest of the holiday.

She'd never forgotten the sudden, annihilating shock of that instant transition from sweltering heat to searing cold. A second after falling through Stella Di Mauro's front door, she experienced it again.

Only this time, a thousand times worse.

The first breath scorched her lungs; then she couldn't breathe at all as the shock sent them into spasm. Her whole body went stiff, as if the cold that had sliced through her had frozen her solid.

She hit the ground; the surface was yielding, gritty and more scorchingly cold than the air. It filled her nose, her mouth, her eyes.

Snow.

Her lungs restarted; she inhaled snow. As she coughed and spluttered the paralysis broke. She rolled onto her back, limbs thrashing.

Snow angel. She's no angel.

Cally got onto her hands and knees, shivering in the wind.

Flat whiteness all around her. No shelter, no cover. Nowhere to hide. Only the wind.

Get up. Move or die.

Yes. Movement would generate warmth. She must find shelter. Build a fire.

Her limbs were stiffening again. The sweatshirt she'd been sweltering in seconds ago was now a pitifully inadequate shield against the gale. Her teeth chattered. She'd begun to shake. *Move or die.*

When she stood, ice crackled on her skin where her sweat had frozen and she almost fell, because the surface she'd been lying on wasn't flat at all. It was a slope, and she'd landed near the top of it.

She'd no idea how high up she was because the hillside below her was lost in whirling white. A snowstorm, filling the valley below. There were vague grey shadows might have been other peaks, but she'd no idea how far or close they were.

The only way is up, baby.

The top of the hill was only a dozen yards ahead; the sky above, black with cloud, limned the crest.

She'd be exposed to the wind on reaching the top, which would be colder still. But she could hear something, over the storm.

Voices. She was sure of it, and raised in something like a song. That meant people. Perhaps friendly, perhaps hostile, but people meant fire, and shelter, and that without those she was dead.

Hunched against the wind, she battled upwards, arms wrapped around herself, chin tucked into her chest. The full force of the wind hit her as she reached the crest; Cally rocked back on her heels, flailing for balance, then lurched forwards until the ground flattened underfoot.

A mist of snow blanketed the hilltop, and the wind howled louder than ever. At first it drowned the singing and Cally was afraid she'd imagined it, but then it became clear again. Dark shapes loomed up ahead through the storm, and in the centre of them was a bright orange glow. *Fire.*

Cally waded towards it. Snow crusted on the hooded top, soaked into her jeans. Her hood was blown back; the wind seared her face; icy claws sank into her scalp and snow clotted in her hair. She tried brushing the worst of it away, but her hands were blue with cold and almost numb.

Keep going. Keep going. Follow the song.

The looming silhouettes were too big to be people, and the wrong shape: they were huge fangs, half-broken columns, rectangular blocks.

Stones. Standing stones.

Where am I, and when?

The orange fireglow lapped across the snow, shining on the grey and black of the two nearest stones and the yellow lichen growing on them. Cally felt the heat, and was about to stumble towards it when she saw three figures standing in a rough triangle – *a Trinity* – around the fire.

They were humanoid, if not strictly human. Despite the cold each wore only a loincloth of animal skin. They weren't singing: it was a chant. The first figure uttered a line, and the other two recited it back. Their squat barrel-bodies, thickly-furred against the cold were heavy with insulating fat, giving them drooping breasts, giving no clues as to their gender. They had low foreheads, wide flat noses, heavy jaws and beetling brows, and their faces were painted red and white and black.

She'd seen one such being smiling down at her in the Pit, as it had gripped her wrists to stop her falling. It might even have been one of these three.

The one who acted as cantor to the others held two human thighbones, sharpened to points and carved with pictographs. It raised them aloft each time it chanted, pointing them down at the fire as the others responded. The words the Cantor was reciting were familiar, too. But also different.

How?

Clinging to one of the standing stones, Cally listened as it began again.

"*Angana sor varalakh kai torja,*" said the Cantor.

"*Angana sor varalakh kai torja,*" the others answered. No different, so far, from the version Cally knew.

"*Angana sor varalakh chor volraan,*" said the Cantor.

"*Angana sor varalakh chor volraan,*" came the response.

There.

Chor volraan, not *cha voran.* Cally heard it repeated several times, till she was certain.

Lightning flashed; thunder bellowed over the wind. Cally's hair prickled and lifted. Static in the air.

No, not static. Something else, some other force gathering and building, ready to be unleashed. The cells of her body seemed to ripple like water, and the earth beneath her too.

An earthquake? No: it wasn't shaking but *vibrating*, as if the earth were purring like a cat. Humming. The sky, the earth, her own body. Everything. A purring cat. A serpent, uncoiling. A sleeper, waking.

The bones rose skyward, then swept back down towards the fire as if drawing the lightning down. The chant grew louder, more urgent. The air was thick and shimmering. Cally felt as if she were shimmering too. Ripples, running through everything. All reality had become like water, to be poured, directed, reshaped.

"Angana sor varalakh kai torja."

"Angana sor varalakh kai torja."

"Angana sor varalakh cha voran–"

As soon as the Cantor said it, their small eyes widened and their mouth became an O of purest horror. Realising a mistake had been made, a slip, the wrong words. They swung the bones above their head and opened their mouth to shout, but the other two were caught up in their ritual's near-hypnotic rhythm, and unthinkingly, they repeated the line.

"Angana sor varalakh cha voran."

The rhythm Cally had felt, in the air and earth and frozen water of the snows, became an erratic judder. The flames turned blue, then white, rushing up to touch the sky. Smoke and steam boiled up from around the fire. Snow and ice evaporated; the earth beneath them thawed then charred to ash. Cracks raced across the ground towards the celebrants. The rock turned red and poured away like honey into a terrible darkness beyond.

Only a hole now where the fire had been, but still the blue flames burned. A column of fire. And then it fell, plunging into the depths like a spear.

The hill shuddered. Lightning blazed above. The standing stones rocked and wavered. Cally stumbled back, out of the circle, into the blackness and the wind.

The air shimmered and swirled. The three priests screamed,

their images no longer shimmering but distorted, swirling like water. The standing stones fell and then the ground caved in, falling, with the priests, into unending blackness.

Wind blew across the hill from all directions, towards the hole in the earth, gathering snow, ice, stones, birds and beasts and hurling them down into the pit. Cally fought to keep her footing. If she fell, she was done. She'd be swept into the abyss with the rest.

A great black shape fought free of the maelstrom, beating its ragged wings, a distorted low-browed face howling in idiot glee in its chest, before being pulled back down.

Cally twisted away, pushing against the wind. It was her only chance. If it was at her back she'd be bowled over and flung into Hogge's Pit. Because that was what she was seeing here: Warden Fell, thousands or millions of years ago, and the birth of Hogge's Pit.

Perhaps she was meant to understand something here, but what good would it do her? She couldn't hold against this wind. In a moment she'd be picked up and–

"No," said someone. A voice she knew.

52.

The blackness was utter and awful; Cally shut her eyes against it. She tumbled end over end, as if floating in space.

Then metal dug into the backs of her thighs; there was heat on her face, and warm orange light shone through her eyelids. The air no longer scorched her lungs when she breathed; it smelt of grass, flowers and warm dry earth.

"Cally?"

It was the same voice that had spoken before. She knew it; of course, she always had, since childhood. It couldn't be. Made no sense. But she knew it, all the same.

She opened her eyes.

She was on the bench in Dad and Lucy's garden. A summer evening: bright without being dazzling, warm without being oppressive. The terrible, numbing cold was gone; her clothes were clear of snow, and dry. Her throat felt parched.

Her father sat opposite her in a folding lawn chair, wearing shorts, t-shirt and Jesus-boots, smiling his warm, pleasant smile. There was a clear plastic bucket on the ground, full of ice water; he fished out a can of Pepsi Max. "Drink?"

Cally popped the tab and drank gratefully. The can was as cold as the snow on the hill. "You're not my dad."

"No." He looked exactly like Owen Darker – the ungovernable waves of thick but greying hair, the bespectacled, intelligent face – but Cally knew it wasn't him. "But we've a lot to talk about, little time to do it in and thousands of years between us. Countless cycles of earth and sun." He touched his forehead. "We're talking mind to mind here. Spirit to spirit. Otherwise, we'd never understand one another."

"Who are you really?"

"You saw me on the hill." A gesture, and it wasn't her Dad anymore; the Cantor was perched on the lawn chair, bare calloused feet swinging back and forth six inches above the ground.

The Cantor smiled at her. By human standards they were grotesque, but conveyed no sense of menace. The small, deep-set eyes were kind, as they'd been when the Cantor had saved her from falling into the Pit in her dream.

"Hogge's Pit," said Cally at last. "That was you?"

The Cantor's face grew so sorrowful Cally almost regretted asking. "Not our intent. There'd been bitter winters, no food. And that winter was the worst and longest of all. It had to end, or my people would. So, we began the working. To wake the earth. Understand, please: we wanted only to bring life. Abundance. Healing. To make spring come again."

"A fertility ritual?"

"A fertility ritual, compared to this, would be... a raindrop to a thunderstorm. What you saw came from months of fasting, sacrifice, prayer. All to prepare the way. Provide a... fulcrum? Yes. A point of leverage. For that final working, to end the winter. Understand, please," the Cantor said again: "we knew from the start it was a vast undertaking, fraught with risk. But it was the only chance remaining, that our people wouldn't perish. Otherwise, we would never have tried. Such workings are... unforgiving."

"Unforgiving," Cally repeated.

"Yes." The Cantor nodded. The voice itself was still her father's, but the speech and cadences bore no more resemblance to Owen Darker's now than its appearance. "With any working, a single error can send everything awry. For a small working, small consequences. The father's breasts give milk, instead of the mother's. A deer falls from the sky, feeding the tribe but breaking the hunter's head. A joke, almost. But should a great working go askew…" The Cantor shook their head. "We were close. But then–"

"You got the chant wrong."

Another nod. "A working is like… pushing a stone up a hill. The greater the working, the bigger the stone, the steeper the hillside. As you push against the stone–" the Cantor pressed at the air with their palms – "the stone pushes back against you. Resistance. It can take many forms. Exhaustion. Injury. Accident. Or error. The closer a working nears completion, the greater the vigilance required."

"Because the resistance will be strongest right before the end?"

"You grasp. We thought ourselves prepared. Vigilant. Yet nonetheless…" The Cantor indicated themselves. "Error."

"*Cha voran* instead of *chor volraan*," said Cally. "Did I hear it right?"

The heavy brows rose. "You have a good ear."

"And that created… Hogge's Pit?"

"A Depth." Cally heard the capital D the Cantor gave the name. "Instead of life, it brought worse than death. A chaos. A corruption. Body and spirit."

"An entrance to Hell." Cally imagined what Millicent would have said, had she known.

The Cantor shook their head again. "Not as you think it. The Depth is a wound in the world. It festers. Corrupts. Spreads its festering to whatever it can touch."

"The taint," she said.

"Yes. But the tainted have done no wrong. No wickedness. Only misfortune. Only wrong place, wrong time. Caught and drawn in."

Cally wasn't sure if that made it better or worse.

"The wound always festers," said the Cantor. "Sometimes it almost closes, but never entirely. Sometimes it breaks open, to spread the taint. As now."

Like a volcano, as Harrower had said. Sometimes deadly, sometimes dormant, waxing and waning in accordance with cycles even the Cantor might not understand. Harmless to CORRAN the urbexer, and those who'd occupied the airbase after the war. But deadly to Tony Mathias and his family, and to Peter Culleton. And deadly to Cally herself.

"But now the danger is greatest. The taint may spread wider. Poison all the world." The Cantor pointed at Cally. "Through you."

53.

The garden had turned cold, the sky grey and sunless; the willow tree at the garden's end was russet and brown, the leaves falling. In a second, it had become autumn.

Poison all the world. Through you. She shook her head, staring at the ground. But she had to listen. The world was Stella Di Mauro. It was Dad and Lucy. It was Ellen.

No more pulling the covers over your head. She looked up. "Tell me."

"The tainted are... an affront to this world. It... resists? *Rejects.* Their presence. So they are cast back into the Depth. They can gain only moments of relief in this world, though for them even moments are enough to be worth the attempt. But now, this time: different."

"Why?" Then she realised: Gowland, Harrower, Woodwiss. "The Trinity."

The Cantor nodded. "The three. The taint wakes and sleeps: it touched these just before it last fell into slumber."

"After Tony Mathias, and Peter Culleton?"

"The lightest of touches, but enough. Rare, but it happens. They are... carriers? The taint lies dormant. Until the Depth wakes again. It works *through* them. They plot and plan. Guide the steps of others."

"Harrower emailed me," Cally said, now understanding the email address: pete56283. Peter Culleton had been twenty-seven. 1983 minus twenty-seven years was 1956.'56 to '83: 56283. "To get me interested. And then the others. All so bloody helpful."

"The taint must grow," said the Cantor, "either in them or others. For two of them, it's no more than that."

Harrower must have been contaminated by Culleton's answerphone messages. Perhaps Tony had inadvertently infected Gowland the same way.

"But the third..." the Cantor said. "The Depth touched him at conception, soured his nature in the womb."

He repelled everyone. That was what Edna had said; what Cally had experienced herself. "That's why no one can stand him, isn't it?" she said.

The Cantor nodded again. "Others sense it and draw away. So he has always been alone. Unloved. Despised. And therefore, full of rage against the world."

Cally remembered Roland telling her about the new boy's birthday party he'd attended the night of the murders. Hoping to make a friend. But he'd been denied that, too. Not because the other children had turned the new boy against him, but because of the revulsion Roland's very presence engendered.

Who wouldn't be full of rage, given that? Cally knew what it was to be despised and rejected from her own schooldays, and it wasn't as though she and her own mother had ever had much time for one another. But she'd still had Dad and Lucy, and while it had taken some time, she'd eventually found people who'd accepted her, loved her even. Roland Woodwiss had never known that, even once. Except, perhaps, with Alison Mathias, who, for whatever reason, hadn't been affected.

Cally remembered the rage she'd felt, remembered wanting to tear down her school and burn it to ash. *Imagine feeling that way about the whole world.* For the first time, she actually felt something other than repulsion towards Roland Woodwiss. She felt – reluctantly, and to her own astonishment – pity.

Although none of that changed what he was, or the threat he now posed.

"He is the worst of them," the Cantor said, "and the strongest. They sought you out. Carefully, over time. You in particular."

"Why? I'm nothing special."

The Cantor shook their head. "You have a strength."

"Strength? Me? Have any of you got the right person?"

"Were you born in my time," said the Cantor, "you'd have been like me. One who hears; one who sees. One able to make a working."

"A working," she said. "Magic. A spell."

"Your words. But a working is not a trick, or child's game. A working is… an alteration to the world."

Magic, she thought again. "Like them? The Trinity?"

"Compared, their power is small. Yours, if woken, could enact a great working. The Depth seeks to use that power."

The Depth.

"When you change, you will make a working, open a way. From this world to the Depth. They intend to release those who inhabit the Depth into this world permanently. But, more likely, the Depth will suck all this world into itself."

"So I'm not only turning into a demon, I'm going to end the bloody world as well? Fucking great."

"Or save it." The Cantor spread their hands. "I am, we are, the dust of souls. I am, we are, the remnants of all those taken by the Depth. Of what we were before. Torn, scattered, cast aside. Mingled. But, at last, drawn together. I, we, have tried, over the years, to warn others, but few can hear. Only echoes. But you? Different."

"Because I'm one who hears, one who sees."

"You grasp."

"*What* do I grasp? I mean, *how* am I different? What can I *do*? I'm halfway to becoming a freakshow as it is–"

"Another Trinity," the Cantor said. "A second one."

"For fuck's sake, make sense."

The Cantor sighed. "Complete our working, and the circle closes. The wound, healed. The Depth – gone. And the tainted…"

"Yeah," said Cally. "What about them?"

"Their suffering ends. Either healed, or they cease to be. Which? I, we, cannot say."

"What happens to me? I'm tainted too."

"The same."

"Healed, or I cease to be." Cally thought of the Dead Parrot Sketch. *She's an ex-Cally. She has ceased to be.*

"You grasp," the Cantor said.

"God, will you stop *saying* that–" Cally shook her head. She'd wanted answers; however brutal, here they were.

"I speak only the truth. I am sorry."

"It's all right," she said. She'd accepted her own death before; she'd only struggled with the process of leaving. She'd a chance of survival now, however small. "Go on."

"A new Trinity," the Cantor said again. "You, two others. Find the mouth of the Depth. Where it began. And perform the working anew. Speak the words. Without error."

"*Chor volraan* instead of *cha voran*," said Cally. "Right?"

A nod. At least they didn't say *you grasp*.

"Where it began," she said. "Warden Fell?"

A nod. "The exact spot."

"So, the entrance to Hogge's Pit."

The Cantor nodded.

"How will I know where that is?"

"You will know."

"If you say so." Cally tried to recollect the ritual she'd observed. "So we position ourselves around it, like a triangle. Then I say a line, the others repeat it?"

The Cantor nodded.

"But... I'm tainted. Won't that make me–"

"Susceptible? Yes. But the one who hears and sees must lead. I, we, shall give you what strength we can. Force back the taint a little while."

"You can't cure me?" said Cally. But if they could have done, they would.

The Cantor shook their head. "Only delay. Hours only, from

when you wake. Until tomorrow's dawn. After that–" They shook their head again. "Once begun, the working itself will protect you."

And if it goes tits-up like the first one? Better not to ask. Cally couldn't imagine a worse outcome than she already faced, but if one existed, she'd sooner not now . "How long does it take?"

"Minutes. Hours." The Cantor shrugged. "As you progress, you will feel both the power, and the resistance to it, increase. If you reach it, you will know the moment the balance shifts."

"If." Few words could promise or threaten so much.

"I will not mislead," the Cantor said. "The danger? Great. You will face the same resistance we did. The working, rightly done, will protect you from the Trinity, but they too will try to trick you into error."

"And if I make one?"

The Cantor shook their head. "As I said, such workings are unforgiving."

That word again.

"No pressure, then."

The Cantor sort-of smiled. "The risk is great, but there is no alternative. You must succeed where we failed."

"Come on." Cally's voice cracked. *Take me home, Daddy. Put me to bed.* "I can't. I'm not strong."

"You must believe yourself capable." There was sorrow in the dark eyes, in that lined, brutish face. "There is protection. Small. But protection, still."

"Okay."

The Cantor told her. "Now," it said, "gather your Trinity."

"Where do I find two other nutters who'd believe all this?"

"They've already found you, love," said the Cantor, sounding like Dad again. "It's up to you now. Remember what I said, and believe you can do it."

"Believe in myself? *That's* the best you've got?" She'd hoped for better from an honest-to-the-gods Palaeolithic shaman.

"A working is... belief. Your will against the world." The

Cantor smiled. "Don't pretend you can't be bloody stubborn."

Despite everything, Cally smiled back. "I suppose."

The Cantor's smile faded. "Off you go, then."

The world around her shattered like glass; behind it, once again, was blackness, and Cally tumbled into it.

Part Four

And All The Souls In Hell Shall Sing

54.
Llanuwchllyn, 36 hours earlier

Ellen Rooke locked her flat door, shot the deadbolt, closed the windows despite the summer heat, and ran to the shower. She was greasy with sweat, and terror-sweat had its own particular, acrid smell, every whiff of which made her recall what she'd just seen.

The *thing* – the Cormorant – had been bad enough in itself, but it wasn't the first such experience Ellen had had. She'd told Cally about her night terrors, but not the three previous occasions when despite being wide awake she'd seen things that couldn't possibly have been there.

They'd all occurred in the month leading up to her breakdown. Once she'd seen a domestic violence survivor standing in her hallway, naked and bloody, face so battered and swollen he couldn't open his eyes. Another time she'd walked into her living room to see a suicide she'd found in a woodland, decomposed and part-eaten, hanging from her ceiling.

The last hallucination had been the least gruesome, but the worst. Two weeks before her breakdown, Ellen had helped arrest a particularly brutal rapist. They'd found him sitting quietly on his bed, hands clasped before him, his scarred, shaven head bowed as if in prayer. He'd looked up at Ellen, his fish-eyed gaze crawling over her body, before she and the other officers pinned him down and cuffed him. She'd showered as soon as she'd got home that night, too, trying to scrub his gaze off her skin.

Ellen came home one night to find him sitting on her bed,

watching her with those cold fish eyes. Like the others, he'd vanished the second Ellen switched the light on, but it had been the final straw. The next day she'd been unable to get out of bed, paralysed by sheer panic.

Her terror tonight had been twofold: firstly of the thing itself, and secondly at the prospect of her grasp on reality had slipped again. Except that the *thing* hadn't disappeared when the lights came on, and Cally had seen it too. And hallucinations didn't smash windows.

In the shower, a fresh panic attack took hold, and Ellen found herself huddled in the corner of the cubicle, arms around her knees, shaking. She wanted someone there to hold her, but the only person who came to mind was Cally, and thinking of her didn't help at all. When she could finally get out of the shower her fingers were wrinkled and pruney; she thought she'd been under there for hours, but according to her phone it had been thirty minutes.

Ellen somehow managed an hour's fitful sleep before her alarm went off. She dragged herself out of bed, dressed and stumbled downstairs to the waiting Juke on autopilot, then drove to the station at Dolgellau.

She'd been paired with Dave Greene again; normally they bickered good-naturedly over who drove, but she was happy to let Dave do that today, unsure she'd stay awake at the wheel. He seemed to assume she was hungover, and Ellen was happy to let him do so, especially as they were patrolling near Bala again. She bought two energy drinks from the Spar in the town, and prayed for a quiet shift.

Her prayers, at first, seemed to have been answered; the morning and early afternoon passed without incident, and they parked up near the lake to try and catch a few speeding motorists, but around three o'clock a call went out: a fire and possible shooting in Fron-Goch.

"Christ," she and Dave had muttered simultaneously, in very different tones. Dave had spent his whole brief police career on this beat, and dreamt of a transfer to a livelier one like Manchester; Ellen knew they were heading into potential danger, and that in her current state she'd surely screw up. And if you screwed up in this job, people died.

But it was all over by the time they got there. Firefighters were still blasting foam and water into the bungalow's charred ruins, but the flames were out, black smoke belching into the air. The neighbours, ordered outside in case the fire spread, muttered and stared.

The firefighters had seen no sign of anyone with a firearm, so Dave canvassed the crowd while Ellen kept them and any passing rubberneckers back. She only caught snatches of conversation, but overheard two people saying they'd heard a shot, just before smoke had started pouring from the bungalow's windows.

"Suicide, I bet," one of the firefighters grunted. "And what d'you call it, self-immolation. Have a sniff."

"Sorry?" said Ellen.

"Can you not smell it? Like roast pork?"

Ellen could, and pressed a fingertip to her chin; an old trick she'd learned to avoid throwing up. "You think he's in there?"

"Bet you any money," said the firefighter. "Set the whole place to go up ahead of time, I reckon. Splash enough petrol around, the shot'd ignite the fumes. Top himself and set this little lot going all at one fell swoop."

"Why do that?"

"Something to hide? Kiddy porn, maybe? That's your end, love. This, though?" He nodded towards the ruins. "No accident. Deliberate arson, any money on it."

Ellen went home exhausted and fell straight into bed, sleeping nearly eleven hours straight. She woke an hour before her alarm was due to go off, but didn't feel rested. She suspected there'd been nightmares, but couldn't remember them. Which was probably a blessing.

She was paired with a different officer that day, an older

guy called Williams. The Fron-Goch business was a CID matter now, but supposedly a body and a twelve-bore shotgun had been recovered from the bungalow; suicide of some kind, they thought. Around ten o'clock her AirWave crackled and she was curtly ordered to immediately report to Bala police station.

Ironically for a police officer, Ellen was used to feeling guilty. Growing up, she'd said or done the wrong thing, as far as her parents were concerned, just by existing, on countless occasions, so she tended to assume she'd done something wrong the moment attention fell on her. It was a bug in her software she'd done her best to get rid of; even so, she'd a horrible feeling that this time she *had* fucked up.

Williams dropped her at the station around ten-thirty; Ellen was told to sit and wait in reception. Her stomach clenched when she glimpsed Dave Greene being escorted down the hall behind the reception desk. And then, at precisely quarter to eleven, her world fell apart.

"Constable Rooke?" A clipped, very English voice: *upper-class* and *public school* were the words that sprang to mind. Didn't sound like a copper, and when Ellen looked up, he didn't look the part either: too ramrod-straight, too lean and hard-muscled, and wearing far too expensive and well-tailored a suit.

He snapped his fingers. "This way." He was very tall, with dark, side-parted hair, a clipped moustache, and grey, gelid eyes more suited to a predatory fish than a human being. He turned and strode off; Ellen followed, struggling to keep up. He was long-legged, and marching double-time. Military, rather than police. Ex-Army turned CID, maybe: old mannerisms died hard.

But he didn't introduce himself, there were no other officers in the interview room, and once she was inside, he locked the door, motioning her to a chair. When he sat down, she saw he carried a pistol in a shoulder holster.

His clothes were tailored to conceal it, which would be well beyond the average coppers' means. He glanced up and smiled, eyes as dead and emotionless as ever. A predatory fish's. A pike's. *Don't tell him your name, Pike*, she thought, and almost giggled.

"Something funny, Constable?" said Pike.

"No, sir."

He smiled again. Then it vanished, wiped away like a wrong sum from a teacher's whiteboard. "I should hope not. You have nothing to be amused about."

The table in front of him was bare, except for a smartphone and a tablet of some kind, in a folding leather wallet. He tapped at the phone's touchscreen. *Recording.* "So, Constable Rooke," he said. "Tell me about Callandra Darker."

"Who?" Ellen was genuinely thrown.

"Feigning ignorance won't do you any good, Constable."

Maybe he was from Professional Standards. "Sorry, can I ask who you are and what this is about?"

"You may not." His smile would've been pleasant if his eyes hadn't remained cold and empty throughout. "What you can do, and really should, before I lose my patience, is tell me about Callandra Darker. We know you and Constable Greene interviewed her on the 16th June."

Hearing the surname again made things click. *Callandra?* "You mean Cally?"

"*Cally*, is it? Are you and she on *intimate* terms, then?"

Ellen didn't like the emphasis he put on *intimate*. She wasn't out to her colleagues, or even her parents. She'd gone out on the gay scene in Aberystwyth a couple of times, and to a meet-up in Caernarfon, but that was all. She thought she'd been discreet; now she just felt painfully exposed. She felt her face reddening.

He's just being a dick. Answer the question. "Nothing like that. She called herself Cally, that's all, not *Callandra*. So did her boyfriend. Ex-boyfriend, rather."

She was on firmer ground now; she just needed to tell the

truth. She outlined the call that had taken her and Dave out to Owen and Lucy Darker's house in Bala.

Pike tapped two fingers on the table-top, a thin, impatient smile on his lips. "And you've had no other contact with her."

"Why would I?"

"You're here to *answer* questions, Constable, not *ask* them."

Had Rav tattled on her? Or Harrower? Pike changed tack. "What about Griff Parry, Constable?"

"Who?"

"You're now pretending you don't know who *he* is? Or was?"

"I don't *need* to pretend." She didn't bother with the *sir* this time. "I don't know the name."

"So you weren't at his house yesterday?" he said, in a slow, patronising tone.

"What?"

"Yesterday, in Fron-Goch? Surely your memory isn't *that* bad, Constable."

He was goading her; Ellen calmed herself with an effort. "If you mean the fire yesterday, I didn't get the resident's name. Dave might have. He was interviewing witnesses. I was on crowd control."

Pike sighed and shook his head; Ellen folded her arms. "You can smirk all you want, mate. It's the truth."

"The truth?" he said. "The truth. I see. I suppose you weren't aware that Mr Parry and Miss Darker were on... *intimate* terms?" Again the slimy, insinuating emphasis on that word.

"What?"

"They've been friends, quite possibly more, for some time. Mr Parry's phone records show several calls between him and Callandra Darker over the past few days, along with emails and social media messaging. Quite a coincidence, that barely a week after her return to the area her boyfriend's house goes up in smoke with him inside?"

Boyfriend? Ellen felt a stab of jealousy, hurt, betrayal, then realised that was exactly the response Pike would want. Parry was Cally's ex; so what? They'd had better, more interesting things to talk about than all their exes.

Unless he wasn't *an ex.*

Pike was trying to make her jealous and angry. Ellen dug her fingernails into her palms. "Are you saying Cally Darker shot Griff Parry and burned his house down?"

Pike sighed. "Again, Constable, *you're* the one here to answer questions. Doesn't it sound a strange coincidence?"

She shrugged. "We're talking Bala and the immediate surroundings here. It's not a densely populated area. If you look for a connection between people, chances are you'll find it. That's all, unless something in those messages suggests Cally was a danger to Mr Parry."

Pike smiled. Ellen's stomach twisted. She'd said *Cally*, not *Miss Darker*. But it didn't matter; if they'd accessed Griff Parry's phone records, they'd have accessed Cally's too.

Pike, with considerable ceremony, put on a pair of reading glasses. Ellen waited for the axe to fall.

"*8pm okay?*" Pike read. "*Want to have a bath and chill first. Kiss kiss.* A text message, Constable, sent from your phone to Callandra Darker's two days after your little house call. While I appreciate dedication to duty, that does seem a little above and beyond." He looked up, that hateful smirk still in place. "Wouldn't you say?"

Ellen dug her nails deeper into her palms.

"And then there's the phone call you made the following evening. *That* transcript makes for rather spicy reading. Darker: *Hi, lovely.* Rooke: *Yo. Fancy eating out tonight?* Darker: *Well, I've had worse chat-up lines.*"

The worst thing was Pike's mocking tone, aping Ellen's shy, stumbling delivery to make her sound stupid, reducing everything between Cally and her to the level of cheap porn. "If you listen to the rest of the transcript–"

"I have," said Pike. "Popping around with a curry to dab

the patient's fevered brow. Most commendable. But still... excessive. You'd only made a welfare check on Callandra Darker – who suffers from a host of mental health issues and whose boyfriend had contacted the police out of concern for her well-being – two days earlier. God knows your closeted little sex-life – if we can call it that – makes pathetic reading at the best of times, but were you really so desperate you had to prey on vulnerable members of the public?"

Ellen's humiliation finally turned to rage. She was used to keeping her head down, staying quiet and taking her lumps, but there were limits, and she'd reached hers. She had some pride, some dignity. "Fuck this," she said. "I want my union rep–"

She jumped to her feet as she spoke, ready to storm out, but Pike lunged under his jacket, and then the pistol was levelled at her, his finger on the trigger. He wasn't smirking now; his thin lips were compressed and white.

Ellen made a thin, strangled noise, something between a whimper and a choked-off scream. The muzzle of the gun seemed very large. Her stomach clenched harder still; she was sure she was about to wet herself, or worse.

"Sit. Down. Now." Pike's voice was taut and came through bared teeth. "Put your hands behind your head, and remain. Absolutely. Still. This is your first and *only* warning."

Her legs were trembling and she was almost hyperventilating. Ellen made herself breathe deeply and sat down, praying her legs didn't give way, then put her hands behind her head as instructed.

Pike rested the gun on the desk. A Glock automatic; standard military and police issue. A seventeen-round magazine, probably loaded with hollow-point bullets for maximum stopping power. For a moment Ellen was certain he'd pull the trigger; he was too distant for her to grab for the weapon, and too close for Pike to miss. Her one hope was that he wouldn't shoot someone in the middle of a police station, and even that felt very thin.

Pike switched off the recording and attached an earpiece to his phone, glancing from it to Ellen. Thin, faint voices came from the earpiece: Hers and Pike's. He pressed the earpiece deeper in, frowning, studying her closely, then pursed his lips and tapped at the phone again. Ellen heard it ring; after a few moments he spoke. "Nothing on mine. You?"

He listened, then nodded. "Not contaminated, then. Just a stupid little cunt in way over her head. Thanks."

He tapped the phone, removed the earpiece and holstered the Glock. "You can go."

Ellen stood. Her legs still trembled; she had to steady herself on the chair. "That's all?" An absurd thing to say, she knew.

"Indeed it is." Pike pocketed his phone and slid the tablet into the wallet. "You're suspended, Miss Rooke. And you won't be coming back."

"What?" she said.

He sighed. "Did you think I was an idiot? That I hadn't checked up on you, and your *girlfriend*? Hm? I knew all about you and your little house calls – and how you'd been making enquiries on her behalf with other officers. All very naughty, but if you'd been truthful at the outset, you might – *might* – have kept your job. Minus any prospects of advancement, of course. Instead, you lied. Therefore you can't be trusted, and therefore you're finished in the police service." Pike smiled brightly. "My advice? Resign, while you can. It'll look better on your CV when you try to get a job stacking shelves at the Co-Op. Because be assured, you *are* done, one way or the other. By tomorrow morning I can have half a dozen of your fellow officers swear on oath you stole cocaine from the evidence store and were high as a kite on duty. Now fuck off. One of your soon-to-be-ex-colleagues will drive you home."

55.
Llanuwchllyn, 4 hours earlier

Dave Greene drove her, looking more miserable than Ellen had ever seen him. As he escorted her from the station, she glanced reflexively at her watch. Eleven o'clock. It had taken Pike less than fifteen minutes to end her career.

Normally Dave was such a joker Ellen sometimes wished him struck dumb, but he'd nothing to say now. Which was fine by her: nor did she.

She felt numb. It was all unreal. At eight o'clock, it had been another day at work; three hours later, she wasn't a policewoman anymore. *You won't be coming back,* Pike had said, and Ellen didn't doubt him for a moment.

I can have half a dozen of your fellow officers swear on oath you stole cocaine from the evidence store and were high as a kite on duty. That was what he'd said. She glanced sideways at Dave. Would he be one of them? He wanted a transfer, after all; everyone had a weak point, a way to be bought or squeezed – or, as in her case, casually destroyed. And Pike, whoever he was, had walked into a police station, taken charge and rooted through Ellen's life like a pervert through an underwear drawer. More than enough authority to buy or squeeze as required.

Like every burglary victim she'd ever interviewed, Ellen felt violated. She couldn't forget Pike's sneering tone as he'd read the transcript, making mock of every private thing. She'd been about to walk out but had wanted to hit him; the last of her self-control had held her back. Even that mightn't have been enough if he hadn't had the gun.

But he had, and he'd drawn it, when all she'd done was stand up. One move and he'd have fired.

He was afraid of you.

Not contaminated, he'd said. Cally had mentioned contamination, too; something Tony Mathias had brought home to his family. That was what Pike had been afraid of. And then hadn't been.

Just a stupid little cunt in way over her head.

Ellen felt her fists clench.

"You okay?" said Dave.

Ellen shook her head. Dave, thankfully, didn't press the point.

Finally, he pulled in outside her flat. Her car was still at the station in Dolgellau. She'd have to get a bus or taxi to pick it up. Then she remembered Glyn Scurlock – a local farmer, only ten minutes' walk away, who owed Ellen a favour; he'd have no problem giving her a lift. Not that she was in any hurry to go near her former place of work; her skin crawled with shame at the very thought.

Still, Glyn kept an old Land Rover, in a barn on his land, the keys stashed under the front nearside wheel arch. He'd let Ellen borrow it for a day or two, if it came to that. For now, she just wanted to fall on her bed and cry.

"Thanks, Dave." Her voice felt like ash.

His face was red. "Sorry, Ell, but I've to come in with you. Search the flat. Any police equipment's got to go back with me."

Was that standard procedure? She'd already given him her warrant card. Pike's doing, maybe, to ensure she couldn't help Cally. "I haven't got any in the house."

"Sorry, Ell. Orders."

He sounded thoroughly miserable; Ellen was tempted to remind him that she was the one who'd just lost her job, but it would have been too much effort. Anger percolated in the depths of her, but it was still buried under numbness and shock, under hurt and violation and a bone-aching sense of failure. Besides, venting her anger might have been satisfying, but Dave was the wrong target.

"Fine," she said. "Come on. Get it over with."

She shut herself in the bathroom, hugging herself and biting her lips on the toilet, listening to doors and drawers being opened and shut. After a while she covered her ears, and concentrated on not crying. She wasn't doing that, not yet.

She jumped when he knocked on the bathroom door. "Ell?" he said. "Sorry, but I've got to search in there too. And I'll, er, need your uniform."

She unlocked the door and brushed past him into the bedroom. Everything seemed a vast effort, but she managed to take off the uniform and pull on a sweatshirt and jogpants. That done, she sat on the edge of the bed, and waited.

Dave waited too, for a couple of minutes, before knocking on the door. "I'm decent," Ellen said, and almost laughed, but couldn't quite.

Dave cracked the door open, eyes lowered, face still red, as if he thought she'd lied. "All right," he said. "That's me."

"Fine," she said.

He gathered up the uniform. Her spare one lay by the front door; as she'd told him, there hadn't been anything else. Dave picked that up too, then opened the door. "Ell, I'm bloody sorry. If there's anything I can do–"

"Yeah." Ellen managed a faint but genuine smile; that was the first and only hint, since that nightmarish interview with Pike, that she wasn't a complete pariah. "Thanks."

Dave nodded, still not meeting her gaze, and let himself out. Ellen bolted the door and went back to her room, so weary she had to grip the walls for support. She toppled full length onto the bed, and finally let herself cry.

After about an hour, she didn't feel better, only a little less numb. She took out her phone and looked at it, half-hoping and half-afraid there'd be a message or missed call from Cally.

There wasn't. Thankfully. Anything Cally sent would be seen by Pike and his loathsome crew, whoever they might be.

Ellen tossed the phone aside, but it had reminded her of something. In her bedside drawer was a little pay-as-you-go phone she'd bought a couple of years ago as a back-up, with five or ten pounds' credit. The battery was dead, of course, but she still had the charger, so she plugged it in. .

She'd no idea when, if ever, she could tell her parents. The only person she could have talked to right now was Cally. What would Pike's crew do if they laid hands on her, if they hadn't already? Pike had feared *contamination* enough to blow Ellen's brains out in a police station. What that meant for Cally she didn't want to think.

She didn't want to think at all, full stop. She'd no idea how to get through today, never mind what came after.

Ellen brewed tea, devoured a pack of chocolate biscuits with methodical, cheerless greed and curled up on the bed. She wanted sleep. Oblivion. But she couldn't stop thinking.

This is hell, she thought at one point. The thought of suicide seriously crossed her mind: to just give up. She genuinely saw no way forward, or of life even being bearable after today. There was no point to any of it. She told herself to get some perspective, pull herself together, but those were hollow-sounding platitudes at the best of times.

Do nothing, then, for now. Don't do anything you can't take back. Just do nothing, and let this pass.

And if it didn't? To feel like this forever would be intolerable.

She shook her head. *This too shall pass.* Wherever she'd heard it, it was true. Everything did, good or bad. You had to relish the good things while they lasted and weather the bad ones, knowing they'd lift.

She had to believe that was true. If not, well, suicide was always an option, if you were still alive.

Unless you end up paralysed and can't do anything—

"Aren't you a fucking ray of sunshine," she told her traitorous mind. She wondered if Pike had bugged her flat. If so, let them make of that little aside what they would.

There was birdsong outside. *With all its sham, drudgery and broken dreams, it's still a beautiful world.* She had a print of Ehrmann's *Desiderata* somewhere; she'd always meant to mount it on the wall and never had. Maybe she'd get around to it now.

How long will you be able to keep the flat, without a job? Stacking shelves in the Co Op? Will you be able to bear that, surrounded by people who remember when you were a copper? Where will you go, if you can't stay here, and what will you do?

Stop thinking, she told herself. Stop *thinking.* But her mind whirled and wouldn't stop, while her body remained dull as clay: she thought of going outside, to the hills, the lake anywhere there was beauty and peace to be lost in, but the effort required seemed too vast.

Outside there was more birdsong but little else; the flat was silent too. The flip-phone bleeped to announce it was fully charged; otherwise nothing.

Then her smartphone buzzed. It was lying inches from her head; the sound and vibration made her jump.

Something to be grateful for, maybe.

A text message, probably. She couldn't imagine one she'd want to read right now, but it would be a few seconds' distraction, even if it was just the police making her suspension official or saying *fuck off, you won't be missed.*

Then she saw the first line of the message, and everything changed. The room went still; so, more importantly, did her brain.

Ellen, this is Cally. I'm sorry for everything. Please don't blame yourself.

"Oh, shit." Ellen sat up. She'd seen messages like that before. Texts and emails; handwritten notes. Heard them, too, in recorded messages, sometimes sounding cracked and broken, other times calm, even happy; the decision to end your life sometimes conferred a kind of peace.

Using different phone, the message continued. *Lost the old one. Wasn't safe. I'm so sorry for everything that happened. Hope you'll be okay now. Take care. Love. X*

For a few minutes, at least, she had a purpose again. She fumbled with the smartphone, to call the number, then stopped. Anything she said or sent would be seen by Pike. Ellen unplugged the flip-phone – *great minds think alike, eh?* – and typed the number into it.

Her thumb hovered over the call button.

You sure about this? You're in deep shit already.

"No," she muttered aloud. "But fuck it."

And with that, she made the call.

56.

Stella Di Mauro didn't try catching the girl when she fell through the doorway. Old bones broke more easily, and old muscles were more easily strained. *Old age cometh not alone*, as her grandmother liked to say. The girl was young, the hall carpet soft and springy; she'd recover from any bumps and bruises fast enough.

Even so, she could hardly leave the poor thing lying there. She obviously wasn't well – hopefully only in the physical sense, although the wild look in her eye hadn't been encouraging.

Stella was still sturdy enough to drag a reasonable weight, so she crouched, grabbed the girl under the arms, lifting with her legs and not her back, and pulled her into the hallway.

She'd done enough first-aid courses throughout her theatrical career to know what to do: get the patient into the recovery position, then call an ambulance. But the last thing the girl had said had been: *I found out. Tony. I found out what happened to him.*

Well, she'd only fainted, probably from the heat; Stella could revive her, perhaps, before calling 999–

Thunk.

Cally's shoulder-bag had slipped from her grasp, and something had fallen out.

Stella had grown up with firearms, and her father had ensured she knew how to handle them safely. As a result, she'd not only handled countless prop guns during her acting career, but had acted as armourer on several stage productions, ensuring any weapons involved were kept safe and used properly. She picked the weapon up, aiming it at the floor where an accidental discharge would do no harm, and

326

keeping her finger off the trigger, then she ran her fingers over the pistol grip and found the magazine release: a button just behind the trigger. She pushed it and the magazine landed on the carpet with a solid *thump*.

She pulled back the slide to clear the breech, ejecting a bullet onto the carpet beside the magazine. Shiny, glinting brass. Stella picked it up. A live round, not a blank. Cally Darker was carrying a real gun.

A trilling sound made Stella jump, dropping the bullet and pistol together. When the noise repeated itself, she realised it was a mobile phone.

"Fucking hell," she muttered. It wasn't hers: that played the *William Tell Overture*, unless her agent called, in which case it played the Imperial March from *Star Wars*. This one was simple and generic, albeit very loud.

The phone was in the girl's jeans. Stella flicked it open. The screen showed a number, no name. She hoped it wasn't that wretched little shit Bernard Gowland. Stella answered the call. "Hello?"

"Cally?" said a soft, breathless voice.

"Who is this?"

"Who's *this?*"

"This is Stella Di Mauro. Who have I the honour of addressing?"

"What? Er, Ellen. Rooke. Never mind that, where's Cally?"

"If you mean Ms Darker, she's currently lying in my hallway."

"What? Is she okay?"

"I doubt it. She practically collapsed at my feet."

The only response to that was ragged, nervous breathing. "Hello?" said Stella.

"Yeah. Er, sorry, what was your name again? Stella–"

"Di Mauro."

"Tony Mathias' sister?"

"You *are* well-informed."

"I was helping Cally. I'm a police officer. Well, was – look, never mind. Listen, you're in danger where you are. Cally is, anyway. There's people looking for her."

"Are there now?" Stella looked down at the pistol on the carpet.

"Yeah. And there's a pretty good chance they'll be heading wherever you are now."

"Should I call the police?"

The other woman hesitated. "These people – they're sort of official. But they're *not* the good guys, trust me."

"I'd be naïve to assume they were, just because they were dressed in a little brief authority."

"Right. Whatever. Look, you need to get her out of there."

"Oh, do I?"

Ellen Rooke's voice hardened. "Even if you don't care about her, she's your best chance of finding out what happened to your brother."

"Fair point," Stella said at last. "Any thoughts on where?"

Another brief pause. When Ellen Rooke spoke again, the breathiness and panic were gone; she sounded steady and authoritative. "I think we'd best put our heads together. Go somewhere you can lie low for now. I'll call when I'm en route and we'll go from there. Okay?"

A great deal was being demanded of Stella in exchange for very little information, but the Darker girl plainly needed help, and Ellen Rooke sounded genuinely afraid. There might be consequences for helping a fugitive, of course, but if meant answers at long last, she'd risk them. "All right."

"Thanks. Oh, and ditch your smartphone. They can trace you through that."

"What fun," muttered Stella, but the phone was dead. "So much for a quiet weekend."

Ellen was surprised how calm she felt: the numbness and paralysis were gone, at least for now. Given time they'd return, but for now she'd things to do. And someone to do them for.

She pulled on her trainers, pocketed the flip-phone, then rushed round the flat stuffing anything of possible use into a backpack. Five minutes' work – which still felt far too long – and she was out of the flat, running downstairs.

The Juke was still at Dolgellau, but that was a blessing in disguise. Pike might consider her an irrelevance now, but her comms, credit cards and vehicle registration would all no doubt be flagged. *What if they were watching her too?* Ellen shook her head; she'd second-guess herself into insanity that way.

With luck, she stood a chance. Ellen took a deep breath; Glyn Scurlock's barn was ten minutes away; less if she ran.

A dirt track ran through farmland near Wagonfield, beside the River Bollin. Stella had had a picnic in the meadow beside it with a gentleman friend a few years ago, during a fine summer much like this. It had been very quiet, and nobody had bothered them. Sitting on the ground – and getting up afterwards – was harder work these days, but they'd been limber enough to manage it. Among a few other things; Stella was a big believer in growing old disgracefully.

The dirt track ended at a line of trees ranged along the riverbank; to her left was a tall hedge, screening off the field on that side. The meadow where she'd picnicked was on her right, its grass yellowed and earth cracked. At the very end of the track, the intersection of hedge and trees created a shady corner, where Stella had parked her well-worn Volvo estate, though it was still stifling inside; she didn't dare wind the windows down for fear of swarming insects.

It was almost half-past five, two and a half hours since Cally Darker had fallen through her door. The girl was in the back of the car, curled up on her side and snoring softly.

Stella hadn't smoked in years, but craved a cigarette now. The girl had been burning hot to the touch when Stella had bundled her into the car, the hair plastered to her face. Stella had peeled the hoodie off, only to see exactly what it had concealed. She'd been briefly tempted to run away screaming, or call the authorities after all to make the problem go away, but she'd inherited her mother's distaste for organisations that made inconvenient people disappear. Besides, Cally said she knew what had happened to Tonio.

Unfortunately, the girl was still dead to the world, head pillowed on her wadded-up hoodie; Stella might have thought her dead entirely if not for the snoring. That, and the occasional movement of the tentacle sprouting from her bristle-haired right arm; hence Stella's general unease and nicotine craving.

The flip-phone had rung twenty minutes earlier; on learning where Stella was, Ellen Rooke had claimed to be no more than ten minutes away. There was still no sign of her, but this spot wasn't easy to find – the track didn't even have a name as far as Stella was aware – so Ellen was probably still driving up and down the narrow Cheshire lanes in search of it. Hopefully, anyway; it was all too easy to imagine other, more sinister reasons why Ellen wasn't here.

Unable to bear the muggy heat inside the car any longer, Stella climbed out and walked into the trees. Birds sang faintly. The Bollin trickled slowly past, wide, shallow and the colour of stewed black tea. The river's smell was overpowering.

As she picked her way back towards the Volvo she heard another car, and hid behind a tree. She felt stupid; it wasn't much of a hiding place. A greyish humped square appeared further down the track; a Land Rover. She gripped the tree till her fingers ached.

The Land Rover halted a few yards behind the Volvo. The engine cut out, and a woman with short chestnut hair got out. "Stella? Cally?"

Small for a policewoman, Stella thought, then took a deep breath and stepped into view. "Ms Rooke?"

"Ellen." The younger woman stuck out a hand. They shook awkwardly. "Where's Cally?"

"Still out for the count, I'm afraid." Stella unlocked the car, leaning in after Ellen as she climbed inside. The policewoman's breath caught abruptly. "What the *fuck*?" She glanced back at Stella and coughed. "Sorry."

"Don't worry, dear. I said much the same. I take it she wasn't in this condition when you last saw her?"

"Think I'd have noticed."

Stella was about to quiz Ellen Rooke more closely, but before she could, Cally Darker let out a gasp so loud and sudden that Stella started, banging her head on the Volvo's ceiling.

Cally's eyes opened. She looked lost, but only for a second. She looked from Ellen to Stella, and a dazed smile formed. Then she spoke, although Stella had no idea what it meant: "Trinity."

57.

The Land Rover's windows were wound down; the air had the muggy closeness that comes before a storm. Above Jericho Hill, the evening sky was black with clouds.

Despite the heat, Cally still wore the hoodie. Ellen hadn't been able to stop staring at the tentacle and hair. Cally couldn't blame her; she struggled not to stare at them herself.

Ellen was currently dozing in the driver's seat, her head against the window-frame. Cally was still exhausted, but didn't dare sleep: she might end up in the Pit again, or worse. It had taken great effort on the Cantor's part to save her before: there wouldn't be another such rescue.

She only had to stay awake a little longer. One way or another, this would end tonight. At worst, she'd hopefully have time to blow her brains out if things went wrong.

And Ellen's? And Stella's?

If there was time. If they wanted it. Hardly an easy conversation to have, although it couldn't be more bizarre than the one that had followed her waking up.

Cally got out of the Land Rover and looked about the yard. Jericho Hill overlooked Jerusalem Heights, the neighbourhood where Stella and Tony had grown up. The Heights were still among the most deprived districts in the country, but the hill retained a rugged, unspoilt beauty. There were two or three farms along the Ridgeway, the narrow lane that ran over the hill from Rishcot; otherwise, it was uninhabited.

Croasdale Farm stood on the crest of the hill. Its name was burned into a battered wooden sign on one gatepost, just below a mud-spattered FOR SALE sign, greening with moss. The yard was littered with rusting machinery and half-empty feed sacks; the house's windows were shuttered or boarded up. Cally wasn't sure how Stella had known about the farm, but it had given them a decent hiding-place, concealed from the road by the tall hawthorn hedges that grew along the Ridgeway.

Cally walked down the drive to the road itself. From there she could see out over Rishcot, huddled in the valley below. Not much to see; grey and brown buildings, a few scattered lights. Other hills rose in the distance, only shadows in the dull, hazy air. She wondered if one of them was Warden Fell.

She hugged herself. *A long way from Bala, and the summer sunshine there.*

Bala made her think of Griff, and she retreated into the driveway; her throat was tight and she couldn't hold the tears back. The road felt too exposed, and Ellen was in the car; the drive was the only privacy she'd find.

Cally leant against the gatepost, shaking. She'd cried a little, when Ellen had first told her, but there'd been too much else to tell and hear. The grief had had to wait its turn; now it had caught her off-guard.

She'd been almost certain about Griff, but Ellen had confirmed it. *No,* cariad, *it's not a dream. I keep trying to wake up and I can't.* Cally shook her head, wanting to remember the good parts: the jokes about nurse's outfits and his undying love for her. *It's even possible you might never come to your senses and marry me, but is it* likely? Except they hadn't been jokes: he'd been a friend, and he'd been in love with her. She'd traded on that, and now he was dead.

The crying finally trailed into scattered sobs, leaving Cally empty. In the yard, the Land Rover's door opened and closed. "Cally?" Ellen called.

"Here." She heard a car coming up the Ridgeway from the town and hid behind the gatepost; a silver Mercedes whooshed past. *Have fun, wherever you're going.* Hopefully the driver was on their way to a night of unremarkable pleasures; dinner, TV, cuddles on the sofa, all worn smooth and easy.

Maybe she and Ellen could have that, if they somehow survived tonight, though it seemed unlikely given the kind of baggage they'd be left with. For now, what mattered was that Ellen was here and determined to help; Cally would need all the allies she could get to stop what she'd inadvertently started. Specifically, she needed the Trinity.

Ellen stood by the Land Rover. Cally wiped her eyes and forced a grin. "Just stretching my legs."

"You okay?"

Cally shrugged.

"Griff?"

"Can't get anything past you."

Ellen nodded towards the road. "I'm guessing that wasn't Stella?"

Cally shook her head.

"Think she *is* coming back?"

"Yes."

"We're fucked if she doesn't."

"Er, yeah, I know."

Probably are even if she does.

The hours since she'd woken seemed to have passed in seconds, while simultaneously having happened years ago. She couldn't recall what she'd said to Stella and Ellen; it had seemed to flow through her from somewhere else. Maybe it had; a last bit of help from the Cantor, to convince the rest of her motley Trinity. She wasn't complaining; whatever words she'd come out with had clearly been the right ones.

"You eaten at all?"

Cally shook her head. "God, not since yesterday." She hadn't even thought about it till now, but having done so, her stomach growled.

Ellen held out a pre-packed Cornish pasty and a bottle of water. "Picked them up on the way. Figured we'd need some fuel."

Which was true. They had a physically demanding journey ahead, if all went according to plan. "Thanks."

She wolfed down the pastie, gulped half the water and handed the bottle back. Ellen reached out as though to touch her, then let her hand drop. "How you doing?"

"Well as can be expected." Cally adjusted her sleeve to conceal the fur on her wrist. Her fingernails were dark grey, as if shaded by heavy pencil; her hands were dry and smooth, like a lizard's skin.

Hours only, from when you wake, the Cantor had said. *Until tomorrow's dawn.* Come the night, Cally was certain, the changes would accelerate, and the Pit's influence grow stronger.

"Where the fuck *is* she?" she muttered.

"She'll be here soon. Said so yourself."

"I don't want to stay in one place too long. You haven't seen those bastards, Ellen."

"Er, *yes*, I have. One of them, anyway."

"Not the Cormorant. The *Trinity*."

"I thought *we* were the Trinity–"

"The *other* one. Woodwiss, Gowland and Harrower. You haven't seen them. Neither have I since last night, which is what's worrying me. No idea when they'll show up. Or where."

"Only when it's dark, I thought you said."

"I've only seen them at night, but I've only seen them once full stop. They just turned up out of nowhere. I don't know how. Did they fucking teleport? For all I know they could pop up here any second. And even if they can't do anything till it's dark, it will be, soon."

"I know." Ellen looked at her watch.

"Time is it?"

"Seven-thirty."

"How long?"

"Two hours, maybe three."

Two or three hours of light remaining, and they still had to reach Warden Fell. They looked miserably at each other; Cally could almost hear the sand whispering through the hourglass.

Ellen forced a smile. "You saw them off before, though, yeah? And you were on your own then."

"And all this got worse." Cally indicated her arm. "If it hadn't been for the Cantor, I might not have got through today. And once it's dark–"

Wind blew through the yard. Rain speckled Cally's face; she looked up at the blackening sky. Dark, but not true dark yet. There was still light left in the world. She had to remember that.

"Cally?" Ellen touched the back of her hand; the blue eyes were wide and serious. "I just wanted to say sorry."

"What for?"

"Running out on you."

"You're here now. That's the important bit."

"Yeah, but–"

"Look, if it'd been me, I'd have run a mile too–"

"I haven't had many, you know, relationships. Not with another girl."

"Please don't tell me you were a virgin."

"Fuck *off*." Ellen laughed. "When I first got to Manchester, I was still in denial, you know? Engaged to an actual *bloke*."

"What happened?"

Ellen snorted. "I *wish* I could say I had a sexual awakening and Steve came home to find me in bed with another girl, but it was the other way round. Went about as well as you'd expect." She grinned. "I'd been a bit of a doormat till then. He really wasn't expecting me to go nuclear. Or chuck all his stuff out the bedroom window."

"Good for you."

"Quite a sight, seeing him run around the front garden trying to grab all his gear before it blew away. Anyway, that's when I found out that sex with me was, quote, like fucking a dead fish."

"How would he know?"

"That's what I said."

"He was obviously just crap in bed."

Ellen grunted. "Well, I *did* tend to lie there and think of England. Finally realised blokes just didn't do anything for me. Even ones in eyeliner."

"He wore eyeliner?"

"No. You mushroom."

Ellen kept hold of her hand but looked down, hunched into herself. Cally slipped her arm around her shoulders, drawing her close. Ellen wrapped her arms around Cally's waist. "I never really came out properly – even in Manchester, which is like Queer City."

"Certainly is."

"The other cops didn't know, or my parents. I'd hang around places like Vanilla–"

"I remember *that* part."

"But most of the time I just watched. Trying to get my nerve up. I had a few girlfriends, but no one loves a closet case, right? No one wants to be the dirty little secret. And then I ran into you."

"Oh yeah. I'm quite the catch."

"Far as I was concerned, you were the package," Ellen said simply. "Everything I wanted. Not just physically. You actually *liked* me, and... I know it hasn't been long, and I'm not gonna say you know me better than anyone, because you don't, but... Everyone else, I have to keep stuff back, hide something. There's no one I feel I could show *everything* to – you know, warts and all. But I felt like I could tell *you* anything. And I dunno if you understand how big a deal that was for me."

"I think so." It hadn't been as big a deal for Cally; she'd long ago reached the point of saying *this is me, and if you don't like it, tough.* But she'd had Dad and Lucy for parents; not everyone was as accepting.

"And the second things got tough, I ran off." Ellen shrugged. "All I could think was what a coward I'd always been. So when you messaged me, I was – even though I knew what that text meant, part of me was *glad*. I know that's horrible, but it was like the world saying *Here's one last chance and this time do* not *fuck it up*. Anyway, it's why I'm here now. I want to say I'm not gonna let you down again, but I'm still scared I might. But I'm going to try as hard as I can *not* to. Hope that makes sense. Sorry if it doesn't." Ellen sniffed. "End of speech."

Cally held her close, trying not to think about how her own flesh was betraying her, warping into new chaotic forms that would destroy her. She shook her head; Ellen looked up, the blue eyes wide. "Makes perfect sense," Cally told her. "Believe me, I get it." She kissed Ellen's forehead. "And thank you."

They stood like that awhile. Flecks of drizzle spat, then stopped.

Ellen raised her head again. "Hear that?"

Through the thick still evening air came a motor's growl. "Yeah."

They didn't move towards the drive. The approaching car could be Stella, or the silver Mercedes returning from wherever it had gone. Or Department Nine, closing in on them at last.

Cally put her hand into her shoulder-bag, gripping the automatic. The car growled closer, slowing down. Tyres crunched and gritted on the drive. Ellen stepped away from Cally and moved forward, fists balled at her side. Cally stepped sideways, slid the Glock from the shoulder-bag and pointed it at the ground, careful to keep her finger off the trigger. At least for now.

58.

Stella's Volvo nosed its way out of the drive, crunched across the pot-holed yard and rolled to a halt. Cally returned the Glock to the shoulder-bag.

Stella climbed out, grinned wearily and laid a two-foot bundle of sacking on the Land Rover's hood. "Mission accomplished. Come see, ladies."

She picked at the thin blue knotted rope that held it shut, wincing and grumbling. "Need a hand?" said Ellen.

Stella sighed. "Yes, you might have better luck." She shrugged at Cally. "The old finger-joints aren't as they were."

Ellen had small hands with nimble, slender fingers; in a few seconds the rope was unknotted and the sacking spread open on the bonnet.

"There," said Stella. "One each."

"They're already sharpened," said Cally.

"Abso-bloody-lutely," said Stella. "I've never tried to sharpen a horse's thigh-bone before and didn't intend to start tonight. That kind of task always sounds simple and ends up taking all night or going disastrously wrong. Better to give it to an expert, I thought, while one was on-hand."

"Got to admit," said Cally, "I wouldn't have known where to get hold of these."

"Benefits of knowing an actor, especially one who's also doubled as a props mistress, as I so often have. You get very adept at procuring the unlikeliest items at short notice. And you'd be surprised how many shows require prop bones or animal carcasses. I've got contacts at half a dozen abattoirs nationwide."

"Seriously?"

"Believe me, I wish I was joking."

Ellen held up one of the bones. At one end, the joint was intact; the last seven inches of the other were honed to a needle point. "We sure this'll do any good?"

"About as sure as we can be," said Cally. "Given the circumstances."

Stella sighed. "I *do* prefer getting my information from more reliable sources than dreams. But needs must when the devil drives. If you'll excuse the expression."

"The Cantor said they should really be human bones," said Cally. "And you were supposed to do it all yourself – killing the victim, cleaning the bones, carving signs on them. Plus sacrifices, rituals and I-don't-know-what. But that'd take months."

"Plus the whole murder thing," said Ellen. "I'm not up for killing some poor bastard and harvesting his thigh-bones."

"Nor I," said Stella.

"Me neither, don't worry," said Cally, although she might have made an exception for anyone from Department Nine and suspected Ellen would at least consider it in Pike's case. "These won't have the power of the real thing, but they'll give us some protection if–"

"If we run into the three cunts," said Stella. She'd met Harrower briefly during the original police investigation, and had liked him no better than Edna or Cally. She'd also met Roland Woodwiss, albeit only in passing as he'd still been a boy; even so he'd made a lasting impression. *Very unpleasant child, even then*, she'd said. *Not surprised he turned out to be a wrong 'un.* "Since they seem to be a package deal, like Hughie, Dewey and Louie."

"So, tell me again." Ellen studied the bone dubiously. "How's it work, exactly?"

"Like a wand, I guess. It focuses your..."

"Mojo?" Stella suggested.

"Will, maybe? Focuses it, anyway. You chant the incantation while you do it–"

"*Mantakha sa niroleph?*" said Ellen. "That one?"

"Yeah, that one." Cally didn't want to imagine what might happen if she used the other.

Ellen still looked sceptical, which was no surprise; it was pretty ludicrous, but it was all they had.

"All I know is I used that incantation against the Trinity last night, and it *hurt* them." Had hurt Gowland and Harrower, at least; Roland Woodwiss had just looked annoyed. "They'd have got me then, otherwise."

"So we just… point and chant?"

"Yeah. Just remember, it's basically a bodge. It'll hurt them, but it won't kill them, and it's gonna have a pretty short working life."

"According to the caveman in your dream."

"Yes, Ms Rooke," snapped Stella. "We're aware it's all inherently absurd. Pointing it out's become old and boring."

Ellen turned red and looked away. "Fair enough. Sorry."

"No. *I'm* sorry." Awkwardly, Stella squeezed Ellen's shoulder. "We both owe you a considerable debt of gratitude."

"'Specially me," said Cally.

"It's just a lot to take in," Ellen said. "You know?"

"Tell me about it," said Cally. "And I've had longer to get my head around it."

"I understand and sympathise," said Stella, "but we haven't the luxury of disbelief now. We need to accept what we've learned, however incredible, and proceed on that basis. We have to end this, tonight, before we pass the point of no return."

"Only if I'm still alive," said Cally.

"Woah," said Ellen. "Cal–"

"Sweetheart, you've got to accept that too. I don't want to die, but if I *do* change, *completely* change, it won't *be* me any longer. I'll be something that needs putting down. And if you *don't,* the Pit'll open all the way, and everything we've seen so far will be like a tea party." She took the Glock out again. "That's why I'm keeping this handy. If all else fails–"

"It won't." Ellen was trying not to cry.

"We can't let that happen." Cally took her hands. "You need to be ready."

Ellen shook her head.

"You're going to have to accept it, Ms Rooke," said Stella gently.

"Fuck off! It's all right for you–" Ellen broke off, shaking her head.

"I understand the pain." Stella touched Ellen's shoulder again. "Believe me, Ms Rooke, I do. But we have to go into this ready to do whatever's necessary."

"Fine." Ellen wiped her eyes. "I promise I'll kill you if I have to, okay?"

"Okay." Cally thought of Griff. If she owed him a death, then so be it.

"Can we get a fucking wiggle on, then?" Ellen said. "Time's ticking."

"Yes. Of course." Stella turned back towards the Volvo.

"We'd better leave yours here," added Ellen.

"What?"

"Police'll be looking for us, remember? Or Department Nine. Or both. If they've traced Cally to your address – and they probably have – they'll know to look for your car."

Although Ellen's face was blank, Cally wondered if there was just a hint of petty revenge there. Stella shrugged. "Fair enough. What about yours, though?"

"Not my car. Hopefully the owner doesn't even know it's gone yet, and even if he does, they mightn't have linked it to me."

"'Hopefully' and 'might not'," sighed Stella. "But that's really all we have, isn't it?"

They piled into the Land Rover and Ellen started the motor.

Stella took the passenger seat and Cally huddled low in the back, the hood pulled up once more over her hair.

The Ridgeway was empty. Ellen drove down towards Rishcot. Beyond that lay the road to the empty moors and hills beyond. The road to Warden Fell.

59.

The route was long and winding, as if designed to make getting there impossible. They saw the hill soon enough, looming above the lower peaks around it with Pendle Hill raised like a grim shadow in the distance, but it never seemed to get any closer.

It was already after eight p.m., far later than Cally would've liked, when Ellen turned off the high-hedged lane onto a dirt trail very like the one beside the Bollin, only far darker and more cheerless. It led into a coppice, and a clearing where she halted the Land Rover before getting out.

Ellen had insisted they stop in Rishcot first. Ever-methodical, she'd taken the time at Croasdale Farm to make a list. Stella always kept a roll of cash handy for emergencies; a couple of visits to late-night stores had done the rest.

Each of them now wore an olive-green cagoule and a backpack containing bottled water, Kendal Mint Cake and a heavy-duty flashlight, along with one of the sharpened bones. Ellen had bought a pair of walking boots and some thick socks; Cally already wore boots, and Stella a pair of sturdy, sensible shoes she'd refused all offers to replace. "I've already got bunions, thank you very much. Last thing I need is a bumper crop of blisters too."

Ellen shone her flashlight across the trees, then on the ground. "Okay, folks. Keep your torches aimed down. Less attention that way. And less likely to trip over something."

Her face looked pinched and white, but composed, too, with a *togetherness* in it that hadn't been there before. This was more familiar territory for her, straightforward and practical.

"Understood," said Stella.

"Go slow," said Ellen. "And watch out for cameras."

"Cameras?"

"Security," said Ellen. "They'd have to have some. But they couldn't have anyone on the site itself, or even CCTV."

"Because it might pick something up, right?" said Cally.

"Yeah. The taint spread to you through the cassettes, but we know Tony took pictures, too. They all went up in smoke, but I bet if any of them *had* made it..."

"They'd more than likely been infectious too," said Stella. "So monitoring the site itself would be counter-productive. Monitoring the *approaches*, on the other hand..."

Ellen nodded. "Set up cameras galore just outside the danger zone just in case anyone's stupid enough to go in."

"How close are we now?" asked Cally.

"About two miles, as the cormorant flies." Ellen flashed a small, tight grin. "Probably further on foot."

Cally's stomach tightened in dread; for a horrid moment she thought the crablike motion in her belly had started again. "How long'll that take?"

"I know, love. We're up against it. But we'll be even more up against it if Department Nine show up. I'm just saying, let's try not to make it any harder than it is."

"Right," Cally muttered. "Fine. I get it. It's just–"

"I know," said Ellen.

"We're with you, Ms Darker," said Stella. "We're determined to see this through."

She had to laugh. "I think you can call me Cally now."

Stella grinned. "I suppose I should, shouldn't I? All right – Cally. Ellen."

Ellen grinned back. "Cheers. Speaking of which – Callandra?"

"Oh, piss off," Cally muttered.

"Perfectly good Greek name," said Stella. "Anyway, shall we discuss that afterwards?"

Assuming there is *an afterwards*, Cally thought. She suspected that had occurred to the others too, as a moment of grim and awkward silence followed. Stella cleared her throat. "All right. Lead on, Macduff."

The trail led through a wooded valley, between two hills. The thick tree growth made the darkness deeper still; when they finally re-emerged into the open air, Cally was surprised how much light remained in the sky.

They crossed two low hills and a stretch of moorland. It rained as they went – a brief shower lasting five minutes, but it felt interminable at the time. They pulled up their cagoule hoods, but the wind blew them back unless they pulled the drawstrings tight, which restricted their vision uncomfortably.

It was harder going than Cally had expected; the past few days' stress and strain, and the mayhem currently being wrought on her body, had all taken their toll, and she almost collapsed at one point; Ellen insisted on a brief rest stop, much to her frustration, but after she made Cally drink water and ate a bar of Mint Cake – which, being almost pure sugar, gave her an instant surge of energy – they pushed on.

And there, at last, was Warden Fell: a broad flat peak with a tangled, wire-like crown of spiky, wind-warped trees. One side of it was thickly wooded, all the way down to the moor.

"There it is." Ellen pointed. "End of the rainbow."

"No pot of gold awaiting us, I suspect, though," said Stella.

"If only."

They'd seen no evidence of hidden cameras or listening devices, but with any luck the Depth's influence didn't extend far beyond the peak, meaning any such devices were most likely hidden on the final stage of the approach: the ascent of Warden Fell itself.

Which would be slow and awkward going were they to have any hope of avoiding detection. And having reached the old airbase, they'd still have to find Hogge's Pit.

Supposedly it had been the site of a mediaeval castle, Edna had told her, *remnants of which survived in certain restricted areas below-ground.* Not that Adrian Woodwiss had been the most reliable source of information.

It was almost nine o'clock. The sky was very dim, with a dull burnt-umber smear at the western horizon where the sun was dying. The torches were essential now, and would be all the more visible to watching eyes. Cally couldn't yet feel the change stirring in her again, but it would only be a matter of time once it was dark.

"Cally?"

"Hm?"

Ellen stared anxiously up at her. Stella, already ahead of them, had turned back, hands on hips, looking downright impatient.

"You ready?" Ellen said.

No, she thought.

"Yes," she said, and strode forward. Ellen fell into step beside her; Stella pivoted on her heel and led the way into the woods.

It was near dark now; as the woods thickened they grew darker still and the brief rain made almost every surface shine like glass; if a camera's unblinking lens *was* tucked away in the trees or undergrowth, they'd scant hope of picking it out.

In addition, the path grew increasingly winding and treacherous; it took all their concentration to negotiate the uneven, slippery ground and avoid the tangled roots and brambles that straggled across it. Both Cally and Stella almost fell several times; only Ellen, the smallest of the group and with the lowest centre of gravity, kept her footing.

So much for slow and steady, Cally thought.

The trail snaked maddeningly to and fro; like the road, it might have been designed to delay their arrival indefinitely. With the thick tree growth, they couldn't tell how far they'd gone or had to go. All Cally could see were the trees around the path, and the trail – if she was lucky – as far as its latest bend.

But finally the trees thinned out again – not completely, but enough that, as the rain began once more, Cally could see the dim sky through them. It still wasn't completely purged of light, and the black ridge of the hilltop stood out against it.

"Nearly there," she wheezed.

The rain intensified, from a light patter to a harder, more insistent drumming.

"I see it," Stella said, breathlessly. Cally was about to ask if she was all right – she seemed healthy enough, but was in her seventies nonetheless – when Ellen screamed, "Get down!"

Gunfire rang out, a hard, metallic chatter. Stella cried out and pitched sideways across the path under the now-hammering rain.

Bullets thudded into trees. Splinters flew. The gunfire swept towards her. *Machine gun*, Cally thought, but couldn't seem to move. Then something slammed into her and she pitched forwards, into the muddy earth.

60.

As Cally hit the ground, something landed on her back, winding her. That was the worst pain, which was odd. A bullet in the spine should have hurt a lot more.

The machine-gun fire stopped, leaving only echoes and rain. Cally realised the weight on her back was muttering: "The gun. Where's the fucking gun?"

Not a bullet in the back, then; Ellen had tackled her.

"Where's the *gun*?" Ellen's hands groped over Cally's arms, legs, ribs, hips. *You're not going to find it there, love.* "Cal, you okay? You hit?"

"Don't think so." It came out as a wheeze. "I'm okay."

"So where's the fucking gun?"

"Backpack."

Stella lay unmoving. Rain rattled on her cagoule.

"Anything?" someone called.

"Can't see," a second man answered.

The hiss and drum of rain. "All right," said the first man. "Move in, chaps." Clipped. Nasal. Public school. "Seek and destroy."

The trees rustled; Cally dug her fingers into the soil. Baked hard minutes before, it was now nearly liquid.

Outgunned and surrounded; no chance of escape, and if Stella was dead, it was pointless anyway.

So let them kill you. You can't become a monster then. Can't end the world. Dad and Lucy will be safe.

The rustling drew closer.

We want the same thing, you stupid bastards, Cally wanted to scream. But they wouldn't listen. She fumbled for Ellen's hand, but couldn't find it. Ellen was rooting inside the backpack, still trying to find the gun. *Pointless, love.*

"Here!" shouted a voice. Light flashed into Cally's eyes, from a light clipped under the barrel of a machine-pistol. A black-clad man, in a balaclava.

A second man appeared beside the first. He had a machine-pistol, too, but she could see his face: pale, with a trimmed moustache and empty grey eyes. The small mouth twitched in a smile. "Miss Rooke. Quelle surprise."

Pike.

"Wait," said Ellen. "Listen."

He smirked and opened his mouth to say something, but that was when the torches on their guns flickered, as did Cally's flashlights.

Wind blew up the slope.

Pike wasn't smiling now. He knew what was coming, even before the chanting began.

"Angana sor varalakh kai torja. Angana sor varalakh cha voran."

Another light shone through the trees below. Not the moon or a torch; a pale cold light, unnatural. Pike's face slackened; if he'd momentarily been afraid of Ellen in Bala, he looked terrified now.

The Department Nine men opened fire, but nothing hit Cally; she wasn't the target now. They were firing at something else, down the slope.

The Trinity had come.

The chanting grew boomed and rang as if from stadium loudspeakers. It almost drowned out the screams. But not quite.

Cally heard things snap like balsa sticks. Wet tearing noises; crackling, gristly pops, like roast chicken legs torn and twisted from their sockets. Liquid, splattering.

Ellen cried out: her face was all blood. But she was wiping it frantically away, cursing; it wasn't hers.

At last, it stopped: there was only the rain's drumming, and the Trinity's chant. The chant faltered and stopped. Someone sobbed and moaned.

"Oh, come on!" she heard Roland Woodwiss shout. "Stop snivelling, you old shit! You knew their bullets couldn't hurt you. Get *up*!"

"Leave him alone," said Graham Harrower. "Christ! Have you had your fun? Did you have to do *that* to them, you sadistic little–"

"Stop it!" Roland's grew almost shrill. "You're spoiling everything! We have to keep going."

"Fine, then. Let's put the silly tart out of her misery. Come *on*, Bernard, on your feet. Sooner it's done, sooner *we're* done."

"All right." Bernard Gowland's voice, still cracked from weeping, was barely a whimper. "Just get it over. Get it done."

A pause, and then the voices rose again. *"Angana sor varalakh kai torja–"*

Something closed around Cally: a fist, jaws, razor teeth. Department Nine was finished; the Trinity's focus had shifted to her.

"Angana sor varalakh cha voran."

Pain erupted in her guts. Scrabbling, serrated razor-legs, tearing her apart.

Embrace. You cannot win. Embrace.

Things moved and unfolded in her. The tentacle writhed against her arm, pulled more of its length out of her flesh. She felt the others growing too.

She had to end it. Cally grabbed at the backpack. Ellen wrestled to keep it; she knew what Cally wanted to do. Cally balled a fist to hit her; she had to get the gun and use it, now.

"Mantakha sa niroleph chir karagh!"

Something blew past Cally like a wind and drove her aside, against Ellen; the two of them fell into the mud.

The hillside shuddered. There was a three-throated roar of pain and rage.

"Insapa veir bereloth! Insapa!"

Cally ducked, pushing Ellen down, as another invisible cannonade erupted down the path.

When she raised her head, she saw Stella Di Mauro kneeling against a tree-trunk, grey hair blowing in the wild wind. Blood trickled from her hairline down the side of her face. Her expression was furious and hieratic: a High Priestess, a witch in her wrath. Her extended right hand aimed a sharpened thigh-bone down the slope; a blue, lambent flame danced around it.

"Maengrepa gir trequefa gla detiresh meirka!"

A shimmer flew through the air; this time it was Ellen who pulled Cally down. Another wounded bellow sounded from below, and the pale glow dimmed.

On the path, their torches flickered back into life.

"Get a fucking move on, you two!" Stella shouted. "Things to do, remember?"

"Yes, Sarge," muttered Ellen, laughing shakily, helping Cally stand.

Stella shouted the incantation again as they blundered up, keeping out of the bone wand's line of fire.

"Stella–"

"I'm all right. Just a nick." The rain had washed most of the blood off Stella's face and she wiped away the rest with her fingers, but her face was white and stretched-looking; her bared teeth chattered with pain and shock. "Give me your bones."

You don't hear that *every day.* "What?"

"Your *bones.*" Stella brandished the wand; the lambent blue flame died, and Cally saw the tip was already charred black. A limited working life, as the Cantor had warned her.

Cally and Ellen fumbled in their backpacks; Stella shouldered them aside, aimed along the trail and shouted the incantation once again. Trees cracked and splintered, swaying; there was another roar of rage. Stella grinned tightly. "Good job I'm still a whizz at learning lines, eh? Right – you two get on ahead, and find this pit."

"No," said Ellen. "Stella, you can't. It's got to be the three of us, remember?"

"What do you think I'm suggesting? I'm not ready for the glue factory yet, thank you." Stella eyed the charred wand. "No offence, Dobbin. I don't know if you've noticed, but the Three Stooges here are doing their level best to ruin our day. So you two go and find the spot we need to use; I'll tie Wynken, Blynken and Nod up as long as I can before retreating in good order. Dunkirk, not the fucking Alamo. Now, if you'll each give me a bone – no tedious jokes, please – and be on your way? We haven't all night."

"All right." Ellen held out her wand; her free hand was wrapped around the Glock. Cally reached for it, but Ellen stuffed the gun into her cagoule pocket. "If we find the Pit," she told Stella, "I'll fire three shots as a signal. Sound okay?"

"Marvellous, dear, marvellous. Now do fuck off."

Stella levelled the wand again as the cold light brightened below. Cally grabbed Ellen's arm; as they scrambled up the slope, the Trinity resumed their chanting. Stella's voice, tiny and reed-like in comparison, responded. Pressure and static built in the air as the rain beat down; another gathering storm.

61.

Roland Woodwiss looked up at the night rain, and smiled.

Night-time was the best time. It concealed things. From most people, anyway, if not from him.

Behind him, Gowland moaned and shook and sobbed; Harrower held him upright. Gowland's face was grey. Hurt and terrified. Pathetic. Roland sighed: neither of them appreciated the gifts they'd been granted. Whinging old fools. But he had no illusions: they were his allies out of fear, nothing more.

Gowland cared only about money; Harrower prized order above all else, although the order he believed in, dying even in the 1980s, was well and truly defunct now, and good riddance to it. Pretty Cally Darker might agree with Roland on *that*, if nothing else. How would *she* and her little policewoman have done back then, after all? Such appetites were broadly accepted now; Roland's still weren't, and that wasn't *fair*.

But it wouldn't have helped even if they'd been what the world called normal, because people loathed him. That wasn't his fault, though for years he'd thought it was. Such a relief it had been, to realise it was nothing he'd done, simply what he was, and to accept, at last, that there was nothing wrong with that. That his rage wasn't petulance or bitterness, but the only sane response possible to a world that didn't want him in it.

He worked hard, after all, and hardly asked anything from life in return. A little companionship and pleasure: not unreasonable, surely? And yet they'd all refused him: the world in general, and women in particular. Beginning with Mumsy.

Not that he'd desired *her*. Ugh. He had *standards*. He'd owed her only vengeance, for all the years she'd kept him down. At least that debt was paid, if not as fully as he'd wanted.

He didn't feel regret, or pain. He didn't feel grief. He didn't. He did *not*.

Alison Mathias had been different. He could guess what Mumsy had probably thought, and anyone else who'd seen Alison in his company: something dirty, something sexual. But it hadn't been. Alison had been pure. Innocent. The sweetest, gentlest creature ever to draw breath. The only person who hadn't been disgusted by him. He had loved Alison. A real, pure love.

When he became a god, if he could, he'd bring her back from the dead.

Cally Darker, though; yes, he'd have loved to enjoy that red hair and milk-white skin. But that couldn't be, even if he won. She was about to become something very different.

Which Roland should attend to now, if he was to enjoy all he'd worked for.

He turned his face from the rain, and back towards his companions.

Cally stumbled out of the woods, towards the summit of Warden Fell.

The last light had gone out of the evening now, and the rain was beating down. Her boots slid on the muddy ground, and she almost fell.

Ellen caught her arm and steadied her. "Easy."

"No time," said Cally. Under her cagoule sleeve, she felt the tentacle writhe. Ellen felt it too, and let go. "Sorry," she mumbled. "But you've got to watch where you're going. Break your leg and we're even further up Shit Street."

"All right." Cally shone her light at the ground. "But we haven't long."

"I can't go on, son," moaned Gowland. "I can't."

Son. As if he'd have given Roland the time of day if not for the Depth, working through Roland and present in Gowland himself. "Yes, you can," said Roland, "and you will. Because believe you me, I can do far worse than them."

He raised a hand. He didn't touch Gowland; didn't need to. The old man let out a choking cry and would have fallen if not for Harrower, who eased him into a sitting position, then turned, fists clenched. "That's enough," he snapped. "You vile little shit."

Roland flinched, but stood his ground. "Then get that withered old twat back on his feet. Once we get rid of the old cunt, the danger's past. There have to be three of them, remember?"

Roland strode forward; moments later, he heard the other two stumbling after him.

He'd thought it was a done deal, once pretty Cally Darker began to change: just a case of protecting her from Department Nine and forcing her through the last stages of her transformation. The first part hadn't been hard: Department Nine had never encountered anything like Roland, and had been surprisingly small in terms of manpower. Most of the job was keeping watch on a hillside, after all. He'd wiped out half of its personnel last night, and now he'd disposed of the remainder. Department Nine was extinct, and the powers that be would never rebuild it: after tonight, they'd be the powers that *were*.

But the second part of things wasn't proving so straightforward, and that troubled him. Nothing, *nothing*, in the past had hinted at any sort of countervailing force, anything that could pose a threat to the Trinity. Only over the past twenty-four hours had Roland realised that something was working against him; that pretty Cally Darker and her little friends might pose an actual threat. All this time and work and waiting, and *still* the balance could tip the other way; still Roland might be cheated of a world in which he could belong.

And *that* just wasn't fair.

But now the Di Mauro bitch was on her own. She had weapons, yes, but nothing the Trinity couldn't overcome. Kill her, and pretty Cally Darker and her policewoman posed no threat. Unless there were three of them, the others could do nothing, even if they found the place they needed.

Roland Woodwiss continued up the path. Gowland and Harrower followed.

Stella heard them chanting, then felt a rising wind, a kind of static in the air, and a slow, building pressure around her that felt deeply unpleasant. She was strongly tempted to run away, but she'd vowed to stand her ground as long as she could.

A cold light shone up the path, turning the rain to glowing mist. Stella steadied the bone in both hands. The chant wormed into her ears, her head; she almost forgot what she was meant to say and almost uttered *their* incantation instead of her own. *Christ, no.* But then she remembered. "*Mantakha sa niroleph chir karagh,*" she said, and the bone vibrated in her hands.

"*Insapa veir bereloth. Insapa.*"

Blue flames danced around the bone.

The three men appeared, silhouetted against that strange, pale glow. "*Maengrepa gir trequefa gla detiresh meirka.*"

The bone thrummed, so violently she thought it would leap from her grasp. A shimmer raced through the air, and the three shapes recoiled. There was a grotesque, amplified bellow of pain. But when she'd used the bone before, it had discharged its force at them at every line of the incantation. Its power was fading.

The glow among the trees began to brighten again. Stella uttered the first line once more; this time a shimmering wave burst at once from the wand. That was heartening. Another discharge of power came on the next line, and another on the next. But the bone was almost entirely black now, pitted and crumbling. It wouldn't last much longer.

As if sensing as much, the three men advanced through the trees. The glow shone brighter than ever, and the chanting swelled. Stella fumbled for the other two bones with her free hand, then aimed the charred wand directly at Roland Woodwiss' smug, plump face, and began to speak again.

62.

Light flared down in the woods; Cally heard Stella's voice; then the Trinity roared in pain, but not as loudly as before. Their defences were weakening; soon Stella would have to fall back.

Or die, and then you're really screwed.

"All right." Ellen raised her torch. "You keep your light on the ground, make sure we don't trip. I'll scan ahead. Okay?"

"All right." Cally swept the torch back and forth, holding Ellen's wrist in her free hand to steer her clear of hazards, but the going was surprisingly easy; the ground, though soggy, was at worst mildly uneven, as if the hill had finally decided to give them a break.

From the hillside came another flash and roar.

Ellen tugged Cally's arm. "Here." Her torch played over a chain-link fence, stretched between twenty-foot concrete posts.

. The beam flitted over the links, plunging into one gaping hole after another. It was like a torn fishnet stocking. Some of the holes were the work of trespassers, but most looked like the result of decay and weather damage. Between the tops of the posts, rusted barbed wire hung like withered creepers. On one post, a faded, flaking sign read: KEEP OUT BY ORDER MINISTRY OF DEFENCE.

"Through here," said Ellen, pointing out a gap easily seven feet high and three wide. Almost like an arch to welcome them. *Do come in; we've been expecting you. Complete your change; open the way.*

Cally drew back. Now, at the threshold, she was uncertain;

what if this was what the Depth wanted, for her to come straight to the hole in the world's heart, thinking she'd a chance of healing it, only to ensure the opposite; what if the Trinity had played her even more thoroughly than she'd realised?

No. That was her fear talking, desperate to find any excuse to turn back. Ellen squeezed her hand. Cally squeezed back, and they stepped together through the fence. As they did, the temperature around them plummeted. Their breath billowed ahead of them like white smoke.

"The *fuck*," said Ellen.

"Yeah," said Cally.

Their torches picked out wooden slats, corrugated tin, the curve of a Nissen hut. The tentacle on Cally's left arm writhed. Under her clothing and inside her, the other growths and changes stirred.

It *was* all a trap, after all. It *was*.

Yes. You cannot win. Embrace. Embrace.

She shook her head. The voice was too eager, too hopeful. It wouldn't need to persuade her if that was true.

Embrace.

"Cally? You okay?"

She wasn't, but she nodded. "*Mantakha sa niroleph chir karagh*," she whispered to herself, soft so Ellen wouldn't hear.

They moved forward, between the huts. Cally wished she'd studied the urbex site more closely, tried to sketch the station's layout. She couldn't get any proper sense of her surroundings, far less of where Greston Castle might have been.

"*Insapa veir bereloth–*" she whispered.

"Where now?" said Ellen.

"The fuck should I know?" Cally was suddenly furious at being asked so stupid a question. Worse, Ellen was distracting her as she tried to stave off the change.

Kill her, then. Get rid of her.

For the worst moment, that seemed a reasonable thought, even – for an instant – after she realised it wasn't her own.

Kill her. Kill her. Embrace. Embrace.

"Fuck *off*," said Cally, then launched herself away from Ellen, remembering as she went to train the light on the ground ahead.

The bone shattered into soot, charcoal and glowing blue embers as Stella completed the chant again.

Laughter rolled up the slope, then gave way to whispering as the Trinity resumed their own incantation.

Ellen called out behind her, but Cally kept going; she had to put distance between them.

Yes. Good. Leave her behind. Now embrace. Embrace! Hear the call and follow. Come. Embrace.

There was something new now: not just the voice or the sensations of movement as her body continued, slowly and relentlessly, to alter, but a kind of light. *Black* light. It shone, or *un*-shone, ahead of her, like a beacon. Her altering eyes – or some other sense – perceived it clearly; the movements inside her and sprouting from her skin quickened in its un-glow.

Follow the call. Embrace.

Cally had still been muttering the *Mantakha* incantation, but now she stopped. After that, it became easier; she wasn't walking towards the blacklight but being reeled in, like a hooked fish. She thought of the stuffed ones in the White Lion: pike, salmon, perch.

Like when she'd met Griff there. *All the better for seeing you, cariad.* He'd still been Griff, then; he'd still had eyes, and human limbs. *No, cariad, it's not a dream. I keep trying to wake up and I can't.* Her fault.

Yes. Embrace. No more guilt, then. No more 'fault'.

"*Mantakha sa niroleph chir karagh,*" she shouted, and kept shouting as she staggered forward, fighting to build her defences back while the voice screamed rage in her head. She'd dropped them just long enough: she'd seen the source of the blacklight.

Stella picked up one of the remaining bones, and waited, rain lashing down around her.

She'd no idea how much time had passed; the battle could have lasted anything from five minutes to an hour. There was no subtlety or strategy here; the Trinity advanced and Stella drove them back. A trial of strength, over and over again.

Below, in the trees, the pale glow brightened.

Whatever you're doing, girls, hurry up and get it done.

Cally was travelling in an almost straight line, veering only to avoid obstacles directly in her path; her torchlight receded and bobbed, but never went out, so Ellen found it easy to keep on her trail.

In the dark, lit only in fitful snatches, the airbase was like a ruined city. Impossible, surely, to find anything here – but then Cally wove around a Nissen hut and across open ground – empty except for a small shed, standing on its own. She cannoned into it almost headlong, and was nearly sobbing in frustration when Ellen reached her, but still muttering *Mantakha sa niroleph chir karagh* as she pounded on the door.

"Easy," said Ellen. "I've got it."

But had she? For all her preparations, she'd never thought as far ahead as getting inside a sealed building. The chain and padlock securing the shed door were rusted solid, but the shed itself looked like plain wooden planking, no bigger or stronger than what you'd find in someone's garden.

Please let looks, this once, not be deceptive.

"Step aside," she said, in her firmest policewoman's voice. "Cally!"

Cally stared blankly at her. *She doesn't know who I am.* But then she blinked; her eyes lost their empty look, and she moved back.

Oh for a Big Red Door key, Ellen thought; had she been on duty, she'd have a portable ram on hand. But she wasn't on duty; never would be again, if Pike was to be believed. Although Pike was dead now, so maybe that wasn't true any longer. But – considering how confident he'd been of getting her colleagues to denounce her as a thief and cokehead – would she even *want* the job back, were it offered?

Irrelevant now: all that mattered was tonight, and getting through this fucking door.

And if Ellen couldn't break a door like this down by herself, she wasn't good for anything much.

She took two steps back, then came forward at a run. She was afraid she'd slip and fall on the sodden ground, but kept her footing and drove the flat of her boot into the middle of the shed door with all her strength, aiming at a point a foot or two beyond it.

The door crumpled inwards and her boot went clean through. The air in the shed was clammy and bitter-cold – Ellen felt it even through the thick boot-leather, and was certain something was about to seize her ankle and drag her inside. She wrenched her foot free in sudden panic, then leant forward, steeling herself, and shone the light through the hole.

There was nothing inside but a few old tools, blotched with rust. Then Cally reached into the hole, tearing at the boards.

"Whoa! Cally, take it easy. I'll – Jesus!" Cally kicked and thrashed; Ellen pushed her aside, then began kicking at the door again, using the heavy flashlight as a club to knock more loose boards clear, till the gap was big enough to enter.

Cally's hands were bloody; her lips moved in that chant. Then she stopped, blinking. "Ellen?" Her eyes were dazed.

"It's okay." Ellen pointed the torch inside the shed again. "Talk to me. What're we looking for?"

Even before the first bone's power started waning, the lulls between attacks had been shrinking, the wand less effective each time. Almost as if the bastards were developing a tolerance.

Well, let's see what we can do about that.

Stella reached down now and picked up the other remaining bone. Maybe a double dose would be more effective: both barrels of the shotgun, instead of one.

Worth a try at least, she thought, and aimed them down through the pelting rain.

Had Cally been able to get through the door, she'd have known at once where to look, but the struggle with Ellen had broken her semi-trance: now it was no longer drawing her in, she couldn't pinpoint the blacklight's source.

She'd been close; she knew that much. At this distance, it shouldn't be hard to feel. But they were *too* close now; the Depth's call was everywhere.

And then she realised. So simple. The shed was the heart of it, else she'd have skirted it as she had any other obstacle, meaning there was only one way to go now. "The floor. Rip up the floor."

"On it." Ellen handed Cally her torch, stepped inside the shed and hefted a pickaxe. "Stand back, okay? I don't want to brain you by accident."

"Just on purpose, eh?"

Ellen grunted. No; the chances of that were next to nil, even if Cally begged her. And Ellen now had the Glock as well.

But that was for later. For now, Cally held the torch as Ellen attacked the floor. The wooden boards smashed and splintered; seconds later, with a loud *crack,* the steel pick hit stone.

The three men, little more than silhouettes against the killing light, advanced. A wind rose; pressure and static built in the air. Stella wasn't sure if they meant to tear her apart or transform her into something from a Hieronymus Bosch painting: either way she wanted none of it.

The Trinity advanced along the path. The static and pressure intensified.

Here we go, all or nothing. Stella pointed both bones at Roland Woodwiss' face, and said *"Mantakha sa niroleph chir karagh."*

Blue fire erupted around the wands; a shockwave seemed to sweep through her, then out through them. The air rippled and shimmered, and she was gratified to see Roland's eyes and mouth widen into O's of shock in the instant before the wave hit. The three men were hurled bodily backwards, and this time the sound they made wasn't a roar but a scream.

"Get in here." Ellen shook her head; her hair was dripping wet. "I need some light."

Cally squeezed into the shed, a flashlight in each hand. Ellen hooked the pick under the splintered floorboards and levered them up, grunting. Again, she worked fast, tearing a wide, ragged hole.

Under the shed was a concrete surface, in the centre of which a metal sheet was bolted into place. Ellen waved Cally back again and hacked at the sheet, using the broad adze-head. The metal dented easily; it was comparatively thin and there was nothing beneath. Turning the pickaxe, Ellen used the sharp spike next, punching through the metal, then shifting her grip and hauling with all her strength.

Stella tasted blood where she'd bitten the inside of her mouth. The glow was shining brighter than ever through the trees; no doubt a counterstrike was on its way. Stella spat to one side and raised the wands again.

The light grew dazzling, and the pressure built once more. She struggled to breathe, but managed, somehow, to force out another chant. This time the Trinity's shriek of agony was louder still; more importantly, it changed from a single unified voice, booming and echoing, into three separate, very ordinary-sounding human ones, and the light cut out.

Both wands were streaked black with soot; tiny blue coals smouldered on each. Rain hammered on the thick tree cover and ran down the path; wind blew through the trees.

"Bloody hell," Stella muttered, shaking slightly. Maybe Cally had underestimated the wands' power. They wouldn't be out of the woods – in any sense – if the Trinity were dead, but their chances would have improved.

There was another cry from below. Not agony this time, but rage.

"Get up," Roland Woodwiss said through his teeth. "Get *up*, you useless old bastard."

Gowland shook his head and curled into a tighter ball. He was sobbing hysterically, and bleeding from the nose and mouth. Roland went to kick him again, but Harrower pulled him back; when Roland struggled, Harrower raised a clenched fist as though to strike him.

Roland flinched, and was furious with himself for doing so, especially when he saw the contempt on Harrower's face. The same old story. Nothing ever changed.

He pulled free and stepped back, glaring, fists clenched at his sides. If he raised them Harrower would smash his teeth in; old or not, the pig was still dangerous that way.

But Roland had other ways to prove his superiority. *That*

had changed: he didn't have to let the world kick him around anymore.

"What the hell bloody good is that supposed to do?" barked Harrower, as if Roland was a child. Like the schoolteachers who'd hated him. Another old man, given power over Roland and then despising him.

But Harrower didn't have power over him, not anymore. None of the old men did, any longer.

"Well?" Harrower demanded. "How'll kicking the daylights out of an old man do you a penny worth of bloody good, eh? Pathetic little shit."

Roland ignored him. "Get up," he told Gowland again.

"No," moaned Gowland. "No."

Harrower crouched beside the old man, then looked up, grim-faced and Roland saw that blood was bubbling not only from Gowland's mouth and nose as fast as the rain could wash it away, but also from his eyes. Something had broken inside him during that last assault. He'd always been the weakest, in every way.

If Gowland died the Trinity was finished, and Roland with it. On his own he wouldn't have the power he required; couldn't be certain of finding the world he so wanted – *needed* – to inhabit once the gates were opened.

All because of the others' weakness, their failure to follow when they were required to.

He could not, would not allow such failure. And he didn't have to. The Depth was with him; its power was in him. It told him what he must do now.

63.

The sheet came up easily; the bolts popped out as if mounted in butter rather than concrete. Almost as if something wanted them to enter.

Better not think along those lines, Ellen decided.

The metal cover peeled back like tin foil. Ellen dragged it out of the shed, and Cally shone the lights on what lay beneath.

"Step away from him," Roland told Harrower.

"What? Oh, bugger off."

"Step away from him, I said." Roland was shocked by the power in his own voice. His own power, not the Trinity's, because he was the strongest of them all. The Depth knew he was its child and would serve it. He was the son of the Chaos and Old Night that had reigned before this world's dawn, and the one who'd restore it. Another Trinity, far greater than this one. The true One Who Was, Is And Always Will Be; the Christian version was just a pale imitation.

But as far as this other, lesser Trinity was concerned, there was one thing the Christians had got right; that Three could become One.

Harrower started towards him. "I've just about enough of–"

"I know the feeling," said Roland Woodwiss, and waved a hand. A casual gesture, but Harrower was catapulted backwards, smashing into a tree.

For a moment Roland worried, but then Harrower groaned and stirred. Still alive, for now. Roland nodded; he only needed the horrible old bully breathing a few moments more. Gowland was the more urgent case; in seconds he'd be gone.

Lightning flashed overhead; a thundercrack shook the sky.

The perfect accompaniment. Roland extended his left arm, and slowly splayed his fingers out.

That was all, but all he'd done a moment ago was gesture with his right hand, and that had flung a grown man bodily through the air. Ordinary faith might move mountains, but his could do much more.

Gowland shuddered and convulsed. His eyes widened, full of a terror far beyond anything the fear of mere bodily death could have instilled.

Roland had thought him beyond speech, but Gowland surprised him, one last time. "No," he managed. "No."

Roland Woodwiss smiled. "Yes."

He closed his hand, and Gowland screamed. It wasn't just his voice screaming, wasn't just a body; a soul was screaming too.

Gowland's eyes curdled, turning white and sightless; then he cracked open like earthenware, from crown to crotch. There wasn't a drop of blood. Inside he was hollow; no blood, bones, or innards. No mind, and no spirit either. Only a red mist, a vapour that flowed out of his broken shell and into Roland Woodwiss' left hand.

Harrower stared at Roland, mouth agape. Despite the deluge, Roland saw with satisfaction that the crotch of the policeman's trousers was sodden and dark.

He brought his fist to his face and opened it, inhaling Bernard Gowland's essence like perfume. He drank it down like wine; felt it infuse into his tissues, its energies brighten the blacklight of his soul. Felt himself swelling with it; felt the seams of his shirt split.

He should have done this long before; the other two men's weaknesses had undermined him. But no longer.

"Graham," he said, smiling.

"No," said Harrower, and turned to run.

"Yes," said Roland Woodwiss, and raised his left hand again.

Another appalling scream; then silence and darkness. The rain hissed and drummed.

Stop dithering and get a move on, Stella thought. *The girls need your help; you're no good to them dead.*

The cold bright glow returned, shining up the path again. The air filled once more with static and pressure, and somehow, now, it was worse.

A wind rose. There was movement in the trees, then the sound of trunks and branches snapping as something huge moved up the path.

"This is it." Cally's face, always pale, was whiter than ever in the backwash of torchlight as the storm battered the shed roof. "It's here."

Recessed into the concrete was a round steel hatch. Cally knelt and gripped the locking-wheel at its centre. It turned smoothly, as if freshly oiled. Ellen knelt beside Cally, and helped her pull.

By the pricking of my thumbs, something wicked this way comes, thought Stella, who'd once played one of the Witches in the Scottish Play. Her fingers were numb with cold and she felt an overpowering urge to run that deepened as something emerged from the trees.

It was vaguely humanoid but impossibly tall, twenty feet if it were an inch. Grotesquely bloated, it was nonetheless horribly fast and nimble, prancing up the hill towards her on tiny hands and feet. It glowed, with the same pale light that had limned the Trinity.

"Mantakha sa niroleph chir karagh!" shouted Stella: the shockwave drove the lumpen, ogreish shape back into a stand of bony silver birches in a cacophony of splintering wood, but the two bones burst into flames. Blue fire engulfed her hands, burning like ice; Stella cried out and let the bones fall. When the fires guttered out, only smoking char remained.

More trunks and branches crackled and snapped. The bloated shape rose, haloed in awful light. The rain boiled into steam where it struck it.

It let out a sniggering, snorting laugh. *Thn-thn-thn.*

"Fuck this," said Stella, surprised how calm she sounded, then turned and fled. Behind her the wind rose, and something vast crashed through the trees behind her, tittering as it went.

64.

The hatch swung back and cold damp air, rank and stale, breathed up from the darkness beneath.

Ellen shone a torch down through the hatchway. Iron rungs. A concrete shaft. She gripped Cally's arm. "C'mere."

"What?" Cally was bewildered and angry, but let Ellen drag her back outside into the rain. The tentacle beneath her sleeve was less easily persuaded; Ellen felt it writhe angrily, and almost let go. But she held on.

"We all go down," she said. "All together, or not at all. No solo expeditions."

Cally scowled, but nodded. "Gotcha. Makes sense."

Ellen drew the Glock, and fired.

Stella heard the first shot as she broke out of the trees, stumbling and sliding in the mud. She could see the ragged fence up ahead clearly; the pale light was far too close behind her, illuminating the hillside. She didn't look back; she was struggling for breath already, and another glimpse of that thing might finish her.

Mother of God, don't go and have a heart attack, woman. Last thing anyone needs right now.

Lightning flashed as she reached the fence; thunder rolled again, and she heard a second shot.

A small, hazy light appeared, just outside the fence, as Ellen fired into the air a third time. Behind it, the Trinity's ghostly glow shone up through the trees, accompanied by the sounds of wood being snapped, crushed and splintered by some vast bulk.

"Stella!" shouted Ellen as the little light reached the fence, and waved her hands in the air, but that would do nothing to help.

Ellen turned to grab the torches, but there was only one left on the ground and Cally was nowhere in sight. Torch-light flickered inside the shaft.

"Fucking hell," she muttered. *Like herding cats*, she thought, *trying to get all three of this sodding Trinity in one place at the same time.*

Only all three of them together would stand a chance, so she needed to get hold of Stella. Then they could go after Cally, and if – please God – Cally *was* still Cally when they found her, they could try and stop this.

By forming a circle and chanting a slogan? What is this, student politics?

"Sod off," Ellen muttered, then grabbed the torch and swung it back and forth, shouting Stella's name.

Cally's descent was maddeningly slow; she was climbing one-handed, the other hand using the torch to find the rungs below her. And with each step she glanced up, afraid Roland Woodwiss' grinning face would appear at the top of the shaft.

So far, it hadn't.

She could hear Ellen shouting, but Cally had to focus on the climb, and on repeating the *Mantakha* incantation over and over, for whatever protection it still gave.

The sound of rain faded. The air grew damper and colder; clouds of breath billowed around her. Climbing became mechanical, unthinking; when Cally stepped down and her foot finally hit solid ground she cried out, and almost fell.

She was on a stone-flagged floor that glistened with moss and slime. Cally was glad of her sturdy boots with their deep treads. The last dozen rungs were set not into concrete but a wall of rough-hewn, thickly-mortared stone. Like the floor, it was wet and slimy, and very, very old.

Greston Castle, I presume.

Hogge's Pit couldn't be far now. Cally inspected the chamber; it was surprisingly small, and seemed bare except for some stone steps leading up to an archway at ceiling level which had been filled in with rubble and mortar.

If Greston Castle had been destroyed to its foundations, this chamber must have lain below its deepest recorded levels. The Roundheads had razed everything above it, obliterated all evidence of the castle's existence, then buried this place under layers of rubble and earth. But where was the Pit?

The torch-beam alighted on another archway, this time at floor level. More importantly, it was clear. Beyond it, Cally saw more a spiral of stone steps, going down.

Wait for Ellen and Stella. It needs to be all three of you.

All true, yet Cally couldn't hold back. Steadying herself against the wall with her free hand, stepping carefully on the wet stone, she descended.

Ellen caught Stella by the shoulder, steadying her before she could collapse. "You okay?"

"Not dead yet," Stella managed between gasps. "Where's Cally?"

Ellen shone the torch into the ruined shed. "She went that-a-way."

Stella peered down the shaft. "Oh, joy to the fucking world."

"Can you manage?" Ellen's face was drawn and scared.

"Don't worry about me."

As if in answer, a peal of thundering laughter rolled through the empty buildings, and a cold pale light shone.

Ellen shielded her eyes. The light emanated from something that floated, balloon-like, above the ground, gliding sedately towards them.

It was vaguely man-shaped, with a huge, bloated trunk and head and doll-like hands and feet. Clouds of steam trailed behind it where the rain struck its engorged body. A wide, smug grin stretched across its beady-eyed face, which was still, just about, recognisable as that of Roland Woodwiss.

Its skin was mealy white, but blotched with spider-webs of ruptured blood-vessels; in places the skin itself had split, releasing an oily, yellow-white seepage that glued a few remaining rags of clothing to the shape. Its arms were outspread, its legs almost – but not quite – pressed together, giving Ellen all too clear a view of the monstrously erect phallus between them.

"Fuck off," Ellen managed, then raised the Glock and fired twice. It had no effect, other than to cause a momentary expression of annoyance to cross the apparition's face, giving way a moment later to cruel amusement once again. As the air rose and prickled around her, Ellen remembered – too late – what had happened to Pike, and anyone else who'd turned their useless weapons against the Trinity.

Get to the shaft, climb down.

She knew she had to, but couldn't move. She'd fired at the thing and now she was rooted by the rising power of its vengeance. She could only stand and wait to be torn apart.

Something caught the scruff of Ellen's neck and hauled her backwards. "Come *on*," snapped Stella di Mauro. "Standing there like a eunuch in a brothel. *Mantakha sa niroleph chir karagh!*" she shouted, almost as an afterthought, as though at an unruly dog. The wind faltered, the Woodwiss-thing flinched and Ellen could move again. Five words in a long-dead language, whose very meaning she'd never know, but they'd achieved more than any bullets.

Stella towed Ellen into the shed. "In there. Climb. *Today*, Ms Rooke!"

Ellen shoved the Glock into her cagoule pocket and started clambering down as the pale light from the Woodwiss-thing washed into the shed.

The policewoman had scurried under cover, like a woodlouse fleeing daylight; now only the di Mauro woman remained.

Roland had never liked her: just another one who'd treated him like something from beneath a stone. But it was *their* turn now to be the insects, trying to hide away from him. And they wouldn't succeed. They were his playthings now; he could – and would – do with them as he wished.

He could, for instance, fuck them to death. Quite literally. And then he'd bring them back to life, and fuck them again. He'd do the same to every girl and woman in the world. In every hole, to death and back, world without end, amen. All the women who'd denied him, rejected him – he could have them all now, any one he wanted.

But not Alison Mathias. He'd restore her, untouched and pure. He'd keep that sweet, precious creature alive and cared for, for all time.

The rest of womankind, though…

Stella di Mauro was a little old for his taste, but he'd make do. And with her gone it would be game, set and match; pretty Cally Darker and her policewoman would have no way to stop him.

The incantations the old bitch was flinging his way were more effective than the policewoman's bullets, but only a little. She didn't have the bones any longer.

It wouldn't take Roland long to end her.

The steps glistened and the walls trickled. Water trickled down the nape of Cally's neck. She shuddered, wanting only to be out of here, away. But that wasn't a choice. Never had been.

Under her clothes, inside her body, things stirred in anticipation. Something thought its time had come.

Stella felt the familiar rising pressure, the familiar static in the air. *Time to be gone,* she thought. But found she couldn't move.

Overconfidence, she thought as the Woodwiss-thing bore down on her. *No fool like an old fool.*

There were words that would set her free, give them a chance, at least, to stop the gates opening. If they didn't, Tonio's death, and Lindsay's, Neal's, Alison's, would all have been for nothing. And there'd be no setting the record straight; no one would be left who knew the truth.

No one would be left, full-stop, in any recognisable human form.

There were words. Only seconds ago she'd used them. Now they wouldn't come.

The Woodwiss-thing grinned and moved its hips, thrusting its bloated member towards her.

For Christ's sake, was that it? A dirty little boy, waving his willy and expecting her to – what? Scream in terror? Fall to her knees and worship it? Was that all it boiled down to, his willingness to annihilate the world? So he could use his dick to make the girls scream?

Fucking pathetic.

Despite her terror, Stella laughed, and anger showed in the Woodwiss-thing's expression again. Perhaps that made its concentration lapse for a moment. Whatever the case, the blankness in Stella's head cleared, and she remembered.

She recited first one line of the incantation – *Mantakha sa niroleph chir karagh* – then the next – *Insapa veir bereloth, insapa* – and it was a true delight to see the grimace on the ogre's face. So much so she was sorely tempted to keep on doing it, but she couldn't. All it had done was to slacken his grip on her, just for a moment, so she could think – and, more importantly, move.

Shutting her eyes to avoid that piggy stare, Stella pivoted on her heel and lurched into the shed, opening them again just in time to avoid falling headlong down the shaft. She pulled the hatch shut after her, twisting the wheel till it locked.

Out of the rain, at least.

Now there was only her torch's fragile beam, and another tiny distant light, bobbing far below. Everything else was darkness, but better that than the light she'd just escaped. Gritting her teeth, Stella climbed down.

65.

Cally wondered how far down the steps went. Maybe they'd never end; maybe this narrow shaft *was* Hogge's Pit, and the Cormorant, Eel and Toad were waiting, somewhere below, to welcome her into their company.

She made one final turn on the stairs and the passageway opened out, the last steps leading down to a level floor.

Behind her, someone called her name. Ignoring it, she descended the steps, shining the torch ahead.

It was a huge, circular chamber, built from heavy stone blocks and buttresses. Thin stalactites hung from the ceiling where mortar had dissolved; thicker, shorter stalagmites dotted the flagged floor. The ceiling was high; between it and Cally were several galleries, with stone parapets and arrow-slits. Anything that had escaped the Pit would have found an army waiting.

An oak-and-steel cover, thirty feet across, occupied the middle of the chamber. Iron stakes had been driven through its outer edge into the stones beneath, and through links in the web of chains that stretched across it. Some of the chains, orange with rust, were clearly iron or steel. Others, which had turned a blackish-green, Cally guessed were silver.

This was the original summit of Warden Fell, where the Cantor and their companions had conducted their ritual. Earthworks had been raised around it, and successive fortifications built on them, to keep the Pit's occupants at bay, of which Greston Castle had been the last. The Roundheads had sealed off this chamber and obliterated everything above it, so that Hogge's Pit would never be found again.

But someone always had to dig. Like Tony Mathias, or Cally herself. Someone always unearthed something, and then someone always had to ensure the Pit's occupants stayed in the depths, where they belonged.

So it's always been, so it always will.

But it *hadn't* always been this way. Before the Cantor's 'working' had gone awry, this had been just another hill. And it could be again.

"Cally!"

"Down here," she called. She was calm now. Hadn't been so calm in weeks or even months. There were footsteps; torchlight flickered, and Ellen joined her in the chamber.

Roland Woodwiss flicked a finger, and the shed exploded in a hail of splintered wood.

Below it was the steel hatch, locked tight against him: Roland made another gesture and the hatch was torn loose, flung away across the hilltop.

Down in the shaft was the di Mauro bitch's torch, a tiny shrinking dot. He couldn't fit through the hatchway now: he'd grown too great, too magnificent. But he didn't need to.

He could do almost anything now – and soon enough, even that 'almost' would disappear, and his vengeance on the world begin. In the meantime, though, he had power enough.

Raising a hand, he sent that power down the shaft.

A cold wind, and a pale light: Stella felt the pressure building round her again and looked up to see Woodwiss' grinning face filling the hatchway like a preposterous moon. She began mumbling the incantation once more.

But her teeth rattled in the deepening cold, the cut on her forehead was bleeding again, and she felt desperately tired.

You're no spring chicken anymore, darling.

Almost out of strength already, and the night's real work not yet begun. But Stella di Mauro was a stubborn old cow, as some smart-arsed young director had muttered when he'd thought her out of earshot; she'd rounded on hm with a look that had shrivelled the little sod's balls, but it was true nonetheless. She wore it as a badge of honour.

Besides: the Pit, the Trinity, Woodwiss – they'd killed Tonio and his family. And that couldn't go unanswered.

Those arsehole Sicilian forebears of hers might have recognised something they approved of there. *Vendetta*: blood for blood. Not pleasant, but if it got her through this, what did it matter?

But it was more than that. Atheist or not, at heart Stella had always wanted to believe there was an order to things. Meaning, pattern, balance. Absurd, yes, but that didn't stop you wanting it. She'd always known someone, or something, was responsible for her loved ones' deaths, and there had to be consequences for that. Balance.

Again, yes, absurd to believe she, or Tonio – *anyone*, really – actually *mattered* on any grand scale. Nonetheless, that belief had got her through. But it might take considerably more to save her this time.

Her eyes began to throb. Roland Woodwiss grinned down at her. *Fuck you, you sick little shit.* She was crying, but the liquid on her cheeks felt thicker than tears.

Blood, Stella. He's making you weep blood.

So this was how it ended? Halfway down a ladder with a super-powered pervert pulling her apart? There'd probably been sillier endings, but that was no consolation. If she died, there'd be no stopping Woodwiss. Even if Ellen kept her word and killed Cally, which Stella wasn't sure she was capable of, all promises aside, Woodwiss would still be in the world and who knew what carnage and havoc he'd wreak before he was dragged back into the Depth?

That was the best-case scenario, if Stella died. The worst? The gates opened, and it was the end of everything.

In which case, obviously, she mustn't die. But there seemed little she could do to prevent it.

Unless...

Stella looked up at Roland Woodwiss through the blood that veiled her eyes and shouted the *Mantakha* incantation with all her remaining strength; just for a second, the pressure on her eased. In that moment, she let go of the rungs, leant back and fell.

The concrete knocked the breath from her. Something cracked in her hip, and she screamed; the pain was blinding. But as she'd hoped, she'd been close enough to the bottom of the shaft to survive the fall. Before the pressure could come down on her again she rolled, bellowing again at the pain from her hip, out of the pool of light from overhead.

A roar of frustration made the room shudder. Stella was in far too much pain for laughter, but managed to bare her teeth in a shaky grin.

Her torch had shattered, but she could make out footprints on the slimy flagstones, leading to an archway up ahead. She dragged herself through, onto the spiral staircase.

Above, the ground shuddered; stone cracked.

She couldn't stand, let alone walk, but Stella painfully dragged herself into a sitting position at the top of the steps. Propelling herself with her arms and steering with her good leg, she started down into the dark.

66.

Roland Woodwiss thrust his frustration aside. No time for raging now; no time for tantrums. Soon he could indulge every whim, tear reality itself apart – but not yet, not yet. There was still work to do.

Roland didn't mind work. He wasn't lazy. But there had to be something worthwhile to gain from it. Money or stability were only a means to an end: the whole point of wealth and a stable anchorage in the world was that you could *do whatever you wanted*.

And for years, he'd been unable to. Mumsy had watched him closely to ensure he had no opportunities. But the lawyers had screwed him worst of all. He'd been *good* at that job, that was the howlingly unjust thing. It would have made him rich.

They hadn't liked him, no, but that hadn't mattered: he'd made them money. Another year and he'd have been a full partner, and invulnerable. Could have done whatever he wanted. *Had* whoever he wanted.

And Rowena Winchcole had been so pretty. Small, thin, a heart-shaped face. Impossible to resist. She'd reminded him of Alison, a little. He'd wanted her, but of course she hadn't wanted him. No woman did; even the ones he'd paid couldn't hide their revulsion. All but the most raddled whores had been unable to go through with the act, had thrown his money back at him and run.

He'd denied himself for so long – ever since that incident in Scorbridge. He'd known so many people who'd seek any pretext to lay him low, prompted only by their instinctive dislike of him. He'd known he'd have to bide his time; work to make himself rich enough, safe enough, to do as he pleased.

His mistake had been assuming he was there already.

Rowena was only a secretary, after all. No one important. He'd been sure, afterwards, she'd never dare tell a soul – he'd half-expected her to crawl straight home and kill herself, unable to bear having coupled with him.

She had, in the end, but not for another three or four years: before that, she'd talked.

Oh, not to the police; Roland had been spared *that*, at least. No, she'd spilled her guts to Sarah Parker, the partner who hated Roland most of all; the only one who'd actually opposed offering him a partnership, despite all the money Roland brought in. Sarah would happily have handed him over the law, but that would have caused a scandal. The firm wouldn't have liked that, and Sarah Parker, an ambitious girl, was determined to reach the top.

So, no police; Roland he'd simply had to quietly resign. Even then, he'd thought it only a setback; he'd had a glittering career up till then, and – again – he was *good at the job*.

But he'd applied to firm after firm without a reply. He'd considered suing them for discrimination; it was ludicrous someone with his qualifications shouldn't at least rate an interview. But it wasn't just them: all his connections in the profession – colleagues and clients alike – ignored his calls and emails, even avoided him in the street. he couldn't even try and set up his own practice.

Costing him his job hadn't been enough for Sarah Parker; she'd had to destroy his entire career. Because Rowena Winchcole or no Rowena Winchcole, she just didn't like him. Nor had any of the others; even if he'd only been fined for littering, Sarah would have made sure he became a pariah, in London and everywhere else.

So he'd slunk back home to Scorbridge to dwell under Mumsy's watchful eye and run a caravan park. A caravan park! *Him!* But he'd always known he was meant for something greater. And at long last, it had revealed itself. When he became a god, he'd mete out such punishments to them all, the living and the dead.

But that, all that, was play. That was pleasure. That was to come.

First, the work.

Pleasurable work, though. Sweet work. Because it would make all those pleasures, the ecstasies of vengeance and plundering at will, possible.

Work more worthwhile than any he'd done before.

But harder than anticipated: the other two were stubbornly refusing to die, the di Mauro bitch in particular. The threat, however small, still remained.

And that wouldn't do.

The shaft, of course, was far too narrow for him now, but that wasn't a problem.

Roland Woodwiss raised his hands.

"Easy." Ellen got Stella's arm around her shoulders. "Cally?"

Cally ran across and caught Stella's other arm. The older woman cried out as they lifted her, but shook her head. "Let's get this done," she said. "Just don't expect me to dance a fucking jig."

"You don't have to," said Ellen, fervently hoping she was right. "Right, Cal? Cal? What now?"

Cally stared back at her, a rabbit caught in headlights. *She doesn't know,* thought Ellen. *All the way out here for nothing.*

"Cally?" said Stella through her teeth. "What now?"

Cally's mouth opened. Here it came: the final defeat, the confession of ignorance. But as her mouth opened, the chamber shook and rumbled. Dust, mortar and stone-chips fell on them from overhead.

"What the fuck?" demanded Ellen. And then the ceiling cracked.

He couldn't bring the chamber down on them; pretty Cally Darker would die then, and pretty Cally Darker had to live a little longer, till she was only a goat's head and tentacles, lizard-claws and breasts with eyes.

Roland *could* have done it, easily. His power was limited only in range. He couldn't strike someone dead from miles away, not yet; he had to be close.

But at such short range, he could do almost anything he pleased.

A crack spread across the concrete slab, radiating east and westward from each side of the hatchway. It kept extending, till it stretched for twenty-five feet on either side; then Roland's tiny hands closed into fists, and it widened.

Like lifting up a stone, he thought, to find the crawling things that hid beneath. He'd di Mauro and the policewoman 'twixt his fingers like beetles, leaving pretty Cally Darker all alone. He'd hurry her change along, then; the Depth would speak through her, the way would open, and–

– Roland giggled, *thn-thn-thn* –

All hell would break loose.

"Oh, *shit*," Ellen yelled, then covered her head with the arm not holding Stella up. Stella moaned in pain; it wasn't easy being supported between two women of different height, especially when one was trying to burrow into the floor while the other stood up straight.

Cally hadn't ducked because she knew, even as the chamber's ceiling split wide and the chilly light spilled through, that Roland Woodwiss wouldn't let anything heavy fall on them – nothing that might kill his golden goose. Or cormorant. He had something else in mind

"*Angana sor varalakh kai torja,*" boomed a vast, reverberant voice. "*Angana sor varalakh cha voran.*"

No, she reminded herself. Not *cha voran*. *Chor volraan*.

That simple: the one tiny error that had bred millennia of anguish.

She'd been paralysed a moment earlier because she'd been convinced there must be more, some detail she'd forgotten, but there wasn't. The ritual was simplicity itself: the three of them, in this place, and a few words. The right words. *Getting* them right over and again, until their aim was achieved.

The chamber juddered. Stone cracked. Dust and fragments fell on them.

"Ms Darker?" Stella's voice was tight with pain. "If you're going to do something, now would be a good time."

The crack in the ceiling widened and more cold light spilled through. Larger chunks of masonry tumbled upwards, sucked towards the light, but Cally was calm. She knew what she had to do.

Cally crossed the chamber to the apex of an imaginary triangle, then pointed out the other corners. "Stella, you're here. Ellen, there."

"I can't stand up." Stella's teeth were chattering: shock and the cold, which deepened as the pale light filled the chamber. Cally's fingers were already numb.

"You don't have to," she said. "Sitting's fine."

Ellen dragged Stella into position and lowered her to the ground. The ceiling gaped wider; the light blazed down, and at its centre Roland Woodwiss' face beamed with dreadful cheer. *"Angana sor varalakh kai torja,"* he boomed again, and Cally felt tentacles writhe and sprout on her skin, felt serrated legs scrabble inside her. Ellen stared up into the light, into that face, mesmerised. *"Angana sor varalakh cha voran."*

"Ellen!" Cally shouted. Ellen's head jerked round, eyes struggling to focus. "Quickly."

Ellen ran to her corner of the triangle.

Roland loomed above them, vast and bright with the

Trinity's power. Cally closed her eyes, picturing the chamber as they'd found it: intact, dark, lit only by torchlight. When she had it clear in her head, she opened her eyes and began.

The sight of Roland's huge, grinning face had very nearly emptied Ellen's bladder, not to mention her mind. He was even bigger now, even more bloated; if only he'd pop, like a balloon.

But he wouldn't. That was the worst thing about him, that stayed with Ellen even as she took her place: the hopelessness. The despair. There was no way anything they did could prevail against *that*. Even the bones had only stung him, and the bones were gone.

There was no point; never had been. They could never have won, least of all by chanting a few words. Who *were* they, after all? A podcaster, an actress, a copper – *ex*-copper – still mostly in the closet. Nobodies. There was nothing they could do or ever *have* done. Why even try? It was pointless.

"*Angana sor varalakh kai torja,*" Cally said.

Ellen knew what she was supposed to do, but what was the point? It wouldn't succeed. It wouldn't matter.

No point even trying.

Easier, far less painful, to give up now.

"*Angana–*" began Stella di Mauro, then broke off, realising she was responding alone.

"Ellen!" said Cally.

Stella said nothing; to her own surprise, a part of her was relieved. She was nauseous with pain; her brain felt close to bursting with fear, anger and disbelief at the impossibilities the world contained. Not to mention all the memories of Tonio and his family that had come flooding back to her, fresh and vivid after all these years.

She was an old woman, dazed, frightened, still grieving four decades on, half-crippled and in pain. There was no chance at all she could complete the task ahead: at least, this way, the failure would be someone else's fault.

However utter and final the defeat.

Give up now, the voice told Ellen, and she almost did, till she remembered where she'd heard that voice before; when she'd felt that despair. It was how Depression talked: it said you were worthless, that all you did was meaningless, foredoomed to failure.

And Depression was a liar; she'd had to remind herself of that over and over, whenever it used some setback to urge her to give up. It had done so a dozen times during her police career–

– *And look how* that *ended* –

– but after they'd suspended her she'd wanted to give up, end it all, rather than face tomorrow.

If she'd given up, she wouldn't be here. Cally would be dead – or worse, the gates would already be open.

The gates. If they failed, everything was gone. Not just her, or Cally, or Stella. Mum and Dad. Dave Greene. Her exes, even the ones she liked. Bala and the lake, Llanuwchllyn. Taylor Swift albums, Indian food; woods in autumn; small dogs with huge dark eyes. All of that would be gone, if she gave up.

It'll be gone whether you do or not.

But that was Depression talking, and Depression was a liar.

"Sorry," she said. "I'm ready."

Cally peered up into the light. She looked drained and shaken, struggling to stand straight. Things moved under her clothes.

Ellen could have punched herself. One error could destroy them all; that was why Hogge's Pit existed to begin with. A miracle she hadn't already annihilated them. They'd been lucky because they hadn't properly begun.

She wouldn't make that mistake again.

Stella was no longer relieved, but furious – not with Ellen, but herself. She was an *actress*, for Christ's sake. Maybe not a Dench or a Streep, a Mirren or a Rampling, but it had paid her bills for half a century nonetheless.

Hand to mouth, yes, at times, but such were the joys and hazards both; not for her the soul-crushing tedium of the nine-to-five in exchange for financial security.

She'd battled on through that season at Birmingham Rep in '83, all through the hellish year that had followed Tonio's death – partly, yes, because she'd had to eat, but most of all because it was who she was. *The show must go on*: cliché or not, there was truth in it.

She could build a character and create a role, but above all, first and foremost, she could remember her bloody lines. The rest was sod-all use if you couldn't do that. Her whole *job* was to stand up and recite someone else's words from memory, with conviction, come what may. Admittedly the standing-up part might be out of the question just now, but if she still had a brain, she could manage the rest.

This time, if she dried or flubbed a line, a prompt or a quick bit of improvisation would be no help. But that aside, it was a part like any other: she was expected to get every word right, every single time.

Challenge accepted, she thought, and as Cally spoke again, Stella's fears and memories receded; even the pain began to dim. All that had to be left behind, once the show began. There were only the three of them, the call and the response. And for Stella di Mauro, the role of a lifetime, with all the world, quite literally, to play for.

The first few exchanges between Cally and the other women were just that; words and nothing more, till she was afraid it had all been pointless after all.

But then something changed.

There was warmth, to fight the bone-deep chill: she felt a wave of it flood into her, and realised it had emanated from the other women. When she spoke again, it flooded out of *her*, redoubled, back to them.

Back and forth, back and forth, it flowed like a tide as they chanted, filling the space between the three of them, and each time it surged, from Cally or back to her, it was with greater strength. It wasn't the equal of Roland Woodwiss' might. Not yet. But it was growing; it was shielding and strengthening them. Soon their Trinity *would* be the equal of the Depth's, and battle would be truly joined.

In the space between them, a golden light began to shine.

Roland Woodwiss clenched his tiny hands, then opened them again, reminded unpleasantly of how Mumsy's hands had clenched in impotent fear and fury on finding him in her room. Despite everything, they'd found the entrance to the Depth; despite everything, they'd survived; despite everything, pretty Cally Darker, human still, led them in that chant.

Fear gnawed at him, even something close to despair, but anger drove them back. How *dare* they try to cheat him of what was rightfully his, after he'd waited so long? He'd show them. It would be a close race, but he was stronger; he'd win. They were tiny: three little figures, one already half-broken, arranged in a triangle on a stone-flagged floor.

"*Angana sor varalakh cha voran,*" Roland cried, and hurled his full power down into the chasm. The oak and iron cover of Hogge's Pit was stored in like matchwood, and from the void below came a roar: the sound of the dark, unleashed at last. And the blackness welled up like ink, like blood in a wound.

The blackness poured out, thick as oil, cold and dead. Like poison gas, like a stagnant water, like cemetery earth, burying them alive. Ellen cried out in terror, but when Cally uttered the next line she responded; so did Stella. Their chant was a lifeline now, all any of them had to cling to.

The blackness flickered: one moment it was the light that shone from Roland's face; the next, the blacklight that Cally had followed to its source. But they were, in the final analysis, one and the same. The colours of the Pit.

But the golden light was here too, growing ever brighter between them: it shone in the darkness, and did not yield to the chill pale glow. It surrounded them, a fragile shelter against the blackness that had vomited from Hogge's Pit, and the things that had come with it.

Ellen's eyes were screwed shut. Cally couldn't blame her. In the flickering blacklight, the Cormorant struck at them again and again, trying to break through the wall of light with its razor beak. The Toad clutched and scrabbled with its claws and the hands sprouting from its eye-sockets for a crack or flaw in their defences that it could wrench open to form a breach. The Eel wound its coils around and around the golden light and tried to crush it. And they were only three among many: all the souls that Hell could bring were there, all the warped and twisted shapes, the agonised hybrids of human and beast, that had once been women and men. All hurling themselves against the golden light, trying to break through.

But still Cally chanted, still Stella and Ellen answered, and still the light shone brighter.

Roland couldn't penetrate their defences by a frontal assault; time for a subtler gambit, then. A whisper in the dark.

"Pretty Cally Darker?" he said. "Do you hear?"

Cally heard him, first in her left ear, then her right. She felt his breath, too, warm and moist; could almost feel the touch of his fat red lips.

"You'll die," he said. "If you do this, you'll die."

She mustn't listen, mustn't be distracted. The Cantor had warned her: the closer they came to the end, the greater the resistance they'd encounter.

"Not even dead, pretty Cally Darker. Not even dead. You'll no longer *be* at all. No afterlife, no eternity. You'll be wiped from existence, as if you never were."

"*Angana sor varalakh kai torja,*" she said.

"*Angana sor varalakh kai torja,*" answered Ellen and Stella.

"Or give in," he went on, slyly, "and I'll spare you and your little policewoman too. You like girls, don't you, pretty Cally Darker? I'll have all the world and forever to rule it; I can spare a corner for the two of you to frolic in. Hm? Give in, and you can live and love in peace."

For an instant Cally faltered; the golden light flickered, the whole universe poising on a knife-edge. It would be sweet, wouldn't it, to live and love? She wanted to, no denying that. So much to see and do; so much love to give and receive. Despite the clamour of anxiety and the gnawing of depression, when it came down to it, she didn't want to die.

But even if Roland Woodwiss' word meant anything, what kind of love would it be? Eternity in a prison-bubble, knowing you'd condemned everyone and everything else to annihilation? Dad, Lucy – and yes, even Millicent. Stella; Ellen's parents. And what kind of love could it be, if neither of you could leave? Even if it was there at the beginning, it would curdle, turn to hate.

To live and love in peace. But Roland Woodwiss didn't know
the meaning of the word. He'd grown so vast, so powerful, yet
remained so tiny: a sad, rageful little boy, terribly alone, and
terribly cruel in that loneliness, that sorrow and that rage. Had
there ever been a choice for him, a chance to be something
other than what he'd become? Cally didn't know, and for that
she felt true sorrow: once again she pitied him even in his
monstrousness; mourned for his innocence, destroyed before
he was even born.

But he was grown now, to manhood and beyond, had
become something that could not be allowed to have its way;
could not be allowed, even, to exist. If Dad and Lucy and all
the rest – yes, even Millicent – survived, that was enough. If
Ellen survived, and Stella, that was more than ample.

And so the moment passed, and Cally Darker said *"Angana
sor varalakh cha volraan."*

"Angana sor varalakh cha volraan," the other women
answered, and there was a sound like huge, rusted gears, long
disused, grinding into motion.

Roland could no longer hear himself – the bitches' chanting
had reached a crescendo, and now there was a creaking,
groaning sound, like the very machinery of the universe.

At *her* command, not his.

It couldn't be – not after all the work, the suffering, the
years of being denied. It *couldn't*. All he'd gone through had to
make sense. He had to be free to take his vengeance, reap the
pleasures he'd been so long refused – and Alison too, sweet
innocent Alison, to restore her from the ranks of the dead. But
he couldn't hear the Depth, its inhabitants' songs, any longer;
he couldn't hear himself.

Eyes screwed shut, he opened his mouth and cried out his
own incantation, a last effort, hoping to tip the balance the
other way.

"Angana sor varalakh kai torja," he bawled. *"Angana sor varalakh chor volraan–"*

Chor volraan

No! No!

Take it back, I take it back, let me take it back–

But there *was* no taking it back: no unsaying what had been said.

And workings such as this one were…

…unforgiving.

Alison, was his last coherent thought.

The machinery of the universe ground inexorably into action; it did its work as efficiently and pitilessly as it would have had the battle gone the other way. Roland Woodwiss screamed as the balance tipped, and then he felt himself first torn asunder and then falling, in agonised but still-conscious fragments, into the dark below.

As he fell, something rose to meet him; a rising dust of souls. As he fell, he saw the Cormorant, the Eel, the Toad and countless other beings like them burst asunder too, and the same dust pour from them. It flowed upwards, either to be healed and made whole again or to blessed oblivion; either way, as it flowed, it sang. All the souls of Hell sang and then were gone, and Roland Woodwiss was alone in the dark of the Depth. And then the Depth collapsed in upon itself, and him, and crushed them both to nothing.

67.

A dozen pains assailed Stella di Mauro, but none were from her hip. Very small discomforts, for the most part. She was lying on grass and, as she'd apparently just woken up, she'd presumably been asleep here for some time.

No wonder you're aching. Silly thing to do. No fool like an old fool, I suppose.

She opened her eyes, wincing and grunting at the morning light.

Above her was a blue summer sky, and no sign of rain. The small aches and pains receded – always a pleasant surprise at her age – and still there was no discomfort from the hip that had surely been fractured at least. Maybe she'd nodded off in her back garden and slid off her chair.

'I woke up and it was all a dream'? Surely not. Pathetic way to end a tale.

Stella di Mauro sat up, and looked around.

Ellen Rooke, still on the edge of slumber, lay curled up on her side. Grass tickled her nose; she could smell wildflowers.

Where was she? A summer meadow, maybe. That didn't fit her jumbled, chaotic memories of what had gone before, but surely those were the stuff of nightmares, not reality.

"Ms Rooke? Ellen?"

A hand touched her shoulder, and Ellen rolled onto her back. A handsome, grey-haired woman knelt, looking worriedly down at her. She knew that face; a moment later, she recalled the name. "Stella?"

"Ellen. Are you all right?"

"Think so."

Stella helped her to her feet.

"Where the hell are we?" There were buildings everywhere of various kinds, though it was impossible to tell which: all were completely overgrown, every one of them engulfed in ivy, and not only that; brightly-coloured flowers rioted all over them, too. She and Stella were standing in thick, waist-high grass, but when Ellen looked further, she saw moorland and valley below, and other peaks nearby. Surely vegetation had no right to be so lush this high up.

"Warden Fell," said Stella. "It must be Warden Fell. The fence. See?"

She pointed. Ellen made out the concrete posts and the chicken-wire, but only just: they, too, were engulfed in vegetation.

"Warden Fell. Yeah. That's right." She knew the name, but where from? What had they been doing here?

"Why the hell are we here?" Stella frowned. "Come to that, how do I know you?"

"I…" There was something. Should be something. "Someone we knew."

Knew?

"Yes. That sounds right."

A pale face. Red hair. Warmth. A gentle hug.

"Cally," said Ellen. "Cally Darker."

"That's right." Stella nodded. "Cally."

Slowly it was coming back. Impossible to forget the events of last night; impossible, too, to bear their memory. Perhaps they'd make themselves forget; perhaps nearly everyone who'd had encounters with the monstrous or miraculous ultimately did the same. How did you function, day to day, after seeing something like that?

Cally.

"Where is she? What happened?"

"Oh Christ," said Stella.

"What?"

"Don't you remember? She told us herself: if we succeeded, the souls trapped in the Pit, all the people who'd been tainted. They'd either be healed or–"

"Destroyed." Ellen looked at the ground at her feet; grass and earth, nothing more. She knelt and pawed at it, looking for the entrance to Hogge's Pit, but there was nothing. Only earth.

Erased, as though it had never been.

She put a hand to her mouth and shook her head. "No."

"Ellen–" Stella reached out to comfort her, but Ellen turned away, stumbling through the grass.

She tripped and almost fell. Steadying herself, she looked down. A woman lay at her feet, dressed in black except for an olive-green cagoule. Bright red hair spilled across the grass.

"Cally?" Ellen whispered, and fell to her knees.

Healed or destroyed. Healed or destroyed.

She turned the body over. The white face was still and empty, eyes closed.

Ellen began to cry.

The tall grass swished as Stella waded through. "Oh, God. Ellen, I'm so sorry."

"Hey," said a familiar voice. "Do you mind? You're dripping on me. And not in a fun way."

"Fucking hell." Ellen looked equal parts relieved and furious as she helped Cally up. "Scared the shit out of me, you mushroom."

"After last night, I wouldn't have thought we'd have any left to be scared out of us," Stella said. "But I suppose some things are in infinite supply. Welcome back, Cally."

Cally Darker hugged her tight, surprising them both, then released her quickly. "Thank you."

"Thank *you*." Stella turned away, wiping at her eyes.

Forty years of mourning, and still not done. Cally thought of Griff: did you ever really stop missing those you'd cared for, when they'd gone away?

Time will tell, cariad.

Ellen tugged her sleeve. "What about you?"

Cally peeled off the cagoule and hoodie. Her pale arms were hairless and un-scaled; nothing sprouted from her skin. "All seems back to normal."

"Happy to do a full inspection later." Ellen turned red and looked down. "If you want, I mean. Just to make sure you're all clear."

Cally reached out and took her hand. "It's a date." She hesitated. "If that's what you want, I mean."

Ellen looked up, and smiled.

"Ahem," said Stella. "Do you think we could make our way back? I've no idea if anyone'll come investigating, but I'd rather not be here if they do."

"With you on that," said Ellen.

"Yeah," said Cally. "Let's go."

But when they reached the fence, they stopped and stared a while. It was impossible not to: Warden Fell, and all the land around, was blooming. Alive with flowers, and full of light. As if spring had come again.

Acknowledgements

As always, I couldn't have done this without my amazing wife, Cate Gardner. Thank you, my love.

Thanks too to my agent, Meg Davis, and all at Ki, to Simon Spanton Walker, Desola Coker, Christiana Spens, Amy Portsmouth, Caroline Lambe, Gemma Creffield and anyone else I may have forgotten at Angry Robot.

Stuart Kenworthy, Steve Balshaw and Kevin Rees all offered advice and background on art and photography; Remy Porter and Simon Farrant helped with police procedure. Any errors are my own.

My trusty beta readers – Emma Bunn, Hannah Dennerly, Rachel Verkade. Lizzy Cooper – once more hopefully stopped me making a complete fool of myself. (If not, blame me and not them.) The music of Dark Sanctuary – especially their latest album, Cernunnos – fuelled me through the writing of this one. Along with many pots of Yorkshire Tea.

Lastly, thanks to every reader who's bought a copy of this or previous books of mine. Hope you enjoyed this one too.